The Last B

Angus Donald is the author of the bestselling Outlaw Chronicles, a series of ten novels set in the 12th/13th centuries and featuring a gangster-ish Robin Hood. Angus has also published the Holcroft Blood trilogy about a mildly autistic 17th-century English artillery officer, son of notorious Crown Jewels thief Colonel Thomas Blood. Before becoming an author, Angus worked as a fruit-picker in Greece, a waiter in New York City and as an anthropologist studying magic and witchcraft in Indonesia. For fifteen years he was a journalist working in Hong Kong, India, Afghanistan and London. He now writes full time from a medieval farmhouse in Kent.

www.angusdonaldbooks.com

THE LAST BERSERKER

ANGUS DONALD

CANELO

First published in the United Kingdom in 2021 by

Canelo
31 Helen Road
Oxford OX2 0DF
United Kingdom

A CIP catalogue record for this book is available from the British Library.

Print ISBN 978 1 80032 187 8
Ebook ISBN 978 1 80032 186 1

Printed and bound in Great Britain by Clays Ltd, Elcograf S.p.A.

For Daisy D, the berserkest

Prologue

The Rekkr limped towards the village, the butt of his long-handled axe dragging a furrow in the sandy soil. He hummed to himself as he approached the gate in the fence that surrounded the tiny settlement by the sea. It was a simple four-note tune, rhythmic, repetitive, hypnotic. An ancient melody. The vibration deep in his throat suppressed the frailty of his much-wounded body and coaxed the Beast once more from its lair within his heart.

He was a huge man, his scarred face toad-ugly under a greasy fringe of hair; his heavy shoulders made bulkier by the fur cloak draped over his back. The filth-matted fur vambraces, which protected his forearms, made his upper limbs appear absurdly large, particularly when combined with the ropes of coiled muscle on display. A loincloth and a pair of leather greaves, sewn with iron strips and strapped over his boots, completed his costume.

Fifty paces from the rickety gate, he hefted the axe on to his shoulder and broke into a lumbering trot, increasing to the full charge as he neared the wooden fence. The humming rose in pitch and volume to become a terrible keening screech, and then an open-throated, piss-curdling scream. At a full sprint, he threw his massive body against the collection of sun-faded sticks held together by thongs and hemp-twine and crunched through the gate, bursting out the other side, into the village itself, in a shower of debris.

The two gate guards, village men armed with no more than fishing spears and wicker shields, were already running by the time he had brushed the splinters from his fur-cloaked shoulders.

The Rekkr threw back his head, lifted the axe high in both hands and roared with mingled rage and triumph.

Then he set to work.

He strode to the nearest house, a slumped hovel of wattle and daub with a sagging turf roof. He ripped the leather curtain aside, swung low and sank his axe into the groin of a man who lunged out at him with a bait knife in hand. He booted the collapsing man's body back into the cottage and, chuckling and calling out a jovial word of greeting, he followed it inside.

The air was ripped apart by the sounds of violence – shouts of anger first, then squelches and cracks, then screams of pain. Finally a woman's voice pleading, begging – cut horribly short. The Rekkr emerged a few moments later, spattered all over with gore, and laughing like a donkey.

He shook the axe head free of its slick coating, droplets scattering, and stumbled on into the heart of the village. A bitch, a big mongrel with a good deal of wolfhound in her, barked at him, and circled, growling, sensing his evil. The Rekkr leapt, fast as a snake, and the animal was swatted away with a single blow, half her ribs crushed. She whined, staggered and fell.

A shield wall had formed, halfway up the only street in the settlement; a dozen men, all the males of fighting age within the village. They huddled together, trembling pitifully, behind three round, lime-wood shields. A few wavering spears and five or six swords pointed in the Rekkr's direction. The intruder loped eagerly towards them, gathering speed, chuckling and swinging the long bloody axe in ever wider loops around his shaggy head.

The shield wall fared no better than the gate. The Rekkr smashed straight through it; then, he hacked left and right, killing with practised ease.

He took a sword thrust to his left side, the steel scraping over his naked ribs, but paid not the slightest heed – the Beast possessed him now and he had no understanding of pain. The long axe hissed through the air and plunged into living flesh. Again. And again. Blood spraying in wider arcs as the blade sank into human meat and was swept back for another strike.

The five unwounded men of the shield wall now ran for their lives, scattering – and the Rekkr let them go. Seven men were curled on the bloody earth, coughing, bleeding, dying. He stamped on a twitching fellow's head, crushing the skull like an egg under his iron-shod boot. Then, unexpectedly, the Rekkr stooped and picked up the dead man's sword in his free hand, an ancient one, but well made by a craftsman; he gave it a few trial swishes.

He smiled.

The Rekkr then set to work on the houses, zig-zagging across the street from one to another to make sure he did not overlook any victims. At each dwelling he kicked open the door, pushed inside and killed, sword in one hand, axe in the other. He slew the old, the young, women and their children.

Slathered in gore, like a dread creature from a nightmare, the Rekkr approached the last and biggest building in the village, a timber longhouse.

The fur of his great-cloak was now utterly soaked; his vambraces were soggy and glistening red. Of the heavy features of his filth-caked face, only his cold dead eyes could be distinguished along with a glimpse of yellow teeth in his mad, almost jubilant smile. He stood for a moment outside the gable-ended longhouse, looking up at its stout beams, and the oak-wood door, no doubt barricaded by now. The window shutters were all closed too, barred from the inside. Blood dripped from the Rekkr's weapons, held loosely in both his hands, pattering like raindrops on to the dust below each blade.

He began to hum once more.

Inside the longhouse, the survivors of the village, no more than a dozen folk, mostly women and children, were gathered on the far side of the hearth. A grandmother clutched two of her dead son's children, a girl and boy, no more than ten and eleven years old, one under each arm. She squeezed them tight, crushing them to her, and tried to still their whimpers.

'Hush now,' she said. 'He cannot get in. He will soon be gone.'

The boy threw off her arm and ran to the side of the house where, after rummaging among the pots and pans, he unearthed a small eating knife.

One matron seized a yard-long cooking spit from the hearth, and swept its iron length clear of soot and grease with one motion of her hand.

Then they heard it. A drone like a swarm of angry bees. Very close. Just outside the door, but now moving – there! – over by the east wall.

An eerie scraping sound; a loud scratching.

'Get gone, demon!' said the matron. 'We're not frightened of you.'

A crash. Another. A splintering.

The girl let out a shrill little wail. The humming grew louder.

'Hush, little one,' said her grandmother. 'He cannot get inside here.'

The Rekkr hacked apart the rough wattle-and-daub exterior of the hall with the axe, kicked through the thin inner planks and burst into the hall. It took him no more than a few moments, and his huge fur-clad shoulders were erupting in the gloomy interior, like a monstrous chick emerging from the egg.

His humming had reached the pitch of fury.

A doddering greybeard tried to stand in his way and the Rekkr skewered him through the loins with the ancient sword and, turning and swinging the bloody axe with his other hand, he hewed the head clean off the howling matron who tried to stab him in the belly with her roasting spit.

The rest of the inhabitants cowered by the long rectangular fire-trough in the centre of the hall, resigned to their fate, all except for a white-faced boy, who charged at the Rekkr from the shadows, yelling shrilly, the sharp eating knife in his hand. The Rekkr killed him with a sideways flick of the axe, a casual, almost friendly blow, which smashed the little boy's right cheekbone into several pieces, driving the shards deep into his small skull.

The Rekkr loomed over the last few folk huddled by the long hearth, breathing from his exertions. His gaze crawled all over them like a fly on a freshly made corpse. Then he fixed on one of the older girls, a pretty blonde.

'Freya, my sweet,' he said. The words were clogged in his throat, as if they were too large or too jagged to come out. 'I have come… for *you*.'

Part One

One year earlier…

Chapter One

The fate of a murderer

The hemp noose around his neck was as prickly as a bramble. His hands, still crusted with flakes of brown blood, were bound in front of him, uncomfortably tight. The stool under his dirty bare feet creaked alarmingly with the slightest shift of his considerable weight. Very soon, they would kick the rickety wooden seat away and he would drop a few inches and begin choking to death, dangling from the broad limb of the ancient sacred oak, until the final darkness came upon him.

Nineteen summers was a pitifully short span for a young man to walk this green Middle-Realm. Indeed, although he was fully grown to look upon, tall and broad, slabbed with springy muscle, he still felt himself to be little more than a bewildered boy – a boy who would never grow any older.

Neither would it be a good death. This was no glorious battle-field; he held no weapon in his bound hands; there was no circle of slain enemies around his feet. No wingèd sword maidens would swoop down to gather his broken body and take it to the Hall of the Slain for an eternity of feasting, ale and laughter. Instead, he would be slung in a hastily scraped hole on the outskirts of his village and left there to rot, if the foxes did not dig him up and feast on his corpse. That would be the last of Bjarki the Fatherless.

He was a murderer, twice over. He had not even bothered to deny it at the gathering of the Bago village elders, the Thing, which had met that morning to settle the matter, and now he must pay the price for his actions.

Yet he had not expected *this*, this slow strangling in the shade of the ancient oak dedicated to the Old One, the All-Father, in the beaten-earth circle where the village collected to see justice done. Outlawry was the time-honoured penalty for murder – a terrible fate, nonetheless. The outlaw was expelled from society, none would aid him, or shelter or feed him, and any man might kill him, like a wild wolf, without cause or penalty.

Olaf Karlsson, the headman and local *hersir*, had spoken vehemently against him at the Thing. Bjarki was no better than a mad dog, he had thundered, waving a finger in the air, an indiscriminate killer of men, one who must be put down lest he endanger them all. Outlawry would not serve.

Only the ale-wife, Fulla, had spoken in his defence. She suggested he should be branded on the forehead with a hot iron and exiled from the Mark. But no. The Thing decided, in its collective wisdom, that it must be death. Only that finality would keep them all safe from his murderous ways.

Bjarki could feel the prick of tears welling behind his eyes. He had sworn that he would not weep. If he must depart this Middle-Realm it would be with courage. But this unmanly sorrow was threatening to overwhelm him. 'All-Father, mighty Odin, give me the strength to die well,' he prayed.

He glared fiercely, and very nearly dry-eyed, at the assembled villagers, his friends and neighbours – well, neighbours; he had few friends in this fishy mud-hole – who had gathered this spring morning to watch him die.

The village lay in the centre of the island of Bago, a mere flyspeck of low-lying land, barely a mile across, which was one of hundreds of islands of varying size that, together with the Jutland Peninsula to the west and the settlements on Scania in the east, made up the realm called the Dane-Mark.

Almost all the denizens of Bago had gathered to see him swing; some sixty people ranging from babes-in-arms to hobbling grandfathers were spread out in a loose semi-circle on the southern side of the ancient oak. Some passed sloshing ale flasks from hand to hand, others chewed on fresh-baked oatcakes sweetened with honey. It was a kind of entertainment, this hanging, for many of them a blessed relief from the back-breaking struggle to wrest a poor crop of barley or rye from their small, often flooded fields; or from the endless casting and hauling of heavy fishing nets.

A miasma of rotting seaweed and burnt fish oil permanently hung over the settlement. Bjarki sucked it in through flared nostrils, savouring the odour like perfume. His last precious scents on this earth. He looked up at the pale yellow disc of sun through the leaves, feeling its small warmth a final time.

The half circle of familiar faces was a smear of white and pink and grey. There was Olaf Karlsson, the *hersir*, his dark pitted face twisted by hatred, staring directly at him; beside him stood his one remaining son, Freki, smirking, as pleased as a man who's won a wager. He would be the heir now, to Olaf's house and his land. Perhaps, he would be the *hersir* one day, if he petitioned Siegfried, King of the Dane-Mark, to grant him the title.

Fulla the Simple was smiling at something inside her own muddled mind. Her baggy body was festooned with leather flasks of freshly brewed ale on cords of twisted hide. From time to time, she passed one over to a thirsty villager, and made a cut on her tally stick with a blade, to record the sale.

There was Thialfi looking sullen; he had lost a morning's fishing to attend the Thing, which he was bound to do as Bjarki was in his charge, his apprentice. Yet he had not spoken up decisively either for or against the boy. He did not care much for Bjarki. He stated only that he had not seen what occurred in the dunes as he was busy mending his nets on the west beach, and while he knew Bjarki had a temper, he had never known him to kill.

There was one face Bjarki did not wish to see; his eyes skidded over it, only noting the bone-white cheeks and blue eyes reddened from weeping.

He fixed his gaze instead on a tall, lean, one-eyed man in a fine leather-lined woollen travelling cloak and hood – a stranger to the village, but one he had seen here a few times before. He was a trader from somewhere up north, perhaps from the land of mountains and fjords, the Little Kingdoms, as the remote settlements across the straits from the tip of Jutland were called. Or maybe he came from the dense forests of the Svears and Gottars further east, or perhaps from the frozen Sami territory beyond even those far-off exotic realms, where the reindeer herds ran in their thousands upon thousands and the sun only peeped above the horizon for half the year.

Bjarki could not recall the old man's name only that he wandered widely and dealt in small items – beautifully carved bone pins and dainty gold and silver broaches, fine silk threads and colourful ribbons, necklaces of glowing amber beads and precious stones, excellent steel eating knives and powerful magical amulets – perhaps in slaves, too.

He had one beside him now. A skinny thrall of perhaps seventeen summers with knife-cropped spiky red hair, a tiny, elfin nose and a small mouth clamped shut. A look of compressed fury blazed in her bright green eyes, as if she wanted to slaughter the whole world and piss on its grave.

The one-eyed trader – Valtyr, the name came back to him – had his hand on the shoulder of the slave, a symbol of possession, and perhaps a safeguard, too, against the girl attempting to flee. Though there was nowhere to run on Bago, and nowhere to hide either. No place where the fugitive would not be captured within a day or two, and then bound, imprisoned and handed back to her master with a reward for the captor. A savage whipping, or even a small mutilation or branding, would be all the slave could expect.

Perhaps a worse fate awaited a runaway captured by a lonely, lustful freeman in a remote farmstead. The girl was a pretty one, after all.

The old man Valtyr was moving now, pushing through the throng to Olaf's side. He leant forward, smiling in a friendly way, showing a bunch of scarlet ribbons in his proffered right hand. He spoke urgently, forcefully to the stiff-backed *hersir*, who seemed irritated at the outsider's presumption.

Bjarki looked away.

His eye fell on the young face he did not wish to see. But once there he could not tear his eyes from it. Freya's face.

It was swollen from her weeping but still perfect and wondrously beautiful to Bjarki. He held her gaze, each staring at the other across the empty space in their mute shared agony. He knew this would be the last time they would ever look into each other's eyes. He could almost feel the love, so often and so urgently professed by both, shrivelling in the space between them, like a hair held to a candle flame. They would never be wed now, despite the oath he had made to her; their cosy talk of a hearth and a home, of babies and the fishing boat that Bjarki meant to build himself – he had already laid the keel – all that was slipping away too fast, dissolving into nothing as even the most delightful dream must upon the waking hour.

This nightmare was the cold reality.

It was for her sake that he would die this morning, under the old oak tree, in the presence of the whole village. Freya's mother – her father was long dead – stood behind his beloved, looking at him over her daughter's thin shoulder, seemingly fearful of him even now. She believed her daughter had had a lucky escape from a life yoked to a killer. Yet did she know what had truly happened? Did she grasp *at all* why he had done what he did?

–

It had begun with the puppy. A glossy, squirming pup a few weeks old and black as a raven, one of the litter Ubbi the Huntsman's bitch had produced. Ubbi lived on his own in a hut in the woods on the north point of the island, a mile or so from the village, and Bjarki had formed the habit of visiting him around noon, when he returned from working the morning boat with Thialfi.

He would rarely speak with Ubbi, for the man disliked all conversation, but he helped him prepare the hides and skins, which the hunter bartered for necessities, scraping them free of fat and flesh, salting, drying and rubbing them with grease until they were supple again. He helped Ubbi most days – when the man had not sailed off to the north on one of his long solo hunting trips – and received a bowl of venison stew as the price of his labour. On a couple of memorable occasions, he had even accompanied Ubbi on a winter trek to hunt the fallow deer in the most northerly part of the Jutland Peninsula.

Yesterday, having seen that the pups were ready to be parted from their milk-drained mother, he had forgone the stew and begged for the glossy little puppy instead. 'I shall name him Garm,' he informed Ubbi, 'after the black Hound of Death that guards the gates of the goddess Hel's realm.'

Ubbi had merely grunted his assent.

Bjarki had swaggered back to the village like a returning raven-feeder, a sea-warrior with a shipload of booty; the puppy nestled in his under-tunic, sleek black head poking out of the square neck-hole under his chin.

He found Freya on the beach, waiting for him on an old blanket in their usual spot, a grass-filled hollow between the high dunes, out of sight of the fishing boats and their owners. It was their special place, where they kissed, made love, and lay afterwards in each other's arms, apart from the world.

Bjarki had presented her with the puppy, Garm, which was received with cries of joy. Then he received his own reward from his loving Freya.

They had finished making love, and with the puppy nosing happily through the mound of their discarded clothing, Bjarki lay back, content, and looked at a slew of chubby white clouds scudding across a limitless expanse of blue. It was time, he thought, it was time for him to take control of his destiny. He rolled over on to his knees, and took Freya's right hand in his.

'My love for you is as wide as the sky,' he announced. 'You are more precious to me than heaven's jewel!' He made a gesture towards the sun.

Freya smiled up at him, naked, unashamed, her eyes filled with love.

She is so utterly beautiful, Bjarki thought. *She is the most perfect woman in the whole world, the perfect mate and companion for a lifetime.*

'I have no silver for a bride-price,' he said. 'I have no father to ask your family for your hand. But I will give you my solemn promise, here and now, Freya Njalsdottir, that I will love you, protect you and keep you safe from harm for all the remaining days of my life. Will you accept my oath?'

'I will,' she said, 'and I also swear to love you until the heavens fall.'

He took her face in his two hands and kissed her deeply. Their bodies moved naturally, drawn together, the one fitting perfectly into the other.

Then Bjarki heard something. A snigger. A guffaw. He broke away from his lover, turned, looked up and saw them. He sat upright abruptly.

There were three young men on the brow of the dune, framed by the blue sky – white-blond Jeki and his even fairer-haired younger brother, Freki, and Ymir, a massive, swarthy, dull-witted older fellow who followed the pair of brothers around like a bond servant or their personal bodyguard.

Freya gave a little shriek and dived for her clothes.

'I always knew she was a willing slut – but I had no idea what a lustful little whore Freya truly was,' said Jeki. 'She's randier than a bitch in heat.'

Ymir sniggered: 'She loves a big cock and no mistake.'

Bjarki stood up. He was completely calm at this point.

'Go away. This is a sacred moment between Freya and myself. It is none of your business. Please take yourselves off and leave us in peace.'

'Go?' said Jeki. 'I don't think Freya would like that. I think she wants to have a nice ride on Ymir's fat one. I think she'd like us all to do it to her.'

Bjarki, still tightly controlled, glanced once at Freya, who was now cowering on her knees with the bundled clothes held up before her, and said: 'Go away. You have no right to disturb us here. Leave us alone. Go. Now!'

'Or *what*?' said Jeki. 'What will you do, eh? Nothing, orphan-boy. We'll have some fun with your little slut, I think. We'll get our pricks wet.'

The puppy, sensing the confrontation between the four young men, charged up the hill, barking sharply. Ymir booted the little beast in the ribs, bowling it back down the sandy slope, little Garm squeaking in pain.

Bjarki felt suddenly very, very cold. He heard a rushing sound like a tumbling waterfall in his ears. That was all he would remember for a while.

When memory returned to him, his face and hands were covered in blood. Slathered. Arms gory right to the elbow. His finger bones burned like fire. Blood was in his mouth, eyes and ears. He spat and wiped. Disgusted.

Ymir lay dead in the sandy hollow, his lower jaw had been wrenched completely free of the joint and flopped over to one side, hanging by a flap of skin. One of his eyes was missing; only a red-brimming hole remained.

Jeki, too, was no more. Higher up on the slope of the sand dune. His face was only red mush, and his spine had been snapped, judging from the flopping head twisted at an impossible angle. His right arm had been wrenched from its socket. The puppy Garm was dead too, trampled in the blood-spattered furrows of sand, destroyed in a battle of which Bjarki had not even the slightest recollection. There was no sign of the other boy, Freki.

Bjarki was aware that behind him Freya was screaming, on and on. He was surprised he had not noticed before. Ignoring her, he sprinted up the slope of the dune and gazed around. The fishermen, half a dozen of them, had all ceased their work on the high-tide line and one of them, his old master Thialfi, was trudging towards him across the sand, his expression grim. Bjarki turned away and looked back towards the village. Freki was running towards it, waving his arms, nearly at the gate. His terrified shrieks carried clearly across the three hundred paces or more between them.

-

The wooden stool beneath his bare feet gave an ominous creak, and drew every eye in the circle. Bjarki stood very still, his neck extended as far upwards as possible, as if that would make a difference when the time came. He looked over at Olaf Karlsson – it was the *hersir* who would ultimately give the order to kick away the rickety stool – or he'd do the job himself.

Bjarki wondered how long he would dangle by the neck before he lost consciousness. He wondered if dying would hurt very much. He had heard tell that hanged men always pissed and soiled themselves when the end was near – a bodily failing completely beyond their control. Let Odin preserve him from that humiliation. He wanted to bargain with the god to ensure that this did not happen but he realised he had nothing to offer. His life? It was forfeit. He had no goods to give up, no birds or beasts with which to make a sacrifice.

'All-Father,' he prayed, mumbling aloud, 'let my death be a sacrifice to your glory. Let me hang here as you once hung from an oak tree, for nine days and nights to gain your wisdom. Accept my death as a sacrifice to you, Lord, even though I did not choose it. I choose it now. Accept my sacrifice and take me directly to your dead heroes' feasting hall in Asgard.'

He could see Olaf approaching, striding towards him with an odd expression on his pock-marked face. This was the time. He looked wildly over at Freya, and opened his mouth to call out to her. But she had turned her face away, and buried it in her hand. He had nothing to say to her, anyway, except that he loved her. She knew that well enough already.

The *hersir* walked over to the trunk of the oak. *Now is the time*, he thought. *One kick at the stool and I will begin to die.* He screwed his eyes shut. *Accept my sacrifice, All-Father*, he prayed. *Make it a good, swift death!*

Nothing happened. He was expecting to fall, to feel the prickly noose tighten horribly around his neck and… and… nothing. He opened his eyes. The *hersir* was fumbling with the rope now, which was secured to a heavy iron stake driven into the flesh of the tree. The village headman slowly loosed the thick knot, taking the hempen rope's end in his hands.

Bjarki was surprised. *He does not have the strength to haul me up by himself. Surely not. I am twice his weight. He cannot be thinking of that.*

Then he saw that the old man, the merchant Valtyr, was coming over to join him by the trunk. *Two of them – that made more sense. The old trader is lean but wiry. He looks strong. The two of them could haul me up, and so achieve my end. But why not simply boot away the stool and let me dangle?*

Olaf put the end of the rope in Valtyr's hand.

'Hear me now, all of you,' he said. 'This man, Valtyr Far-Traveller, has offered to pay the *wergild*, the blood price for the deaths of my eldest son Jeki and his bondsman Ymir on behalf of the murderer Bjarki Bloodhand. He has agreed to pay me a fair weight in silver, enough and more to ease my grief and suffering and compensate me for my loss. Therefore I hereby renounce all vengeance against Bjarki for myself – and for this village.'

There were murmurs of surprise and, perhaps, relief, from the villagers. Freya was now staring at Bjarki, a hesitant smile quivering at the edge of her wet mouth. It disappeared soon enough. Wiped away by Olaf's next words.

'But Bjarki is declared outlaw from this time forward and for ever. He is exiled from the island of Bago, and from the whole Dane-Mark. He may not return to this land on pain of death. Furthermore, he is now made thrall. His freedom is stripped from him; he shall henceforth be given into the hand of Valtyr Far-Traveller as a slave. This is the law. I, Olaf Karlsson, Bago law-speaker and *hersir*, have spoken. Let all the gods be my witness.'

Olaf put the end of the rope into Valtyr's hand. Bjarki heard Freya crying out his name. But he looked instead at his new master.

'You prayed to the Old One in this sacred place. I believe he has heard you,' said Valtyr in a kindly voice. 'Get down from there, lad. We must be far from this village by nightfall; and we've a long, hard road ahead of us.'

Bjarki's legs collapsed under him. He crashed down on the stool, splintering it to kindling, and tumbled unconscious to the ground.

Chapter Two

A mismatch in the marketplace

Tor didn't much care for the look of this new fellow, the lumbering fisher-boy that Valtyr had acquired in the one-dog hamlet on Bago that morning.

He was too big, too clumsy and too ugly to make a pleasant travelling companion for either of them. She did not know what Valtyr had been thinking. He had paid half a mark of good hack-silver for this oaf – an outrageous amount – and Valtyr had even gone so far as to cut his bonds and remove the rope from his grubby neck before they got on the stinking fishing skiff that took them five watery miles west from Bago to the mainland, the Jutland Peninsula. Since they had disembarked, and taken the main road heading south, this Bjarki fellow had been allowed to walk freely beside them, trudging along side by side almost as if he were their equal.

Valtyr seemed even to encourage him in that belief, talking quietly with the great oaf, apparently comforting him. Telling the newly outlawed slave that his old life was over but that many exciting prospects lay ahead. The oaf walked in silence, like a sleepwalker, or as if he had been stunned by a swift, hard blow to the head, but Tor guessed he was at least half-listening to the old man's soft, continuous blather. Occasionally, the youth nodded in agreement. After about five miles, his chin lifted a fraction, his eyes seemed to focus, and he began to look with a little more interest at his surroundings.

He's probably never been off that fly-speck isle in his life, Tor thought.

It was Tor's turn to make the evening stew when they stopped to camp in a stand of silver birch off the road some hours later. As she stirred flakes of salted herring and oats into bubbling water in the pot, she watched the two of them, sitting like old comrades on a log on the far side of the campfire.

Valtyr was still talking away quietly and, finally, she heard the oaf speak. It was to ask a question: where are we going? As she was shifting the over-boiling pot off the hottest part of the fire, she only half-heard the reply.

She heard the old man say the name Fyr Skola and knew that Valtyr was describing their ultimate destination and what they meant to do when they got there. No doubt filling his head with tales of the legendary heroes, the Rekkar, making promises, and persuading this oaf to accept this path.

He's wasting his time, Tor thought, *as well as his precious silver*. This bumpkin had nothing of the unusual about him, not that she could see. He had killed some local fellow in a brawl, the son of the *hersir*, apparently, but that hardly made him a candidate for the heights of the Fyr Skola. He was also too meek to make a proper warrior, too biddable. This clod would nod and nod and agree to everything Valtyr suggested; then, in a day or two, run off and try to get back to his mud-pie village – the fuss that bedraggled chit made when they took their leave from Bago! Embarrassing for everyone. Wailing, weeping, begging him to stay. Saying he was promised to her. The silly cow had only stopped her noise when her mother dragged her away.

The oaf would run, she was sure of it – and, when he got back to Bago, his neighbours would hang him. It was only a question of whether the big lump would try to cut their throats and rob them before he sneaked away.

She put a hand on the seax that hung horizontally over her loins. She would sleep one-eyed tonight, she decided, with her blade unsheathed.

After they had eaten the fishy porridge and were lounging by the fire, bellies full, with the trunks of the birch forming a ghostly palisade to hold back the darkness, she was surprised to hear the Bago youth speak again.

'Tell me more of these Groves of Eresburg,' he said to Valtyr. 'Tell me about the place we are going to. Is it true that the gods walk there?'

'They do walk there, my friend, but the gods – and the spirits of the wild – are *everywhere* in the world. They can be discerned in every hedge, in every field and wood; in every stream, beside every mountain path,' said Valtyr. 'They are, perhaps, even here with us in this copse, on this night.'

Tor saw the oaf shudder and glance quickly over his shoulder at the yellow firelight flickering on the pale bark of the trees all around them.

'But I shall tell you more about the Groves of Eresburg, if you wish.'

Bjarki nodded.

'Well then,' said Valtyr. He shifted his position on his thick bedroll to make himself more comfortable. 'Once, when the world was fresh, before the first men were made, before even the gods came into being, there existed but a single tree, a mighty oak called the Irminsul. The Northmen, of course, call the One Tree the Yggdrasil, for like the gods it has many names, but by whatever name it is called, all agree the One Tree is so huge, so vast, it connected this Middle-Realm with all the other eight worlds of the universe below and above, its massive trunk running right through the centre of all.'

'Everyone has heard of the One Tree,' said Bjarki.

'Just as they should, son,' said Valtyr. 'Just as they should.'

Tor reached for the ale sack, took a long, cooling gulp and passed it over the flames to Valtyr. She felt sleepy. This rendering of the familiar tale made her feel oddly comforted. Almost like a little girl again. She shook out her big, ragged wolf-fur cloak and wrapped it round her narrow shoulders, leaning back and resting her cropped red head on the bulk of her back-sack.

'For an age before the coming of men, the Irminsul was all alone in the empty world, and she was magnificent. Growing taller and thicker in time, becoming strong and also, perhaps, a little lonely, she desired companions. So she scattered her acorns over the fruitful earth and they took root and made more trees, many children in her image. Thus, after many centuries, she created a vast woodland that covered the world like a thick blanket.

'In due course, the hundreds of thousands of new trees in this First Forest also spread their seed and they grew thicker and closer than the hairs on my beard. And the Irminsul was the mother of all trees, all plants, even grass and wildflowers; she was the wellspring of all life in the whole world.

'Then came the men, with their axes and their fire. They came to cut and to build, to burn and clear the ground for their animals and their crops.

'Before the men came, not even light could penetrate into the heart of the First Forest, which was itself alive, and at its centre was the mighty Irminsul, the Mother of Trees. Yet the coming of the men meant the slow death of the great forest. They cut down many of the Irminsul's children with their bright axes and burnt their bodies for fuel. They stripped the earth bare and planted their barley and their rye. They made beams from the ash, alder and oak and built their longhouses. The First Forest began to die.'

'But it did *not* die,' asserted Bjarki, yawning.

'No, it did not, and I shall explain why. Now where was I… Ah, yes! The arrival of the gods. Of course, along with their axes, and their fire, when the men first came into the First Forest, they brought all their gods with them – Odin and Thor, Tiw and Freyr, Loki and Hel and Heimdall and all the rest of them – drawn into the Middle-Realm by the worship of the people. But the spirits of the First Forest, who were more ancient even than the gods, resented this intrusion and a terrible war began between the different deities.

'After much conflict, much destruction of both folk and forest, a truce was called between the gods of men and the spirits of nature, and to ensure a lasting peace, Odin, the greatest god, called the All-Father, offered to sacrifice his own life for the sake of harmony between Man and Nature.

'So he gave himself up to the Mother of Trees, allowing himself to be hanged by the neck from one of the Irminsul's sacred boughs. There he hung for nine days and nine nights as still as a corpse, and yet it was not truly so – the Mother of Trees was tricked by Odin. The cunning god had swallowed a bar of iron and the rope by which he was hanged could not crush his neck with the iron lodged deep inside it. Odin did not die. Instead, on the ninth day, he cut himself down, spat out the bar of iron, and was reborn, stronger, wiser and even more cunning than before – because, of course, by his sacrifice he had gained the wisdom that comes from cheating Death itself.'

Tor could feel her eyes closing. On the far side of the fire, close enough to feel its warmth, the blanket-less youth was curled up on the turf, barely awake.

'The Mother of Trees was tricked by Odin,' repeated Valtyr, 'yet she was not angered by the god's subterfuge. Instead, she was impressed and amused by his antics. She forgave the god, and a true and lasting peace was then made between the ancient spirits of the forest and the new-come gods of men. It was agreed that, every year, the Irminsul would render up a few of her many children for the needs of men, for their fires and their fields, to build their dragon-ships and their houses. And deep in the heart of the First Forest, a high place known as the Groves of Eresburg, where the Irminsul still grows between the nine worlds, would remain sacred for ever.'

'That's where we're heading?' Bjarki's voice was a drowsy murmur.

'It is, son. Now it's time for sleep. We'll need our strength tomorrow.'

–

After a cold breakfast of the remains of the fish stew and some twice-baked barley bread, the three travellers resumed their southward march.

Tor had slept soundly, in spite of herself, and was mildly surprised to find the oaf still with them in the grey light of morning. But there he was, noisily swilling out his mouth with ale from the skin, scrubbing his teeth with a chewed birch twig, and spitting voluminously into the dew-wet grass.

They passed through a flat, pleasant countryside as they walked, fields of sprouting rye, a few verdant sheep and cow pastures, sticking always to the main road that took them south. Away to their left, a mile or two to the east, they occasionally glimpsed the sea, a strip of white-flecked blue.

By midday Tor could see the flat, dirty, brown smoke bank above a substantial settlement at the mouth of a glittering tongue of sea, and Valtyr, stopping them briefly, passed out barley bread and cheese and said they would shortly enter the town of Flens where he hoped to do a little trading.

'You are both to behave yourselves,' he said. 'No fighting; even if you are sorely provoked. Do you hear me, Bjarki? If they call you a milksop or a low-down dirty dog – you do nothing at all. You smile and walk on. Yes?'

'Smile and walk on,' said Bjarki, nodding. 'What else would I do?'

'Don't forget this. I will not pay *wergild* for you a second time. And you, Torfinna Hildarsdottir, you had better behave yourself too, my girl.'

It was a market day and Flens was teeming. Hundreds of farmers and their families had come into the town from miles around to exchange their goods: milk curds, preserved fruit, pickled vegetables, fresh fish and dried, and cuts of fresh meat, new-brewed ale, wool and cloth, linen shirts, as well as a variety tools, nails, knives, hammers, cooking pots, bowls and kettles.

Valtyr found a spot in the corner of the main square and laid out a blanket on the ground on to which he set out his wares:

rows of delicately carved bone hairpins and combs, bunches of coloured ribbons and amulets on leather thongs blessed by magicians from the frozen north and guaranteed to ward off marsh fevers or ensure that blades could not pierce your flesh.

Tor and Bjarki sat down beside the blanket, munching hot mutton pies that Valtyr had purchased, and watched the crowds as they passed by – red-cheeked, brightly dressed, cheerful countrymen and women, prosperous folk, enjoying a day of spring sunshine and a chance to swap gossip with their more distant neighbours. Valtyr, too, did not seem particularly eager to sell his wares. He greeted several of the townspeople by name, and was seemingly well known and liked here. He chatted to a sheep farmer about his flocks and the damage caused by packs of hungry wolves coming out of the southern forests in winter; he exchanged news with a *hersir*, very stern in his mail and polished helm, leaning on his spear. They spoke at length about the Dane-Work, the mighty earthwork fortification that King Siegfried, ruler of the Mark, was repairing and extending in the south, on the Saxon border.

Madness, the *hersir* called it, for Siegfried was offering cold, hard silver from his own treasury to any workers who would help complete this monumental task, labouring alongside his thralls. All the young freemen of fighting age, the *hersir* said, were flocking to join the work gangs. Warriors were turning themselves into ditch-diggers. Where was the honour in that?

Valtyr spoke to a jolly ale-wife about the shocking price of barley per bushel due to last year's rain-soaked harvest, and praised her fresh brew extravagantly – Tor thought he might even be flirting with her. He sold a clay love amulet to a youth with a face marred by a plague of angry pustules who was hovering nervously near the selling blanket. The amulet, if placed under the pallet of a sleeping girl, would compel her to fall in love with the first face she saw upon waking. *Pity the poor girl, if she ever saw that pimpled face looming over her in the light of dawn*, thought Tor.

Through all this, Bjarki just sat on the beaten earth beside the selling blanket and smiled, eyes closed, his big, stupid face tilted up into the sunshine – still apparently savouring his continued existence after the close brush with death. Once she saw him put a hand to his neck and gently touch the angry red mark under his chin that the hemp noose had made there.

The young man's unnatural serenity began to irritate Tor. Who was he to be so content? He had nothing to his name – not even that wench who wept so embarrassingly at his departure from Bago. He didn't even own a pair of shoes, a blanket or eating knife. He was a thrall. A big dolt who this time the day before had been almost hanged like a stray dog. Tor could not imagine the circumstances in which she would allow herself to accept such a bad death, such ignominy – and at the hands of her friends and neighbours, too. To suffer such a miserable, cowardly end was too shameful to bear.

'Let's take a look around,' she said. 'Come on, oaf, stir yourself.'

Bjarki opened one eye. Then the other. He glanced over at Valtyr, who nodded briskly at him and snapped: 'Best you remember my words, lad.'

The two of them set off together to explore the market.

–

Bjarki tried not to gawp. He had seldom been much further than a few days' travel from Bago, except on Thialfi's small fishing craft, and then only to visit other bedraggled villages on the coast of the various islands, which were all remarkably similar to his own; even the faces of the people seemed to be the same. But Flens was at least ten times larger than Bago village, and was home, he supposed, to at least five or six *hundred* folk. Today there seemed to be at least that many just walking in the streets, calling out to each other merrily, peering at the wooden stalls that held the mounds of shining herrings, fingering the dry goods, joking with the stall holders. A group of three young local lads, all painfully near manhood, swaggered past them in a line, taking up nearly the whole muddy street. Bjarki put his hands on Tor's shoulders, guiding her to the side of the street to allow the three youths to pass by unchallenged, and she rounded on him, eyes blazing, spitting fury.

'Take your filthy paws off me! You think I need *your* protection?'

Bjarki was taken aback. He lifted both hands, palm out, in surrender.

'I meant no harm,' he said.

They continued walking in angry silence. Tor stopped at a stall selling knives, a handsome collection of seaxes: bone-handled, sharp steel blades as long as her forearm, housed in beautifully engraved leather sheaths. Bjarki wondered if she had any money to spend. He had none. For a tiny moment he considered stealing a seax. Then rejected the thought as unworthy. Also, he suspected that in big towns like this, thieves were hanged for their crimes. One experience in the shadow of the noose was more than enough for him.

Bjarki turned away from the stall and saw on the far side of the street a large open space in which two big men, stripped to their waists to expose oiled, fish-belly-white chests, were grappling with each other. The space had been marked out as a rough square with long, slender hazel branches, denuded of their foliage, marking each of the four sides.

The two men were not fighting in earnest, Bjarki knew immediately. One man threw the other, almost gently, then stepped forward to help him back to his feet. A small chattering crowd was forming outside the hazel square. So Bjarki left Tor with the knives and crossed the street to join it.

The taller man, with hair the colour of dirty straw, stepped outside the hazel square, leaving the other man inside, and said: 'Who fancies a bout? Who here is man enough to take on Black Svein in bare-handed combat? A silver penny to compete, a purse of ten if you manage to throw him. Ten times your wager! Haven't got a penny? A loaf of bread for ten loaves in victory. Who will place a stake on his own strength? Who will fight?'

Black Svein, a squat, raven-haired bruiser with a mat of chest hair, was strolling around the square, flexing his impressive muscles, rubbing grease into his shoulders and arms. Grinning at the crowd. Striking poses.

Three youths to the left of the hazel square were shoving each other and laughing, making jests; the same ones who had swaggered past in the street.

'How about you, young warriors? Got a silver penny to wager on your prowess? Nothing a pretty maiden likes more than a brave fighting man. You, young *hersir*, can you best Svein? Can you throw him in the mud?'

One of the youths had accepted the challenge, and was stripping off his tunic. He was half a head taller than the dark-haired wrestler, ten years younger, strapping and well made. He stepped into the square to the cheers of his two friends, lifted his hands in the air as if anticipating an easy victory, and winked lasciviously at a pretty girl holding a basket of bread.

Bjarki turned away to see where Tor was, only for a few moments, and missed the whole bout. When he looked back, the young man was lying on the ground with Black Svein standing over him holding his right arm vertically in a complicated twisted position, which was evidently painful.

'Best of three,' said Black Svein, helping his scowling opponent back to his feet. The youth shook his head and went back to his convulsed friends.

It was soon clear that none of the other onlookers wished to try their luck, despite the pleading of the straw-haired man.

'Tell you what – wager a single egg and receive a dozen if you can win. No? Nobody? How about a free bout, then? Any man who wants to have a turn, with bare hands, blunted swords or just the quarterstaff, any man brave enough to step into the hazel-wood square with Black Svein, come now, step forward. No charge, no wager – just for the fun of it.'

There were still no takers.

'How about you, son? You look like a strapping fellow. Care to try your strength?' Bjarki realised the tall blond man was speaking to him.

He shook his head.

'No need to be afraid. I'll tell Black Svein to go easy on you.'

'I'm not afraid,' Bjarki said.

'Then come inside the hazel square and prove it.'

Bjarki shook his head. He smiled.

The straw-haired man turned away. 'There must be one or two here today who are not snivelling cowards,' he said, his back turned to Bjarki.

Bjarki stopped smiling. He felt suddenly cold. He took a step forward.

'He's not a coward,' said a voice at his elbow, a cool hand there, too, restraining him. 'He just doesn't want to fight your friend today. And calling him one won't change his mind.'

The straw-haired man turned back and looked at Bjarki – and Tor, who was now standing beside him.

'You his girl then?' he said. Then to Bjarki: 'Aren't you a one – getting your little girlie to speak for you. I see *now* why you won't fight.'

'He won't fight your friend,' said Tor, 'but I will. You said you had quarterstaffs? Yes? All right then, I accept your challenge.'

The straw-haired man was nonplussed. This scrawny young woman, with arms like kindling sticks, was about half of the weight of Black Svein – and a head shorter than him, too. It was a ridiculous match.

'You can't fight him,' he said.

'Oh yes? Why is that? Is he afraid of me?'

That started a howl of laughter from the crowd, which had thickened considerably by now. The straw-haired man flushed pink with irritation.

'You cannot fight him, girlie. It would not be a fair contest.'

'What if I go really easy on him?' said Tor. 'I promise I won't hurt him all that much – hardly at all. I'll be as gentle as a lamb with the poor idiot.'

The crowd was roaring with mirth by now. Straw-Hair was scowling at her like a man who would like to commit murder. 'No, no match.'

'Perhaps it is your friend Svein who is the snivelling coward,' said Tor.

Bjarki whispered: 'Enough, Tor, you've made your point. Let's go.'

'Or maybe it is *you*,' said Tor, 'who hasn't the stomach for the fight.'

The man leaned in and hissed: 'You've just earned yourself a beating, you silly bitch. If he breaks your skull, you've only yourself to blame.'

'Don't do it, Tor,' said Bjarki. 'He'll kill you. I'll fight him for you.'

'Fuck that. I accepted his challenge. I'll give this troll a fine spanking.'

And Tor stepped over the hazel branch and into the square.

–

The quarterstaff was taller than she was. An inch-thick pole of oak, six feet long. Tor held it in both hands, seemingly taking the measure of its great heft. Bjarki watched with increasing alarm. On the other side of the square Black Svein was twirling his staff with one hand, spinning the wood in a blurred circle just with his strong fingers. Grinning. This joke had gone far enough. Bjarki wondered if he ought to step into the square and plead with the straw-haired man to cancel the bout before Tor was hurt, or even killed.

The crowd was thick about the space now, with people calling out jests and encouragement to the fighters. One man shouted out: 'Kill the little slut!' Bjarki glared at him, memorising his features for future punishment.

'Fight!' Straw-Hair gave the command and stepped away from the two combatants. Black Svein attacked, a slow, lateral swipe at Tor's upper body. He was treating this like a child's game. Tor put the vertical staff across her body and blocked the swipe easily with the upper part of her wood. Then she reversed the blow and struck Svein's leg, hard, with the lower portion of the heavy staff. The staff smacked into Svein's thigh with a noise like a clap.

A couple of men in the crowd laughed.

The dark-haired man was stung, more shocked than hurt. But he didn't go down, as a weaker man might have. He stepped back quickly out of range and rubbed his limb. His face changed. The grin was long gone, and his eyes seemed to fill with new-found wariness. He attacked, a series of short, fast blows alternately striking at Tor with the top and the bottom of the staff.

The girl blocked each strike – clack-clack, clack-clack – with her own pole. She easily anticipated where the blow would fall and her own staff was there just before his. She was quick, Bjarki saw, very, very quick. And she obviously had trained with the quarterstaff before – and trained with serious opponents. She fought like a man, in fact, like a seasoned warrior. But nothing could make up for the superior strength of her opponent. Each whack from Black Svein's weapon drove her back a pace, and now she was on the far left-hand side of the square, by the hazel branch. All she had to do to end the bout was step beyond the barrier, and it would be over and done.

Bjarki opened his mouth to tell her to do exactly this – and stopped.

Tor dived forward, rolling over her own staff, which was tucked tight into her middle. She passed under Black Svein's heavy, swinging blow, bobbed up on the other side quick as a hunting stoat, and delivered a thudding, double-handed thwack of her staff across her opponent's buttocks.

Svein howled with pain and humiliation.

Tor was bouncing on her toes, laughing openly at her red-faced foe.

He swung at her, full strength, using the staff like a long club. If the blow had landed it would have split her skull in two. But Tor ducked, flicked the lethal strike harmlessly over her head with one end of the staff, and neatly swept away Black Svein's weight-bearing right leg with the other.

The big man flew up in the air and thumped down on the beaten earth full on his back, winded and utterly astonished.

Tor, leaning casually on her staff, said: 'Best of three?'

'That is enough, Torfinna,' said a voice beside Bjarki. 'Stop bothering that poor man. Put the quarterstaff down and come here. We're leaving.'

Chapter Three

Mountains made by men

The new shoes felt strange on Bjarki's feet. He had never owned a pair before, although he had once tried on old Thialfi's greasy, fish-smelling boat slippers when his master was asleep and Ubbi the Huntsman had loaned him a spare pair of warm, dry, reindeer-hide boots when they went out last winter in the snows on one of the rare hunting expeditions he was invited to join.

He disliked not being able to feel the earth properly beneath his toes, and he felt clumsy and unsteady wearing them, as if he might slip over and land flat on his arse at any moment. Anyway, the soles of his bare feet were now as thick and hard as any shoe leather, so that he had long ago stopped feeling any pain even over the stoniest terrain. But he rather liked his new possessions, he glanced at them often, with quiet pleasure as they marched, and was determined to learn how to walk in them as well as Tor and Valtyr.

The shoes, along with a cheap iron knife in a wooden sheath, and a wooden plate, spoon and cup, an ale flask and a thick woollen blanket, were gifts that Valtyr had purchased for him at the market in Flens before they left. He carried them in a new wood-framed oiled-linen pack on his back, along with a couple of loaves of bread and some other dried food items, and a linen-wrapped package with a strong scent of lavender, which Valtyr said was soap. It made him feel like a man of substance to be so encumbered.

They marched south along a highway on a low, flat-topped ridge known as the Ox Road, sleeping the first night in a ditch under a blackthorn hedge beside a cow pasture, and moving on at dawn, past hamlets and farmsteads, but meeting few folk as they travelled. On the second afternoon, an hour before sunset, the Dane-Work became visible, a bar on the horizon.

It looked like a series of small barrows or hillocks marching across the southern skyline. Even from half a mile away they seemed to loom menacingly over the flat countryside like a vast series of waves about to crash on to the shore. There were evidently a great number of people living here too. The smoke from cooking fires was thick over the gap between two long mounds of earth, already lightly stubbled with grass and weeds, where the high road was leading them. And Bjarki could see men toiling on the mounds of earth further out with baskets of dug earth strapped to their backs. There was a township of grubby tents and turf-roofed houses – many hundreds of them, some already showing lights in the gloaming – laid out at the bottom of the mounds on both sides of the Ox Road by the gap.

'That is Hellingar,' said Valtyr. It was the first time any of them had spoken since the midday meal. 'It's a dangerous place. Be on your guard.'

'Why dangerous?' said Bjarki. He was greatly in awe of Valtyr and, more recently, of Tor as well, since she had displayed her quarterstaff skills.

For a moment, Bjarki thought that Valtyr would not answer him. They were, as a rule, a group who travelled in silence, like a patrol of stealthy warriors scouting for signs of the enemy. Since they'd left Flens, Bjarki, who was now fully recovered from his near-death ordeal in Bago, had been a bubbling cooking pot of questions, but Valtyr largely ignored them, or snapped single-word answers and told him to be quiet, and Tor had given him a furious glare in reply to his whispered enquiries. Soon Bjarki resigned himself to silence and they trudged along all day like a trio of mutes.

'There are more than a thousand men living in Hellingar,' said Valtyr, 'very few women, and they are all far away from their villages and families. It is like an army camp or a long siege. The men labour all day on the Dane-Work for King Siegfried. At night they drink and fight over the handful of drabs foolish enough to join them in this place of mud, muscle and sweat.'

'Why – why do they come here to live like this?' Bjarki wondered if he was pushing his luck.

'For greed, oaf.' Tor's tone brimmed with contempt. 'For the love of silver, men who might be warriors grub down in the dirt of the Dane-Work.'

'But why?'

'Odin's arse,' muttered Tor. 'Because they're fools, that's why.'

Bjarki opened his mouth but before he could speak, Valtyr said: 'The King of the Dane-Mark is building an earthen rampart here, but he is also cutting a huge ditch, an artificial river, if you like, on the other side of that huge rampart – you cannot see it from this side – but it's a waterway that runs from the port of Hedeby on the Schlei inlet, about two miles that way—' Valtyr pointed eastwards '—all the way to Hollingsted Fort on the River Treene, which flows into the Eider marshes, eight miles that way.'

The old man indicated the west.

'Siegfried calls the ditch the Mark-Channel. He doesn't have enough thralls to do the work so he's paying poor freemen to do the digging for him. And before you ask me why, like an accursed infant, Bjarki, I shall tell you.

'Imagine that King Siegfried takes his grand fleet west cruising down the coast to raid the Frisians. And, in his absence, he hears that the down-trodden fishermen of Bago have rebelled against his irksome rule or, more likely, that the brutal Svears—' here Valtyr winked at Tor '—have taken to their dragon-ships and are merrily robbing and burning the king's lands in the east; playing pirate in the home islands while the mighty sea-lord of the Danes is away with his fleet. Siegfried must return and crush his enemies as swiftly as he can. Yes? But to get his ships from the West Sea to the Eastern Lake he has to go all the way around the north tip of the Jutland Peninsula and, just perhaps, past enemies lying in wait in the fjords of the Little Kingdoms. That journey by the whale's road might take him one or two weeks – even if he's unmolested on the way there. Think what damage a couple of shiploads of Svear raiders could do in that time among all the peaceful fishing villages on Fyn or Lolland. So Siegfried is making himself a short cut, a route right across the base of his peninsula, and when it is completed, he can move easily his ships along the Mark-Channel from the West Sea to the Eastern Lake in a matter of days. Understand now, son?'

Bjarki nodded. He had so many other questions to ask – how could King Siegfried afford to pay out so much silver? If he had so much silver to spend, why not just build more ships and have fleets in both the West Sea and the Eastern Lake? – but he decided, perhaps wisely, to hold his tongue.

He thought about the Svears attacking his village on Bago: burning the houses, killing the men, raping the women. The prospect seemed quite plausible. He wondered what Freya was doing, right at this very moment. Did she miss him? He wished, desperately, painfully, that she were in his arms; the two of them on their blanket in the dunes. He wished that golden moment, frozen in time, were the reality. That all this – his near hanging, his expulsion from Bago, these two strange companions – was just a bad dream. He thought fleetingly of his oath to Freya. And felt a shaft of raw pain in his guts. That promise – meant to last a lifetime – had died in less than a day.

They were approaching the sprawling town of tents now: Hellingar. The first ones were the meanest ones, set up either side of the Ox Road, some of them not much more than a cloak or blanket hung over a rope tied between two stakes in the ground. Men, young men, all very dirty, peered out at the travellers as they passed. They looked hostile, wary. And dog-tired.

Bjarki looked straight ahead, avoiding meeting their hard, challenging gazes. The earthworks seemed more oppressive close up, steeper and more unnatural. They must be at least five times the height of a man, Bjarki reckoned, and he wondered how long it would take to move so much earth, to hack it from the ground and haul it up to the top of these extraordinary man-made mountains. No wonder all these labouring men looked so exhausted.

His eye was drawn to a huge wooden fortress, set out right in the middle of the gap between the two central earth barrows, barring the main road. He saw a thick circular palisade of sharpened wooden poles, and the shingle roofs of several long-houses visible inside the walls. The road they were on – here made more substantial with rows of logs embedded in the mud, led straight to the gatehouse in the palisade – and Bjarki saw soldiers in helmets watching their approach from a roofed gallery above the gates.

He expected Valtyr to turn aside before the fortress gate, to lead them to some large tent or turf-roofed house where they would rest. Night was falling; a washed-out wafer of moon was already visible over the brow of the western barrow. But the old man did not. He took them straight up to the portal of the fortress and, staring up at the soldiers above, said: 'Open the gates, open them quickly for Valtyr Far-Traveller and his followers. I claim guest-friendship of Jarl Snorri Hare-Lip, the Master of Hellingar Fort.'

They were admitted. The gates creaked open and the three of them walked inside to be greeted by a cheerful red-headed soldier in leather armour, with a hand-axe in his belt and a spear. The soldier who, it seemed, was more of a guide than a figure of authority, led them into the fort.

Once inside, Bjarki was immediately astonished by the regularity of the layout. He was used to people building their houses and barns and animal pens and workshops wherever they wished, as long as it did not impinge on their neighbours' space. But this place, this great fortress of Hellingar, was laid out with strange precision, all straight lines and sharp corners. He muttered something of this nature to Tor, who gave him a look of icy scorn.

Valtyr, seeing his surprise, leaned over as they walked along and hissed into his ear. 'The master has fashioned Hellingar in the Frankish style; he's aping our enemies. Now keep your mouth shut and eyes open.'

Bjarki did not understand. But he knew how, and when, to obey. He kept his mouth closed and took in the sights of the extraordinary settlement.

The circumference of the perfectly circular fort was marked by a man-high earth bank, topped with a double-thickness palisade of split pine trunks, twice that height, sharpened at their ends. A walkway ran around the inside, allowing a sentry or defender to stand with most of his body protected by the stout palisade, with only head and shoulders exposed above the pine spikes. A defender could shower missiles down on any attacker, or use sword, axe and spear from a commanding and well-protected position inside the walls.

Once through the gate, a log road led due south straight across to the other side of the fortress two hundred paces away where there was another double gate. Another log-paved road, running east to west, intersected the north–south road, creating four distinct areas, quadrants inside the circular fortress. Each of the four quadrants contained four large longhouses arranged in a square or box, with one longhouse on each side, and it was to the nearest quadrant, to the immediate right of the gatehouse, that the soldier-guide led the travellers. They entered the nearest longhouse through a door in the gable end, and came into a large hall filled with warmth, wood smoke and the usual pungent household odours, and several dozen strangers.

The red-headed soldier stopped a passing steward, a harassed-looking middle-aged man in a gold-trimmed scarlet tunic, and asked where Jarl Snorri was. The man gave the grimy travellers' rags one contemptuous glance and said the jarl was busy. He nodded towards the end of the hall, where a pair of wooden screens partitioned off the final third of the long building. So the soldier took them to the benches at the side of the hall and left them sitting there, saying the steward would look after them from now on.

Valtyr nodded his thanks. Bjarki was already feeling slightly uneasy, overwhelmed to be inside such a huge, bustling place. There seemed to be more people inside this one long room than in the whole of Bago village.

They sat in a row on the bench, watching the people moving about the great hall. Warriors in leather armour reinforced with iron strips sat on the benches on the other side of the hall, their swords across their knees, drinking from horns and joking with their fellows; women with embroidered aprons, their hair tied up in white kerchiefs tended steaming cauldrons of soup that bubbled over the rectangular central hearth fires; in one corner a group of a dozen children was being told a story by a skinny grandfather, who acted out all the parts of his tale, the firelight casting shadows on the bare wooden-plank walls of the hall as he became, in turns, a terrifying frost giant, then an innocent blushing maiden, then a hideous mountain troll.

In a little while, a fat matron with a large tray brought them bowls of leek soup and fresh bread, and a scabby youngster, a thrall by the iron collar he wore, brought wooden cups and an ale skin. They ate, drank and waited.

Finally the screen shifted aside and a man came out of the space behind it. Bjarki had never seen anyone like him before. His face was angular, kindly and wise, with bright blue eyes, and his blond hair was tidily cut in the shape of a ring that ran all the way around his head, but the top part had been shaven to expose his sun-browned pate. He wore a long robe of undyed wool so pale it seemed to shine in the gloom of the hall. He carried no sword, nor a knife. He had few adornments on his attire, merely a rope belt and thong round his neck from which hung a plain wooden cross.

'Who is *that* man?' Bjarki whispered to Valtyr.

There were two men coming out behind the bald fellow, men with steel helmets tucked under their arms, and grey scale-armour visible under long black cloaks. Black tunics, black trews and black leather boots. They wore two swords at their belted waists, a yard-long one on the left and a shorter one on the right, and the ever-watchful expressions of hard men tasked with warding the precious life of another.

'That,' said Valtyr, in a bleak tone, 'is an apostle. A Christian priest – what we would call a *gothi*. His name is Livinus and he is an Angelcynn missionary from the lands across the West Sea. But what he's doing in the hall of one of Siegfried's most important jarls, I do not know.'

'And what—' began Bjarki.

'An apostle is a holy man of the Christian god, a fanatic, who seeks to force the whole world to submit to his foul doctrine. That one is also a lord of warriors, who controls much land; he is, in short, a dangerous enemy.'

The Christian apostle and his two hard-faced bodyguards were shown out of the hall by the steward, who bowed and bobbed along beside them obsequiously, as if he were in the presence of the king of the Mark himself.

Bjarki watched them leave, fascinated – both attracted and repelled by the pale-clad priest and his grim entourage. Then they were gone, and the hall seemed a good deal darker. He could feel the hot soup pleasantly filling his belly, and the long day of walking began to take its toll. His eyes began to droop. After a little while, the steward came to them and announced that His Excellency Jarl Snorri would deign to see Valtyr Far-Traveller now.

Valtyr relieved Bjarki of the strongly scented package of lavender soap – an expensive gift for the jarl's wife, apparently – and left his two young companions drowsing on the wide wooden bench while he walked to the end of the hall and disappeared into the dark space behind the screen.

Valtyr's conversation with the jarl did not last very long at all, perhaps less than a quarter of an hour. Nor was it satisfactory, judging from the dark expression on the old man's face when he rejoined them on the hall bench.

'I thought he might have one or two good prospects for me from among the men on the Dane-Work,' Valtyr said to Tor.

'But no. The mean bastard took my soap, called me a demon-worshipper and told me to be off.'

–

They slept on the benches and woke before dawn. They breakfasted on well-watered ale and oatmeal porridge sweetened with honey and, before the sun was above the horizon, they had left Hellingar by the southern gate and were making their way across the bridge of land that spanned the Mark-Channel.

Bjarki stopped in the middle of the causeway and looked left and right. Of all the wonders he had seen in his life, this was the most extraordinary. An enormous trench had already been excavated on either side of the narrow land bridge, a monstrous muddy ditch more than twenty paces wide. And the diggings were already half filled with rainwater. The scale of this mammoth undertaking was, to Bjarki's mind, almost inconceivable: that a man, even a great ruler such as Siegfried, could order a ten-mile river to be dug from one side of his realm to the other, and demand a high earthen rampart to be built behind it, and that all this would actually be accomplished. It was awe inspiring, stupendous. While the sun was not fully risen there were already hundreds of dirt-smeared men along the edges of the Mark-Channel, wielding their picks and spades, with the overseers bawling instructions…

'Don't dawdle, oaf,' snapped Tor. 'We haven't got all day for you to stand around and gawp at these scurrying river rats.'

Bjarki broke into a trot but he was surprised to see Valtyr standing on the far side of the land bridge looking back thoughtfully at the long broken shapes of the man-made mountains on the bank of this artificial waterway.

'Take another look, Bjarki, if you wish to,' the one-eyed old man said. 'You may not see the Dane-Mark again for some time. Since the peace was made, this place now marks the frontier between the kingdom and Saxony.'

'Siegfried and the Saxons were at war?' said Bjarki.

'Until last summer. Theodoric of Saxony and King Siegfried have been butting heads in this region for many years – mostly squabbles over the theft of cattle and sheep by border folk – but they are now fully reconciled. They made the old sacrifices at Hellingar last year, agreed that this was the border between their territories and feasted like heroes. Duke Theodoric's eldest son, Widukind, was married off to Siegfried's daughter Geva to seal a peace. And this, the Dane-Work, is a monument to the alliance they made then.'

Tor made a scoffing noise.

'Take a last look yourself, Torfinna, and save your scorn. Siegfried is a wise ruler and favours peace. But not peace at any price. This channel will prove a fine passageway for his ships but it is also the Mark's best defence, its moat and ramparts in one, which may one day save us from our enemies.'

Chapter Four

A forest of bones

They walked for seven days without sheltering under another roof. For the first two days they passed through low-lying farms, pastures and patches of pretty woodland that to Bjarki's eyes very much resembled his homeland.

He had half expected – now that he was in Saxony – that everything would look different. This part of Theodoric's realm, just south of the Dane-Work, was the home of the Nordalbians, one of the four main Saxon tribes, Valtyr explained to him over supper that first night. Westphalians were the most powerful tribe who occupied the lands south of Frisia; the Angrians were horse-rearing folk from the Weser Valley in the very centre of Saxony; and the Eastphalians hailed from the wild borderlands along the River Elbe.

'And Theodoric is king of all these different tribes?' asked Bjarki.

'He's no king,' replied Valtyr. 'But all four tribes acknowledge him as their war leader. They submit to him because they share a common enemy.'

'That Christian apostle?'

'Very good, Bjarki, I see you *have* been paying attention. Yes, the Christians are our enemies but it's not a few wandering apostles peddling their stupid religion that the Saxons fear. It is the Franks. The Franks are devout Christians but they also have armies. Powerful armies. Thousands of warriors. The Franks encroach on Saxon lands in the south and west. They seize territory, slay the people and construct their accursed churches.'

‘What is a church?’ asked Bjarki, who was scraping out the last remnants of supper from the porridge pot, eating the curls of dried-on oats. Marching made him permanently hungry and there was never enough to eat; something that both Tor and Valtyr seemed to find endlessly amusing.

‘It is a large building in which the Christians pray to their absurd god,’ said Valtyr. ‘They also pray to their god’s son who was nailed up on a tree.’

‘They pray to their gods *inside* a building?’ Bjarki was intrigued. ‘Do they not fear that their gods will not be able to hear them through the walls?’

‘None of it makes any sense, lad. Don’t even try to understand it.’

‘If Theodoric doesn’t like it, why doesn’t he just burn their churches?’

‘Because they don’t just build a church. They build a fortress around it, with high walls, and they fill it with hundreds of their soldiers. That’s why.’

Bjarki put down the empty pot. His belly gave a hollow gurgle. Valtyr was still talking about these dreaded Franks. He seemed to have a bee in his bonnet, but at least the talk might take Bjarki’s mind off his half empty stomach.

The Franks, Valtyr was saying, had a vigorous new leader, a young fellow named Karolus who, it was whispered, had murdered his own brother in order to rule alone. This new Frankish monarch, a fanatical Christian with many warriors, had vowed to spread his religion and make all the people in the lands of the North believe in his god. *That’s stupid*, Bjarki thought. *How could you force a whole people to believe something, if they did not want to?*

–

The march south was monotonous, more than anything else. They would arise at dawn, eat a few scraps of bread or the remains of last night’s supper, if Bjarki had left any, and then march till midday when they would stop for an hour, eat bread, drink from their flasks, rest, tend to their blisters and the sores from the chafing packs, then, grudgingly, get up and march till dusk.

The food ran out after three days and Tor produced a short bow from her pack, strung it and carried it always in her right hand as they walked. She took pride in effortlessly demonstrating her skills as a hunter again and again. She could raise the bow, nock an arrow and loose in less than a single heartbeat. And it was seldom that she failed to skewer even a swift-running hare or high-scampering squirrel. She could even hit a pigeon or waterfowl on the wing three times out of four. Valtyr too demonstrated his knowledge of foraging in the many marshlands and rivers they crossed – catching eels, fish and frogs with a surprisingly youthful agility; he also had a fine instinct for where to dig for edible roots, or find banks of wild garlic to flavour soup.

Bjarki was allocated the unpleasant task of skinning or plucking and cleaning the creatures Tor and Valtyr killed, and threading them on nodding hazel sticks to roast over the campfire. But he was not unhappy with this role. And while he was usually hungry, never quite full, they rarely slept without something in their bellies. Which had not been the case in Bago.

The countryside changed as they travelled. The sleepy villages they sometimes saw in the distance – Valtyr did not allow them to stop and investigate them, not even to beg a little fresh bread – petered out, the land began to rise and they began to enter wilder, less populated areas.

Ahead of them was a thick band of green, the sad remains of the once vast First Forest, Valtyr said, yet it seemed to Bjarki as big as an ocean when viewed from the top of a rise, with the occasional mountain or range of hills poking through the mossy blanket.

At night they heard the music of wolves. Their path took them south, always south, and the handful of people they did meet on the road began to speak in a different way. The language was very similar to the northern tongue all three used – whenever they *did* talk – and while the speech was comprehensible, the Saxon dialect seemed heavier, more brutal in the mouth.

On the morning of the sixth day, they came at last to the edge of the First Forest, and Valtyr stopped them. He leaned on his walking staff, unlaced and took off one of his shoes to rid himself of an irritating pebble.

'From now on, we must be completely silent,' he said. 'We should not attract the slightest attention. And any folk or… or other creatures… we encounter we must regard as very dangerous unless they prove otherwise.'

Bjarki looked at the forbidding wall of the woodland, thick ancient trunks, oak and ash, alder and birch, all gnarled, twisted and knitted together, armoured with moss and lichen, the undergrowth in places as thick as a hedgerow. There did not seem to be a road or path leading into the forest at all. And there appeared to be strange patterns of branches growing over the surface of many of the trunks of the ancient trees. Tiny branches, twigs even, arranged in parallel patterns, almost like ribs, like little skeletons…

'Bones,' he said. 'Animal bones.'

'Not just animal,' said Tor, and she pointed at an oak as wide in girth as a wagon's wheel. And Bjarki saw the complete outline of a man's inner framework, picked clean of flesh and somehow fastened to the huge trunk.

'A forest of bones,' he said, wonderingly.

'Sacrifices,' said Valtyr. 'People in these parts nail up living flesh here as an offering to the spirits, to keep them all safely *inside* the woods.'

'And we're going in there?' Bjarki was suddenly appalled.

'This is what is left of the First Forest, which once covered the whole wide world,' said Valtyr. 'The Groves of Eresburg are its beating heart, once the core of the Middle-Realm, so naturally they nestle in its bosom.'

'And the Fyr Skola?' said Bjarki.

'Yes, yes, the Skola is in the groves. Now, shall we get on?'

The First Forest was strangely noisy. Once the travellers had penetrated the outer wall of trees, following a path so faint it might have been made by a particularly light-footed mouse, it was noticeably gloomier, with only a few reed-slender shafts of sunlight breaking through the canopy above.

Yet Bjarki was surprised at how much life appeared to be all around him, all the time: the ancient trees had many birds clattering and quarrelling through the branches, magpies and pigeons, cawing rooks. A plump red squirrel squeaked and chittered its outrage at them from a low moss-covered bough. A black scuttling grouse hurried away from their approaching feet through the thick banks of rustling leaves, giving out sharp cries of distress. There were rabbits, too, in a few of the grassy clearings that they saw from time to time, and on three occasions that first day they saw two elegant spotted deer looking at them from behind trees less than a dozen paces away with their lovely liquid eyes. Tor had raised her bow but, swifter than she, Valtyr seized her wrist and snapped that she was not to kill any creature – not one – without his permission.

Neither, apparently, were they allowed to make a fire, even a small one. They stopped in late afternoon, when it was already nearly too dark to see five paces ahead. Bjarki was not sure if they had been following a path *at all* in the past two hours; they might just have been blundering aimlessly in the half-light, pushing through shoulder-high ferns and low snagging branches.

So, no comforting fire when they stopped for the night, and precious little to eat, too. The remains of a roasted hare from the day before, now cold and greasy, and a handful each of raw, half-dried mushrooms, gritty from the bottom of Valtyr's pack. The three of them sat with their backs against a fallen log, already wrapped in all their bedding but still damp and chilly, chewing on the leathery mushrooms and staring out into the early darkness.

'How far must we travel before we reach the Fyr Skola?' asked Bjarki.

He was only slightly cheered by the answer. 'Not far. Tomorrow… or the next day.' Valtyr seemed strangely uncertain.

'If we don't starve to death before then,' muttered Tor.

Hours later, swathed in his new woollen blanket, tired from the march but unable to sleep, Bjarki listened to the sounds of the First Forest all about him: the creaking of an old tree; the rustle of some small creature fossicking through dead leaves. He tried not to think about the ancient spirits of the forest who surely still lived there, those beings who were so fearsome that they needed to be placated with living offerings nailed up on the tree wall.

He remembered something Valtyr had said to him on the first night after leaving Bago – that the First Forest itself was alive. He now believed it.

The moon rose, a glossy fresh cheese just visible above the highest branches of the treetops, and the pure darkness below was slightly alleviated.

Bjarki found he could now make out the individual tree trunks around him. In a way, it was far worse than the impenetrable black. There were shapes out there that he could not imagine were natural in any way. He was almost sure that the thing over there was a bush or a young alder tree, but its twisted black shape against a dark grey background looked exactly like a bent old man, wearing a floppy travelling hat and leaning on a gnarled staff.

He half-expected it to speak. He shifted his position and now the bush, or whatever it was, looked like a rearing horse, a fine stallion, frozen in time.

He even imagined he could hear it breathing. Heavy, snuffling breaths.

Something *was* breathing out there. Something very large.

And it was not the bush-stallion.

A stick cracked. A sharp report. There was no way of explaining it away. It was not his imagination; his night fears. Something heavy, much heavier than a man, had trodden on a substantial dead branch and snapped it.

Bjarki rolled out of his blanket and stood up. He felt for the cheap iron knife at his belt. But he had removed it to sleep more comfortably. It was somewhere in the leaf litter by his pack. He would not find it until morning.

The thing – whatever it was – was moving closer. Bjarki could smell it now, a musky, earthy, animal smell overlaid with a scent like old rotting meat. He could make out a shape in the darkness to his left, a vast creature on all fours, broad as a door, flat-headed, two red-glinting eyes…

'Do not make any sudden movements,' Valtyr's whisper was only just audible. Bjarki could feel the old man's presence, a warmth behind him. He could hear the rustle and crunch of leaves as Tor emerged from her bedding.

'When I say run – we all go and in different directions. To confuse it.'

There was a rattle of stick on stick, then: 'Put your little bow down, Tor,' Valtyr hissed in the darkness. 'You will only irritate this noble beast.'

Bjarki felt light-headed, cold and then hot, he heard a rushing sound of water in his ears. He felt an urge to approach the monster, to reach out and touch its fur. He took a faltering step. And another. He stretched out a hand.

'We mean you no harm,' he said quietly. A massive coughing grunt was the answer, like an explosion. It seemed to shake the heart in his chest.

'We do not wish to hurt you.' His words were much louder this time.

The creature suddenly reared up on its hind legs, it was twice as tall as a grown man. It roared. A meaty blast of sound, like a hundred trumpets. Bjarki felt the storm of it blowing on his face and hair; it almost forced his body back, like walking on the shore in a wild sea gale. Instead, gritting his teeth, he took another nervous step towards the huge animal.

'Brother Bear,' he said, and he knew not where the words came from, 'we greet you as a comrade; Brother Bear, we respect your strength and wisdom. Have mercy on us, Brother Bear, we weak creatures, we foolish children of men. Grant us safe passage through your wood, your kingdom.'

The huge animal roared again, another hurricane of noise, and Bjarki braced himself for the lumbering charge, which he knew would come next.

But, instead, astoundingly, the animal suddenly dropped on to all fours again and, making a low moaning noise that sounded almost like a weird singing, it turned around and shambled away. Bjarki could clearly hear it blundering through the crunching undergrowth, loudly grunting to itself from time to time, growing quieter until there was no sound from it at all.

He turned around and looked at his two companions, just able to make them out in the grey shafts of moonlight.

'I do not think he truly meant to hurt us,' he said, in a tone that was almost apologetic. 'He was just a little taken aback to find folk in his wood.'

'We should have brought some heavy hunting spears,' said Tor.

Valtyr laughed in relief. 'And a dozen warriors to wield them!'

They settled down again, wrapped once more in their blankets. Bjarki found his knife-sheath in the leaf litter and threaded it once more on his belt. But he did not feel afraid. He had not felt any fear since the huge animal had gone. 'I think he has granted us his permission to be in his forest,' he said.

'Or maybe he has gone to find some of his friends, to invite them all back here for a nice feast of man-flesh,' said Tor, laughing far too heartily.

They all sat against the log for a while in silence. Yet not one of them was in the mood to sleep.

'The words you spoke to the bear, Bjarki,' said Valtyr, 'who taught them to you? Who taught you to say those exact words?'

'I was not taught them. I have never spoken them before in my life.'

'Is that so?' said the old man. 'Interesting.'

-

They did not sleep again that night. They sat in a row, backs against the log, and talked quietly of bearish things. Valtyr spoke of the great white bears he had encountered in the frozen north, who would, if they were desperate, hunt and kill people for food. They would wait outside the remote Sami cabins and pounce when the folk emerged to relieve themselves, as if the people were unwary seals coming up from a hole in the ice-bound seas. Tor spoke of a cousin of her mother's neighbour in Svearland who claimed to have known a hunter who found a motherless black bear cub and raised it to its full strength with great patience, love and tenderness.

'Then, during a hard winter, the bear killed the man who cared for it, and ate him up, down to his boots,' she said with a wholly false chuckle.

Bjarki said little. He was still savouring his brief encounter with the magnificent beast. He truly believed that a kind of communication had taken place between him and the wild animal. He hugged that idea to his chest.

The next day, after several hours of struggle through the thick forest, up steep mountainsides and down vertiginous slopes into deep valleys, during which on at least two occasions Bjarki was convinced they were utterly lost, the three travellers emerged from the green gloom into bright sunlight on a high, narrow ridge overlooking a long valley that ran roughly northeast to southwest. There was a wide, sparkling river wending down the middle of the marshy, treeless glen, and a sort of island, a huge oval outcropping of earthy rock, bursting out of the ground on the far side of the silvery waters.

The rock outcropping, which was five hundred paces wide and a little more in length, thrust out from the valley floor, rising more than a hundred paces straight up in the air above the south bank of the river, and its wide flat summit seemed to be completely covered with dense green foliage. Trees.

It looked like a round, inch-thick griddle cake placed on a table top. Bjarki could see buildings, too, on this strange valley-island. Through the green smudge of leaves, he could make out thatched and timber-built houses and even the tiny figures of people walking about outside them. There was a village of sorts on top of this strange geological formation but one the like of which he had never seen before. A man-high palisade of sharpened logs had been constructed around the whole outcropping, pierced by only one gate that Bjarki could see, with a rutted track that led up to it from the valley floor. But strangest of all, to his eyes, were the trees, the ancient oak, ash and beech trees, which were *inside* the palisade on top of the valley-island.

They had been shaped into neat patterns, cut or cultivated into long, curving lines to make a design clearly visible from the high ridge they were standing on more than a mile to the north. The tree lines made a clearly defined configuration that consisted of three interlocking leaf-shaped lobes, each equidistant from the other two, and all meeting in the centre, where there was a massive patch of dark green, rising much, much taller than the rest, in the rounded triangular space at their junction. This was a block of dark foliage the size of the whole village of Bago. It took Bjarki a moment to realise that the towering green mass in the middle triangle formed by the three interlocking lobes was made up of a single gigantic tree. It was the Irminsul, he realised with a shock.

'Behold the sacred Groves of Eresburg,' said Valtyr, speaking slowly and portentously, like a skald at a royal feast. 'Home of the Fyr Skola.'

'About time, too,' said Tor. 'I'm digesting my own stomach here.'

Chapter Five

The Fyr Skola

They were intercepted by half a dozen well-armed men before they had descended a hundred paces down the side of the ridge into the valley. Dressed in woollen tunics and fine leather-lined cloaks, long seaxes slung across their bellies, the men emerged silently out of the forest from all sides and surrounded them with a ring of deliberately pointed spears.

It was neatly done, even Bjarki could tell that. These troops were well trained. One moment the travellers were alone on the steep path, the next, they were completely at the soldiers' mercy. He looked questioningly at Valtyr. Should they resist these warriors? Should they try to fight them off?

No. Valtyr was grinning broadly at the captain of these men-at-arms, a middle-aged Jutlander named Bragi, who seemed to know Valtyr well, in fact he seemed to be an old and trusted comrade. The spear points swiftly lifted.

As the soldiers led the travellers down the narrow path to the valley bottom, Bragi aimed a stream of questions at Valtyr about the outside world: was the peace holding between Siegfried and Theodoric? Was the Dane-Work completed yet? Was there any sign of fresh Frankish incursions?

To Bjarki's greater surprise, Valtyr answered them all: the peace with the Dane-Mark was intact, but Christian missionaries, protected by Frankish troops, had built a wooden church in the far west, inside Theodoric's realm on the east bank of the River Ijssel, at a little place called Deventer.

Valtyr seemed to be carefree while chatting with these soldiers, as if a burden had at last been lifted from his shoulders. Without obviously staring, Bjarki scrutinised these ordinary-looking men-at-arms while they scrambled down the valley side on well-worn footpaths. Could these men really be the famous warriors of the Groves of Eresburg – the Rekkar, the heroes who knew no fear in battle, whose skin could not be pierced by any blade, who wielded their weapons with the skill of wizards and strength of ten men?

Bjarki did not believe it. They looked like commonplace *warriors* to him. Perhaps that was their secret: they looked ordinary but somehow transformed into the legendary frenzied fighters when battle was at hand.

'They don't look very special to me,' he muttered to Tor. They were walking through the lush meadows at the bottom of the valley, beside the chuckling waters of the river. 'I thought at least they'd all have decent furs.'

Tor gave him a look of deepest contempt. 'These are not Rekkar, you idiot,' she hissed. 'These are not Fire Born. They are just... men.'

One of the younger Eresburg soldiers raced off ahead to give warning of the three strangers' arrival and, as they splashed over the shallow waters of the river, which barely came up to their knees, and began to climb the track that led up to the high valley-island, Bjarki lifted his eyes to look at the place that Valtyr had promised to lead him to, the sacred community where, if Bjarki were blessed, he would remain for months undergoing the rigorous training the old man promised would change his whole life: the Fyr Skola.

It looked completely different from the eagle's-eye view on the ridge, where the interlocking pattern of the three leaf-shaped groves could clearly be discerned, and the Irminsul unified the whole in the centre of the design.

He could see a low earth wall and lichen-smeared log palisade, not dissimilar to the one that protected the Hellingar Fortress, indeed it was not all that different from the one at Bago – although thicker and higher. The most obvious difference was that the palisade surrounded the mass of trees on the summit, as if *that* was what it sought to protect. Usually, a village had woodland on the *outside*. It was a bizarre inversion of the order of things.

When they reached the top of the track and passed through the open gates, they found that a crowd had already formed. Bjarki was taken aback. He was not used to his arrival being a cause for any kind of gathering. He glanced at Tor and saw her grubby face filled with a glow of happiness.

There was a large group of people waiting to meet them, about a hundred men and women ranging in age from greybeards to girls on the cusp of womanhood, and they were all singing. It was a melody that Bjarki did not know, and yet it seemed familiar nonetheless: it was solemn and slow and in a language he did not understand, and so beautiful that he found the fine hairs on the back of his neck rising with the song's emotion. He realised that Valtyr, standing beside him, was singing along, and the old man had tears pooling in his empty right eye socket and streaming down his cheeks.

The crowd parted and formed a corridor and Bjarki and his companions stepped forward, passing between two wings of singing Eresburg folk. He found himself walking towards the Irminsul, the sacred heart of the Groves.

Close up, the One Tree's size was staggering. The gnarled trunk of the ancient oak was so massive that twelve tall men clasping hands would be unable to make an unbroken ring around its girth. It soared up, up and up into the sky, its distant topmost branches out of sight and each of its many curving limbs and sprouting twigs was bristling with new leaves, so dense the sunlight that managed to filter through to the earth had a greenish tinge.

Bjarki and Tor found themselves alone, in a little patch of space under the faint emerald light of the tree, when the beautiful music finally ceased. They stood there, feeling more than a little foolish, as a tall, lean and lovely woman stepped forward, holding a newborn lamb in the crook of her arms.

Bjarki had never seen anyone who was as thin as her before – yet the lady did not seem malnourished, nor faint with hunger. She seemed calm and serene, a crown of white hawthorn blossoms and other spring flowers was set on her long, reddish-gold hair, and she wore a gown of some fine material, green as moss, light as gossamer, which fell to her ankles. In her right hand she held a long, black, iron staff with an intricate head of spiralling strands of metal forming a small egg-shaped cage below a large iron knob.

'Welcome, weary travellers,' she said in good, clear Norse, but with a slight Saxon accent. 'I am Skymir, Mikelgothi of the Groves of Eresburg. I bid you welcome to this sacred place. I, and all my fellow *gothi*, and all the servants of the Groves here gathered, pray you may discover your true selves here, and find a knowledge of your inner power, and furthermore that you will learn to use what strength you gain here for the benefit of all mankind.'

Valtyr stepped forward. 'Greetings, Mikelgothi, may the gods shower their blessings on the Groves of Eresburg. I bring you Bjarki Bloodhand of Bago and Torfinna Hildarsdottir of Svearland, who seek the honour of enrolment as novices in the Fyr Skola. May you find them both worthy.'

'Our thanks to you, as ever, Valtyr Far-Traveller. Not all who enter the Fyr Skola are blessed by the gods; but all may render good service to them.'

Then she said, in a surprisingly deep, booming voice for someone so slight and slender: 'Irminsul, hear me! Mother of Trees, bear witness!'

The crowd began to hum, a thrumming in a hundred throats, a simple, four-note repetitive tune. It made Bjarki's arms immediately goose-pimple.

'Do you freely choose, Bjarki Bloodhand and Torfinna Hildarsdottir,' the priestess intoned, 'to join our community this day as novices, to enroll in good faith into the ranks of the Fyr

Skola, and to solemnly swear in the presence of all these good folk that you will accept and keep all our laws and practices, and take them as your own; that you will cherish and protect the Fyr Skola and its customs, keep its secrets, and guard the Irminsul and the ancient spirits of the forest from all enemies as long as you both shall live?'

There was a slight pause. Then the priestess smiled and said, in a more normal, friendly tone: 'You *can* say "No", if you want to. We will feed you and clothe you and send you safely on your way, if you do not choose to join us. Think hard before you answer. This is a serious and binding oath.'

Tor immediately said: 'Yes, lady, yes, I choose and so swear.'

Bjarki said: 'I don't know what your laws are here. So how can I swear to accept them? I know hardly anything about you or about the Fyr Skola.'

'Just say yes, you dunderhead.' Tor's voice was too loud. 'Don't you *want* to become one of the Rekkar? Don't you *want* to become a legend?'

The weird humming had stopped. The crowd was muttering now.

'You may refuse to take the oath, Bjarki Bloodhand, it is entirely your choice,' Valtyr's voice was soft and kindly. 'I hereby free you of thralldom and will take you back to the Dane-Mark, if you wish it, to face whatever the Fate-Spinners have in store for you there. But you may *not* know the secrets of the Fyr Skola before you make your decision. You must swear the oath *unknowing*; you must trust us blindly. Or not. Just as you choose. All I will say is that I think this is the right path for you, the right place for you to be. I would not have brought you here if I did not believe that with all my heart.'

For a moment or two, Bjarki did actually consider going back to the Mark. Freya would join him in his exile, he was sure of that, and they could hide out together in the forests in the north of the peninsula, or on one of the more remote islands, and be safe from the wrath of the Bago folk. But then what? The miserable life of an outlaw, a despised outcast, freezing in winter, hungry much of the time, constantly in fear for his own life and Freya's?

He took a deep breath. 'All right,' he said. 'I choose and so swear.'

'Good! Let the great Irminsul and all servants of the Fyr Skola witness these solemn oaths made today,' said the Mikelgothi, 'and let the making of them be marked now, and for all eternity, in iron and death and blood.'

She passed the iron staff to another *gothi*, held out the newborn lamb in one hand and plucked a short knife from her belt with the other. She sliced quickly through the lamb's neck with one movement and held the struggling creature over the thick roots of the ancient tree so that the blood spattered and gushed down on to the gnarled wood. Bjarki stepped back to stop the hot gore splashing his new shoes. The lamb made not a sound as it died.

The ceremony was over. The priestess handed the limp carcass to an attendant and received a linen towel from another to wipe her bloody hands clean. Valtyr grasped Bjarki by the elbow and gently led him to one side.

'You did well, son,' he said, patting his shoulder. 'Oaths are a serious business and a serious man should never swear one lightly nor unthinkingly – but I do not think you will regret what you have promised on this day.'

Bjarki thought of the oath he had made to Freya in the dunes: the promise to love and protect her all the days of his life. The knowledge that he'd broken that solemn pledge was a knife in his heart. But he said nothing.

The crowd was dispersing now, streaming away in all directions.

The Mikelgothi came to them; she was taller than Valtyr, perhaps even as old as he was. Certainly they were of an age. She had a tattoo in the centre of her forehead, Bjarki saw, a long black triangle inked between her brows.

'Have you any thoughts about the Lodge to which they should be assigned?' she said. 'Or should I ask the Dreamers to pronounce on it?'

'He's Bear Lodge,' said Valtyr, indicating Bjarki. 'My life on it.'

'I must be assigned to Wolf Lodge,' said Tor, emerging from behind Valtyr's back. 'It has to be the Wolf Lodge. My father was *ulfhethnar* – Hildar Torfinnsson, you will certainly have heard of him. He died gloriously in battle a few years ago, slaughtering his enemies, terrorising his foes. He left me his Wolfskin before he was gloriously sent to the Hall of the Slain.'

Tor was now rummaging in her pack.

'Hildar Torfinnsson! I have not heard that name in a long time,' said Skymir the Mikelgothi. 'I did not know him well myself. I was Boar Lodge and our paths did not often cross. He was Wolf-chosen, for certain. And we know that the blessing of the *gandir* is often passed on through the blood.'

Tor was now holding out the slightly raggedy and moth-eaten old skin that she used as a sleeping blanket. Skymir took it gently from her hands.

'You may *not* wear this,' she said. 'Not yet. The Wolfskin is for those who have passed through the flames and emerged as Rekkar. For the Fire Born. It is not fit for novices.' Bjarki saw the rage blaze in Tor's eyes, like a dry haystack put to the torch. He wondered if she might attack the priestess.

'But,' continued the Mikelgothi, 'I shall assign you to Wolf Lodge for your training. In time, if the gods allow it, perhaps the Wolfskin shall be returned to you. Then you may wear it in honour of your father's memory.'

–

Valtyr took his leave of them shortly after this. Bjarki found himself close to tears when the one-eyed old man embraced him and told him that he would be gone by first light and they should not see each other for some while.

'They will look after you well here,' Valtyr said. 'And we shall surely meet again. Obey the Mikelgothi in all things, serve the Fyr Skola faithfully, and look for truth deep inside yourself. Farewell. May the Bear guard you.'

Tor had already been led away. She had not said goodbye. And Valtyr was now striding across the space with the Mikel-gothi without a backwards glance. Bjarki saw, with a little jolt of surprise, that they were holding hands.

'Hey, you must be Barney, the new one,' said a voice.

He turned round slowly and saw a young man a year or so older than him; a round face with a wide mouth grinning at him from under a mop of greasy hair. The stranger wore a plain blue tunic and trews, gartered below the knee, leather shoes and a belt from which hung a short knife and purse.

'It's Bjarki,' he said. 'But, yes, I am newly come to this place.'

'You've been assigned to Bear Lodge, which is this way. Come on, hurry up, we're about to eat. I'm Gunnar, by the way, your Elder Brother.'

Bjarki looked at the stranger. He looked quite normal; nothing odd or mad about him at all. Yet he seemed to think he was a blood relative.

The young man seemed to read his mind. 'My job is to look after you for your first few months as a novice, show you how things work, where to go, what to do. They call me your Elder Brother although, obviously, I'm not. Anyway, tell me about yourself, Bjarki, where are you from? What trade do your parents follow? How was the journey? See any monsters in the forest?'

The youth loosed a string of questions at him as they walked away from the Irminsul, heading into one of the leaf-shaped groves, but he did not seem to listen properly to any of Bjarki's answers. He threw out items of interest, nuggets of Fyr Skola knowledge, from time to time, but Bjarki was barely able to take them in. After a few hundred yards they approached a longhouse, thatched with straw, the heavy end-beams carved in wonderful designs, all of them depicting bears in various poses – bears snarling, bears reared up ready to fight, bears sleeping curled like dogs. At the apex of the roof, at both ends of the hall, were attached two huge, bleached, bear skulls.

There were several broad wooden tables set up outside the longhouse in a large sun-lit area of beaten earth. A fire was burning merrily in a pit to one side of this space over which the glazed carcass of an enormous wild bull, an aurochs, was turning. The smell of roasting beef was intoxicating.

'They feed us properly here; it can't be denied,' said Gunnar. 'Grab a seat, there's ale in the jug, help yourself, I'll be back in a moment. I'd better report to Angantyr that you are here. Sit. Sit down over there. I'll be back.'

Bjarki sat down at a pine bench that was parallel to the largest table.

A short, middle-aged man with cropped grey hair, naked above the waist, his upper body covered in swirling tattoos, was sitting on the far side of the table. The youth nodded and said, 'Greetings, sir, I am called Bjarki.'

The older man just stared at him – not *at* him, through him, as if he were not really there at all. His eyes were an indeterminate muddy colour and curiously opaque, almost blank. Between them, above his squashed nose, Bjarki noticed a tattoo of a triangle – not the same shape as the one Skymir possessed, this one was less pointed and of equal length on all three sides. It was only one of many curious markings that this strange man bore.

Bjarki saw that his squat muscular body, where it was not tattooed with serpents and stars and animals and the outlines of large-breasted women, was thick with scars – pink ones that curved round his ribs, short greyish bars of hard tissue, wide glossy patches of skin that looked like terrible burns, as if he had rolled in the hearth coals. Half of one ear was missing and a white crevasse joined his right eyebrow to the right-hand corner of his mouth.

But for the fact that his muddy eyes were open, Bjarki might have believed the man fast asleep. Then he moved. His right hand shot out with the speed of a striking snake and he grasped a pottery jug that was on the table in front of him. He slopped some brown drink into a cup and shoved it skidding across the table towards Bjarki. It stopped exactly in front of him.

'Ale,' he said, in a thick, dusty voice that sounded as if it came from deep within a centuries-old tomb. 'Drink some ale, lad.'

This, surely, thought Bjarki, was a Rekkr. The odd fellow could not possibly have looked more like one of the fabled warriors if he'd tried.

'See you've met Brokk,' said Gunnar. 'He's halfway to being Galálar and so not terribly talkative for much of the time, but if you give him enough drink he can be quite amusing. Angantyr, the Lodge Father, will be out with the others in a bit, and I'll introduce you to everyone. Sling me over that ale jug, Brokk, there's a good fellow, I've got a burning thirst on me today.'

The food at the Fyr Skola was more than abundant. Bjarki had at first assumed that the wooden plate piled high with dripping, bloody beef that was placed in front of him was for the whole table to share. But it quickly became apparent, as other similar plates were slammed down on the board and were claimed by other members of the Bear Lodge, that it was a portion for him alone. There was bread and cheese, too, huge raw radishes and onions, boiled mashed turnips, and some sort of greens wilted with butter and served in a – Bjarki could think of no other suitable word – bucket.

He gorged. He ate till he could eat no more, and washed it all down with copious amounts of nutty, freshly brewed brown ale. The conversation around the table was loud and bawdy, old jokes were cracked, the language was shockingly filthy, and his new Lodge mates were teased, mercilessly teased, but it all seemed to be perfectly amicable and extremely congenial.

Brokk said nothing at all. He lowered his face over his platter of beef and ate like a starving wolf, smiling up at Bjarki in a weird mechanical way from time to time with his beef-blood smeared face, as if he had been told to do so by some chiding inner voice. After the privations of life on the road – the gritty mushrooms, the salty fish porridge – Bjarki felt he had died and gone straight to the Hall of the Slain. He swilled and gorged with the rest of them, forcing himself to eat beyond his stomach's usual capacity, fully determined to do all honour to this unexpected and quite magnificent feast.

That was his second misunderstanding – this was no feast, no special celebration. This was the ordinary midday meal, taken a little after noon on every day of the week when they were in the groves. Bjarki could barely comprehend such extravagance. When he muttered something in this vein to Gunnar – who was sitting beside him – the young man mumbled, 'Got to keep your strength up,' through a gigantic mouthful of half-chewed beef.

When Bjarki tried to express his gratitude to Angantyr, the Father of the Lodge, a massive warrior with an entirely bald, shaven head, and a tattoo of a snarling bear on his smooth sun-bronzed chest, the man smiled over at him in a cool but friendly way and said: 'Eat hearty, youngster, and drink up your ale – you'll soon be earning that meat and drink, I promise you that.'

Bjarki looked at him enquiringly, smothering a belch, and Angantyr said: 'Tomorrow morning, lad, you enter the Fyr Pit. We'll see what you are made of then. Tomorrow, my little bear, you'll fight for the very first time.'

Chapter Six

Into the Fyr Pit

In the afternoon, Bjarki began his training: he attended a Voyaging session with the Bear Lodge's Dreamer, a middle-aged matron called Nikka, who informed her charges that the search for true knowledge began inside every one of them. 'Delve deep into your heart,' she said, in an odd, soft voice. 'The truth will emerge like the magnificent butterfly from its drab cocoon.'

Bjarki was so sleepy then, after his gargantuan midday meal, that he had great difficulty staying awake for the duration of the lesson.

There were seven novices in the group sitting at her feet inside the Lodge, at the western end, near the wall that was plastered with lime and painted with images of wide dark forests and huge bears, with stick-like human figures armed with spears running between the trees.

'The truth is inside you all,' intoned Nikka. 'Every one. And while I cannot say what that truth may be,' she continued, 'whether you are found worthy or not, I can say this: if you find your inner strength, if you do indeed find the true fury of the Rekkr, it will derive from the Bear, not from you.'

Bjarki puzzled hard over this. So did a Rekkr's strength come from inside the warrior or from outside – from this Bear that she spoke about?

By the end of the hour, he thought he had a better understanding of it. A Rekkr was possessed by a *gandr*, a kind of animal spirit – in Nikka's case the Bear spirit – which came into the body of the Rekkr during the ordeal of Voyaging, and took up lodging there in his or her heart. When the Rekkr was called upon to fight in battle, the *gandr* was unleashed, and this spirit granted the Rekkr all the power and ferocity and fearlessness of a wild beast.

Bjarki noticed that Nikka too had a small triangle tattooed between her bushy eyebrows, the same shape as those of Brokk and Angantyr.

After some conversation with Gunnar immediately following the Voyaging session, Bjarki also felt he was beginning to get an idea about the different types of people who made up the full membership of the Bear Lodge.

There seemed to be about forty men and women living in the smoky longhouse but, of these, only four or five were actual Rekkar. They could be distinguished by the tattoo they bore on their foreheads, a triangle with equal length sides. Gunnar had explained that each lodge had its own shape of triangle for their Rekkar. The Wolf Lodge had a triangle with two long sides and one short one at the top, supposed to resemble the face of a wolf; the Boar Lodge had a very long triangle, to mimic the elongated face of a wild pig. The Bear Lodge, of course, had a triangle with three equal-length sides.

'The Bear Lodge is the senior Lodge,' said Gunnar. 'It was the one which was founded first and which gives the common name to all Rekkar – the Bear Shirts, *berserkir* – because they wear the fur of a bear as armour.'

Gunnar leaned in closer. 'It is also the best Lodge by miles, in my opinion. But I am not entirely impartial,' he chuckled. 'The Wolf Lodge prize speed and teamwork; the Boars – the *svinfylking* – think they are the bravest and the most stubborn in a long fight. But we Bears have by far the greatest strength and ferocity – and that's what *really* counts in a battle.'

'So when will you become a Rekkr?' asked Bjarki. He liked Gunnar. The young man had a fine sense of humour and an air of irreverence that was appealing. And, although he had been already enrolled in the Lodge for more than a year, he did not brandish his superiority over the newcomer.

'Next year, perhaps. Only the All-Father knows. Odin loves all the Rekkar – and he decides who will be chosen, and when. But there are all sorts of mystical tests and difficult lessons to be learnt first, and complicated hoops for you to jump through. Then you must go out Voyaging into the First Forest alone and meet your very own Bear spirit. There's also the Fyr Ceremony in front of the whole assembled Skola – that's the final test. And it's brutal. You have to leap into a blazing inferno and come out the other side – that's why the Rekkar are called Fire Born. They undergo a rebirth in the sacred fire. Some don't survive that. They get burnt to a cinder. On second thought, I hope to become Rekkr the year after next, or even the one after that.' He chuckled. 'Until then we might as well enjoy ourselves.'

After Voyaging with Nikka, they had a two-hour lesson on Warcraft in the cool evening in a flattened area of ground outside the longhouse. The middle-aged man in charge, who was called Hymir, was *not* a Rekkr – no head tattoo – which intrigued Bjarki. The man was obviously a fine warrior.

Hymir demonstrated the correct use of the spear and shield in dazzling combinations to the seven Bear Lodge novices and a few of the younger men-at-arms, too, calling on a beanpole youth and a sturdy woman to come out and show the less-experienced the more complicated moves. This pair were frighteningly competent, jabbing at each other like lightning with their blunted spears, blocking with the shields in a thoroughly professional way.

Gunnar whispered in Bjarki's ear that Hymir was a master of all known arms – but he had utterly failed to find his own Bear spirit when Voyaging. Therefore he could not become a Rekkr but, instead, had been given the important role of teaching the Lodge members the use of commonplace weapons, and guiding them to become skilled fighters. Hymir was also the captain of the Lodge's twenty-strong company of Barda, or Grove guards.

The Barda, none of whom were Rekkar, made the daily patrols in the countryside around the groves – such as the one that had intercepted the three travellers the day before. They also fought in battle, in an unbreakably solid shield wall behind the Rekkar, if the groves were ever threatened – or if they were sent away elsewhere to fight on behalf of the Eresburg community.

'You two seem to have a lot to say to each other,' Hymir bellowed. 'Maybe you two noble *hersirs* feel you don't have need of my instruction?'

Bjarki blushed and hung his head. Gunnar just grinned up at the furious master-at-arms. 'Since you don't want to listen to *me*. Why don't you two would-be heroes come here and show us what you know about the spear.'

Bjarki found himself clutching a long blunted spear and a heavy round shield and facing Gunnar, who was similarly equipped, in front of the class.

'Fight!' commanded Hymir.

Bjarki stepped forward and poked at his new friend, half-heartedly.

Gunnar took the weak blow on his shield, tried to stab Bjarki back as a counter attack; and missed completely, the blunted spear going harmlessly under Bjarki's right arm. Gunnar blundered forward, impelled by his own momentum, and crashed into Bjarki, knocking him off balance, and they both ended up on the ground in a laughing tangle of spear-shafts and limbs.

'Hopeless, both of you,' said Hymir, 'completely hopeless. Sit down, keep quiet, unblock your ears and try at least to learn *something* today.'

–

Gunnar woke him early the next day for a breakfast of boiled eggs, ham, cheese and bread, and watered ale – all in similar quantities as the midday repast of the day before. He had slept deeply on the benches in the Bear Lodge, on a pile of blankets and furs, and he felt strong, rested and, for the first time in a very long while, absolutely and utterly content.

After breakfast, an hour or so after dawn on another beautiful, warm spring day, Gunnar took him over to the Fyr Pit, which was beyond the clearing of the Irminsul, in part of the groves that Bjarki had not yet seen.

It was a large square pit, sunken to the height of a man, fifteen paces by fifteen, walled with blackened stone slabs. The floor of the Fyr Pit was a tamped-down surface of fine grey ash and cinders. Indeed, the whole Fyr Pit strongly resembled an enormous empty cooking hearth in some giant's hall.

'They will pick out someone roughly your height and weight,' said Gunnar. 'But it won't be one of your Lodge brothers, so don't feel you have to hold back in the slightest. If you feel the Beast stirring inside you, that's good. Embrace it. Let it have control. If you hurt your opponent, or even kill him, you won't be punished. This is the Fyr Skola: casualties *are* expected.'

'Seriously?'

'Yes. You won't have weapons. You'll also fight barefoot. And the Ropers are there to stop the bout if one of you goes completely Galálar.'

'Ropers? Galálar?'

'Sorry, I forgot that you don't yet know all our jargon. Galálar is probably not the right word anyway. It means that the Beast inside you takes over completely. You stop being a man and wholly become a wild animal. It happens – but only rarely – to some of the Rekkar. They cannot come back from the place they go when the Bear spirit – or the Wolf, or Boar – rises up inside them. You met Brokk? He's gone Galálar a few times. But they have always managed to bring him back; so far, anyway. If someone goes that way completely, they must be put down immediately or we're all at risk.'

Bjarki was transported back to the Thing at Bago, and Olaf Karlsson, the *hersir*, saying Bjarki was no better than a mad dog, an indiscriminate killer of men, who must be put down immediately lest he endanger them all.

'And the Ropers?' he asked.

'Those men over there. They are the… well, sort of the judges. They will all work together to stop a fight, with any luck, if it gets out of hand.'

Bjarki looked at the group of four bulky warriors on the far side of the Fyr Pit. Hymir, the Bear Lodge master-at-arms, was one of them. He wished he had been more attentive in the Warcraft class the evening before; not that it would help him. The four men, the Ropers – none of them Rekkar, as far as Bjarki could tell – were conferring together, they each had a coil of rope looped over their shoulders, and carried nets made of thick knotted hemp.

'And I have to do this?' Bjarki felt suddenly cold and sick.

'Oh yes, every novice must do this. Sorts out the wheat from the chaff. Think of it as an initiation. May the gods bring you victory!' said Gunnar cheerily, slapping him on the back. 'Don't forget, Little Brother, fight your absolute hardest: the other fellow will almost certainly be trying to kill you.'

Tor walked towards the Fyr Pit with a large, chattering, laughing crowd of her fellow Wolf Lodge mates. She had never felt more alone. Her reception in her new home, in the community she had long dreamed of, in the place where for years she had longed to be, had not gone well. Quite the opposite.

When Valtyr had left her under the Irminsul, she had been collected by an older girl, perhaps nineteen years of age, a tough-looking creature with bulging arm muscles, hairy tree-trunk legs and a thick, much-broken snub nose, who introduced herself grumpily as Helga, her Older Sister.

She whistled for Tor to follow, as if she were a dog, took her over to the Wolf Lodge, where she abandoned Tor to fend for herself at the dinner table. Despite the mountains of food available, Tor found she was really not very hungry at all and she only picked at her meat. Her Wolf Lodge brothers and sisters looked at her as she ate it but no one spoke directly to her.

Tor realised that, as was her habit, she was glaring ferociously at any person who happened to catch her eye. But somehow she could not prevent herself from doing this. She found, much to her surprise, she was actually missing the company of that dull oaf Bjarki, and when she thought of the comforting silence of one-eyed Valtyr, she felt like weeping into her plate.

She had attended a class on Stealth, with a small, balding idiot who mumbled endlessly about how to move in various terrains without being spotted by enemies, using the ground, and any natural features, how to break up the outline of your body using twigs and leaves shoved into your belt and clothing. But it was all obvious, childish stuff to Tor – she had been taught these exact skills from a young age by some of Svearland's finest hunters.

She grew bored during the long lesson; feeling she was somehow being shunned. Nobody in Wolf Lodge seemed to be at all interested in her.

After the miserable old buffoon had finished his Stealth lecture, the junior members of the Lodge and some of the servants went off to perform a sacred rite to propitiate the spirits of the forest at dusk – it was the Wolf Lodge's turn to do this, apparently. During the whole ceremony, Tor had not the slightest idea what was going on, and nobody saw fit to explain it to her. They spent hours delicately trimming the branches of long rows of beech and alder trees with bronze sickles all around the three groves, carefully collecting up the leaves and cut branches as if they were rare treasures.

Then they returned to the middle, to the Irminsul, where a pair of bound chickens were ritually slaughtered and their blood sprayed around the One Tree's massive trunk in a pair of circles, one sun-wise, one widdershins.

There was some chanting, some more of the eerie four-note humming, and the Wolf Lodge Mother, a decrepit little hag, quite clearly as mad as a moon-frog, by Tor's reckoning, lead the prayers in a voice so soft Tor could not make out a single word. Then they all went back to the Lodge for supper.

After she had finished her bowl of chicken soup – all the sacrifices were eaten by the Lodges who supplied them, after the deities had had their invisible share – she decided it was time to take matters into her own hands.

She stood up on the bench and kicked hard on the table edge with her boot to attract attention. The forty-one people who were in the Wolf Lodge at the time stopped eating and talking and turned in astonishment to stare.

'I wish to introduce myself to the Lodge,' she said. 'I am Torfinna Hildarsdottir – you may call me Tor. I'm honoured to join your community.'

'Sit down, you ninny, and be quiet,' hissed Elder Sister Helga from across the table. 'Learn your proper place, you silly girl.'

Tor ignored her. 'I want you all to know that I am the daughter of Hildar Torfinnsson, who was once a famous Rekkr of this Lodge, and I am proud of my connection with him. I plan to become Fire Born myself, with your help. I hope I'll bring as much honour to the Lodge as my father did.'

There was an unpleasant silence following her words. Then somebody guffawed. Then another person laughed too. A huge scarred warrior at the end of the table slapped his dinner companion and said: 'As much honour as Hildar Torfinnsson – ha-ha! – *that* shouldn't be too difficult to achieve.'

Helga was now tugging at her leggings. 'Get down, Tor, down now.'

The Lodge Mother rose, coughed wetly, and fixed Tor with her raw-egg eyes. Between wheezes, she said: 'If you wish to remain a… member of the Wolf Lodge… you'll sit in your allotted place… and be… silent.'

Tor sat down quickly. Her face was burning. The hag, though, was not finished. 'Furthermore… you will not again speak the name of… Hildar Torfinnsson… within this Lodge… on pain of… immediate expulsion.'

When Helga informed her in the chilly light of dawn, after a wretched sleepless night, that she must attend the Fyr Pit and fight, Tor welcomed the idea. She would show them. She would prove to them that she was more than worthy of a place in the Wolf Lodge. And if they no longer respected the memory of her poor dead father – so what? They would come to respect *her* when they saw her prowess, the fruit of her hard training, at first hand.

And although Tor didn't like to admit it to herself, her heart leapt when she saw Bjarki, standing with another lad at the edge of the Fyr Pit.

'Hey there, oaf, ready to show them your mettle?' she called out a little too loudly. Almost before the words were out of her mouth she knew they struck the wrong note. Bjarki looked terrified. It had genuinely not occurred to Tor that the oaf might not be as eager for his first public bout as she was.

'Tor,' he said dully, merely glancing at her. 'How do you fare?'

She saw that the other Bear Lodge youth, a grinning mop-headed idiot, was whispering in his ear and he was looking at the other side of the Fyr Pit where the tall older woman, the Mikelgothi, was speaking to a young man, about the same age as Bjarki, a bare-chested, squat, muscular fellow, very big, even running to fat, who was surrounded by a ring of Boar Lodge folk. She knew them as Boars by the forehead tattoos their two Rekkar bore.

Bjarki was now stripping off his linen shirt, pulling off his shoes, and wearing only his threadbare trews, he was climbing down the ladder that led to the floor of the Fyr Pit. The plump Boar Lodge fellow was also entering the arena. Four large men with heavy ropes coiled on their shoulders were taking their places on the four sides of the pit. The crowd was now thick on each of the four sides, talking excitedly. It seemed that almost the whole of Eresburg had come out today to see this contest, to evaluate these fighters.

Skymir the Mikelgothi stepped to the edge of the Fyr Pit.

She said: 'The first match today is between Bjarki Bloodhand of Bear Lodge, and Ivar Knuttson of Boar Lodge. Under the spreading shade of the Mother of Trees, and in the presence of the All-Father, let them demonstrate their battle-courage and prove their worthiness to remain here as novices in the sacred Groves of Eresburg. Novices – fight!'

Suddenly, Tor felt a chill spreading through her belly and loins. The other novice fighter, the heavy Boar lad, looked terrifyingly dangerous. He was advancing on Bjarki in a strange crabwise manner, kicking up little puffs of ash with every slow, shuffling step, his meaty hands opening and closing convulsively, his large ugly head twitching a little with every step.

She could see a little creamy white spittle already collecting at the edges of his slack lips. Bjarki was just standing there; his hands dangling, looking horribly frightened and lost. She had an almost overwhelming urge to jump down into the pit and go to Bjarki's aid – to help him escape this massive twitching freak, who was now bearing down on him. But she knew she could not do it. The oaf must fight his battle. *Fight, idiot. Attack now.*

Ivar Knuttson let out a long, wordless grunting roar – and charged.

He came thundering forward with his arms outstretched, fingers spread as if he wished to seize Bjarki's pale flesh and wrench it from his body.

On pure instinct, Bjarki ducked under the heavy reaching arms and spun away, and as he turned he punched the other lad in the side under the ribs. It was a solid, punishing blow, yet the Boar didn't even seem to notice.

Ivar charged again, this time swinging his big fists in great arcs. Bjarki ducked again, punched him again, this time in the belly, and tried to step back out of his opponent's reach. He stumbled, righted himself and caught a huge swinging blow full in the face that knocked him flat on his back.

Then the Boar was on him. He pinned one of Bjarki's arms with his knee and began to batter his face with both fists; big, pounding blows of extraordinary power, which rocked Bjarki's head from one side to the other.

Bjarki tried to fend off the blows with his one free arm, but the ferocity of the onslaught was too much for him. Punch after punch evaded his increasingly feeble one-handed blocks and landed on his battered face and neck and upper chest. The blood was flowing rich and thick from his mashed nose. There was no martial skill displayed here, as far as Tor could see, it was just a raw outpouring of animal rage as the Boar smashed again and again into his opponent's head and body. Then Ivar flung back his head, and gave a massive bellow of rage – and agony. Bjarki had somehow managed to get a knee into his groin and was driving it up, again, and again. The Boar released, rolled quickly off the Bear, but immediately bounced to his feet.

As a partially stunned Bjarki struggled to rise, Ivar kicked him savagely in the side of the head with the sole of his bare foot, snapping his enemy's body back down on to the ashy floor. The Boar rushed forward again and seized Bjarki by the ears, lifted his head and smashed it down hard, once, twice, on the unforgiving ground. Then he bared his yellow teeth, there were strings of white spittle flying as he jerked back his head, he lunged in, bit down on his face, incisors clamping into a patch of Bjarki's cheek flesh. The Boar flung back his head, ripping a chunk of flesh free of Bjarki's face.

He spat it out on to the pale ash, a gobbet of red; then grunting and snuffling in his crazed swinish joy, opened his gore-slimed mouth very wide, seeming to grin, and went in for his second massive bite…

The loop of rope dropped over his shoulders, a jerk tightened it around his upper arms, and Ivar Knuttson was hauled back off Bjarki's prone body, just in time, his teeth snapping on empty air, a bare inch from Bjarki's nose.

The Boar fighter thrashed wildly, his body twisting and turning, but another loop of rope caught his arms and neck, the new noose tightened and pulled him in another direction. Ivar was still thrashing like a beached salmon, secured by two taut cords, kicked-up ash flying everywhere, when the third Roper cautiously approached him and flung a stout web of hemp rope netting over his writhing body. Gradually, as the young Boar became further entangled in the net, he grew less violent, a few massive twitches and he was still. His Lodge mates – a dozen of them, all crying out in joy at his victory – jumped down into the pit and rushed forward to congratulate him.

Tor vaulted down and sprinted to Bjarki's body. She was aware that the other Bear Lodge man was hard on her heels. They both skidded to a halt beside the still body. Bjarki was breathing, at least, light shallow gasps. His face was covered in blood and he did not respond when Tor called his name.

'The Bear spirit, the *gandr*, did not choose to come into him,' said Gunnar. 'Unlike the Boar – and he was already half-crazed when he entered the Fyr Pit. That was cunning, oh yes, to prepare himself that way. Ivar must have taken an infusion of the Red Spot, a fat dose, at least half an hour ago – which is clear against the rules, of course, and reckless, too, although I doubt anyone will chastise him for it. Poor old Bjarki never knew what hit him.'

'Out of my way,' said Skymir the Mikelgothi. She knelt down beside Bjarki and wiped away some of the blood with her sleeve. She peered at him closely, examining the raw welling hole ripped in his right cheek. She lifted up his eyelids and looked at his pupils, then put her hand on his heart, and her head right down close to his face to listen to his thin, labouring breaths.

'He'll live,' she said to Tor. 'We have the best healers in the Groves, young one, full of cunning and magic. He'll boast a beautiful scar after this.'

They bore him into the shade of the Irminsul on a padded wooden stretcher and a team of *gothi* and servants, mostly older women, cared for him, packed his cheek wound with cobwebs and stitched it closed. Then they gently washed and bandaged up his poor battered and swollen face.

Tor sat beside him on the ground and listened to him breathe. He had never been very good-looking, she thought, but he was going to look truly hideous now. Poor oaf. He should not have come to this dangerous place. He would never make a Rekkr – never – he just did not have the strength in him.

There were two other bouts in the Fyr Pit, one short and the other longer – Tor could hear the cheering and the occasional scream of terrible pain. But she did not observe them. She sat and watched over Bjarki, feeling close to tears – for him, and strangely also for herself.

Then she was called for her own bout.

There were disconcerting patches of fresh blood on the powdery ash floor of the pit. But Tor ignored them – and pushed all thoughts of Bjarki from her mind, too. He would live – the Mikelgothi had promised as much. She needed to do well in this match. She must be victorious. She would show the indifferent Wolf Lodge that she was indeed her father's daughter.

However, when she saw her opponent climbing down the ladder into the Fyr Pit, Tor had to smother the urge to burst out laughing.

She was an emaciated waif with spindly arms and legs. She might be about the same age as Tor, seventeen summers or thereabouts, and she probably weighed only slightly less. But Tor had been training in all the methods of warfare since she was seven years old, when she first became fully conscious of her absent father's fame and prowess. Tor might be slim – but she was wiry and as tough as twice-boiled leather. She had trained all day, almost every day, for a decade: recently sparring with full-grown warriors in Svearland, and had bested more than a few of them, her weight and height notwithstanding. She could fight. But the person facing her across a stretch of blood-spotted ash was, well, she was just a girl.

For a moment Tor was nonplussed. She dimly heard the Mikelgothi announcing her match – the waif was a member of Boar Lodge, called Frigga or Hrigga, something girlish like that – and then the fight began.

The Boar girl ran at her, kicking and punching, screaming insults. Tor easily fended off the wild blows and neatly snap-kicked her in the stomach, knocking the wind out of her. The waif sat hard down on the ground, holding her belly, gasping like a landed fish. Tor had absolutely no idea what to do next. Should she kick her again? Wait politely for her to get up?

The girl was game, that could not be denied. She clambered up to her feet and charged straight at Tor, trying to ram her with her blonde head.

Tor sidestepped, and gave the girl a downward shove on the back as she passed, and her opponent, crashed face first into the gritty ash. She got up again, brushed the smeared cinders from her grazed face and attacked once more. Tor punched her in the face this time, a piston-hard straight right to the nose. The girl was stopped dead in her tracks; and Tor followed the blow with a hard clubbing left hook to the side of her jaw, which immediately knocked the female Boar sprawling to the ashy ground again.

But the girl wouldn't *stay* down. She rolled on to all fours, shook her head, dazed, and slowly got to her feet. She ran at Tor again, but slowly, tottering, groping for her opponent, and Tor seized her by one flailing arm, twisted it, dipped her shoulder and flipped her down to the pit floor again.

This was ridiculous. The poor thing had no battle-skill at all.

Frigga – or Hrigga – rolled over, her face and body grimed in grey ash, looked up at Tor with hot, pinhole eyes. She tried to rise again, and faltered, slumped back down – and then suddenly she began to cry. She just sat there on the ash floor at the bottom of the pit bawling her little blue eyes out.

Tor looked around at the people watching from above her on the lip of the Fyr Pit. There were few of them left, and not one of them looked very impressed. This was evidently the last bout of the day. She saw the ancient Wolf Lodge Mother, staring at her, leaning on her stick. Tor half-lifted a hand in greeting, and shrugged at the crone as if to say: 'What could I do?'

The hag ignored the gesture, turned on her heel and shuffled away.

The Mikelgothi was now beside her in the sand. 'I think that will do,' she said, striding towards the two girls. Tor plucked at her flowing sleeve as she passed. 'Forgive me, lady,' she said, 'what will happen to her now?'

'Oh, I believe she may still usefully serve the Groves – but I do not think she is destined to be a Rekkr. Wouldn't you agree, Novice Torfinna?'

–

Tor returned to Bjarki's pallet under the One Tree. She felt ashamed of her one-sided scuffle with the waif, as if she were the village bully, a persecutor of the weak and helpless. How was she supposed to have acted? It had been an unequal match. Should she *not* have beaten her opponent? Let her win?

She looked at Bjarki and saw that, where it was not covered by the swathes of bandages, his skin was a much better colour, a little pinker, his eyes were fluttering open too. In a few moments they were wide and staring.

'Freya?' he said, looking at Tor with a puzzled expression.

'Freya's not here,' she said, suddenly hating the silly trull, the one who had made such a fuss at Bjarki's departure. 'It's Tor – your frien— uh, I mean, I was your companion on the march down from the Dane-Mark.'

Bjarki closed his eyes and shook his head slightly. It evidently hurt.

'My face is on fire. He *bit* me!' he said. 'What am I doing here?'

'This is the Fyr Skola,' said Tor, 'you came here with Valtyr and me. We picked you up on the island of Bago and brought you here. Remember?'

'I know *where* I am, Tor,' he said, opening his eyes. 'I was wondering what I am *doing here* – among this vicious gang of blood-drunk lunatics.'

Chapter Seven

A little help from a friend

Bjarki sat by the hearth-fire in the Bear Lodge wrapped in a thick blanket, sipping a horn of ale. It was past midnight and the other members of the Lodge were all asleep. Bjarki stared into the flames, watching the shifting shapes and colours. His bitten face throbbed badly, preventing sleep, as if the Boar Lodge fellow was still gnawing at it, indeed, his whole body ached from the savage pounding he had received in the Fyr Pit that morning.

He was thinking about Freya – his one true love. Had it not been for that insane incident in the dunes during which he killed Jeki and Ymir, and of which he could not remember a single thing, he might have been with her now. Perhaps lying in her arms by another warm hearth, perhaps discussing the design of the boat he had planned to build, or the places they meant to go in it, or the life they intended to make together in Bago or on one of the other bigger islands. He might even have already gone through a simple betrothal ceremony in front of the whole village, and they might be formally joined together, in a solemn binding union recognised by their community.

He might even be happy.

Instead, he was here in this strange, frightening place, surrounded by a gang of vicious madmen who glorified violence and pain, who sought out spirits of the wild and encouraged them to turn decent people into savage, bloodthirsty monsters. When Valtyr had spoken about the Fyr Skola and the Groves of Eresburg, he had spoken glowingly of heroes and traditions and transforming himself into a living legend. Bjarki had seen himself becoming one of those heroes, and with the magnificent name and fame that went with it, of returning in triumph to Bago, after a year or so, to reclaim his woman and his old life. He had imagined striding into the Thing space under the sacred oak tree, where they had tried to hang him, resplendent in furs and armour, with a sword at his hip and a blazing aura of glory all about him. The *hersir* Olaf Karlsson would have fallen to his knees and begged him, weeping, to return home to lead the men in battle in his place. And Freya, as wife of the new war chief of Bago, would have been loved and revered by all the other women – as his queen, and as the mother of all his tall sons.

It could still happen, he thought. He could still return to Bago one day wreathed in glory. But first he had to find a way to rise in this community of lunatics, this blood-obsessed brotherhood, and that meant one thing. He must become a *berserkr*. He must strive to join the elite ranks of the Fire Born. Could he do that? Did he have what was necessary inside? He did not know.

He became aware of a figure shambling out of the darkness towards the glow of the hearth and recognised with a sinking heart the battered face of the maddest of all the blood-drunk lunatics in the Bear Lodge.

It was Brokk. He came into the firelight and gazed blankly at Bjarki for a moment. The flickering red light played over his tattoos, his burns and the scars on his face and his naked upper body, twisting them into weird shapes, with dark hollows and strange, unexpected lumps and bumps. He stood there for a moment, seeming to be as solid as a boulder and just about as sentient.

His blank gaze ran all over Bjarki, stopping at the fresh dressing that covered his cheek. It was clear that he had no recollection of who Bjarki was, and it seemed likely that he did not care to find out either. He bent and thrust out a spade-like hand and seized the large, half-full ale jug that sat by Bjarki's feet. Once again his movements were swift as a hunting snake.

The Rekkr did not bother with a horn. He drank straight from the heavy jug, pouring a couple of pints of the strong ale directly into his open mouth.

Bjarki watched him with mingled awe and disgust. Was this really what he hoped to become, he asked himself, a fell creature only partially human?

Brokk belched and sat down beside Bjarki on a stump of tree-trunk that served as a stool. He casually dropped the empty jug on the earth floor.

For a long time the Rekkr stared into the flames, silent, barely seeming to breathe. Bjarki felt no inclination to attempt any conversation with him.

Then, to his surprise, Brokk spoke: 'He took the Spot.'

For a moment, Bjarki thought he was imagining the words.

'He what?' he said.

'The Boar, the one who bit you, he'd taken Red Spot. That's bad.'

Bjarki had no idea what to say to this. 'You saw the fight today?' he said, and then realised that it was a stupid question. Of course Brokk had.

'You take the Spot first time,' Brokk growled, 'you always need the Spot. Every fight. Every battle. Every time. You'll never find your *gandr*.'

Bjarki was still not entirely sure that he was not imagining this whole conversation. Had he perhaps fallen asleep by the hearth? He took a fold of the soft flesh on the inside of his forearm and pinched it. No, he was awake.

'Will you tell me, Brokk, how it was that you found your *gandr*?'

Brokk's head turned and he looked sideways, straight at Bjarki. His muddy eyes were no more alive than before but something very strange was happening to the right corner of his mouth. It was twitching, jerking. Was he having some sort of fit? Bjarki realised the man was trying to smile at him.

'I know nothing of all this,' Bjarki said. 'It would help me understand if you told me how you became a Rekkr. If you don't mind speaking of it.'

'Fetch more ale,' said Brokk.

–

'I was Barda,' said the Rekkr, when Bjarki had replenished the jug from the huge barrel in the far corner of the Lodge. 'I could fight, but I had no *gandr*. Three years I waited. No *gandr*. I hummed daily. You know how to hum?'

'I don't know anything.'

'They will teach you. Pay attention. And practise. You hum to summon the *gandr* to you. The vibrations reach out to the otherworld, they say, and call it, like… like whistling for a dog. But not always. Your *gandr* is not your dog. Not at all. Better to say you are the *gandr*'s dog.'

Bjarki looked at him uncomprehendingly.

'Listen to me. Sometimes a *gandr* is angry with you. Sometimes it wants to tease you. Play games. Sometimes it just doesn't want to come…'

'You speak with your *gandr*?'

'It speaks to me. It speaks to me like… like my dead mother.'

Bjarki made an explosive little noise, a hastily smothered laugh.

Brokk looked at him again. His face twitched on the right side again.

'You think this funny? It *is* funny. My *gandr* has my mother's voice. Funny, but also true. But not all *gandr* are the same. Nikka says her *gandr* is like the wind rustling through the leaves of an ash. Each one is different.'

'So when did it come to you?'

'I'll tell you. More ale.'

Bjarki passed over the jug.

'I was a Barda and we went to help the Eastphalians – far to the east on the River Elbe. They have a problem with the Sorbs. You know the Sorbs?'

Bjarki didn't.

'Slav tribesmen – very fierce. They live in the marshes. Damp villages. They all stink bad. Like rotting wool.'

Brokk took a massive pull from the ale jug.

'Our Saxon friends wanted to punish the Sorbs for raiding across the river. They had stolen some cows, I think. I don't remember. And the Eastphalian chief – Hermann was his name – he said we should go across the Elbe and burn their villages, take back his cows. Or maybe it was sheep.

'I was taking a shit – I went away from the camp, a little way, and dropped my trews. It was the middle of the night. And that's when the Sorbs attacked us. A dozen of them. They had been watching us in secret. They killed everyone. Even our Rekkr – Arnulf – he was killed in his sleep. Two arrows punched through his blankets. He never even woke up. Hermann was killed too. They took his head off with an axe. And – you will think this very funny – if I had not been taking a shit, I would be as dead as my own dung.'

Brokk's cheek twitched again at the memory. Bjarki was fascinated.

'I saw the attack, my trews round my ankles. I shouted a warning. But they were all killed. Zip, zip, zop. They heard me, and they came looking for me. I didn't even have my sword. I pulled up my trews, picked up a rock and began to hum. I hummed – I should have fled into the darkness. But, no, I hummed the summoning tune. My whole body was vibrating like… like a harp string. I could hear the Sorbs approaching. And then my *gandr* came to me. And you know what it said? First thing my *gandr* ever said?'

Bjarki shrugged.

'You didn't wipe your arse, you dirty boy!'

The face was twitching wildly now. Bjarki, too, began to chuckle.

'It was my mother's voice. And she was scolding me. And since then whenever I summon my *gandr*, I hear my dead mother. That silly old bitch.'

Brokk was laughing openly now, making a strange harsh noise like a cawing crow. And Bjarki could not help but join in the merriment. When he had at last recovered his poise, regained his wind, and wiped his streaming eyes, Bjarki said: 'And what happened next? With the Sorbs, I mean?'

'Oh… them,' rumbled Brokk, and Bjarki felt him slipping back into his normal boulder-like state of blankness. 'I fed them all to the ravens.'

-

As spring expanded into summer, and Bjarki's face healed, he settled into the rhythm of life in the Fyr Skola. And, as the pain and shock of his brutal encounter in the Fyr Pit faded, he began to appreciate his community a little more and find the virtues of the unique group of people that surrounded him.

Each day began with prayers to the spirit of the Bear, lord of the forest, and to the Irminsul, the One Tree. Most of the Bear Lodge attended these simple rituals, which involved a call and response led by the Lodge Father, although there were always a few members away, detached on other duties.

'Hear us, Brother Bear, and grant us your strength, your courage and your wisdom as we undertake the labours of this day,' Angantyr would intone, both hands, palms facing out, lifted high above his big, shaven head.

'Hear us, Brother Bear, hear us this day,' the Lodge would reply.

After the prayers would come breakfast – eggs, bread, butter, cheese, ham, ale and sometimes oatmeal porridge – eaten informally on the benches around the sides of the longhouse. Gunnar always sat beside Bjarki during this first meal of the day, and usually passed on snippets of gossip or news or advice about Lodge members – 'Never ask Hymir about his Fyr Pit fight with Elendri, the ancient Mother of the Wolf Lodge, she beat him half to death more than twenty years ago – and he still hasn't quite got over the embarrassment of being knocked out of his skull by a skinny old woman!'

The five members of the Bear Lodge who *were* Fire Born were treated like royalty, Bjarki discovered. They never had to do any of the day-to-day chores, none of the cooking or washing, or fetching water or firewood, which was done by the handful of Lodge servants and the younger novices.

Three of the Rekkar were men: Angantyr, the Lodge Father, half-mad Brokk, who heard his dead mother's voice, and Edmund, an Angelcynn from across the seas, who spoke Saxon with an odd accent but apart from that seemed an ordinary man. Two were women: Nikka, who taught Voyaging, and Sif, a burly matron who, according to Gunnar, had an eye for handsome novices, and wasn't above trying to fondle them when she got the chance.

'Watch out for Sif,' Gunnar whispered. 'I've seen her eyeing your arse when you walk out of the Lodge. Stay out of her way, unless you *want* to bed her. Although I've heard it's quite the experience. Whatever you do, Little Brother, don't make her lose her temper. She has slaughtered more than twenty trained warriors in battle and never once took a serious wound.'

After prayers and breakfast came the physical training, which was mandatory for every member of the Lodge except the servants, who were too busy to participate, and the five Rekkar, although they most often joined in anyway, sometimes leading those exercises that they particularly favoured.

There was a special area just outside the Bear Grove, set up for the whole of Eresburg to take exercise in. But the Bear Lodge training always began with running: novices, Barda and Fire Born all jogging off out of the gate, down the track to the valley and then up the steep wooded hillsides and running a loop of eight or so miles before returning to the exercise yard.

Then came exercises to strengthen the body, lifting and throwing heavy boulders or man-sized logs with handles cut into the wood, these wooden weights, polished smooth by antiquity and the hands of long-dead Rekkar, were decreed sacred and Gunnar claimed that the logs were, in fact, the first children of Irminsul to be sacrificed after the war between folk and forest.

'That's obviously a load of horseshit,' Gunnar added, 'all wood starts to rot after a few years in the rain. And the gods' war is supposed to have taken place a thousand years ago. A lot of what they tell you is rubbish. But you have to pretend to believe it or you'll get in trouble and be punished.'

Any punishment, though, was absurdly light by Bjarki's standards. In Bago, his master Thialfi would thrash him bloody with a fishing rod when he was mildly displeased, which was several times a month. Once, when Bjarki had crushed an old lobster pot by accidentally stepping on it, Thialfi and two other fishermen had beaten him unconscious with cudgels – Bjarki had been twelve years old at the time. He was regularly forced to sleep outside Thialfi's hut in the cold with no blanket for very minor transgressions.

Here at the Fyr Skola, chastisement meant being made to run round the outside of the Grove palisade three times – about three miles in distance – or being denied a meal. Bjarki didn't mind a bit of running and the meals were always so enormous that skipping one was sometimes even a great relief.

There was a powerful sense of belonging, even of living in a close-knit family, that came with being a member of the Bear Lodge; something Bjarki very soon came to recognise and to luxuriate in. He felt accepted; he felt part of an important whole. His life on Bago – even his fierce longing for Freya – was becoming a mere memory. He threw himself into the life of the Lodge.

The Bear family was very proud of its five Rekkar, the champions produced by the Lodge system, who were unquestionably the finest warriors in the world. A single Rekkr, so the Groves saying went, was the equivalent of ten ordinary warriors. A Bear Lodge *berserkr*, Gunnar solemnly informed Bjarki, was worth at least twenty.

Therein lay Bjarki's greatest fear. His face wound, although painful, healed swiftly under the ministrations of Eldar, the Lodge *gothi*, and he soon became fit and strong, with large quantities of food and strenuous exercise, but, deep in his heart, he doubted he truly belonged in this collective of exceptional folk. He secretly feared that one day he would be discovered to be a fraud, a man who would never be able to summon the divine spirit – the *gandr* – which gave the Rekkar their fabled strength and reckless courage.

His *gandr* had not manifested itself when he fought the Boar Lodge fellow – Ivar Knuttson – who had so easily humiliated him in the Fyr Pit. He had felt nothing, not even rage, during the fight, not even when the Boar man had bitten him. Neither did the spirit of the Bear come to him during the next few weeks, when he fought mock battles, sometimes drawing blood, with his fellow novices during their daily weapons training under Hymir.

Whatever the nature of the madness that possessed him when he killed Jeki and Ymir on that red day in the dunes outside Bago, it never returned.

He went to see Nikka the Dreamer and asked her advice. She told him, once again, to search inside himself and gave him a series of humming exercises to do in the quiet of the evening after supper. Closing his eyes and making the simple four-note tune in his throat, and letting his mind wander along the secret paths into the thick forests of his own imagination.

'The Bear will surely find you, if that's what the gods decide,' Nikka said. 'Greet him as a brother, salute his strength and courage, and humbly ask for his protection. And be patient, Bjarki – no one can truly say when your *gandr* will come to you. Perhaps tomorrow, but perhaps… never.'

So Bjarki sat quietly after supper outside the Lodge, away from the jests and the old stories and the singing by the hearth-fire and the evening ale jugs coming round and round, and hummed and tried to imagine he was in the First Forest alone, walking down a path in the gloom. He soon nodded off and dreamt of Freya and their lovemaking, and the sweet puppy Garm.

He tried again the next night. He did this for seven days in a row and, on each occasion, he swiftly fell fast asleep, and woke up cold and stiff long after midnight with the faint snores of the Bear Lodge buzzing in his ears.

As the weeks passed he began to despair. Surely they would find out soon he was not blessed – how could they not? – and he would be expelled from the Fyr Skola or perhaps relegated to the humiliating role of servant.

He decided that, even though he had been Valtyr's thrall, he could not bear to live as a Lodge servant, bringing the ale, and pouring it for the fighting men. He vowed that, if he could not attain the heights of a Rekkr, he could become a Barda – he had strength and courage enough for that, surely.

So, in his sixth week at the Fyr Skola, Bjarki went out one long, warm evening and walked over to the Wolf Lodge to find Tor and ask for her help.

Tor was somewhat surprised to see Bjarki – but also, if she was honest, rather pleased. His face was healing well: a scar with a deep indentation on his right cheek was the only evidence of the fight with the Boar novice.

She had spoken to him a few times since then, once after a ceremony for the whole Fyr Skola at the Irminsul, and a couple of times at chance meetings around the Groves. Each time, she had found it hard to know what to say. Their conversations had been awkward, brief and embarrassing. They were not really friends. They were just two people who'd travelled together.

Yet when Bjarki came to seek her out at the Wolf Lodge, she was oddly happy to see him. She would never admit this to herself – it would seem like a grave weakness – but she was lonely. She was aware that most of the members of her Lodge did not like her and, while they had been surprised by her skills when she demonstrated them during Warcraft sessions, good warriors were commonplace in the Fyr Skola and they never warmed to her.

Even Helga, her Elder Sister, had now abandoned her – although Tor had to admit it was for a very good reason. Helga had dreamed of the Wolf on three nights in a row; in the fevered dreams, her *gandr* had called to her, howled for her to come and join the spiritual pack, and on reporting this to the ancient Lodge Mother and the Wolf Dreamer it had been swiftly agreed that Helga was ready to undertake her Voyaging.

Helga had been stripped naked in front of the whole Lodge, washed in icy river water brought up from the valley, while the Mother of the Lodge chanted over her, and the rest of the community hummed the summoning tune. She was marked with a triangle on her forehead in her own blood. She was given a Wolfskin, a belt and a knife and, thus equipped, she set out into the forest to seek her destiny.

'How long will she be gone for?' Tor asked one of her Lodge mates, a clumsy and thick-headed young man called Floki who would never make it as a Rekkr, in Tor's opinion, and was unlikely even to be allowed to serve as a common Barda. If they didn't expel him soon, he would become a servant.

'Till she finds her *gandr*,' said Floki.

'But how long does that take? A week? A month?'

'I don't know,' said Floki angrily, shuffling away from her. 'Don't ask me all these stupid questions, Tor; I don't want to be seen talking to *you*.'

Through shameless eavesdropping, Tor discovered from her fellow Lodge members' conversations that a novice's Voyage was never less than three days long and had been known to last up to several months.

A good number of novices who were sent out into the wild, on their own without food or proper clothing, *never* came back. They starved or froze or went mad or became lost, or were eaten by wild animals, perhaps even by their own *gandir*. It occurred to her that the First Forest might well be full of half-mad, starving Voyagers – no wonder the terrified villagers in the settled lands to the north nailed up sacrifices to keep the spirits inside.

Bjarki, typically, was straightforward about his request.

'I don't believe I will ever be able to summon my *gandr*,' he said to her. 'I'm beginning to think I should be content to be a Barda – but I'm not even very good at combat. Hymir the master-at-arms says I'm slow and that I don't move my feet enough. I know you are very good at this sort of thing, Tor, and I want your help. You're my friend. Teach me how to fight.'

Tor was on the edge of asking what was in it for her, if she were to put in all the effort of teaching him what she knew. But she bit her tongue. She was floundering, frankly, and alone. Even that imbecile Floki did not want to be seen talking to her. But this sad oaf genuinely thought she was his friend.

And so they began.

Every night before supper they trained for an hour. She taught him the twelve basic strokes of the sword, the blocks and parries, the strikes and lunges, making him repeat them over and over until they flowed naturally. Then they worked on sword and shield together, which was more difficult, but which he mastered after only a week or two. Then axe and shield; then axe and sword. They made a strange pair, the hulking young man, red-faced and sweating and the lithe girl, half his size, snapping out orders and making him do the time-honoured battle combinations again and again and again.

People stared. Ivar Knuttson, walking past one evening with a pair of Boar Lodge cronies, pointed and laughed at them: 'It's the girl with a man's name teaching the man who fights like a girl!' But they ignored the frequent and hurtful jibes and taunts and continued with their crucial sword work.

Night after night, day after day, they practised. Hymir, the master-at-arms, was the first outsider to notice an improvement at the end of the first month when Bjarki knocked Gunnar off his feet with a convincing sword feint and surprise shield barge during the daily Bear Lodge Warcraft lesson.

'You've been paying attention, little bear,' Hymir said approvingly. 'We might even make a warrior of you – in about twenty years' time.'

Gunnar lying on his back and spitting dust out of his mouth said: 'I took him under my wing. Taught him everything I know. *This* is how he repays me. No gratitude, Hymir, that's the problem with young folk today.'

One day, in late summer, when Bjarki was called out in front of the class to demonstrate a complicated sword and axe sequence,

Hymir said: 'Just do the simple routine that *I* teach, little bear, don't go showing off.'

Bjarki rushed to meet Tor that evening, with joy in his heart. When he saw her he flung out his arms and hugged her. For a long, long moment, the two of them embraced each other tightly. Then Tor put her right heel behind his, twisted her torso and pushed and Bjarki crashed painfully to the ground.

'Can't believe you fell for that old trick,' she said, half-laughing. 'It's time, I think, that you learnt something about unarmed combat.'

A new session began.

Afterwards, dusty, sweaty, a little bruised but pleasantly tired and sharing a jug of fresh ale, Bjarki told Tor about the Warcraft session and Hymir's backhanded compliment. He was expecting Tor to be pleased with him but she was strangely silent. He asked her what was wrong and, after only a little pestering, she said: 'It's this – this thing we do every night. We're preparing to be Barda. To be *less* than Rekkar; to be second best.'

'It's better than being servants,' said Bjarki. 'And much better than being sent home.'

'Is it?' said Tor. 'I came here to be a greater Rekkr than my father. I don't want to be a stupid camp guard – doing boring patrols, fighting in the shield wall with all the other oafs. I want mine to be a name to remember.'

'Maybe you will be – no one knows when the *gandr* will—'

'Helga came back to the Lodge this morning,' interrupted Tor, the hot words now spewing out. 'Six weeks she was out there in the forest, six fucking weeks – gods know how she survived. She is half the weight she was, half-healed cuts and scratches all over her body. And very strange in the head; in the way she talks now. But the Wolf came to her in the end. Her *gandr* came. She has been examined by the Lodge and will undergo the Fyr Ceremony the day after tomorrow in front of everyone in the Groves.'

Tor was talking very loudly now. 'She will be made Rekkr. And what am I? I'm personal tutor to the world's ugliest and most dull-witted oaf.'

Bjarki ignored the insult. 'I know. I heard about Helga. And she's not the only one doing the Ceremony. Ivar Knuttson – the fellow who bit me, remember? – he has made his Voyage, too, just three days, apparently, and the Boar spirit came to him; he's passing through the Fyr at the same time as Helga. But, here, listen to me, Tor: her success doesn't mean you've failed.'

'You don't understand. You can't understand. My father was a great man – they still tell stories of Hildar Torfinnsson in the halls of Svearland. I grew up with glorious tales of him ringing in my ears: Hildar the Rekkr, who charged alone and broke the shield wall of the King of Vestfold's jarls...'

Bjarki said nothing. He had nothing to say. He knew nothing of his own father or his mother. He had been abandoned as a three-month-old baby by the gate in the palisade of the village of Bago – that is what he had been told by the *hersir* Olaf Karlsson, anyway – unwanted, a useless mouth that some young mother did not wish to feed, or could not. Even old, childless Thialfi had not wanted to take him on as an apprentice fisherman. They had drawn straws in the village – every freeman was made to draw – and Thialfi lost.

They sat together in silence as the shadows lengthened.

Finally Bjarki got up. 'See you tomorrow – at the Fyr Ceremony.'

Tor said nothing.

'*I'm* grateful, you know,' said Bjarki. 'For your help. And if it is any comfort, *I* will always remember your name – for your kindness to me.'

Tor sighed. 'That's nice, oaf. But it's not exactly a seat beside the All-Father in the Hall of the Slain, is it?'

Chapter Eight

The forging of a Rekkr

Bjarki was late for supper and the board inside the Bear Lodge that held the evening soup had long been cleared away. He was resigned to a hungry night when Gunnar waved him over from the far end of the longhouse and produced the heel of a rye loaf and a lump of hard yellow cheese from under his cloak that he had saved especially for his hungry Little Brother.

As Bjarki sat eating contentedly Gunnar gleefully gave him the gossip.

'Some folk are saying he's a fake,' he said. 'A liar. That he cheated during the Voyaging and went to a village just outside the forest where he hid in a pigsty for three days. That's his Boar spirit – a farmyard porker.'

'What are you talking about?'

'The one who tried to eat you in the Fyr Pit – Ivar Whatsisname.'

'Knuttson. They say he's a fake? How can that be – the Lodge Father must have examined him, and the Boar Lodge Dreamer, too.'

'Maybe they did. But we all know the stories. It wouldn't be too hard to make up a convincing tale. A giant boar that came snuffling round you in the dead of night – a conversation in a deep and holy, but still thoroughly porcine, voice. The Boar calls you to become one of his chosen warriors. "You are to be my Rekkr, Ivar Knuttson, I claim you as my own!" I'm sure I could make a tale like that sound pretty authentic – I bet Ivar could too.'

'But that would be sacrilege. Surely the gods would severely punish anyone who did such a terrible thing.'

'I sometimes wonder, Little Brother, whether you are deliberately trying to be stupid. You can't be that naive. Gods do whatever they like.'

Bjarki said nothing. He took another mouthful of bread and cheese.

'We know he took the Red Spot before your bout with him,' Gunnar continued. 'We both know he will bend rules to get what he wants.'

'I don't like him either but I can't see him doing something so wrong.'

'Have it your own way – maybe he's pure as a field of snow and is as beloved by the Boar spirit as he is by that pen full of household swine.'

'I would prefer to believe that,' said Bjarki.

'Although I do know that the Boar Lodge is down to two Fire Born – and they're desperate to create some more. We have five, as you know, and the Wolf Lodge has four. The Boars must feel they're falling behind us.'

'I thought the Boars had more than two Rekkar. What happened?'

'They sent two *svinfylking* west to Theodoric. The Duke of Saxony sent a message to Skymir requesting troops for an attack on the Franks' new fortified church at Deventer – you heard they had the cheek to build another one of their temples on Theodoric's land, on the east bank of the Ijssel?'

'The Far-Traveller said something about it.'

'Well, Theodoric offered to pay well for the service of some Rekkar. The Mikelgothi sent him two Boar Lodge Fire Born and a dozen Barda.'

Bjarki was aware the Rekkar often fought as highly paid mercenaries. It was, after all, the main source of wealth for the Groves. The lavish food and drink they all enjoyed daily came from the bags of silver and the wagonloads of fresh provender that were provided for the Groves folk by grateful clients.

There were also the offerings in gold and silver donated by the local people wishing to honour the old gods of the forest. Beside the Thing House, where the Grove leaders met in council, there was an ancient stone building that was stuffed with bags of coin, broaches, rings, swords, pins, buckles and plates. They called it Odin's shrine, to mark the place where the god was said to have rested after his nine-day ordeal on the One Tree, but it was more like a royal treasury. No one was allowed to enter it but the Mikelgothi.

'Both the Fire Born were killed?'

'I'm surprised you haven't heard. Truly heroic deaths, a fine bloody battle for the skalds to recount in all the mead halls for years to come.'

'Go on.'

'I'll tell you if you admit Ivar Knuttson is a lying, cheating shitbag.'

'I'm not going to say that. I'll ask someone else to tell me the tale.'

'All right. Admit that it's just possible he cheated.'

'Tell me the saga of the two Rekkar – I know you secretly want to.'

'Admit the possibility of there being a possibility that he cheated.'

'Fine. There is a possibility, of a possibility, of a possibility…'

'Was that so difficult?'

Bjarki punched him in the upper arm – hard. 'So… tell me now.'

So Gunnar gave him a detailed description – some of it perhaps even true – of the battle in which the two Rekkar had perished. After the attack on the church at Deventer, which was a long, bloody fight but successful in that the offending Christian outpost had been burnt to its foundations, the Franks sent swift cavalry after the retreating Saxon army in reprisal. There was an ambush sprung by a contingent of *cabellarii*, as the Frankish armoured horsemen were called, on part of the retreating Saxon force.

The enemy had charged in overwhelming numbers. Hundreds of cavalry against a handful of Saxon infantry, many wounded or exhausted from the battle the day before.

Many of Duke Theodoric's troops were surprised and surrounded. They formed a defensive circle. It was a fine, heroic last stand, Gunnar said. A flock of ravens circling above the dead and dying, turning the air black with their wings. The two Rekkar, the last two men standing, slaughtered dozens of the Franks before succumbing to their terrible wounds; the final words on their lips a plea to the great Boar spirit to take notice of their magnificent deeds.

Bjarki nodded approvingly.

'Or maybe they just got heroically drunk after the battle, fell over in the dark and broke their silly Boar necks. You'll admit, it's a possibility…'

Bjarki punched his arm again – but much harder this time.

–

The Fyr Pit had been transformed. During the day – a rest day, a day of complete idleness for all the Lodges, declared so by the Mikelgothi herself – something that looked remarkably like the shell of a small dragon-ship, with a high, carved prow at the end nearest the Irminsul, had been constructed inside the ashy pit. This ship, though, was not filled with fighting men eager for plunder and glory but with stacked lengths of cut wood, drenched in oil.

The whole population of the Groves of Eresburg had turned out at dusk to witness the Fyr Ceremony. The Mikelgothi wore a long black robe and held in her right hand her long, black iron staff of office. Her face was painted a shocking white with a chalk paste and three triangles were drawn in fine black charcoal across her forehead – one for each of the three Lodges.

Every Rekkr who attended had donned the armour particular to his or her Lodge. Bjarki saw that Angantyr's shaven head was covered in a helmet made from a huge bear's skull, reinforced with bolted-on plates of iron, his red face framed below and above by the jaws and long yellow teeth of the long-dead animal. Angantyr stood to the right of the Mikelgothi, at the north end of the Fyr Pit, a heavy bearskin cloak hung down his broad back, almost to his heels. His brawny forearms were encased in thick fur vambraces, and heavy leather greaves were bound to his shins above his stout leather boots. Apart from a soft leather loincloth, the rest of his body was naked, his lean, muscular torso, upper arms and thighs glistening with bear grease, his scars – so many scars! – discreetly highlighted with a fine charcoal dust.

He looked terrifying. Bjarki felt a pang, knowing in his heart that he could never be so magnificent, so filled with the true essence of the Bear.

The two candidates for the Fyr Ceremony were completely naked.

They stood at the far end of the square pit, the furthest side from the Irminsul, at the rear of the ship, and they could not have looked more different from each other. Helga had lost about half her body weight in the six weeks of her Voyaging, her breasts sagged flatly on her emaciated chest, her once glossy blonde hair had turned to limp grey, and she looked at least ten years older than she had before her ordeal. She was standing still with two Wolf Lodge *gothi* positioned at her flanks. Her expression was dull, vacant; face smooth and blank as if her mind were in a faraway place.

Ivar, on the other hand, seemed to be bursting with youth and vitality, he was still a little overweight, if the truth were told, his white limbs were fleshy, doughy even, a thick roll of fat hanging over his private parts. But he was bouncing on the balls of his feet like a man about to embark on a foot race, and eager to begin. His jaws were moving slowly but constantly as if he were chewing something very tough, like a particularly obstinate piece of gristle. The two Boar *gothi* beside him had their hands firmly on both his shoulders as if restraining him, as if he were, in fact, their prisoner.

The Fyr Ceremony began with a prayer to the Irminsul, to watch over this ultimate test of courage, and to the three spirits of Bear, Boar and Wolf, imploring them to watch from the Otherworld and give aid to the men and women who sought their approval and wished only to humbly serve them.

There was a hymn, sung in the old forest tongue, which was only partly comprehensible to Bjarki, even after months of lessons in that dead language – but which he noted that Gunnar belted out with excessive enthusiasm. And then the four-note humming began, an exercise that all members of the Lodges learnt and used to summon the *gandir* to this mortal realm.

Bjarki hummed along with the rest of the folk gathered by the Fyr Pit, feeling the vibrations in his throat ripple out through his chest and into his limbs and out into his whole body, to his very toes and fingertips – it was an odd sensation, as if his whole frame were an iron bell, gently but repeatedly struck with a padded hammer.

He could see no sign of Tor, but assumed she was with the rest of the Wolf Lodge gathered on the side of the Fyr Pit adjacent him. He and the folk of the Bear Lodge were on the north side, nearest the Irminsul, the Wolf Lodge always took their place on the west, the Boars always on the east.

The humming finished and the Mikelgothi launched into another long prayer – speaking about the holy cleansing fire burning away their corrupt human shells and allowing them to be reborn in the form of their true selves.

However, Bjarki was not giving the Mikelgothi's wise words his full attention. He was looking at Ivar – who was wide-eyed, full of energy, head jerking as he looked from side to side. Bjarki thought about what Gunnar had said to him the night before. He wondered if Ivar had once again taken a strong dose of Red Spot or one of the other varieties of mushrooms and toadstools that some Rekkar used before battle to bring them to a frenzy.

Each Lodge had considerable stores of dried herbs and plant medicines, gathered by their *gothi*: some were poisonous fungi. But in the Bear Lodge, at least, they were kept locked in a chest in the Lodge Father's quarters. For a moment, Bjarki wondered if that might be the cunning path to take. If he took a dose of Red Spot himself, would that help him become a Rekkr? He immediately dismissed the idea as unworthy. He remembered Brokk's words that night by the hearth: 'You take the Spot first time, you always need the Spot. Every fight. Every battle. Every time. You'll never find your *gandr*.'

No, absolutely not. If he could not find his *gandr* by natural means, he would resign himself to the life of a humble Barda. And that was not so bad. Truly it wasn't. It was a better life, anyway, than he'd endured in Bago.

There were a dozen servants from all three Lodges now down in the pit with burning torches. They were setting fire to the black oil in the ship, the wood beginning to crackle and smoulder, a thick choking smoke now rising.

Skymir the Mikelgothi said: 'Let both candidates prepare their bodies for the ordeal of Fyr; and let the first to test herself in the sacred flames be Helga Haraldsdottir, of the Wolf Lodge, on my command, let her step forward and willingly offer her life to Wolf spirit…'

She stopped abruptly. Bjarki's eye was drawn to the far end of the pit. Ivar Knuttson had thrown off the restraining hands of his two warding *gothi*. He stepped forward to the edge of the pit, raised his hands and called out in a huge voice: 'The Boar calls me. The Boar compels me. I throw myself into the sacred fire, the cleansing Fyr – and into your loving care, Great Spirit!'

He jumped on to the rear deck of the burning dragon-ship and began to walk quickly along its length, through the black billowing smoke.

There were immediate shouts of protest from all sides of the Fyr Pit. The fire had only just been set, mere moments ago. It had not yet fully caught the planks of the ship, nor the oil-drenched stacks of wood inside the belly of the craft. There were thick drifts of oily smoke, but little yet in the way of flames and heat.

'Told you he was a cheat,' whispered Gunnar into Bjarki's ear.

Ivar had already reached the carved dragon's head and now he leapt out on to the ground, where two servants immediately drenched him in cold water, dipping buckets into barrels and hurling the contents over the youth.

Ivar lifted his hands in the air: 'The Boar claims me,' he yelled. His fat, wet naked body, though a little sooty, seemed to be untouched by the flames.

'This is all wrong; he went in far too early,' shouted Angantyr, pointing an accusatory finger at Ivar. 'He cannot truly be named Fire Born.'

The Boar Lodge Father was suddenly at hand, resplendent in a boar-skull helmet with long up-curling tusks, thick pale leather vambraces and greaves, and ankle-length cloak made from tough hairy pigskin. 'Do not disparage the Boar!' he yelled. 'Ivar Knuttson has shown himself Rekkr.'

'He mocks the *gandir*!' Angantyr raised his fists, menacingly.

'You lie! He walked through the Fyr. He has completed the ordeal.'

For a moment it seemed that the two Lodge Fathers – Boar and Bear – would throw themselves at each other, both exploding into bloody violence.

The tall, skinny form of Skymir the Mikelgothi stepped between the two huge men, holding out her iron staff horizontally to keep them apart.

'Ivar Knuttson has walked through the Fyr,' said Skymir. 'He passes the test. He is Fire Born. Look! Helga Haraldsdottir will make her attempt.'

Every eye around the Fyr Pit was drawn to the far end, where Helga, naked as a baby, had stepped forward. She raised her hands, gave one long piercing scream and leapt into the roaring blaze on the dragon-ship.

The flames had by now fully caught the wood stacked in the body of the ship. Bjarki could barely see her through the crackling flames. Helga ran at full tilt down the centre of the burning ship, her bare feet moving in a blur. He saw her long trailing grey hair catch in the heat and explode in a single brilliant flash, but by then she had crossed the fifteen paces of the ship's length and was at the far side, and leaping desperately for the edge of the pit.

She made it, just, and was immediately drenched by the two servants by the water barrels; she lay gasping on the ground, curled in a protective ball as they poured bucket after bucket over her steaming body.

'No! No! Stop her!' the Mikelgothi was shrieking, and she pointed her iron staff at the stern of the ship. 'Seize her now! Somebody!'

Bjarki turned his head, already dreading what he would see. And there was Tor dressed in her usual leather trews and jerkin on the edge of the pit, in the act of leaping into the crackling holocaust that was the dragon-ship.

'Noooo!' Bjarki did not even know he was screaming. He watched in horror as Tor began her doomed run. That stupid, reckless, impossible…

Her short, spiky red hair took longer to catch than Helga's and she was almost past the halfway point, the ship's mast, before it vaporised in a single yellow flash. Then she tripped, her booted foot caught on a crackling log and she fell face first on to the burning deck.

Bjarki was suddenly freezing cold. He heard a sound like a torrent of water roaring in his ears and acted without a single conscious thought. He let out a roar and leapt forward. He seized the bottom edge of Angantyr's heavy bearskin cloak in both hands and ripped it clean off the back of the Lodge Father. He swirled it around his head and shoulders and jumped into the burning ship at the prow end, landing with both feet in the sea of fire, feeling the half-consumed planks cracking and snapping under his weight.

He charged forward, howling as he felt the flames lick hungrily at his hands and forearms. He reached Tor in three strides, bent down and scooped her up, wrapping her in the heavy fur and turning in one smooth movement he hurled the girl with all his strength up, up and back towards the edge of the Fyr Pit. She flew high through the air, and landed with a thump on the ground, still entangled in Angantyr's heavy bearskin cloak.

The water-barrel servants drenched her immediately.

Now, screaming with pain as the fire licked all over his body, Bjarki took two stumbling, running steps and jumped after her.

He almost made it.

His chest crashed into the stone lip of the pit, all the breath knocked out of him. The shirt on his back was burning, the skin blistering and bubbling under the linen. He felt himself slipping backwards, back towards the fire.

Two powerful hands seized him under the arms and he was jerked upwards and found himself face to face – their noses inches apart – with the head of a giant bear, with Angantyr's angry red face somehow clamped between the beast's open jaws. A bucket of cold water hit him squarely in the chest and another quenched the smouldering shirt on his back. More water cascaded down, blessed in its coldness, agonising in its heavy touch.

But he was alive. And so, he realised, looking over at the small writhing figure, rolling and jerking back and forth on the sodden bear cloak, was Tor. Angantyr's face loomed back into his vision. The Lodge Father was stooping down to peer into his eyes. 'That, little bear, was the single most stupid, reckless and idiotic thing I have ever seen in my life,' he said. 'And by far the bravest.'

Chapter Nine

The trumpets sound for war

Five days and nights of unimaginable pain. Bjarki lay on a pallet in the rear of his Lodge, feverish, moaning, dreaming of bears and fire, of dragon-breath shrivelling the skin on his naked body. Eldar, the Bear Lodge *gothi*, had given him the juice of the mandrake root and infusions of henbane for the pain, as much as he believed the young man could take without succumbing to death. He administered other potions and ointments, unguents and salves, using all his talents. But his skills could not entirely quench the agony.

The skin on much of Bjarki's back and legs fell away in long strips, leaving raw oozing flesh behind, his hands and arms were blistered and red. His singed head, too, was pounding with an ache that speared from temple to temple. But he lived and, thanks to the *gothi*'s magic, he was beginning to heal. The first lucid dawn, when he managed to drink down a bowl of warm beef broth without vomiting, he asked after Tor.

Eldar sucked his yellow teeth and kept his counsel. Gunnar, who was sitting cross-legged beside him whittling a knot of elm wood, sang out: 'Oh, she's in bad trouble, Little Brother; that girl is in very bad trouble indeed.'

'But she lives?' said Bjarki.

'She lives – she was roasted almost as crisp as you – but she's alive. For now, anyway. They treated her wounds in the Wolf Lodge. I hear she's on her feet again. But she will face a full tribunal tomorrow night. All the Rekkar of the Lodges and the senior *gothi* will gather in the Thing House to decide her fate. I wouldn't be surprised if they decided to put her to death.'

'She made a mistake – it's just that she so badly wants to be a Rekkr.'

'She profaned the mystery of the Fyr Ceremony, Bjarki. Made it a free-for-all. Her jumping into the Fyr Pit uninvited. Idiots like you diving in after her. A time-honoured ritual became a joke, a funny story to tell around the Lodge hearth late at night. The Mikelgothi will *never* forgive her for that.'

'What about Ivar Knuttson? You were right. He was a cheat. We all saw him go before Helga – and before the dragon-ship was properly alight.'

'That has already been decided by the Thing council. He is declared Rekkr. Angantyr made a big fuss – shouted and raved, apparently – but the Boar Lodge carried the day in the end. Ivar Knuttson is officially a Rekkr.'

Bjarki said nothing to this. He lay back in his pallet, exhausted.

'That's enough talk for this morning,' said Eldar. 'Let him rest now.'

Bjarki insisted on attending the Thing House tribunal the following evening. His raw back and legs were dressed with bandages thickly smeared in the Bear Lodge *gothi*'s concoction of goose fat and soothing herbs but it was still horribly painful for him to move. He tried to ignore the agony long enough to walk the few hundred yards to the Thing House, which was near the exercise yard on the west side of the Groves.

When he hobbled into the barn-like space, gripping Gunnar's shoulder tightly, he was surprised to hear a tremendous cheer break out. He stopped and looked around him in total surprise. The Thing House was a rectangular, thatch-roofed building, with racks of stepped benches rising on all four sides so that all might be seated and still see the speakers in the centre of the open space. The benches were about three-quarters full when Bjarki came in, and he saw that men and women on all sides were standing up, one after the other, tugging their neighbour's sleeves, pointing at him, shouting his name.

'Bjarki... Bjarki... Bjarki...' The sound came at him in waves.

It was terrifying at first. His instinct was to turn and run – and had he not been so crippled with pain he might well have done so. Then he realised they were actually acclaiming him, praising him for his actions at the Fyr Ceremony – and it became suddenly overwhelmingly embarrassing.

Bjarki wanted to curl up in a hole and hide.

Gunnar raised his own arm to acknowledge the chanting on his friend's behalf and led Bjarki to a bench in the front row to the left of the entrance. The bench was full but the occupants shoved each other aside to make room for their hero. A few moments later, the Mikelgothi came in, dressed in a severe black hooded gown, followed by a half a dozen lesser *gothi* and the twelve Rekkar – not on this occasion dressed in their full animal-skin battle finery but, in stark contrast to the sombre *gothi*, wearing their finest clothes.

These important folk made up the Thing council, and they would make the final decision about Tor's fate. Angantyr was dressed in a rich robe of purple velvet, fringed with little gold tassels, with a bright yellow satin cloak thrown over the top – no doubt a tribute or gift from some wealthy potentate he had served as a young Rekkr. Even mad Brokk had managed to wrap himself in a tattered crimson cape that was held in place with a heavy golden broach.

The Mikelgothi sat in the middle of the bench opposite the entrance, and the *gothi* and Rekkar sat on either side of her. Bjarki noticed that Ivar was wearing plain leather armour – probably, he guessed, because he did not yet possess anything in the way of finery. When they were all settled on the bench, Skymir stood and raised her staff, immediately quieting the House.

'We are met today,' she began, 'to consider the future of one novice among us who has transgressed the ancient laws and practices of the Groves of Eresburg, and together we shall determine the most suitable punishment.'

A roar of anger erupted from the whole Thing House.

Skymir bellowed: 'Quiet! Quiet, now! Bring in the prisoner!'

The big door opened and little Tor came in, accompanied by two burly Wolf Lodge Barda carrying spears. Bjarki was shocked to see her like this. It had not occurred to him until now that she'd be under guard, a wretched prisoner. Her face was gaunt – Bjarki knew exactly how much pain she must be in from her burns – and she looked even skinnier than before. Her bald pink scalp was covered with a faint crop of ginger stubble. Her expression, however, was fierce. She glared like a demon at the assembled crowd, looking this way and that, as if daring any of them to do her wrong.

'Torfinna Hildarsdottir, you stand accused by this Thing of profaning the sacred mystery of the Fyr Ceremony, the burning heart of the Fyr Skola, by leaping unsanctioned into the holy flames,' intoned Skymir. 'You are accused of polluting the Fyr Ceremony by your actions, of disrespecting the gods, this community and even the great Irminsul – and thereby breaking the solemn oath you swore when you joined our company. This sacrilege was witnessed by almost every person now gathered here, including myself. Do you dispute your actions – or deny your guilt?'

Tor said nothing. She glared even more fiercely at the Mikel-gothi.

'I ask you again. Do you dispute your actions? You *will* answer me.'

Tor remained silent. But she shook her head very slightly.

The Thing House made a collective growling sound, like a riled animal.

'Do you wish to say anything in mitigation of your crime?'

Tor shook her head again.

'You have nothing to say at all? No plea for clemency?'

Tor dropped her eyes and stared at the ground.

'Very well. Since there is no dispute, no denial, and since you make no claim for mitigation, nor plea for clemency, we shall pass on straight away to your punishment. In the Fyr Skola, there are three serious punishments allowed by our ancient laws: you may be stripped of your rank as novice and reduced to the status of servant; you may be exiled from this place, banished for ever from our company; and the final punishment, reserved for the worst crimes of all, is that you may be put to death. I tell you now that this is the option that I personally favour. Since you do not choose to speak up in your defence, the Council of the Thing shall now deliberate on your fate…'

'Wait!' Bjarki did not know what impelled him to do this. He only knew that he must. He could not allow them to kill her. He climbed painfully to his feet, he could feel the stuck bandages tearing at his half-healed flesh. He ignored the searing pain and, holding up one bandaged hand as if he were at a Lodge lesson, he said: 'Since she will not talk, with your permission, Mikelgothi, I would speak a few words on Torfinna Hildarsdottir's behalf.'

There was a growing murmur on the benches, and Skymir looked left and right. No one on the council bench objected. She nodded.

'I know Tor better than anyone in the Fyr Skola,' Bjarki began. Then the words withered and died on his tongue. It felt strange to be speaking thus to a large audience, terrifying – yet Tor's very life was at stake. He tried to imagine how Valtyr would talk in such a situation, or the Mikelgothi for that matter. He gripped his shyness, straightened his back, and took a breath.

'Tor and I travelled down from the Dane-Mark together in the spring and, for many weeks now, we have been practising our battle skills together every evening – as some of you will have observed. And, in all that time, she has never said anything that might be thought of as disrespectful to the Fyr Skola or contrary to her sacred oath.'

He paused and took another breath. *Don't fret; just speak the truth.*

'In fact,' he continued, 'Torfinna Hildarsdottir venerates this place and all that it stands for. Her most fervent desire, many times expressed to me, has been to become Rekkr. That is all she wants from her life, to serve the gods as one of the sacred warriors of the

Groves of Eresburg. Everything she says or does, and I do mean *every single thing*, is a way of getting closer to that one ambition. It's her life's dream. I think you must all recognise that.'

There was more rumbling on the council bench as *gothi* and Rekkar muttered to each other.

'She has a strange way of showing it,' shouted Ivar Knuttson. 'By desecrating the Fyr Ceremony, she has made fools of all of us Fire Born.'

'She should not have done that,' said Bjarki. 'It was clearly wrong. But she did it out of desperation – she wants so desperately to become a Rekkr that she was prepared to take the risk of passing through the Fyr without the proper rituals and permissions. She dared to risk her own life—'

'And yours, too,' shouted someone from the crowd.

Bjarki ignored the interruption. 'She risked her own life in pursuit of a nobler aim – to realise her dream and become a Rekkr. She has shown great courage and, in a strange way, great dedication to the cause of the Fyr Skola. Surely that must count for her when it comes to deciding her punishment.'

And he sat down again.

Tor turned her head and glanced briefly at him. Her expression was unreadable. Beside him Gunnar said quietly: 'I had no idea you were so eloquent, Bjarki – you spoke like a royal skald just now. Very moving.'

Bjarki shook his head. 'I spoke from the heart. That's all. Someone had to say something. She's stubborn – too stiff-necked to save her own skin.'

Skymir the Mikelgothi got to her feet.

'Thank you, Bjarki Bloodhand, for your wise words. The council duly takes note of them. Now, does anyone else have anything they wish to say?'

Ivar Knuttson got to his feet, his leather armour creaking as he stood.

'I believe I, too, shall say my piece today. Bjarki Bloodhand's sweet words notwithstanding, that girl has deliberately made a mockery of the Fyr Ceremony – I see her intrusion on the sacred rite as a personal insult to both me and to Helga Haraldsdottir, a gross and indelible slur on our honour.

'We two became Rekkar that day, this is true, but the antics of Torfinna Hildarsdottir have for ever tarnished our achievement. The Fyr Ceremony is about more than running through a burning ship, it's the culmination of months, sometimes years of hard work, pain and struggle, it is a holy thing, a sacred rite, and having that irreverent hoyden prancing about in the flames does not make her a Rekkr – and never will! She has shamed me; she has shamed the Fyr Skola, she shames all of us. Her punishment must be death!'

Angantyr stood then. He was clearly very angry. 'You dare to speak to us about your *honour*, Ivar Knuttson, you cheating little toad—'

The Mikelgothi shut him down. 'You will be silent, Father Angantyr – *that* issue has already been decided. Sit down. Now.'

The Bear Lodge leader subsided. Red-faced and muttering oaths, he plonked himself back down heavily on the council bench.

The Thing House had grown noisy, most were calling for Tor's death, a few others saying Ivar was indeed a cheat, and it took the Mikelgothi several moments to quiet the assembly. 'Does anyone else wish to speak?' she said.

A figure stepped out from the shadows at the back of the Thing House, a tall, lean figure in a stained cloak and hood. Bjarki saw then with a little leap of joy and relief that it was his former travelling companion, Valtyr.

'It is clearly not my place to dictate any punishment that may be due to Torfinna Hildarsdottir, for I did not witness her crime, nor am I a denizen of the Groves of Eresburg. But I know her – and I know all of you. And I shall say only this to you. It must *not* be death. I brought her to the Fyr Skola, and I believed the Groves were the place for her to discover her true nature. If she has transgressed against your laws, then the fault must partly be mine. I accept that responsibility. I will also say this to you now. If you do not care for this brave, this clever, this battle-skilled – this most *extraordinary* young woman I brought to live among you, then I shall take her away. My advice to the Thing is that her punishment, if she even merits one, should be exile.'

Skymir smiled at the old man. 'Thank you, Valtyr Far-Traveller. Does anyone else wish to speak? No? Then I believe I have come to my decision.'

She lifted her iron staff high in the air and waited till the Thing House had grown quiet again. 'Hear me, Torfinna Hidarsdottir, as the Mikelgothi of the Fyr Skola, chief servant of the Irminsul, who is guided by the gods and spirits of these ancient groves, I hereby sentence you to exile for life. Our friend the Far-Traveller shall take you away from this place before the next sun dawns and you may never return, on pain of death. Do you have anything you wish to say before you are expelled from the Fyr Skola?'

Tor lifted her head, glared at the Mikelgothi and said: 'I want my Wolfskin back. I want the skin of my father, Hildar Torfinnsson the Rekkr, which you took from me some months ago. I demand its immediate return.'

'It shall be done,' Skymir said gravely. 'The Council of the Thing has spoken its mind and delivered its verdict, I now move to dismiss this—'

'If I might just say a few more words, Mikelgothi,' interrupted Valtyr.

Skymir stopped; she frowned but made a small gesture with her staff that implied that he might do so.

Valtyr bowed. 'Since almost the whole Fyr Skola is gathered here at this hour, I have tidings that I must impart to you all. And an invitation.'

'Speak, Far-Traveller,' Skymir said.

The old man straightened to his full height. 'Last month, the Franks came north in numbers, accompanied by a strong force of *cabellarii*. They occupied a piece of territory deep inside Westphalia, previously governed by the *hersir* of Thursby, in the far southwest of Duke Theodoric's realm.'

There was angry muttering all around the Thing House.

Valtyr ignored the hubbub and continued. 'They put the *hersir*, an old man by the name of Brand Thurlsson, and most of the adult male inhabitants to the sword; they have enslaved all the rest, seized their goods and beasts and burnt several villages to the ground. It is an outright act of war. They are now building a church and fortress, next to the charred ruins of Thursby.'

There were shouts of rage. 'War, by the gods! A declaration of war!'

'Those are my tidings,' said Valtyr. 'Here is my invitation. Theodoric is out of patience with these Frankish incursions. He has swallowed enough insults in recent months from Karolus, King of Francia, and he cannot allow this fresh outrage to pass. He seeks to make a fine example of these intruders.

'Theodoric plans to descend on the region of Thursby with a mighty army in one month's time, to destroy this new church before they have even finished building its surrounding walls, to burn the settlement to the ground and to slaughter all the Franks he can lay his hands on. He invites the Fyr Skola to join him in making war on these servants of the interloper Karolus. So… will the Thing Council accept Duke Theodoric's cordial invitation?'

In an instant, almost every man and woman in the Thing House was on their feet cheering, hooting, whistling, calling out their affirmation.

They were going to war.

Chapter Ten

A shock for a sleepy sentry

Hymir was dubious. 'You sure you're fit, lad?' he said. He had said it several times. 'Strip and give me twelve star jumps, right now. Go on!'

Bjarki slowly took off his tunic and trews, removed his few remaining bandages, and obediently jumped up and down to show the Warcraft teacher his wounds were almost healed. He offered to fight any of the Lodge Barda, with sharpened weapons, if necessary, to prove the matter beyond doubt.

Three weeks had passed since Valtyr's surprise intervention in the Thing House and, in truth, Bjarki *was* fit enough – almost entirely back to his considerable full strength. Valtyr had disappeared with Tor before dawn the next day – in keeping with the Mikelgothi's terms of immediate exile – and Bjarki, exhausted by the emotion of the Thing and his own part in it, not to mention the very severe pain of his wounds, had returned to the Bear Lodge and slept long and deeply and so missed their dawn departure.

He felt a little irritated that neither Valtyr nor Tor had come to bid him farewell – particularly since he had spoken out on her behalf at the Thing. But they had not visited him, and he must swallow his resentment.

Tor must have a great deal on her mind – shame, anxiety for the future – and although she had been spared death, she would be destroyed by the sentence of exile. So he forgave her and, over the next few days and weeks, he focused his mind on preparing his half-healed body for his first campaign.

He had Gunnar salve his wounds every morning and night with the goose-fat and herb concoction and did light stretching exercises immediately afterwards to make sure his new-growing skin was coming back supple.

After a week, he began running again, every morning with the rest of the Lodge, to the astonishment of his fellows. Those morning runs cost him a good deal of pain – the chafing of even his loosest clothes on raw skin was almost as bad as the original burns. But he stuck with it grimly, running right through the agony, determined that he should be included in the Fyr Skola force sent out to join Theodoric at the muster at the Troll Lake Stones, which would take place on the day of the full moon at the end of the week of the Harvest Feast Day.

It had been decided that three Rekkar should be sent to serve the Saxon warlord – one from each Lodge – a significant proportion of the Fyr Skola's strength; and that each Lodge champion should be accompanied by three trained Barda, and also three strong camp servants, who would carry the food, equipment and spare weapons. There had been fierce competition in the Groves over who would be chosen as part of the twenty-one folk who made up the force, the assumption being that they would earn lasting glory for themselves and bring great honour and wealth to the Fyr Skola.

Bjarki desperately wanted to be picked to join this elite company.

Brokk had been chosen as the Rekkr to represent the Bear Lodge, and two experienced Barda, a young man called Ugo and an older woman named Thorn had already been selected when Bjarki petitioned Hymir, the master-at-arms, to allow him to be the third Bear Barda chosen.

Hymir told him openly that he was in two minds: Bjarki, after his weeks of intensive training with Tor, was shaping up to be one of his best fighters, and his courage had been proven beyond doubt by the heroics of the Fyr Ceremony; but he was still injured, and the ceremony had displayed a previously unrecognised reckless streak in the lad, which Hymir found troubling. A wild disregard for personal safety was expected, of course, even demanded of a Rekkr, but the Barda had to hold together in the shield wall, and a cool head, unshakeable loyalty to comrades and iron self-discipline were the crucial qualities required for these soldiers of the Groves.

In the end, however, Hymir reluctantly agreed to let him play his part.

'You may go, Bjarki, but I want no reports of your rashness. Obey your orders, stay with the other Barda and keep the wall intact in the face of the foe. Let the Fire Born do all the bloody work. May the Bear guard you.'

–

The three chosen Bear Lodge servants – two older women and a young man – were folk who had been passed over not only as potential Rekkar, but also as Barda, some years previously. However, one, a youth from Frisia called Per, said he hoped to make a name for himself in the fighting, to redeem himself in the Lodge's eyes and perhaps be accepted as a raven-feeder.

He confided in Bjarki that he was fed up with sweeping the Lodge, chopping firewood and hauling water all day, and asked that he put in a good word for him with the Lodge Father, and with Hymir, if his service on this campaign was satisfactory. Bjarki assured Per that he would help if he could.

They travelled southwest along the river valley for a whole day, an easy march, and then set out up into the tangled depths of the First Forest, the path climbing in altitude and, more often than not, narrowing and forcing them to travel in single file. The country became less thickly wooded the higher they climbed and they crossed many small rivers, some little more than streams, and passed several large mirror-like lakes. After three days of hard marching, the twenty-one-strong Fyr Skola company arrived at the Troll Lake Stones, exactly on the agreed day of the full moon.

Duke Theodoric's force was waiting for them.

The paramount leader of all the Saxon tribes had dispatched more than a hundred of his best warriors to gather at the ancient standing stones – nine tall granite menhirs arranged in a broken circle beside a long, black, sinister-looking lake. A dozen *hersirs* attended the muster from right across Saxony, each commanding a handful of solid men-at-arms. Yet Bjarki was disappointed that the Duke of Saxony himself had not come, in all his pomp and glory, but instead had entrusted this force to a man called Jarl Harald, an elderly warrior, tough as leather, one of the king's most trusted followers.

Bjarki had, in truth, been expecting a larger muster. This gathering of a hundred fighting men was, to his eyes, hardly a 'mighty army', as Valtyr had put it in the Thing House, it was more like a powerful raiding party.

'Fewer is better,' said Ingvar, the Wolf Lodge Rekkr, a squat, shaggy brute whose terrible facial scars gave him a permanent lopsided snarl, and who was in command of the whole Eresburg contingent. Thorn, the Bear Lodge woman, who had charge of the nine Barda, agreed.

'We'll travel more quickly and give less notice of our presence to the enemy,' she said.

'More glory for each of us, too,' added Ingvar, with a happy chuckle.

It was late summer, almost autumn, with the mornings already crisp, the nights chilly and the days each growing a little shorter than the last – the final weeks of the campaigning season. After a speech of welcome for all the contingents – delivered by Jarl Harald, who appeared to be heroically drunk and was balanced perilously atop one of the smaller menhirs – the Eresburg folk made their camp a little way from the rest of the army between the eastern side of the black lake and the fringe of the First Forest. They were to march at dawn, Jarl Harald said, and should get as much sleep as they could.

In the small Eresburg encampment, the Rekkar of the three Lodges huddled closest to the campfire after the evening meal –

Brokk, silent as usual, sharpened his long bearded axe, but Ingvar and the Boar Lodge Rekkr shared a skin of mead and a jest, laughing together in the firelight.

That was a stone in Bjarki's boot: the Rekkr chosen by the Boar Lodge. The champion they had picked was Ivar Knuttson, the man who, he finally had to admit to himself, had grossly cheated in the Fyr Ceremony.

Bjarki had tried to find things to respect about Ivar but he found it impossible. It was not because the young man had so easily bested him in the Fyr Pit – and bitten a chunk out of his face. It was because Ivar seemed to have no respect for the institutions of the Groves of Eresburg.

This contempt for the Fyr Skola was revealed by the fact that he had used trickery to gain Fire Born status. His rank dishonesty made something that had been to Bjarki good and holy now seem tawdry. Indeed, he made everything about their community, their way of life and their beliefs, seem grubby and, in Bjarki's bleakest moments, even fraudulent. If Ivar Knuttson had successfully cheated to become Fire Born, how many others had done so?

Then there was also Ivar's demeanour: he made his Barda carry his battle weapons, his bearded axe, long sword and heavy round shield, which neither of the other Rekkar did. He had his servants set up a cosy tent for him to sleep in every night, in a comfortable cot slung from the tent poles, while everyone else – even Ingvar their captain – slept on the cold, stony ground, wrapped in cloaks or blankets with no more than a clothing bag for a pillow.

Ivar also behaved with an obvious sycophancy towards the Rekkr captain, laughing exaggeratedly at Ingvar's feeblest jest, flattering him by admiring his impressive collection of scars, and echoing his orders, shouting them, in fact, and berating anyone who did not instantly leap to obey.

It seemed to Bjarki that Ivar did not understand the true ethos of the Groves; or, if he did, that he distained it. He was behaving like a well-born *hersir*, or even like a king's jarl. There was a hierarchy in Eresburg, yes, but also proper respect between the different ranks. Servants such as Per had once been candidates for the honour of becoming Rekkar. Although Per had failed the test, he was still one of them: a man of the Groves – now serving their community in a different capacity. Ivar Knuttson treated Per like a dirty thrall; like a mere *nithing*, unworthy of even the slightest degree of respect.

When Ingvar had told Bjarki after supper that it was his turn to take the first watch that night, Bjarki had merely nodded his assent and begun to walk away. Then Ivar, quite unnecessarily, had bawled after him: 'And don't fall asleep, you dozy fool, or I'll cut that fat head of yours clean off!'

It was a small thing, a silly, childish threat, and Bjarki knew he must ignore it, but it irked him. He wished that Gunnar were with him; they could have joked about the stupidity of the Boar Rekkr and made each other laugh like donkeys. But Gunnar had not even been considered to join the company.

Gunnar was still a novice. He had not been enrolled in the ranks of the Barda by Angantyr – a decision that was entirely the Lodge Father's to make. Gunnar was the oldest of the novices by a year and more but in the grizzled old Rekkr's opinion he was not yet ready to fight. Perhaps Bjarki's friend never would receive that honour. Perhaps he was destined to become a Lodge servant. Yet Bjarki admired him, despite his lack of ambition, and sorely missed him. Gunnar would have made him feel better. He would also probably have made him admit out loud that he loathed Ivar Knuttson.

'Want me to stick a knife in his kidneys when he's asleep?' whispered Per as Bjarki stumped off furiously to begin his sentry watch. 'I'd be happy to do it for you, Bjarki. Honestly, it would give me the greatest satisfaction.'

That wasn't the answer. Ivar was still a comrade, even if Bjarki hated him. But neither could Bjarki be bothered to reprimand the servant for his joke.

–

It was chilly, sitting out there on the fringe of the camp a few yards from the edge of the First Forest, staring into the wall of black trees. Bjarki pulled his excellent cloak tighter around his body. He did, in fact, feel dangerously sleepy after a day's march and a large plate of mutton stew for supper, but he was certainly *not* going to fall asleep. Even though he knew Ivar would not actually cut his head off. He couldn't allow himself to fail his comrades.

He adjusted the position of the hilt of the sword in its sheath, which was digging into his waist. That was one of the best things about being a Barda – they had been handsomely kitted out before they even left the shade of the Irminsul. They had each been issued leather-lined woollen cloaks, good lime-wood shields with iron bosses, and each Barda had received a steel helmet, a boiled-leather cuirass, a pair of leather greaves reinforced with iron, a sword, a hand-axe and an ash-wood spear – a long single-bladed, broken-back seax, too, for those like Bjarki who did not possess one already.

He had even been issued with thick-soled fighting boots, since the cheap leather shoes he had acquired in Flens were already falling apart. The Fyr Skola company was better equipped even than some of Theodoric's poorer *hersirs* – and much better than most of the ordinary Saxon soldiers. Bjarki hoped that, when the time came, he would prove worthy of his weaponry.

He could definitely feel his eyelids drooping and, rather than risk slumber, he got to his feet and began to pace around the perimeter of the camp, trying to avoid looking at the high-piled campfire in order to preserve his night vision. Just one more hour, he told himself, just another hour, and he could wake Ugo for his turn as sentry and climb into his own warm blankets.

He wondered what battle would be like when they came to the church. He had few doubts about their victory – they had *three* of the legendary Rekkar with them. They would be surprising a sleeping enemy, numerically inferior, and sheltering behind half-built walls. He wondered if he would have to kill anyone in the coming fight – and what that would feel like. He had no memory at all of the killings he had done in the dunes. He found, when he thought about it, when he thought properly about the snuffing out of another human life, that he was not as eager for gore and glory as he had been in the Bear Lodge. But he must not show cowardice before the others.

'Psst!'

Bjarki stopped dead in his tracks. He was standing a few paces from the wall of the First Forest, with the camp at his bank. Had he imagined that?

'Psst! Bjarki.'

A jolt of terror flashed from his scalp to his soles: the First Forest was calling to him. Valtyr had said it was alive. Or some spirit or animal demon living in the darkness of its interior was calling to *him*. He found he had the drawn sword in his right hand, shield in the other, legs braced for impact. He opened his mouth to scream out the alarm. Whatever fiend was out there, he would fight it. He felt suddenly icy cold; the rushing was loud in his ears…

'Bjarki! I'm over here, you half-blind oaf. Wake up! It's me.'

–

'You must be the world's worst sentry,' said Tor. 'I've known logs of wood that were more aware of their surroundings. Those *menhirs* are more alert.'

'I'm well, thank you, Tor,' said Bjarki. 'Burns all healed up. No, no, truly, there's no need to thank me for speaking for you at the Thing House. Or to say goodbye. No need at all. Your gratitude is not necessary at all.'

Tor gave him a long, hard look.

'Bitterness doesn't suit you,' she said. 'Or were you attempting to be funny? Anyway, I did come to thank you before I left and I was told – in none-too-friendly terms by your pal Gunnar – that you were exhausted and sleeping like a baby. Did he not tell you that I came to say farewell?'

'No. Oh. All right, never mind. So… what are you doing here?'

'I'm starving, if you want to know. Got any food?'

'Plenty, thanks for asking. We had a magnificent supper in the camp – hot mutton stew and buttered turnips, followed by apples and fresh cheese!'

They were sitting just inside the tree wall of the First Forest, looking out over the sleeping Eresburg contingent. Bjarki reckoned he could still keep a good watch for enemies and talk to Tor at the same time. He reached into the pouch at his waist and pulled out a few hard, dusty strips of dried beef, the remains of a snack, which he handed over to Tor. She mumbled something that almost resembled thanks with her full, fast-chewing mouth.

'What *are* you doing here?' Bjarki said after a few moments.

Tor wiped her lips. 'I'm Voyaging.'

'What?'

'You know, I'm wandering the First Forest with no food, all alone, tying to contact the Wolf spirit. I'm trying to discover my *gandr*.'

'Don't you ever give up?'

'There's been a set-back, for sure, being kicked out of the Fyr Skola was unlucky, but there are always obstacles to overcome. I *shall* be a Rekkr like my father. That's what I set out to do. That's what I'm going to do.'

Bjarki was slightly awed by her determination.

'What happened to Valtyr? Where is he now?'

'He's gone east, I think. We had a disagreement. He said I should go back to Svearland, become a warrior, join a jarl's retinue. I decided not to.'

'So you plan to live in the forest until you meet the Wolf, is that it?'

'That's the plan. You know there have been Rekkar in the Middle-Realm since the dawn of time, don't you? Long before the Fyr Skola was created. Some folk have always been able to summon their *gandr*, or call up the Beast inside their hearts. There are natural Fire Born, you know. I don't need the Mikelgothi or the Fyr Skola or even Valtyr to reveal my destiny.'

'You will starve to death – or be eaten by something. Or both.'

Tor shrugged her thin shoulders.

'Listen, just come into the camp and let me get you some proper food. Forget this Voyaging nonsense. You can sleep warm by the fire. You won't be breaking any rules. This is not the Fyr Skola. You can march beside us, eat with us at night, and the Mikelgothi need never know about it.'

Tor gave him a steely look. 'I have made my decision.'

'I can see that. Look, I have to get back to the camp, I need to wake Ugo. Please, stay close to us. We march tomorrow for Thursby; I can bring food. Watch me, I'll leave something out for you. May the Bear guard you.'

'I *am* going to do it, oaf; I *am* going to become a Rekkr. You'll see.'

Bjarki said nothing. He clambered to his feet, briefly gripped her bony shoulder and stepped back out of the wall of trees into the encampment.

Chapter Eleven

The bloody gift of Tiw

Bjarki peered out through the dense foliage of the old oak tree. He was about halfway up the trunk, lying along a thick limb, out of sight of anyone more than a few paces away. It was an hour before dawn on the second day after his meeting with Tor at the Troll Lake Stones – and he'd not seen her since.

Before he left the lake, he had hidden two loaves of bread, a dried sausage, a wedge of hard cheese and some dried apples in a sack under the exposed roots of a tree in the place they had met, and hoped she had been able to recover them. But he knew, deep inside himself, that it would not make the slightest difference in the end. The food might last Tor a couple of days, but she would die alone in the First Forest, one way or another. He wished he had tried harder to persuade her to take another course – although he knew well that when she made up her mind there was no changing it.

He pushed thoughts of her from his mind. He had a task to do. Before him lay the new Christian church and its fortified compound. Half a mile behind him, hidden inside a large wood, was the Saxon force under the command of Jarl Harald. His task – a signal honour granted to the Fyr Skola company, and thence given to Bjarki – was to scout out the enemy position.

The combination of the church and its defensive walls, watchtowers, barracks, storehouses, kitchens, a blacksmith's forge, stables, granary, and so on was called a *castrum* by the Latin-speaking Christians, he'd been told.

He had never seen anything like it before. It reminded him in its unnatural regularity of the Hellingar Fortress, which guarded the Ox Road that passed through the Dane-Work. But, instead of a circular design, the Frankish *castrum* was a perfect square, each side a hundred paces long, with a square tower at each corner and a large gate in the centre of the north wall.

The walls were made of pine logs, twice the height of a man, as thick as his thigh, and each sharpened at the top into a wicked spike. He could see some Frankish soldiers – spearmen with dull red cloaks, round red shields and steel helmets – patrolling along the walkways that ran along the inside of the walls. He dutifully counted all the men-at-arms he could see – twenty-four. There were four soldiers in each tower and two patrolling each of the four walls, pacing slowly up and down. All of them seemed awake and alert.

This would only be the night watch, Bjarki reckoned. He had no idea how many other folk might be asleep in the buildings inside the wooden walls. A hundred? Two hundred? More? He felt a shiver of premonition. This attack on the *castrum* was going to be more difficult than they had assumed.

He looked left and right scanning the whole area. To his left, to the east, it was clear that the inhabitants of the *castrum* had been industrious. A large area of the First Forest – the size of three or four barley fields – had been cleared of timber and undergrowth. It looked naked, unnatural, and felt like a desecration. Bjarki wondered what Valtyr would say about this mass slaughter of the children of the Mother of Trees. These Franks clearly had no great respect for ancient woodlands of the North. They had chopped down hundreds of fine trees – many more than they needed, surely, and some of which had taken several men's lifetimes to grow – and used their fallen carcasses to build this big wooden fortress and the many buildings inside.

The main structure inside the *castrum* was the large building at its very centre. This was the church of their Christian god. It was a long rectangular shape with a pair of stubby square arms extending on the north and south sides, making the shape of a cross, their holy symbol, according to Valtyr.

The church was built of thick, straight planks, painted with shiny black pine pitch and the building was situated on a raised-earth platform about three foot above the packed earth of the courtyard. The long pointed roof of the church was covered with tiles the colour of dried blood and adorned, at the eastern end, with a large golden cross, which was already catching the first rays of the rising sun and glowing as if it were made of molten metal.

From Bjarki's oak-tree lookout, a hundred paces from the northeast corner of the *castrum*, he could see a big square window, its wooden shutter flung wide open, set in the eastern end of the church, high under its blood-tiled roof. Valtyr had once told him that Frankish churches were all orientated this way, east–west, and had a large window facing the dawn.

Bjarki could see a man standing on the other side of the open shutter, presumably on a platform or on an upper story of the church, and looking out to the east, watching the sun as it rose above the far horizon. Something about this figure was familiar to Bjarki; he'd seen him before…

The man was tall, well built, regular-featured and bald but for a fringe of hair round his ears. He was dressed in a pale robe, which almost seemed to shine. Then Bjarki recognised him. It was the apostle, the Christian priest he'd glimpsed walking through Snorri's hall in Hellingar all those months ago. Even at this distance he was sure of it. That was a strange coincidence.

As the sun came up, filling the interior of the *castrum* with light, the man lifted his arms up in front of him and pressed his palms together. He seemed to be saying something – or perhaps singing – but Bjarki was too far away to hear.

The sunrise told Bjarki it was time to get down from his tree before he was spotted. He took one final look at the buildings in the area inside the *castrum*, at the kitchens with blue trickles beginning to waft upwards from the smoke holes – clearly the breakfast fires were being lit. He watched a red-cloaked Frank emerging from what looked like a barracks, a long, low, log-built building, his steel helmet tucked under one arm. The soldier yawned and called up something indistinct to one of the sentries. There was a wide, open-fronted stable over by the far, southern wall but Bjarki could only see one horse inside, and one tiny stable boy – the lad rubbing his sleepy face, stroking the far bigger animal's silky black neck.

The *castrum* was waking up. It was time to return and make his report.

–

'I cannot be precise, lord, about the strength of the enemy,' said Bjarki. 'But from the size of the two barracks I saw inside the fortress, I should guess at a total of about one hundred and fifty warriors. Perhaps more.'

'Hmm,' said Jarl Harald, 'more than us then – but they don't have, I would say, all *that* much of an advantage. What do you think, Ingvar?'

They were gathered, half a mile north of the new Frankish settlement, in a loose circle under a tall ash in a wood, Harald, the three Rekkar and half a dozen *hersirs*. Bjarki had told them all that he had seen – reporting that the *castrum* had been sited not far from the burnt-out ruins of the Saxon village of Thursby. The fields of barley and wheat to the west and north of the *castrum* had recently been harvested and were covered with golden stubble. So the Franks had already provisioned themselves for the coming winter.

'Tell me again, lad, about the stables,' said Ingvar. 'Not a single horse in them, did you say?'

'I saw one horse only. But there was enough stabling for two score at least. No sign at all of any of the other mounts. The stalls seemed empty.'

'You saw no *cabellarii* at all?' asked Brokk.

Bjarki shook his head.

'They've gone on a raid,' said Ivar Knuttson. 'They've ridden off to plunder the surrounding lands and left the *castrum* without any protection.'

'Maybe,' said Ingvar.

'By Tiw, that's it!' Jarl Harald slapped his knee. 'They're out foraging. I'll wager they've taken a few of their Red Cloaks with them, too. We've caught them with their trews round their boots, having a morning dump.'

'If they *have* gone, lord,' said Bjarki, 'might they not come back?'

'That's enough, Barda,' said Ivar, scowling at Bjarki. 'None of your cowardly talk at the council. Hold your stupid tongue till you're spoken to.'

Bjarki glared at the Rekkr. Harald seemed oblivious to the exchange.

'Yes, it is surely a gift from Tiw,' he said. 'The war god shows his favour. We must attack. This morning. Before the *cabellarii* return from their raiding. Now, the walls – twelve feet high, did you say, young fellow?'

Bjarki nodded. He was still fuming from Ivar's rebuke.

'But there is a great big gate, yes?' Harald seemed excited. 'Could the Rekkar get inside and open it for the rest of us? You could, couldn't you?'

Ingvar seemed to be infected with Harald's enthusiasm. 'As you command, lord. We can open that gate. Yes, we could certainly do that.'

–

The four of them sprinted towards the double gate: Bjarki and Brokk, Ugo and Ingvar; two Barda, two Fire Born. Four warriors to storm a fortress.

They were spotted the moment they left the tree line. A sentry on the walls began calling out the alarm when they were still a hundred paces from the gate, and before they had gone even a few strides further, whistles were blowing and trumpets sounding all along the line of the fortifications.

If they had ever had any chance of surprise, it was gone now.

It was the phrase 'cowardly talk' that had made Bjarki immediately volunteer to be one of the Barda who would assist the two Rekkar to open the big gates. *Why?* he wondered as he ran with the other three. They were just jabbing words spoken by his enemy. Well, it was too late for regrets. As he pounded forward towards the Frankish fortress, the iron rim of his big round shield battered at his lower back, the long sword-scabbard slapped painfully at his legs. It was quite different from the usual unencumbered morning runs in the groves. This was battle. This was the real thing – today they would find glory. Or death. Best not to think about it. Best just to run.

Bjarki had felt a jolt of icy fury when Ivar Knuttson had refused the invitation from Harald to be one of the two Rekkar charged with opening the gates. Ivar had demurred, feigning modesty, and insisted that the honour must go to Ingvar, since he was older, wiser and more experienced than he.

It was a sensible decision, logical, and no one could usefully disagree. But Bjarki could not help but feel that Ivar was just weaselling his way out of an extremely perilous – possibly even suicidal – mission.

'I shall command the main Fyr Skola assault force,' Ivar said grandly. 'Once Brokk and Ingvar have done their duty, when the gates are open, my people and I shall charge through them and slaughter the garrison to a man.'

Nobody argued. No one sane would ever accuse a Rekkr of cowardice.

So it was the four of them – Bjarki, Brokk, Ugo and Ingvar – who were now sprinting towards an alert, ready, and well-manned Frankish stronghold. Bjarki could hear Brokk and Ingvar begin to hum the summoning tune, even over the thudding of their heavy boots. He began to hum along too...

At fifty paces out, the first arrows began to flick past the running men; one snagged in Brokk's left vambrace, stuck in the thick fur and leather; another pierced the bottom of Ingvar's Wolfskin cloak. At thirty paces out, a javelin slammed into the ground an inch from Bjarki's right foot.

The shiny steel helmets on the battlements were multiplying; first it was ten men on the wall on either side of the big gate, then a score, now two score. Officers in plumed helmets were barking orders, war trumpets blared. More men were running along the inside of the walls, helms winking in the sunshine, coming to join the thickening line of defenders above the gate.

An arrow clanged off Bjarki's own helmet; the blow felt like a hammer strike. But they were only ten paces away now. Bjarki could see the knots and whorls in the rough bark of the logs that made up the wall. They had made it. In the last few steps he and Ugo raced ahead of the two Rekkar, turned at the last minute and slammed their backs against the solid wall of logs. It was a manoeuvre they had practised dozens of time in the exercise yard at the Fyr Skola, taking turns first to be 'booster' and then 'jumper'.

Bjarki laced his fingers together, cupped his hands at the level of his knees. Brokk did not even break his stride, he stepped with his right foot into the stirrup made by Bjarki's interlinked palms and the instant Brokk's boot touched Bjarki's hands, he heaved his comrade upwards with all his might.

Brokk flew up into the air; he got his left hand on the top of the wall and hurled himself over. And a Rekkr was now among his enemy. Like a terrier hurled into a pit full of scattering rats, Brokk began his bloody work.

From the foot of the wall, Bjarki could see very little of the epic fight going on above him: but he immediately heard the screaming, and the meaty thuds as the Rekkr's axe bit into flesh, the crack of bone under his heavy blade, the shouts, the curses, the clang of steel on steel, and he certainly felt the gentle red spray that pattered down on his shoulders. A fine bloody rain.

He looked across nervously at Ugo, on the far side of the gate, who had also successfully launched his Rekkr on to the wall directly above him. For a second their gazes locked. Then Bjarki jerked around as a severed head thumped down on to the ground next to him, still wearing a steel helmet and an expression of astonishment. A full-length severed arm was next, dropping like a tossed log and bouncing once on the bloody earth.

He looked up, saw a Red Cloak at the point of hurling a javelin down at him and leapt aside. The launch never came, the man was snatched away from sight, then seemed to leap from the battlements and soar up briefly into the blue sky before crashing to earth. He twitched only once and lay still.

Bjarki looked up again and saw Brokk, leaning over the wall, one long simian arm draped down over the rough logs. 'Come, little bear,' he said.

True to his Fyr Skola training, Bjarki did not hesitate. He made a gigantic leap upwards, his right arm reaching out at full stretch. He felt Brokk's iron hand grip his wrist and he was whisked upwards, as if fired from a catapult. A moment later, he found himself with one boot on the walkway and the other inside the sliced-open chest of a lifeless Frank.

There were dead and dying men all around him; body parts were everywhere too, and glistening wet blood painted every surface.

In some places the corpses on the walkway were piled three men deep. Down below, in the open space before the church, two score or more red-cloaked enemies were gathering, in a disciplined company, spearmen, archers, some armed only with swords – and they were staring up at Brokk in astonishment. To Bjarki's left, he saw that Ugo was also on the wall, but cringing slightly behind a blood-drenched Ingvar, who was frothing at the mouth and grimly chopping his way through a pack of terrified Red Cloaks.

'Come on,' growled Brokk. 'You open gate. I kill these foreigners.'

Bjarki saw that the Bear Lodge Rekkr, too, was slathered in blood, and guessed that a good deal of the glistening red was his own. Brokk was still humming, the four-note summoning tune. He was gashed several times on his half-naked torso, some wounds deep, an arrow was stuck right through his left thigh, and a slash to the face had opened up a purple flap of skin below his right eye. But the Rekkr seemed to be oblivious to his wounds.

'Open the gate,' he said again.

Then Brokk resumed his humming – and Bjarki felt a corresponding shiver pass down his own spine. Brokk jumped from the walkway, landing like a cat on the packed earth floor of the *castrum* courtyard. His humming grew in volume, rose in pitch and became a giant's roar and, streamers of white froth flying from his lips, bearded axe in one hand, bloody seax in the other, he waded into the mass of Franks, heedless of their bristling weapons.

It was like watching a tiny autumn whirlwind driving through a pile of dry leaves. Brokk bored into the ranks of enemies, axe and seax swinging and slashing, gore flying, blood spattering, men falling away, jumping back, shouting, screaming, dying… Bjarki tore his eyes away from the appalling slaughter and stumbled down the set of stairs by the gate on jelly-like legs.

He reached the gate and, in the sunless gloom behind it, he suddenly saw a Red Cloak spearman come out of a little log room at the side. The man, an older fellow, his unshaven jaw stubbled blue, lunged at him with his long spear. Bjarki, who had his own sword out by now, knocked the point aside with his shield rim, entirely by instinct, then came inside the man's range and hacked down into the fellow's neck, half severing it, dropping his foe like a sack of wet sand. He stared down at the twitching strangeness of the fallen body. His first battle kill. So easy. He felt nothing. Nothing at all.

He was aware that Ugo was now beside him, chattering manically, saying something quite unintelligible about the barred gate, and waving his sword, and Ingvar – limping and as gore-slathered as a slaughter man – was hurrying over to join Brokk in the writhing, bloody scrum of their enemies.

But there were no foes within a dozen feet of the two Barda.

'Help me lift the bar,' said Bjarki.

Together they lifted the heavy twelve-foot-long oak beam from its brackets, hurling it aside. And then, taking a door apiece they began to drag the heavy portals open. An arrow twanged into the wood beside the iron bracket, then a second shaft thudded home higher up; he heard someone else calling an order at him from somewhere on his left in a weird but oddly intelligible accent – the man seemed to be shouting 'No! No!' at him.

Bjarki ignored it all, he hauled on the massive door, scraping it through its curved earthen groove, jerking at it madly when it stuck, and – finally – with a heave, he flung it wide.

He stared out at the space in front of the *castrum*, which should have been filled with a hundred charging Saxons, led by Ivar Knuttson and the rest of the Fyr Skola contingent, his people coming to the rescue, and saw…

Nothing.

There was no one there. The area in front of the gate was quite empty.

Chapter Twelve

'We shall oblige your king'

Bjarki stared out of the open gate in astonishment: not a friend in sight. Inside the *castrum*, a Frankish soldier was running at him from the side, perhaps the officer who had been shouting at him a moment earlier. Red plumes on his steel helmet. The man had a short, wide sword and round red leather-faced shield, decorated with a pattern of metal studs.

He stabbed at Bjarki, a short, low, professional killing stroke. Bjarki got his own shield in the path of the blade just in time. He swung his own sword, which was blocked by the officer's shield; then Bjarki barged into him, thrusting up from the knees, shield to shield, using his weight to knock the red-plumed officer down. Ugo darted in from the right side, yelling, and skewered the sprawling man through the groin with the point of his sword.

He turned to look at the courtyard of the *castrum*, both the Rekkar were down now, with two heaving knots of Red Cloaks around each of them, stabbing down with wet-bladed swords, spearmen thrusting in their long shafts, again and again, slicing into the huddled masses of twitching meat that had once been two Fire Born – the pride of the Bear and Wolf Lodges.

Ugo gave a strangled cry and Bjarki whirled to see the young Barda had an arrow right through his neck, the dark-dripping shaft protruding six inches from the back of his jaw. He immediately lifted his own round shield, hunching instinctively behind it…

He was alone. It struck him like a blow. His comrades were all dead and he stood in the gate of the *castrum* with scores of enemies before him.

The space before the gate sucked at his back. He could run. He *should* run. The Red Cloaks were advancing; two or three glaring right at him. His sword and shield felt like lead weights in his hands. Run. He *must* flee now.

Then he heard the roar of many throats. He turned very quickly and looked and there, out there in the bright morning, was an army, a Saxon horde, charging towards the still wide-open gates. More than a hundred men and a few bold women, too, warriors all, were sprinting straight towards him. He felt a wash of relief, his heart lifted by the sound of their war cries.

In the front rank was Jarl Harald, brandishing a long sword and urging his people on. He was surrounded by a pack of *hersirs*, in war helm and grey mail, their own sworn men following behind. The Barda were there, too, on the left, and even the servant Per had come with them, armed with just a long seax and a wicker basket as a makeshift shield. And, by all the gods, was that Tor he could see, running beside them, her lithe body wrapped in nothing but her tatty Wolfskin with a borrowed spear in her grubby hands?

The Red Cloaks had finished dismembering the two Fire Born at their feet; they could see the charging Saxon horde coming for them and all the plumed officers were screaming for them to form a defensive line.

Bjarki stood well back by the open door, hoping not to be noticed. He was not to be so lucky. An arrow thumped into his shield, and he looked up at the battlement on the far side of the *castrum* where a pair of Red Cloak archers was targeting him – and only him. One man was in the very act of drawing his short bow, the other pointing a deadly finger directly at Bjarki.

He tucked his body behind the open door, just as the steel-tipped arrow clattered against the little log cabin wall, missing him by inches. But the Jarl's charging men were now roaring through the gates, shouting, shoving, a Saxon avalanche, well armed, high hearted and lusting for the slaughter.

Bjarki caught a glimpse of Tor's white face, contorted in fury as the jarl's army swept past him. He saw Ivar, too, in the middle of the pack, safely towards the rear of the phalanx, in all his Boar Lodge finery – pig-skin armour, a boar's head helmet – waggling an axe, yelling for blood. *So much for Ivar Knuttson leading the main Fyr Skola assault*, Bjarki thought.

The Saxons crashed into the loosely formed Frankish troops, driving a wedge right into the heart of their lines, and killing as they came. The clash of arms was deafening, like a thousand blacksmiths battering at their anvils in unison. Even above that terrible din, Bjarki could hear the bull-bawling of Jarl Harald, encouraging his Saxon fighters, to kill, kill and kill some more.

The Saxons had the numbers now; the Red Cloaks were weakened and demoralised by the two Rekkars' terrifying assault. Brokk and Ingvar must have claimed the lives of at least two score enemies between them before they finally fell. Now the enemy were cringing before the Jarl's fresh onslaught, Frankish soldiers running for the buildings, trying to escape the blood-drunk heroes of the lands they had so recently invaded, who chased them, hounded them, mocked them and mercilessly hacked them down.

Tor, wielding her long-bladed spear was slicing down men twice her age and height with precise, sweeping blows, cutting through hamstrings and tendons as they fled. She stabbed them, too, with short punching lunges, piercing enemy flesh, but never allowing her spear blade to become wedged tight in ribs or spine. Bjarki watched in deep awe as she cut the legs from under a red-plumed officer, slicing through the back of his knees just above the man's greaves, with a single sweep of the spear's keen blade, then finished him as he was going down with the spear-point jabbed up under his sword belt.

Bjarki roused himself for battle. He must fight. He knew that. He came out from behind the log door, sword brandished, shield high.

And stopped dead. The doors of the huge church in the centre of the *castrum* were opening slowly, and he could see a great mass of dark moving shadows inside. A trumpet sounded, a ripple of notes that shivered down his spine – and out of the Frankish church came a clattering, snorting cavalcade.

Some thirty black-clad *cabellarii* charged out of the dark interior of the House of God in a pack. They wore heavy, ridged steel helms and thick black cloaks over their scale-mail hauberks. They bore nine-foot lances with wicked, needle-pointed blades, carried round black shields, and each *cabellarius* wore two straight swords, one long, one short at his belted waist.

One of these horsemen, however, was differently attired – a flowing golden, blue, white and scarlet vestment worn over his brilliantly polished armour; a pointed white cloth hat with a golden cross at the forehead, and no sword or long lance for this shining *cabellarius*, instead his hands held a heavy war mace, a lethal spiked metal club. His long teardrop-shaped shield was painted pure white, a large forbidding black cross at its centre.

Under the cloth mitre, a round steel cap, and under this, Bjarki saw, the face of the tall Christian apostle he'd seen praying in the dawn's first light.

The Frankish *cabellarii* did not hesitate for a moment, coming up to the canter the instant they were clear of the church's wide-open doors.

They dropped the points of their lances and smashed into the scattered melee in the courtyard, skewering running Saxons with an ease born of great skill and many, many hours of practice. Then, lances embedded in enemy flesh, the *cabellarii* drew their long swords and, riding through the throng, began cutting down enemies left and right.

The charge of the Frankish horsemen turned the tide of the battle.

Here and there, the bravest Saxon *hersirs* planted their feet and stood their ground and defied the mass of mounted men. They swiftly died. Jarl Harald, wrong-footed by the sudden appearance of the cavalry, was bawling for a shield wall, urging his men to band together. The lance took him in the pit of his roaring mouth and burst blood-slick from the back of his neck.

Harald sank to his knees. Toppled, died.

The Red Cloaks who had fled from the initial Saxon charge, those who had tried to find refuge in the barracks and stables and buildings around the edges of the courtyard, came swarming back out like rats, their rage vastly reinvigorated by the experience of their terror. They rushed to the slaughter.

The Saxons were dying now, all around. Some were fleeing, too.

Bjarki saw Per hacked down by a pair of Frankish horsemen, his body jerking with every thudding sword blow; Tor was fending off a lance thrust with her own spear, fencing with it, the lance-point jabbed, just missing her shoulder. Another *cabellarius* was circling behind, sword raised to strike.

Bjarki saw Ivar Knuttson viciously chop his axe into the back of an unsuspecting Red Cloak, then look wildly about him. And what happened next… Bjarki could hardly believe the evidence of his eyes. He saw the new Rekkr abandon the axe blade in the dying Frank's spine, turn empty-handed, and run – sprint, in fact, full pelt – for the open gates. Bjarki watched in astonishment as Ivar hurtled past him, running through the double gates, his ornate Boar headdress pushed back and bobbing against the back of his neck, the champion heading for the trees as fast as his legs would carry him.

Bjarki felt the rage and sorrow mushroom inside him. His people were all dying, or were dead; everywhere he looked, his friends were being cut down. A fine trap had been laid in this *castrum* by their foes – and sprung.

All was lost. The enemy was everywhere triumphant in the courtyard.

They were all going to die, and die today. He saw that two Frankish *cabellarii* were efficiently chopping down the last of the Saxons, calling exultantly to each other as they worked; Red

Cloaks were cornering the last desperate Barda against the fortress walls and gleefully hacking them apart.

Bjarki felt suddenly icy cold, freezing all over his body; he heard the sound of rushing water in his ears like the noise of a giant cataract. He found he was instinctively humming, deep in his throat, that simple, four-tone tune. His mind was spinning, whirling; time seemed to crawl, his vision blurred, became tinged with red – then suddenly sharpened. He felt something huge and ancient growling deep inside his chest, he felt his heart begin to swell and engorge, he could feel the blood pounding slow, ominous drumbeats in his hot, wide veins. He felt light, buoyant, stronger than ever, as if he could leap whole mountains in a single bound, reach out and touch the sky itself…

–

The lance missed Tor by a hair, it slid past her shoulder as she was turning. She reacted instantly, grasping the shaft with her left hand and pulling. The spear jerked free of the surprised horseman's grasp. Tor flipped it one-handed and thrust it into the ground between the horse's legs, the animal stumbled, limbs tangled, snapping the lance shaft, and while the Frank tried to control the frightened horse, Tor jabbed her own spear up into his groin.

She sensed the breath of wind from behind her, ducked instinctively, and a *cabellarius*'s sword skimmed over the top of the ginger fuzz on her head. She left her spear deep in the first knight's loins, drew her seax and leapt at the man above her. She got the knife in the man's shoulder, the point bursting through the scales on his hauberk. But he shoved her away, hard, and she fell back, landing with a breath-stealing thump on her back in the dirt of the courtyard.

The Frankish horseman was gone, swept away by the churning melee that was all round her. She got to her feet, bent and picked up her seax.

All was lost. There were only a handful of her Saxon comrades still fighting; none of the Barda yet lived. It was time to make an end now, such an end that would earn her a place in the Hall of the Slain beside her father.

She had killed half a dozen men, at least, this day, and if she could just take one of the Frankish chieftains down with her, that should earn her enough glory for a seat in the hall. Any of the red-plumed officers would do.

Then she saw Bjarki.

He was standing near the open gate, his legs straddled wide, his head thrown back and he seemed to be screaming madly at the heavens. But she could see no wound on his body. He dropped his head and she saw that his blue eyes were huge and wild, almost seeming to glow; his lips were drawn far back to reveal his uneven white teeth, a thread of spittle hanging from the corner of his mouth. He held sword and shield, one in each hand but flung the shield away from him with extraordinary force. The shield smashed into the leg of a Red Cloak, the pop of bone audible from twenty paces away.

Bjarki drew his new seax from his sheath, and holding sword in his right hand, shorter blade in his left, he screamed again – then he charged.

Tor was stunned into immobility by the extraordinary transformation. She stood and gaped, battle forgotten. She had never yet seen a *gandr* come into its Rekkr. Part of her was genuinely terrified, part awed, part fascinated.

This was what they had hoped and dreamed of for so long. This was the true spirit, the full, glowing ambition of the Fyr Skola. Bjarki had attained it. The Bear was inside him, now; wholly possessing him. He was Fire Born.

Bjarki ripped into a knot of Red Cloaks, half a dozen men, wielding his sword and seax with blurring speed. He moved inside a wet, scarlet cloud of savagery. He tore the Franks apart, leaving them staggering and bleeding, screaming, some already dropping to the ground, two without heads. One man curled up crying over his own slashed belly. One moment there were six fighting Franks, the next a pile of men, broken and bleeding in the dirt.

Next Bjarki hurled himself towards a passing *cabellarius*, lopping off the horse's head with one massive sword blow and swarming over the dying creature and its rider, his seax stabbing, stabbing like a piston. He killed the rider in moments, plunging the blade right through the man's scale armour, ripping it sideways, tearing the man's ribcage apart. He bounded from the dying man, leaping like an ape, throwing himself at another rider.

Every eye in the courtyard was on him, and the Red Cloaks were rallying. In moments, Bjarki was surrounded by furious enemy swordsmen, and even as he slashed and hacked and killed them, more came rushing forward; the press around him grew ever more thick. He was at the centre of a jostling, shouting mob of foes. A *cabellarius* spurred forward to the edge of the crush and over his comrades' heads he jabbed a lance into Bjarki's shoulder. The Rekkr shrugged the blade aside, surged toward the man on the horse, killing two Red Cloaks to get them out of his path. He dropped his sword, swarmed up the horse, savaging the rider with his seax alone.

But his foes were too many; they pulled him back down, arms reaching out, swords battering down and coming back crimson.

A Red Cloak blade clanged off Bjarki's steel helmet like a bell, and he went down for a moment, disappearing in the midst of the mob, then he was up and killing, snarling with rage, teeth snapping, gripping and tearing with his free hand, spraying blood with every vicious sweep of his lethal seax.

'Bjarki – I'm coming,' yelled Tor. 'It's me. We'll kill them together.'

She charged into the circle of Red Cloaks around the Rekkr; she sliced the hamstrings of one tall fellow, then jammed her seax blade into the side of his throat as he sank down gasping in breathless agony. He hacked another Red Cloak across the face; sent him reeling away, noseless and screaming. Tor and Bjarki were now at the centre of a ring of enemies. They seemed to be the only ones of Jarl Harald's force left alive in the *castrum*.

Bjarki had been wounded half a dozen times, he crouched low, panting, blood streaming down his legs, shining wet on his leather cuirass, puddling around his booted feet. He was weaponless but his hands were red to the wrists, the fingers slick with gore and flesh. Still they feared him. Tor glared at them all, her seax clutched in her right hand, her left clenched in a fist.

Not long now, but they would sing of this battle for ever, their fame would last till the heavens fell. Tor and Bjarki: heroes of the Fyr Skola.

Not long now.

Yet the ring of enemies around them seemed to be growing wider; the enemy were moving back, edging away, giving the skinny girl and the big gore-slathered growling man a little more space. One of the Red Cloaks was ordering them back, back. Telling them to keep their distance. *What? Why?*

An arrow slammed into Bjarki's cuirass, stuck fast in the thick leather; another tinked off the iron-reinforced greave on his right shin. He screamed at his retreating foes, took a few stumbling steps. Tor went forward with him. Bjarki's face was ghostly with blood loss. He tried to lift his fist, but it drooped; the Rekkr seemed to be shrinking, deflating, his rage draining away.

'Stand tall, oaf,' Tor ordered. 'We can take a couple more with us.'

But Bjarki was done. An arrow whistled past Tor's ear. Another sliced through the skin of her upper arm. Bjarki mumbled something, it sounded like an apology, he seemed to be saying sorry, over and over again. He was diminished now, ordinary again. The savage aura gone. He slumped to the ground. Tor moved closer, straddling his body with her legs. She bent quickly and scooped up a short sword abandoned by a Red Cloak.

'Come on, you pig-fuckers, let's be having you,' she growled, a blade in each hand. 'One at a time – all at once, I don't care. Let's get this done!'

'Wait!' called a voice, a voice of command. 'Archers, stand down.'

A man in a pointed white hat, in an extraordinary dazzling robe of gold and scarlet and blue, spotted here and there with fresh blood, was pushing through the ranks of the Red Cloaks. He held a nasty-looking mace loosely in his right hand, the vicious spikes stained with hair and clotted matter.

'This is one of their famous sorcerers – do not slay him. Nor the girl.'

The language was close enough to Saxon to be intelligible, although it seemed more flowery and musical than the ordinary Fyr Skola speech.

'Bring ropes and bind them,' said the dazzling man, gesturing to a Red Cloak officer. 'The king will enjoy viewing them – a wizard-demon of the North and his witch-servant. It will greatly amuse His Majesty, I am sure.'

He is irritatingly good-looking, Tor thought.

'I'm not his fucking servant,' she said loudly. 'And any man who comes near me with a rope is going to lose more than a hand.'

'You would rather die, witch? Very well. Archers, nock!'

The handsome fellow stepped back; the Red Cloaks were also pulling away. On the *castrum* wall, Tor could see a dozen archers, bows drawn.

Now she could die. Right now. She could leap at the nearest Frank and try to get in one last killing blow. But she found she could not move. She was frozen to the spot over Bjarki's still body. Death, a glorious death, was hers for the taking; a place in the Hall of the Slain finally within her grasp.

And she found, in that crystal moment, that she did not wish to perish. Not yet. She opened her two fists and the blades clattered to the ground. 'Very well,' she said as grandly as she could manage, 'if this king of yours desires the pleasure of our company, we shall graciously oblige him.'

Part Two

Chapter Thirteen

All roads lead to Aachen

Tor had been certain that Bjarki would die. He was wounded so grievously, and in so many places, that his body must surely surrender. But he did not and, she reasoned afterwards, it must have been his *gandr*, the Bear spirit that came into him so unexpectedly during the fight at the *castrum* that kept his chest faintly rising and falling and the blood trickling through his veins.

She had heard all the stories, of course: the tales of Rekkar who could not be killed, whose flesh was impervious to steel, and those divine warriors who could survive even the most terrible wounds and continue slaying their enemies. But she had only half-believed them – until now. Any normal man would most likely be dead after the many cuts and punctures that Bjarki had suffered all over his body. But he didn't die, the wounds did not go bad and begin to stink, and his much-mangled flesh soon seemed to be knitting well.

After she had surrendered to their dazzling leader – a *gothi* of the Christian god, she assumed – and allowed them to tie her hands, she and the unconscious Bjarki had been herded into an empty wooden horsebox, watched over the open top of the half-open door by six Red Cloaks with drawn swords. After an hour or two, when the courtyard had been cleared of bodies, an ancient healer of some kind came in to look at their wounds.

Bjarki was stripped of his torn and bloody clothes and armour, washed all over with wine and water, his wounds were filled with honey and then stitched and bound with clean linen strips.

The old healer tutted and clucked over the half-healed burns on Bjarki's skin, muttering about the 'natural hardiness of healthy young barbarians', and smeared a salve over the large areas of his skin that were still raw. Bjarki remained unconscious during this process, which was a blessing from the war god Tiw, since it must have been appallingly painful. Certainly when the old man tended Tor's own wounds it had hurt her almost as much as if she were back in the burning ship.

Though, of course, she could not allow herself to show the pain.

They rested for several days in the horsebox, sleeping on clean straw under a pile of red woollen military cloaks and given surprisingly decent fare – small amounts of meat, and even some wine to drink. But always guarded, every moment, by at least six Frankish soldiers with drawn blades.

On the third day of their captivity, Bjarki awoke and abruptly sat up – unwisely, as it happened, for the blood started fresh on the white cloths that swathed him. But he was able to relieve himself into a bucket, with a little help from Tor, and drink a quantity of watered wine with honey, and sops of barley bread dunked in the mixture. The healer came again that afternoon and cleaned and re-bandaged his wounds, and he seemed greatly impressed by the speed with which Bjarki's flesh was healing. He gave them a pair of rough red woollen tunics to wear, and lengths of rope to cinch the tunics round their waists.

On the fifth day, Bjarki stood up all on his own, doddering like an old man, and shaking top to toe with pain and the effort, but upright on his own two feet. At this development, a dozen archers were immediately added to the contingent of guards outside the horsebox that held the two prisoners.

On the sixth day, the Frankish leader, stripped of his impressive multi-hued war cloak and wearing only a plain undyed robe, came to see them. He stood outside the box, leaning his forearms on the open top half of the door as he fondly regarded his two prisoners lying on drifts of loose straw inside.

'You have been well treated? Yes?' he asked, smiling in a friendly fashion. 'Do you require anything? Your wounds are properly tended to?'

His accent was strange but Tor could understand him perfectly. Bjarki was asleep, lying on his back in the straw, mouth open and snoring gently.

'Who are you?' said Tor, getting slowly to her feet. 'Are you the chief of these Frankish warriors – their jarl?'

'I am their Father,' the man said.

Tor frowned at him. 'What – all of them? You *have* been busy.'

The man laughed. It was a light, musical sound, pleasing to Tor's ear.

'That is what I am called by my people – Father. I have no children of my own seed. Yet I am the spiritual Father of all of the faithful Franks here, and a few of the Saxons, too. I am a missionary of Our Lord Jesus Christ, a humble man of God. However, my lord and king, Karolus, has placed me in command of this conquered region of Saxony. My given name is Livinus.'

'The rightful lord of Westphalia is Theodoric,' said Tor, thrusting out her chin aggressively. 'This is his realm. You are the interloper here.'

The man took no offence. 'It is true Duke Theodoric was once the lord of this new part of Francia. But that is no longer true. What is *your* name?'

For a moment, Tor did not wish to tell him. But it seemed pointless, cowardly even, to refuse even to name herself to this odd, smiling man.

'I am Torfinna Hildarsdottir – called Tor – and that big snoring fellow is Bjarki Bloodhand. We are both fighters from the Groves of Eresburg.'

'Ah, yes,' said Livinus. 'I have heard of that nest of sin. Your friend is a sorcerer, a wizard – how do you say it? – a *berserkr*? Is that not the case? A man who becomes possessed by a demon from Hell in the heat of battle?'

'He's a Rekkr,' said Tor proudly. 'As I shall be, if I live long enough.'

'Fascinating. And you believe in – what? – all the usual nonsense about trolls and elves and so-called gods of trees and hills and rivers and so forth?'

Tor was struck speechless. This man – this missionary of the Christ god or Father or *gothi* or whatever he was – seemed genuinely interested in the Groves of Eresburg and the ancient gods and spirits but, at the same time, contemptuous of them, as if they were merely her people's amusing foibles.

She had once seen a misshapen pedlar, a dwarf, in Uppsala, the largest town in Svearland, who had a comical little goat-pulled cart filled with jars of strange creatures floating in liquid. There were two-headed lambs, and mandrake roots that looked like people, weird eyeless fish and a pair of half-formed human babies joined together at the hip – an unborn monster, ripped from some unfortunate's womb. It seemed to Tor then that Livinus regarded her and the sleeping Bjarki in much the same way that the crowds of slack-jawed Svear yokels had gawped at the dwarf's murky jars.

She did not like it at all.

'You asked if we had been well treated,' said Tor. 'We have been fed. Your healer has tended us. But we would like the freedom to take some exercise in the courtyard. We have been mewed up here for nearly a week.'

'Out of the question,' Livinus said. His smile disappeared. 'But you will be leaving here soon. We shall take you into the presence of King Karolus at Aachen. You shall be shown to him. It will be a great honour.'

'I'm sure it will be. And we shall be pleased to bestow that honour on your king. Till then, it would aid our healing if we might take exercise.'

The smile came back, just a flicker. 'You are pleased to joke. That's good. The king himself enjoys some amusements, from time to time.'

And he turned and walked away.

On the seventh day of their captivity, a strange vehicle came into the *castrum* courtyard. It looked like a hay wagon, a platform on four wheels, drawn by four oxen, but the sides were a lattice-work of oak bars as thick as a man's wrist, and the top was covered over with inch-thick planks. It was, in effect, a cage on wheels. And it was to be their home for the next ten days.

–

Tor envied Bjarki's extraordinary ability to sleep almost as much as his newly revealed Rekkr powers. He slept for almost the whole of the journey to Aachen, waking only in the late afternoon, when the cavalcade stopped and hot food was prepared in big brass cauldrons for the whole column. Bjarki would mumble and roll over, then a few moments later, sit up sniffing the air like a dog, and say something oafish like, 'Oh, is it time for supper?'

Tor found him intensely irritating. All day long she was jounced around in the wooden cage on wheels – stared at by the Red Cloak guards, a score of archers and spearmen, who marched alongside, their eyes never off her – while Bjarki lay on a pile of blankets and snored like a contented pig. He seemed entirely unconcerned that they had been captured; after the first few days his wounds apparently ceased paining him, and he slept like a worn-out child, only roused himself in the evenings to slurp down a bowl of hot soup, or eat some bread and stew, before curling up and going to sleep again.

They were fed bread and ale at dawn before the cavalcade set off again, and the smelly wooden bucket for their evacuations was emptied, and they were fed again just before dusk when they stopped for the night. At first, Tor spent many hours, and more than one sleepless night, considering how they might escape from their rolling prison. But they were never allowed to leave the wooden cage – not for any reason. When Tor pretended to have a fit, aping an old Gottar madwoman she had seen on her travels and rolling about the cage, frothing at the mouth and shouting gibberish, the guards gathered around the cage and watched, and she heard them placing bets on whether she would die, soil herself or beat her brains out on the bars. After a while she became embarrassed, and stopped, curling into a ball and feigning sleep.

As the guards walked away, she heard one ask if they should check she was alive. The reply from his officer filled her with impotent fury: 'She's of no account, trooper. Lives, dies, don't matter to the good Father. It's the male he's interested in. He means to show that devil-worshipper to the king.'

She could see little of the company in which they travelled: she counted three dozen Frankish foot soldiers, two of them officers; the apostle in his simple, undyed white robe she glimpsed occasionally, and two other priests with their pates shaven on the top in a similar manner to Livinus. For so-called humble servants of their god, these priests travelled in high style – on horseback. There was no doubt that they were in command of the column.

There were also mounted scouts, a handful, she could not be sure of the exact number – small mud-spattered lancers with green cloaks on swift ponies who occasionally cantered past the bars of their cage. There was a supply wagon, which carried the food, and a couple of donkey-carts, which transported who-knew-what. Booty from Saxony, perhaps.

They travelled west, with a little southing too, as far as she could make out from the sun, soon leaving the Saxon lands behind and coming down from the hills into the soft, cultivated regions of Francia. Once they had crossed into the country of their enemies, the roads began to improve, from the muddy, mountainous tracks of Saxony, in which the wagon was thrown all around by pot holes and rocks half buried in the surface muck, to an even, dead-straight thoroughfare more than a long spear's length wide, the slightly curved surface hardened with flat, square paving stones. She once heard the guards refer to the highway as the Hellweg – but what sort of name was that for a road? It meant the way to the world of the dead. A very bad omen.

Occasionally other roads joined the Hellweg, like tributaries joining a mighty river – and more than a few people joined the main route from these arteries – pedlars, peasants, soldiers, priests

– almost all going in the same direction – to Aachen. It seemed all roads eventually led to Aachen.

They came to an actual river – and a mighty one – on the fifth day. The Rhenus, the guards called it – even Tor had heard tell of it. The Rhenus ran through the Frankish heartland from the snow-capped Alps to the West Sea.

Tor hoped they might be allowed out of the cage for a little while when they crossed over this wide river, perhaps to board a boat or a ship, and that this might present an opportunity for escape. But they remained confined the whole time and, instead of boarding a boat, they trundled over a gigantic bridge towards a sprawling town under a smudge of smoke on the far bank.

Both Tor and Bjarki, in one of his rare periods of wakefulness, stared out through the bars at the grey expanse of flat water as they crossed the massive bridge – some four hundred paces in length from shore to shore – looking in awe at the trading ships and smaller craft that passed under their cage. It made Tor feel insignificant. She had believed she had already seen much of the Middle-Realm in her short but adventurous life and was privy to many of its deepest secrets. She had travelled with Valtyr for nearly a whole year before they met Bjarki. But this journey had shaken her iron self-belief.

Once they had crossed the Rhenus, Tor asked Bjarki, who was now at least partially recovered from his wounds, if he could summon the *gandr* and break open the bars of the cage with his Rekkr's strength. But Bjarki merely shook his head sadly. He claimed not to remember very much of the fight in the *castrum*. He had no inkling why his *gandr* had chosen that particular moment to manifest itself in him. He said he had no idea how to summon it.

To please Tor, he sat that evening in the cage and did the humming exercises that they both knew so well, trying to burrow inside his heart to find the lair of the Beast. Nothing happened. Some of the off-duty Red Cloaks gathered around to watch him – they assumed he was praying to his heathen gods, and muttered as much to each other – but soon they drifted away, one by one, bored. Finally Bjarki stopped. Whatever had occurred in the battle at the *castrum*, it was not something Bjarki could control himself.

'I simply don't know how I did it,' he confessed when Tor lost her temper and called him a useless lump of goat turd. But, for her sake, he gave it another try later that night. With the darkness, and Tor's body, shielding him from the Red Cloaks' gaze, he attempted to pull two of the oak bars apart, and then to wrestle one of them free. But they might have been iron set in stone for all the effect his efforts produced. That exertion started the wound in his shoulder bleeding again and Tor felt a spear of guilt as she mopped the leaking wound and bound it with the same dirty bandage.

They were now passing through peaceful farmlands, and large estates with gangs of slaves at work bringing in the crops – wheat, rye and barley – and past mansions, built from blood-red bricks and tiles, with lush, shaded gardens, tinkling fountains and soaring stone columns in rows at the front.

She had never seen houses like them before. They were simply huge. And she wondered how many people lived in them – they could easily have accommodated the population of a good-sized Svear village. Yet the houses all seemed strangely empty with only one or two people glimpsed as they passed, or none at all, except for those who were obviously over-worked slaves.

She might have believed them the homes of kings or princes, such was their grandeur, had she not passed a half dozen of these palaces on the road during the time she and Bjarki lived in that bastard cage. Surely Francia could not boast that many princes in the slice of territory through which they passed.

They lumbered through humble Frankish villages, too – which were not unlike the northern settlements she was used to, except with low brick-built dwellings with red-tiled roofs instead of wood-and-thatch longhouses – and through larger settlements, often at crossroads, with churches built to honour the Christian god, then actual towns – they stopped in one of these on a warm autumn night, seven days into their journey, and were given roasted lamb on trenchers of fine-milled bread for supper. But they were not allowed to leave the cage. Never that. And the eyes of the Red Cloaks did not stray.

They were going to Aachen; this was all they knew. After nine days of hard travel, they overheard comments that suggested they were close to their destination. One of the Red Cloaks spoke warmly to his friend of a wine shop in Aachen he intended to visit the next night, of a girl who served there.

'What do you think their king wants with us?' Bjarki asked her the next morning as a company of spearmen, at least a hundred strong, every man wearing a moss-green cloak and steel helm but no other armour, trotted past them without a second glance. They had seen three companies like this already that day. Each company was roughly the same size of the force – the 'mighty army' – that Theodoric had sent to attack the *castrum*. Bjarki found himself unnerved by this evidence of the manpower at Karolus's disposal.

'The priest Livinus seems to think you can summon up foul demons from the realm of the goddess Hel, whenever you choose to,' said Tor. 'I think he means to show us off like exotic wild beasts to the king and his jarls. We'll be paraded, prodded and peered at until they get bored with us.'

'What will they do when they discover I can't really call up demons? Or even bring out my own *gandr*? That I'm not really a Rekkr. What then?'

Tor looked at him. She was remembering the shambles in the *castrum* courtyard after the battle. All the Saxon wounded had been dispatched with sword blows to the base of the skull, some of the dying Red Cloaks, too. She knew how little their lives would be worth if Bjarki could not summon up his *gandr*. 'You're quite right, oaf,' she said. 'We need to make a plan.'

Chapter Fourteen

The palace of the king

Bjarki was so astonished he could not speak. The building was simply enormous, far bigger than any human-built structure he had ever seen before. It was far bigger than the church at the *castrum*. It was a kind of hall, he guessed, but it was nothing like the thatched-roofed longhouses of home.

They had passed large dwellings on the journey, mansions even, and, as they travelled into Aachen, they had passed large churches, substantial barns and broad warehouses, huge market squares paved with stone slabs with big houses on all four sides, and one circular structure on the edge of the city, built of ancient crumbling stones, which the guards called the amphitheatre.

This hall, however, was a mountain of a building, fifteen times the height of a man, just as wide as it was high, and as long as a decent-sized barley field – more than fifty of a tall man's strides. It was constructed of bright red bricks with two decks of huge arched windows along the sides. At the eastern end was a massive square fortified tower, taller even than the hall it guarded, at the western was a semi-circular extension with a domed roof.

They entered this massive building by a portico in the long north wall, having come through a bustling street market to reach it – and this was only the most northerly part of the Frankish king's sprawling palace complex, Bjarki learned. Once the Red Cloaks had pushed him into the interior of the enormous hall he was even more impressed. It was a cavernous space, with high timber beams supporting the distant roof, the lime-plastered walls painted a pure brilliant white where they were not covered with rich woven tapestries, with human figures and animals depicted, along with several huge golden crosses and a scatter of silver stars and other symbols. The hall's floor was made of grey flag stones – no cut rushes or beaten earth underfoot in here – and, even more extravagantly, gold candleholders, dozens of glittering crown-like arrangements as wide as the span of a man's arms, were suspended at two-stride intervals from the ceiling, lit beeswax candles shedding a yellow light throughout the space, even though it was broad day!

There were colonnades inside along the north and the south sides of this vast rectangular space, creating two internal thoroughfares of a kind, where scores of people were now wandering up and down, greeting each other and stopping to gossip. Both men and women were present, clad in robes of silk and satin and velvet, and many were heavily laden with rings, brooches and fine jewels. Their faces were grave and beautiful, Bjarki thought, and they moved gracefully and murmured quietly with each other, as if engaged in some kind of intricate dance. But not all were so refined. A few of them wore the same undyed robes in white or brown as Father Livinus and had wooden crosses on their chests and sported the cleric's tonsure. There were also half a dozen fair-haired folk he spotted in Saxon and even more northerly styles: furs and leather, wool tunics and cross-gartered trews.

'What is this place?' Bjarki whispered to Tor. 'It must have been built by giants!' They were both unnecessarily wrapped in heavy iron chains from shoulder to wrist, weighed down and clinking, and forced to move forward by a squad of Red Cloaks who poked at their backs with their spear butts. But, at least, for the first time in ten days, they were out of that rolling cage.

'Behold the manifestation of the earthly glory of Karolus Arnulfing!' said Livinus, who was walking beside them in a proprietorial manner. They had barely seen him on the road but, now that they had arrived in Aachen, it seemed, he wished to be more closely associated with his two captives.

'This is the council hall of the royal palace of Aachen,' he said, 'the northern seat of Karolus, son of Pepin, King of Francia, lord of lands from the rocky Breton coast to the dark forests of Moravia, ruler of men from the stinking marshes of Frisia to the snowy mountains of the Spanish March!'

The pride in Father Livinus's voice was apparent. 'This palace complex – impressive as it must seem – is far from complete. And no giants built it, young wizard,' he said, smiling at Bjarki, 'mortal men, like me and yo— uh, well, anyway the faithful Frankish people constructed this marvel, with their strong hands and broad backs, as a tribute to their beloved king.'

'The *northern* seat,' said Tor. 'Does your king have one of these draughty barns in the south, west and east of his domains as well?'

Father Livinus seemed to be taken aback by Tor's irreverence. 'This region is the hearth and heartland of the Frankish tribes. This royal palace is Karolus's capital, his home. But, yes, he has several other palaces in Paris, Lyon, Strasburg, he is building one in Regensburg, on the Bavarian border.'

'Just the five palaces?' said Tor. 'How *does* he manage?'

Father Livinus's handsome face contorted into an ugly scowl but he said nothing. He jerked his head at the nearest red-cloaked spearman, who jabbed Tor with his spear butt, forcing her to take a dozen stumbling steps forward.

-

Bjarki looked ahead at the west end of the council hall. As they approached it, shuffling and clanking in their ostentatious chains, he could make out a pair of golden thrones, raised up on a dais. And two people sitting on them.

A fine lady occupied the right-hand throne. She wore a beautiful gown of cream silk and green velvet, and a headdress shining with golden and silver thread. Her jet-black hair was curled and oiled and just peeking out on either cheek from under the headdress. The effect framed her face enticingly and made her slim white neck seem impossibly long. She was very slender, although not in any way malnourished, and her large dark eyes sparkled with intelligence. As Bjarki drew closer he realised she was very young under her finery – a girl – perhaps a year or two younger than he was.

Beside her, on a second throne, was a richly dressed young man – this fellow was roughly Bjarki's age. He had the same dark hair as the lady, the same long neck – a family resemblance – but his expression, in contrast to her cool stare, was petulant, even slightly bored. He fidgeted with a golden tassel on his enamelled belt, drummed his fingers on the arm of the throne.

Father Livinus stepped forward and made a low bow. The Red Cloaks shoved the clanking pair of captives to their knees, and retired a few paces.

'Your Highness, greetings,' said Livinus. 'May Almighty God bless you all your days. I see your husband His Majesty has not returned from his travels. Nevertheless, it is an honour, my queen, to stand before you—'

'I think you mean "Your Highness*es*",' said the young man. 'Am I not sitting here too?' He had a whining tone, a voice designed for complaining.

'Not now, Gerold,' said the lady. 'Let dear Father Livinus speak.'

'Thank you – ah, yes, Your Highnesses – it is a great honour to stand before you *both* today. I salute you, Queen Hildegard, and you, Duke Gerold.'

'Was that so difficult, man?' Gerold said, smirking down at priest.

'Be *quiet*, Gerold,' said the lady. 'Must I send you from the court?'

Bjarki, chained and kneeling, watching from under his brows, saw the young man's face darken with blood, his forehead knit. But the duke held his tongue at the younger lady's words. *Brother and sister*, Bjarki thought.

There were two other figures, he saw, standing behind and slightly to the side of the seated pair. The man on the left was a giant, nearly seven feet tall and thick in the chest and arms. His face was covered in a thatch of dark beard that almost joined his two bushy eyebrows, and the little skin that could be seen was raw-red and covered with flakes of dried skin. His eyes were small and sunken, black and brutish, his nose red and swollen with drink. But he stood perfectly still, unnaturally so, upright as a lance.

The black-bearded giant reminded Bjarki a little of Brokk, in his animal otherworldliness, in his latent strength and violence. But this huge fellow was clearly no Rekkr; his attire proclaimed him as a Frankish soldier: he was bare-headed, his skull covered with a cap of cropped black hair. But he wore a black iron breastplate with a white cross emblazoned on the metal, scale-mail shirt underneath, a kilt of strips of leather laced with iron, and black iron greaves. A dark cloak fell from his shoulders to his hairy calves. He had a short, broad stabbing sword on one side of his waist and a long cavalry sword – a spatha – sheathed on the other. As if that were not enough of an armoury, he leaned on a long vicious-looking pole-arm: a tall weapon with a heavy wooden shaft and a shining axe, hook and spike at the head.

He caught Bjarki's eye and held it, staring back at him impassively, measuring his worth or assessing the young man's potential as a threat.

The second figure was short, plump and dressed in a robe of blue, red, white and gold, very similar to Livinus's war mantle, although far more ornately decorated. His brown hair was shaved on top like the other priest's. He held a giant golden shepherd's crook in one chubby ring-covered hand. A huge golden cross hung down to his drooping breasts from around his neck.

'You are back from the realm of the heathen, Father Livinus,' said this gaudy little fellow. 'You must doubtless have a full report for me to read.'

'Indeed, I do, my lord bishop,' said Livinus, bowing to the little man, 'it shall be in your hands directly. But, of greater import, I believe, is the fact that I bring from the Northlands these two barbarian prisoners of war.'

'I will decide what is important to the Church, Livinus. I have not had a word from you for six weeks. You were told to report every sennight—'

'I crave your indulgence, Lord Paulinus, but sending dispatches from barbarian lands is no easy matter. I shall render a full accounting in due—'

'Six weeks, Father, I had begun to wonder if you'd been martyred—'

'This is all *utterly* fascinating,' said the queen. 'Yet perhaps, my lord bishop, you could discuss the minutiae of episcopal communications at another time. Who are these wretches, Livinus? What are they doing here?'

'My lady, they're barbarian warriors from Saxony. I captured them.'

'I can see that, Father Livinus,' said Hildegard. 'I can even smell them. May I ask why you've brought these two filthy specimens before the court?'

The arrival of Father Livinus, the Red Cloaks and the two prisoners in chains had caused a stir in the general thoroughfares beyond the arches and columns. People were drifting towards the dais, in ones and twos, gathering in a loose semi-circle behind the four figures looming above Bjarki and Tor.

'They really are quite disgusting,' said Duke Gerold. 'Dirty. No doubt riddled with diseases – crawling with lice and worms. We should have them scrubbed in boiling lye before they bring a plague down on the whole city.'

'*Why* have you brought them to me, Livinus?' said Hildegard. 'If they are prisoners of war, they are slaves and should be sent to the pens. If you wish to execute them as a warning to the rest of their kind, be my guest. You don't need my sanction as regent. Our beloved king would surely approve.'

'Your Highness,' said Livinus, failing to hide his deep pleasure, 'these two undoubtedly noisome prisoners are, nonetheless, rather special.'

He paused for effect. 'They hail from the devil-ridden lair called the Groves of Eresburg in the forests of south Saxony, from the beating heart of their heathen world. The big ugly one is, in truth, one of their beast-warriors, a shape-shifter, a *berserkr*, in their heathen tongue. I saw him in battle. And since there has been much discussion at court of whether these wizards truly exist, I thought Karolus might like to see the truth of the matter for himself.'

Father Livinus's words had a marked effect on his growing audience. There were gasps; a few of the fainter hearts drew back a step. One lady gave a little shriek of fear, before smothering her cries with a linen kerchief.

The lovely young queen leaned forward in her throne and peered down at the two filthy prisoners lying in chains at her feet.

'Beast-warriors? Can this really be true, Father Livinus?' she said.

'I saw them both in combat with my own eyes, Highness. The male one slew or badly injured a score of my Red Cloaks – he killed some of them after he'd been wounded half a dozen times, bleeding, and deprived of weapons. A devil or demon of some kind possessed him. I saw it myself.'

'The one on the left is only a skinny little girl,' said Duke Gerold.

'I could kick *your* soft white arse, sunshine, with one hand tied behind my back.' Tor's unexpected words set off a gale of twittering in the crowd.

A Red Cloak stepped forward and thumped the butt of his spear into the side of Tor's head. Her skull banged hard against the flagstones of the floor.

'Somebody give me a sword, and I'll kill the insolent witch right here, right now,' said Gerold. Everyone ignored him – except the dark giant who began to fumble at the hilt of his short sword, half drawing the blade.

'Put that away, Grimoald,' snapped the queen. 'Don't play the fool, Gerold. Nobody is going to touch these two until the king has had a good look them. You know he's always been interested in this type of savage.'

'We should kill them now,' rumbled the giant. 'Better to be safe.'

'So these barbarians can speak our language… in a crude fashion,' said Hildegard, ignoring the giant. 'How intriguing! Animals with the speech of men. Can you make them transform before our eyes, Father?'

'As I understand it, Highness,' said Livinus, 'they only change into wild beasts in the heat of battle. I am not sure if it is a voluntary process or if some malign outside agency inhabits them. There's a great deal to learn.'

'How exciting!' said the queen. 'Our very own beast-warriors here in Aachen. My husband *will* be pleased with you, Livinus. We must arrange a suitable demonstration of their wizardly powers when His Majesty returns.'

'I do not think that would be entirely proper,' said Lord Paulinus, peering down at the pair in front of him, 'it would, indeed, be a grave sin. We would be abetting the foulest kind of witchcraft. "Thou shalt not suffer a witch to live", it says in the Holy Bible, Deuteronomy, um, chapter, ah—'

'In Exodus, my lord bishop,' said Livinus. 'Chapter twenty-two, verse eighteen.'

Lord Paulinus gave the priest a poisonous look. 'The point is that I agree with our friend Lord Grimoald here. We should execute them now.'

'You're such a spoilsport, Paulinus,' said the lady. 'We are certainly not going to destroy them before the king has had a good look at them.'

'They are a living abomination, my lady, an affront to Almighty God. The Church is abundantly clear on this matter: all forms of witchcraft and wizardry, shape-shifting, demon worship, what-have-you, are forbidden.'

'Nevertheless,' said the queen, 'I say we shall keep them securely till Karolus returns to Aachen. That, my lord bishop, is the end of the matter.'

The cell they were put into was large enough to house a score of prisoners. It was one of many such big, dank chambers connected by a wide passageway in the underground part of the vast, circular, half-ruined building they had passed on the way to Aachen, which they learnt was the amphitheatre.

There were no windows and only three solid walls. The fourth wall was a progress of vertical iron bars set into the stone floor and brick ceiling a hand-width apart and joined by horizontal flatter bars to make a cage-like effect. They could be observed at all times in this open-fronted brick box. There was a single, heavy iron door set into this front wall of bars and no furniture or fittings at all. A mound of straw had been piled in the corner and Tor, nosing about in the corners, restless and newly freed of her chains, found the remains of dry, crumbling bones.

'They used to keep lions in here,' said their gaoler cheerfully. He was a fat, pale, elderly man named Henk, a Breton who had been taken as a slave when he was a mere boy some sixty years ago, when his country had fought a series of vicious wars with Neustria, the northwestern province of Francia.

'Of course, that was long before my time,' Henk said, passing a pile of thick blankets to Bjarki through the bars of the cell. 'No one has seen a lion here for hundreds of years, not since the Romans had charge of the place, back in the old days. Nowadays it's mostly for prisoners. More's the pity.'

'You would *like* to have a lion down here?' said Bjarki.

'If we could get 'em. But you just can't get lions any more. Bears, yes, we've housed several bears. Wolves too. We had a small pack in the end cell yonder only last year – God knows how they captured them alive.'

'What do they do with these animals?'

'They make them fight each other to the death, in the amphitheatre – the arena above our heads, didn't you know about that, young fellow?'

'Why do they do that?'

'Our new king is mad keen on all things Roman. Obsessed, they say. He claims he's going to remake the Roman Empire – now, in the modern age! All his courtiers must learn to write proper Latin – by royal decree – and he's got a house full of monks over in the palace busy copying out all the old imperial texts. Karolus revived the *Venatio* – the beast hunt – three years ago, after his coronation. They said he was a fool – but he did it anyway. It's always hellishly expensive but we put on a good show. The people *love* it.'

Bjarki looked at him blankly.

'The people of Aachen flock to the amphitheatre to watch the animals fight each other. It's a wonderful spectacle. But we don't do it so much any more. Karolus is far too busy – and, as I say, it costs the earth. But when we do put on a *Venatio*, you should hear the cheering. Wolves against bears, we've had. That was a good one. Hunting dogs against a wild auroch. But no lions, sadly – we haven't had a lion here since the days of Emperor Romulus. The biggest wild cat we ever had was a she-lynx from Moravia two years ago. It died after a day or two – I don't know why. The master of *Venationes*, old Malleus – he's the big chief in the amphitheatre – he said it died of loneliness. I don't know how that's even possible. Known plenty of lonely men, lonely women, too – by the Blessed Virgin, *I'm* lonely – but I never heard of anyone who actually died of it.'

'Will we be given any food today, sir?' asked Bjarki, very humbly.

'Food?' said Henk. 'Oh yes, yes, God bless my soul, yes. Humboldt's cooking up a nice rich pottage down in the kitchens as we speak: cabbage with bacon fat, lovely. You will certainly be given food. Not going to starve you, are they? Not with what you will very soon have to do in the arena.'

'How about ale?' said Tor, coming over to stand at the bars, facing the shapeless sack of a man on the other side. 'Got any ale in the kitchens?'

'No, no ale. I don't think so, no. I could bring you a wine flask, if you like. An honest Aquitainian; sweet and dark. You'd like some wine, yes?'

'Thank you, Henk,' said Bjarki. 'You are most kind.'

The old turnkey blushed. 'Not at all. It's a pleasure to have such a pair of distinguished wiz— ah, two such famous beast-war— no, I mean such noble Saxon guests as you, in my charge. A pleasure. Now let me go and see to your supper. Make yourselves comfortable and I'll be back in a wink.'

The gaoler shuffled away down the passage, and Tor turned to Bjarki.

'Thank you, Henk?' she said, her voice full of scorn.

'He was being kind. I don't see the point in annoying him – or any of them, to be honest. What's wrong with that?'

'They are our mortal *enemies*, oaf! They are keeping us prisoner in a lion's cage. Treating us like filthy animals. Have you gone soft in the head?'

'Have you?' said Bjarki. 'Do you think they will respect us if you are rude to them? Do you think your discourtesy or your rude behaviour's going to frighten them into – what – letting us go? They think we're animals – I really believe they do think that – and snarling at them is what they expect.'

'Well, why don't you have a cup of *honest Aquitainian* with the old man, since you like him so much. Why don't you give him a big wet kiss.'

'That's what I was thinking, too. Well, not the kissing part. But I would like to know what these people have planned for us. I want to know more of them. Be polite to the old man, Tor, be friendly. What harm can it do?'

'You be friendly to him. I'm going to sleep.' She plucked a blanket from his hands and went over to the pile of straw in the corner of the cell.

–

When she awoke several hours later, Bjarki was sitting with his back to the brick wall, a blanket over his knees. She thought it must be a little past midnight. Bjarki had left a cup of wine and bowl of cabbage and bacon stew for her beside her straw pile – it was stone cold by now, of course. But she was stiff, chilly and starving and so ate it with some measure of enjoyment.

'So what did you learn being all lovey-dovey with our friend?' she said at last, scraping the last of the grease from the bowl with her wooden spoon.

'In three days' time, when the king returns to Aachen, we must do battle in the ancient amphitheatre above our heads,' he said. 'It's to be a trial by combat according to the old Frankish laws. We have been accused *in absentia* of murdering the king's men at the *castrum* in Thursby. Their god will judge our guilt or innocence by the result of the battle. We're fighting other captives, warriors from the east, not Franks, they're Av-somethings.'

'I think they must be Avars,' said Tor. 'Valtyr has told me all about them. Fierce people. Horsemen, mostly. Well, that was to be expected. A demonstration of our combat skills. Good. Nothing to worry about, Bjarki. I'm sure we can handle a couple of Avar tribesmen between us. You're pretty much healed, aren't you? It is *good* news, oaf. If we want respect, we'd better show 'em that we're Fyr Skola folk, and not to be trifled with.'

'It is *not* good news, Tor,' said Bjarki. He looked extremely sad rather than frightened. 'And it's not just a couple of Avar warriors.' He looked at Tor. 'We have to fight forty of them.'

Chapter Fifteen

A matter of faith

Bjarki made the most of his new friendship with Henk, talking to the old gaoler for many hours each day. He was naturally curious about the people who had received them in the council hall on their arrival in Aachen, and their talks took his mind off the coming battle in the amphitheatre.

'Queen Hildegard is the king's second wife,' Henk told him. 'Karolus had a lovely, sweet-tempered Lombard lady before, from north Italy, Desiderata she was called, but, well, the Lombards are really not quite the thing just now. Heretics, they say. Arians. I'm told the king means to go to war with them soon, to sort them out. So he put away sweet Desiderata, had the match annulled by the Holy Father in Rome. And he married Hildegard last year. She's already given him a son – a baby Karolus – what a good wife she is! And she came with *such* a dowry. Her father was the Duke of Swabia and had vast lands in Neustria and in Alemannia in the mountains on the borders with Lombardy. A dazzling match – she's almost as rich as he is!'

'And the young lord – Duke Gerold – he is her relative?' said Bjarki.

'He's her older brother – and after his father died, he became the new Duke of Swabia. She's the regent here when Karolus is on his travels – which is often, he has a lot of territory to oversee, of course, and a lot of local lords to keep in line. But Gerold claims that he should be Karolus's viceroy in Aachen on account of his wealth and power and, ah, because he's a successful soldier and the king's lieutenant in battle, and his sister… isn't. Many girls would defer to him. But not Hildegard. She knows her value.'

Henk looked over his shoulder at the empty corridor.

'I shouldn't gossip like this, Bjarki, but I don't suppose it matters much. You won't tell anyone, will you, and in a couple more days, well, you'll probably be—' The fat old gaoler stopped and turned beetroot.

Bjarki felt a twinge in his belly. In two days he and Tor would be dead.

'Who was the angry little fellow with the golden shepherd's crook?'

'That's Lord Paulinus, Bishop of Aachen and Karolus's chaplain and chancellor, his right-hand man. The queen might be the regent – and what she says goes when the king is not here – but our Karolus relies on Lord Paulinus to run his whole kingdom efficiently for him. He keeps the regional vassals, all the dukes, counts, bishops and abbots honest. He's got spies everywhere and he always knows what's going on long before anyone else.'

'So Lord Paulinus is Father Livinus's master then?'

'Yes, and some say his greatest rival. Father Livinus has his own networks of friends and allies; he's been appointed Count of Westphalia, as well as a priest, and apostle – and his self-proclaimed mission is to bring all of the pagan lands of the North into the light of Our Lord Jesus Christ. I've heard that Karolus likes him, trusts him. And he's supremely ambitious.'

'You seem to know a lot about these high and mighty folk, Henk.'

'Been here a long time, Bjarki. And old Malleus, he relies on me – he's not so well these days; it's his old heart, he says, and I spend a good deal of my time nursing him, bringing him hot wine. He doesn't go out much so there are always people coming in and out of his apartments, you see he still has some influence here despite his health. I pick up scraps here and there.'

'Tell me about that huge warrior, Grim-bold or something like that. He looks like a very interesting fellow.'

The usually loquacious Henk fell strangely silent.

After a pause he said: 'Lord Grimoald is his name. He's the King's Shield, captain of the *Scholares*, the royal bodyguard – or the Black Cloaks, some call them because of their… I'll say nothing out of turn about *him*.'

'Come on, Henk, as you said, it's not like I'll ever see him again.'

Henk shot a frightened little glance down the corridor. 'He's a wicked man. Born a pagan but he's come to Christ under Karolus's guidance. They say he's personally killed more men than the plague. He too has spies…'

'He certainly looks fearsome enough.'

'He is the knife in the darkness, the slow agonising death on the rack. There are some lightless cells in the eastern part of this very amphitheatre that his Black Cloaks use for their interrogations…' Henk shuddered. 'I've said too much, lad. Must get on. Can't chatter here all day like a fishwife.'

And he turned and hurried away.

–

While Tor was quietly scornful when Bjarki conversed with the old gaoler, she did at least refrain from antagonising him. Henk was indeed a lonely man and despite his abrupt departure that morning, he enjoyed Bjarki's company and he returned in a happier mood later that day, bringing food and wine and little comforts of various kinds – a table and two stools, more blankets, hot water, soap and a towel, clean clothes, and a steel mirror and razor so that Bjarki might make himself presentable for the king when he had to stand before his presence in the amphitheatre for the trial by combat.

'In the old days, in the days of the Empire, before the Church put a stop to it, we regularly used to have barbarians and slaves fighting to the death in the amphitheatre. Couple of times a year, at least, according to the old Latin scrolls I've read. But the Holy Father in Rome banned it, hundreds of years ago. The Church decreed that it was barbaric – but I always thought, yes, but they are barbarians, so of course it's barbaric. But never mind that, those days are long gone – as I said we don't even do the beast-hunts that often. So your trial by combat will be quite the event. Sure to be a good turn out.'

'My death will make you happy?' said Bjarki.

'Not *happy* – you seem like a nice lad. And it need not be the end.'

'Death is not the end?' Bjarki sounded mystified.

'Our Saviour has promised eternal life to all who come to him in faith.'

'I think I'd rather have eternal life by… well, by not dying.'

'No, you miss my point. Those barbarians who fought to the death in the sand before the mayors of the palace – that's how the royal family were called, of course, before they ascended to the rank of king – they dedicated their souls to God before battle. They received Jesus Christ in their hearts.'

'Even though they were about to die?' said Bjarki. 'They forsook their own gods on the eve of battle?'

'Their *false* gods,' said Henk. 'There is only one true Lord of Hosts.'

Bjarki said nothing. He glanced at Tor who was sitting on a stool at the table, munching bread and cheese. Tor rolled her eyes at him comically.

'And they *all* did this, did they? They all honoured their enemies' god before they fought here and died?' Bjarki found this very difficult to believe.

'It might sound strange. But traditionally the king, or the mayor of the palace, pardons all who fight well, but only if they are believers in Christ.'

'Oh, I see. So if the slaves won their fight, if they survived that is, they would be pardoned by the king and set free, is that what you mean?'

'Only if they accepted baptism and were reborn as true Christians.'

'That makes a lot more sense,' muttered Tor.

Later when the gaoler had gone, Tor and Bjarki discussed what they might do to survive the amphitheatre.

'Forty Avars! Forty hardened warriors,' said Bjarki. 'We might hope to beat half a dozen, even ten. But forty? We're dead. Done. Finished.'

'Maybe your *gandr* will come again. It might do. You've been practising your humming, yes? And we'll both be armed, that's what Henk said, we won't be defenceless.' Tor seemed unworried by the numbers against them.

'I've been humming till my throat bleeds. And not a thing happens. Why aren't you more concerned about this horde of Avars, Tor? Why?'

'What is the point? Worrying won't change anything. We're going to fight. We're probably going to die. But if we can put up a decent fight, die with valour, the Wingèd Ones will come and take us to the Hall of the Slain. That's *our* eternal life. In Valhalla. One thing I won't do is bow down before their stupid Christ god like a craven right before the blood begins to flow.'

Oddly, Bjarki was rather encouraged by Tor's nonchalance. They *were* probably going to die. But they could die well. And maybe, just maybe, they might fight well enough to earn a place in the All-Father's eternal feasting hall.

–

They received a visitor on the last day, the evening of the third day. He was an unusually tall man, in his mid-twenties, with short red-gold hair and he looked fit and strong, with large expressive eyes. His defining feature was a long, curved nose, like the beak of an eagle. So quietly did he move that he seemed to suddenly appear at the bars of their cage like a magician, and he stared at them for some while before he spoke.

Bjarki approached him. 'You wish to speak with us?' he said.

'I came to ask if you have everything you require before the trial?' said the man. Bjarki noticed that he had pale blue eyes.

He saw Henk hovering down the corridor, lurking, in truth, and keeping a close watch over them all.

'Everything but our freedom,' said Bjarki, with a friendly smile.

The tall man smiled back. 'That, I am afraid, I cannot grant you. Is the food to your liking? Is it sufficient to nourish you, keep up your strength?'

Bjarki glanced at Tor, who appeared to be asleep, rolled in a blanket on the straw mound next to a pile of assorted war equipment provided by Henk from the amphitheatre's comprehensive, if elderly, armoury. He had a good idea who this fellow was – it must be Humboldt the slave in the kitchen who prepared their food each day. He was dressed simply in a grey woollen tunic and cross-gartered trews, with a belt with a golden buckle around his slim middle: a rare treasure for a humble cook, a gift from a rich patron perhaps.

'We have no complaints,' said Bjarki in a soft voice. He did not want to awaken Tor in case she said something rude or aggressive and angered the man who fed them so lavishly. 'Indeed, we thank you for your kindness.'

'Kindness?' said the man. 'I've not been called kind in many years.'

'Your generosity, then. We are truly grateful.'

Humboldt frowned. 'Tell me about yourself, if you will,' he said. 'You hail from Saxony, I understand? Does your father owe fealty to Theodoric?'

Bjarki laughed. 'No, I'm an orphan. I only saw Saxony for the first time this spring. I come from Bago, which is an insignificant island off the Jutland Peninsula. My master is, I guess, Siegfried, King of the Dane-Mark.'

'Indeed? And how came you to be fighting the Franks in Thursby?'

It seemed an odd question from a cook. Bjarki began to feel unsure.

'You ask about my master. May I ask who yours is?' said Bjarki.

'My master?' said the man. 'I suppose you could say that I serve God and the Kingdom of Francia. My masters are the peoples of these lands.'

Bjarki nodded: a public slave. He'd heard of these kinds of thralls, owned by the community rather than an individual; now cooking in a prison.

'You were telling me how you came to be at Thursby,' said Humboldt.

So Bjarki told the cook his story: how he had killed two boys in a rage over an insult to his girl and been taken to the Groves of Eresburg; how he'd trained there to be a warrior, but only found his *gandr* in the big fight at the *castrum* at Thursby. Then he had been wounded, captured and brought here.

Humboldt did not interrupt once: he seemed fascinated by the long tale. When it was done, he said: 'And how many fighters are there, like you, at these groves?' Bjarki felt another prickle of uncertainty. He did not know this man and he had sworn an oath, he remembered belatedly, to protect the Fyr Skola and keep its secrets. He should not be blurting them out to cooks.

'Oh,' he said, 'hundreds. About five hundred like me, maybe more. A thousand. Now, if you will excuse me, I must sleep. I bid you a good night.'

'Now, you are lying,' said the tall man, although he did not seem to be angry. 'But lying for the first time since we met, I believe. There are not five hundred more like you. Nor yet a thousand. I believe you are rather special, if not actually unique, my friend. I can always smell an outright lie. It is my greatest gift; and my curse, too. But I'd truly like to know *why* you lied?'

Bjarki actually blushed. 'I remembered too late that I swore an oath not to reveal the secrets of… that place. Yet I fear I've said too much already.'

'Then you must say no more about the matter. I like a man who is true to his oaths. I shall ask no more impertinent questions. God be with you.'

The man began to walk away down the passage. After only a few steps he called back. 'If you need anything before tomorrow, ask the old turnkey. I'll make sure he supplies you with whatever you need before the combat.'

'You know who that was, don't you?' said Tor sleepily from her nest of blankets.

'He was the kitchen slave, Humboldt. The man who cooks our food.'

Tor laughed. 'Did he tell you that?'

'No, but I guessed. He asked about how we enjoyed his food.'

'That was the king, oaf. Didn't you recognise that great beak – the famous long nose of the Frankish royal family? Never seen it on a coin?'

'I've never owned a coin.'

'Well, that was Karolus. That was the man who ordered this trial by combat, who will doubtless relish watching us being slaughtered tomorrow.'

Bjarki stared down the empty corridor.

Tor yawned. 'Do you want to sleep?' she said. 'If you don't, I have an idea how we might make the contest more even tomorrow. Want to hear it?'

–

They walked out of a dark tunnel and into the brilliant light of the amphitheatre.

Tor wore a leather breastplate, a kilt of leather and iron strips, leather vambraces and greaves over bare feet and a steel cap on her head – the best combination she could conjure of protection without too much weight.

She needed to be fast.

She had armed herself with a six-foot spear, tipped with a razor-sharp leaf-shaped blade, a short stabbing sword of the kind favoured by the Red Cloaks, and a seax hung horizontally over her loins. But for her bare feet, she would not have stood out in any military muster in the North. She also looked small, skinny and dull in her old leathers, almost insignificant.

Bjarki, by contrast, was a sight to behold. He had spiked with honey and dried pig's blood what remained of his thick blond hair, after the cruel burns he had suffered at the Fyr Ceremony, which made it stick up in mad-looking reddish clumps all over his head. His face was painted dead white with a paste of flour and chalk, provided by Henk, with black and red circles drawn around his eyes to make them seem unnaturally huge and unnerving.

He wore a long mail hauberk and mail leggings, but patches of fur had been sewn into the links of the metal, here and there, to make it seem as if he were an animal bursting out from under the mail. His shoulders were made even broader with rolls of a thick fur cloak. Tor had sewed dozens of animal bones to his sleeves and the edges of his mail, which rattled eerily as he walked.

He was armed with a long, bearded axe, a sword at his waist and a seax, slung over his groin. He also had a large round linden-wood shield bound with iron – but no helmet. They had quarrelled over the lack of proper head-protection. But Tor had insisted their enemies must see his terrifying face.

The brightness of the amphitheatre, when they emerged from the dark tunnel with a dozen bow-wielding Red Cloaks at their back, was almost overwhelming; as was the sudden wave of noise from the packed benches that rose up on all sides. Henk had been right: this trial by combat was quite the event. Bjarki stared around, gawping at the packed citizenry, stacked tier after tier – there must be tens of thousands of people here, he thought, and then rejected the idea. No settlement, even a Frankish city, could boast such a vast number of inhabitants. But the noise of the crowd was like the noise of a stormy sea, rumbling, growling, crashing down on him in wave after wave.

Thousands of folk, anyway. And all seemed to be screaming the same thing: 'Beast-man! Beast-man!' Bjarki realised that they were shouting for him. Calling him a monster. That he wasn't even human in their eyes.

Tor, standing beside him – a slight, drab figure – was ignored by the crowd. It was the fabled 'beast-man' they had come to see: the wizard-warrior of the North who could transform himself into a terrifying creature, a killer impervious to pain. Bjarki desperately wanted to piss; his mouth was dry as ashes. He was terrified. He wanted to scream: 'I can't do it! Please, I cannot. I'm an ordinary man just like you. This paint and fakery is not me.'

Tor nudged him in the ribs; she said something but it was impossible to hear over the screams and roars of the huge crowd. She jerked her head at the bank of seats in the middle of the amphitheatre. Bjarki looked at a large box draped in thick, golden cloth, at the figure seated in the throne there…

It was the man he had thought was the cook Humboldt.

Tor had been right, as usual. The king was better dressed this bright autumn morning, in long purple robes embroidered at the hem and neck with golden stitching, a golden crown encasing his brow. Behind him stood Lord Grimoald, the King's Shield, and the Bishop of Aachen, Lord Paulinus.

Karolus was leaning forward to say something to his wife, Hildegard, who was seated on a golden bench in front of his with her brother. She was twisting her long neck around to hear him; smiling, excited. Duke Gerold merely looked bored. He began to clean his fingernails with a small knife.

Bjarki felt a presence at his side and turned his outrageously decorated head to see Father Livinus beside him: the priest was in his colourful war garb once more, a mantle of gold and blue and scarlet and white, and close up, Bjarki could see symbols of his Christian faith inscribed on the rich cloth – crosses, and fish and the arrangement of rune-like letters. Livinus was holding up his two arms, as if in triumph, receiving the tumultuous accolade of the crowds in the packed stands. In one hand, he held a large spiked mace. The crowd was chanting for him now: 'Liv-in-us… Liv-in-us!' On and on. An accolade for something, but what, Bjarki wondered. The priest had done nothing special. What had he achieved to deserve such public acclaim? Then it struck him: the accolade was for capturing these half-human barbarians.

Tor had also seen the triumphant gesture from the priest. She scowled.

Now Father Livinus was ushering the pair of them towards the centre of the arena and under the box containing the royal family. There was a row of fifty Red Cloaks, armed with spears and bows, standing at the edge of the nearest seats. Bjarki looked up into the box. He felt ridiculous with his white and red painted face and blood-and-honey clumped hair. Like an entertainer, a mountebank at a travelling market who will dance to amuse the crowds.

Livinus shouted up: 'Hail, great king! Hail, Lord of the Franks! Hail, Karolus! I bring before you a wizard of the North – a savage creature of the wilderness. Behold the beast-man of Saxony and his witch-servant of that same benighted land. They have been accused of the murder of several of your loyal servants at a place called Thursby in my county of Westphalia.'

Karolus, the supreme ruler of Francia, rose to his feet.

'We meet again, my friend,' he called out, smiling down at Bjarki. 'You have been accused of a terrible crime and the court has deemed that you must prove your guilt or innocence on the field of battle. God Almighty will be your judge – he will spare you or punish you according to His will. Are you ready to show us your skill and prowess in this place of judgement?'

'I thought you were a cook,' mumbled Bjarki, too quietly to be heard.

Father Livinus gave him a shove on the arm. 'Answer the king!'

Bjarki looked down at his feet. Tor muttered: 'Do we have a choice?'

'They are ready, great king,' the priest boomed. 'They put their trust and faith in Almighty God and accept the wise decision of the royal court.'

'Before you hazard your lives,' said the king, 'do you choose to save your souls? Will you renounce all superstition and embrace the Heavenly Father, the Holy Ghost and His only Son, Jesus Christ, as your Saviour?'

Bjarki shrugged. Tor hawked and spat on the sand.

'You need only say a few words to Father Livinus,' the king called down, 'and you will be saved. Say only: "I renounce sin and all the works of the Devil. I turn to Jesus Christ and accept him as my Lord and my Saviour".'

Bjarki said nothing.

But Tor stepped forward: 'I piss on your god, O King. I piss on his only son and his false promise of eternal life. Tomorrow, Bjarki Bloodhand and I, Torfinna Hildarsdottir, will be feasting in the Hall of the Slain. Today, we will show you how folk of the North can fight – and how we can die.'

'Brave words,' said the king, sitting down. 'We shall see if your actions match them.' He gave a flourish with his right hand. 'Let it begin!'

Chapter Sixteen

Blood on the sand

A trumpet sounded, and then a dozen more, a bold and joyful fanfare. At the far end of the amphitheatre an enormous iron-studded double gate swung slowly open. And Tor could see a dark mass of people emerging through it.

Father Livinus left them, walking towards the line of Red Cloaks, which parted immediately, and a little door opened in the wall of the arena. The priest disappeared through it and, a few moments later, he reappeared in the royal box and took up his station just behind the king's left shoulder.

Tor closed her eyes, and breathed a silent prayer to all the gods and spirits: grant me vengeance, ancient ones. For a brief instant, she imagined being loose in that absurd gold-swathed box, armed as she was and free to kill and maim as many as she could before the Red Cloaks put her down.

Then she dismissed this fantasy and turned her attention to the Avars.

They were slight, sun-darkened men in loose dun-coloured clothes. They wore no armour but for spiked steel helms over their dark, bearded faces, and carried small round metal shields, also spiked in the centre. Each man had a long, slim, curved sword and a curved dagger stuffed into his leather belt.

There seemed at first glance to be a great deal more than forty of them, and then she realised there were twice that number of Red Cloaks behind the Avars, urging them into the amphitheatre at the points of their spears.

The Avars spilled out into the centre of the amphitheatre, spreading out into a loose semi-circle, every man staring at Bjarki and Tor. The gate closed behind them; the Red Cloaks retreated and took their places against the wall.

'Ready?' she said to Bjarki, who nodded. He looked terrified under his odd white paste, ringed eyes huge with fear. 'Remember what we agreed?'

Bjarki said: 'We will show them who we are. And what we are!'

'Can you feel your *gandr* close by?'

'No, nothing. Even if I could summon it – look how many they are. It is over. This is the end for us, Tor; and I just want to say thank you for—'

'Oh shut up, you soppy oaf. Let's go and make a start on killing them.'

They began to crunch across the hard-packed sand of the amphitheatre towards the waiting enemy. Bjarki gripped his bearded axe handle tight, he thought about the mad plan Tor and he had come up with the night before.

Tor walked behind Bjarki, to his left, holding the spear casually over her shoulder, trying to stay out of the line of sight of the Avars in Bjarki's massive shadow. The sun was to her right, low over the southern side of the stands. It was two hours before noon, she thought. A day of pure blue skies.

They stopped, facing a wall of Avars. One man in the centre of the line, a black-bearded ogre, very thick in the chest although of short stature, was gently swishing his curved sword to and fro in the air in front of him. He was a killer, Tor knew it, a leader of men. He'd be the first to taste her spear.

'Work your way towards the southern part of the arena,' she muttered to Bjarki. 'Circle to your right. Keep the low sun in their eyes, if you can.'

There was another peal of trumpets, and suddenly there were Red Cloaks running everywhere; hundreds of them, and dozens of big men in scale-mail with black cloaks, too; the *Scholares*,

Karolus's royal bodyguard. They formed a thick line of bristling spears between Bjarki and Tor and the mass of the now very surprised-looking Avar warriors.

They heard Father Livinus's voice, well aided by some sort of brassy speaking trumpet, echoing out over the hot dry circle of the amphitheatre.

'The king declares this contest to be manifestly unfair. The numbers are grossly unequal,' Father Livinus boomed. 'His Majesty has decreed the two heathen sorcerers shall face only ten of the Avar – the best ten. The two fighters from the North will fight only the last ten Avar standing. Let the battle to determine which ten Avar men shall have that honour begin now!'

'That will set the cat among the starlings,' said Tor.

The crowd around the edge of the amphitheatre was cheering, some were laughing, and calling out that the king was a man of wisdom and wit, a few were even throwing nut shells and pieces of half-eaten fruit down on the heads of the Avars to taunt the eastern warriors, who were now completely surrounded by hundreds of Frankish troops with lowered spears.

The Avars appeared bewildered by this turn of events. Bjarki wondered if they had understood the meaning of the priest's booming words. They were, after all, even more alien in this strange city than the two fighters from the Groves of Eresburg. They came from lands far to the east. Their language was utterly different to the tongues that Bjarki, Tor, Livinus and the king spoke.

But some of the Avars had understood the message.

Bjarki saw a man inside the ring of Red Cloaks pull a dagger from its sheath and ram it into the belly of the man standing next to him. Blood blossomed on the victim's loose brown tunic; he stared uncomprehendingly at his comrade and sank to his knees, his life spilling and spurting on the sand.

His murderer was immediately cut down from behind by another man's sword, which severed his head from his neck. In an instant, it was mayhem inside the circle of Red Cloak spearmen.

The Avars fell upon each other with cries in their strange language and the clash of steel. A few moments later, and half of the Avars were down, and desperate men were duelling everywhere inside the ring, slashing and hacking at their friends in a frenzy.

After the initial cull of the unsuspecting, the last remaining men fought with grim determination, cut and riposte, blades clanging on steel shields, the screams of the wounded, and stench of opened bowels filling the air.

It was done inside a hundred heartbeats. The last few remaining men, eleven of them by Bjarki's swift count, stopped fighting, panting, gore-spattered… A man in the centre of the fallen, who was wounded in three or four places and swaying, but still on his feet, looked about him desperately. Three of his comrades advanced on him at the same time. The swords arced down on him; an arm was lopped. He toppled to the sand.

There were ten Avars still standing. Many of them wounded. The crowd was cheering wildly. Sweets and flowers were raining down all over the sand. The trumpets sounded once more: a recall to barracks. The Frankish troops formed a line and trotted away. Bjarki stared in disbelief at the carnage before him, the pathetic humps of broken men lying on the sand, some still gasping, moaning, bleeding away the last moments of their lives.

'Now it's our turn,' said Tor, giving him a little push. 'Go, oaf, go.'

Bjarki roared. A mighty battle call to shake the branches of the One Tree itself. He charged at the nearest Avar. The man was half-turned away and wiping his bloody sword on the brown cloak of one of his fallen comrades when Bjarki's axe smashed into his shoulder, slicing through flesh and bone and plunging deep into his chest.

Tor, right behind him, half-obscured by his bulk, leapt out and skewered another Avar who was staring in shock at the bellowing apparition with dead, white face, weird spiked hair, and mad red-and-black ringed glaring eyes.

Bjarki was already terrifying the next fellow, exchanging cuts of axe and sword, the blades battering at each other's shields. Tor was a darting demon in leather, killing with a swift miraculous skill, leaping out from Bjarki's shadow, slicing with the spear, cutting tendons, dropping Avars here, there, and reversing the pole and punching the spear down into them when they were sprawling on the sand. Meanwhile, Bjarki roared and stamped and battered at the lightly built easterners with his superior weight and strength. The much-practised blows and combinations of the Fyr Skola flowed naturally through Bjarki's powerful limbs: he smashed opponents out of his path with great sweeps of the axe; he hooked the bearded blade over the small Avar shields, pulling his opponents forward to be met with a terrible bone-crunching punch from the steel boss of his own wooden shield.

He howled and gibbered like a madman, and capered crazily when he remembered to, stepping in between the corpses of the fallen as he danced, and roared, Tor's cunning words of the night before still echoing in his ears: 'You distract them, Bjarki, I'll be killing. Draw their eye; I'll do the rest.'

Tor killed like a striking serpent: precise, swift, a flickering steel blade sheathed in glistening red. When her spearhead eventually became trapped between the bones of one Avar warrior's spine, she abandoned it in the body, whipping out her short sword and seax and laying about her with renewed fury. So the slaughter continued. Bjarki found he was humming as he bellowed and stamped and smashed at the swarming enemy, hacking with his long axe, and his heavy shield doing equal damage to his foes. Yet while his hot blood was definitely singing in his veins with the commonplace joy of combat. He could not sense the dark, inhuman presence that he craved.

He took several crunching blows to his well-armoured arms, legs and back, and felt them like kicks from an angry horse, one man spiked him with his shield point, but none of them managed to pierce his iron-link mail.

And still his *gandr* did not come.

Until, quite abruptly, it was all over. Tor dispatched the last wounded Avar with a lightning lunge to the throat, the point of her short sword hacking through one side of the man's neck in a horrible shower of red.

The battle was done.

The noises from the crowd were ear splitting. Every man, woman and child in the amphitheatre, it seemed, was on his or her feet, roaring their joy and approval at the slaughter. Flowers floated down on them from all sides as the Franks of Aachen showed their appreciation for the spectacle, just as their old Roman ancestors had in the days of the barbarians and beast hunts.

The cry of, 'Beast-man, Beast-man,' sprang up once again and this time Bjarki did not find it nearly so demeaning. It was a hymn to his victory. To the victory he and Tor had won. He dropped his battered shield and stood swaying, head drooping, leaning on his long gore-clotted axe, white paste mingled with sweat dripping on the sand, his body trembling uncontrollably.

Three paces away Tor sank to her knees, panting. She had a bad cut along her jaw line, and fresh blood dribbled from the point of her chin on to the ground. But otherwise she seemed more or less unharmed.

They looked over at each other and grinned.

–

They were relieved of their weapons and armour and immediately ushered by the Red Cloaks into a horse-drawn wagon, with Father Livinus on the bench up front, and a squad of guards all around, and transported the short ride southwest along a fine main road to the sprawling palace complex.

The Red Cloaks helped them to dismount and Bjarki looked around at the fine buildings of pale stone and red tiles – some of which were still in the process of being constructed. He could see the long council hall in all its magnificent bulk away to his right, and the tall square tower at the end, and all the other buildings of the palace, connected by red-roofed galleries. Slaves, soldiers and tonsured clergy bustled here and there. A light fog of dust gathered over the half-built areas of the palace and the music of workmen's hammers tinked in the air. They were conducted into a low square building, with colonnades on all sides and a shallow, open-air tank of gently steaming water the size of a small lake in the centre of the space.

'This is the imperial baths of Aachen,' said Livinus, 'built by the old Romans in the days when it was called Aquae Granni. The waters here were considered sacred by the pagans, and do indeed contain healing properties.'

Father Livinus left them, and the Red Cloaks retreated out of sight, and they were stripped and washed, and allowed to soak their bruised bodies in a great square marble tank, which they discovered was filled with delightfully warm bubbling water, although it smelled slightly of rotten eggs. When they were thoroughly washed and clean, they relaxed on soft pillows on thick cool marble slabs in the colonnade and a matronly slave sewed up Tor's cut face, muttering about scars and ruining her pretty looks. Tor ignored her and the pain of her needle; she was already half-asleep, drowsing at peace. Some hours later they were fed royally, various kinds of meat and fruit, given hot sweetened wine to drink, and they were massaged by a pair of burly half-naked slaves, blinded at birth so they would 'see' better with their fingers.

It was just the right side of painful, deep kneading strokes, and while Tor was initially wary of allowing a bald, beefy Moravian to manipulate her scrawny body, she eventually relaxed and allowed the sensations to engulf her. Bjarki fell fast asleep almost as soon as he lay down on the marble slab.

In the evening, Father Livinus reappeared, now in his usual plain white robe, and they were dressed in fresh Frankish attire and, with only a pair of Red Cloaks in attendance, led along a brick path in the cool dusk over to the square tower at the east end of the council hall. They were ushered into the spacious room on the second floor, a chamber hung with silk tapestries showing scenes of the hunt and lit by scores of golden candle holders.

They were, Bjarki realised, in Karolus's personal quarters.

The priest, obviously brimming with pride, bowed low before the king and presented his two charges with suitable aplomb.

'I salute you both as victors,' said Karolus, who was lounging on a couch, eating a peach. 'I cannot remember,' he said, smiling happily at the pair of them, 'when I have seen a nobler display of courage and prowess combined. God has judged you and found you innocent of all charges.'

The king was flanked by Lord Grimoald and Lord Paulinus, both standing stiffly behind the long couch. A score of black-cloaked guards in full armour lined the walls – the much-feared *Scholares*. Karolus was as plainly dressed as the night before when Bjarki had mistaken him for a cook: clean brown tunic, plain leather belt and cross-gartered hose. But he wore a gold circlet that glinted in the candlelight and kept his red hair from his face.

Father Livinus stepped forward and spoke for them: 'My friends are deeply honoured by His Majesty's gracious praise for their pagan valour.'

Bjarki glanced over at Tor, worried she would say something rude, but she just rolled her eyes. He suddenly felt an overwhelming urge to giggle.

Lord Grimoald said: 'Majesty, it is my duty to tell you that I do not think this course at all wise, as I said before it is a dangerous indulgence—'

'I'm aware of your opinion, Grimaold,' said the king coldly, twisting his neck to stare up at the soldier. 'And while I thank you for sharing your wisdom with me, it is unnecessary for you to repeat it.'

'They *must* acknowledge the true Faith,' said Lord Paulinus. 'I cannot allow Your Majesty's proposal to proceed unless that vital condition is met.'

'*You* cannot allow it?' said the king, raising an eyebrow. 'Are you saying that you would step down from your position as my chaplain and chancellor if I were to proceed without your blessing, Paulinus? Because, if that is the case, I would with the greatest regret give my consent – and immediately begin considering who might be chosen as your successor.'

'No, no, Majesty, I'm content to continue to serve you in my present capacity… I would never presume… I meant… I merely suggest that these two heathens must admit the truth that Jesus Christ is Our Saviour before any offers of mercy are made. It is the law of Francia, and the law of Holy Mother Church. If we were seen to be relaxing our vigilance against pagans and heretics, demon-summoners and the like, then… well it would set a dangerous precedent, as well as damaging the soul of the nation.'

'I hear you, Paulinus. But I also must remind you: I make the laws in Francia – not you, and not the Church. Anyway, let us hear what our two heathen heroes have to say about this matter. Then I shall make my decision.'

The king fixed Bjarki with his pale blue eyes and said: 'I am minded to bless you with a signal honour, in recompense for the indignities you have suffered here and in recognition of, and reward for, your remarkable victory in the arena. Are you willing to receive a great honour, my young friend?'

'I would much rather be honoured than dishonoured, Your Majesty,' said Bjarki. 'But since I do not know what this honour is, I can't say more.'

Karolus laughed. 'This is what I would do: I would invite you, and your brave friend, to join the ranks of one particular *scara* of my army, that is, to join a regiment of my troops, a special unit known as the Auxilla.

'This *scara* is part of my royal household but it is made up of non-Franks, men and women who are not natives of Francia and who do not owe me service through their territorial lords. You would be housed in Aachen and fed, armed and paid, and I would employ you in special duties, nothing too arduous, in the main as a guard of honour in this palace. You would also have the right of personal audience with me, as members of my *familia*.'

The king paused, and looked sternly at Tor, before turning back to Bjarki. 'However,' he said, 'you would be required to swear an oath of allegiance to me. But I give you my word you would not be required to fight your own folk, to shed the blood of Saxons or warriors of the Dane-Mark.'

'What about Svearland?' said Tor.

'Svearland?' said the king. He looked enquiringly at Lord Paulinus.

'It is a remote land of ice, snow and darkness far to the north and east of the Dane-Mark. The people are savage barbarians, heathens all and—'

'Yes, yes, all right,' said the king. 'So… you will not be called upon to fight Svearlanders either. I give you my word. However, I shall require you to acknowledge the true Faith, and accept the Lord God and Jesus Christ into your hearts through the sacrament of baptism. Now, what do you say?'

'What if we do *not* accept your offer? What then?' said Tor.

'Then,' said Lord Paulinus, with a horrible smile, 'you will be accused of witchcraft and devil-worship and returned to your lion's den under the amphitheatre until we decide your fate. Or until you see the light of Christ.'

'It is a huge honour for you,' rumbled Lord Grimoald. 'One I do not believe you truly merit. But the king desires it. So, now, you must choose.'

Bjarki and Tor glanced at each other.

'We accept,' said Tor. 'Now, shall we discuss suitable rates of pay?'

Chapter Seventeen

A very special scara

'Are we doing the right thing?' said Bjarki. 'Acknowledging the triple Christ god? Undergoing their washing ceremony – pretending to believe in it? What would the Mikelgothi say about our actions, I wonder, or Valtyr?'

They were sitting in a tiny anteroom outside the king's private chapel, on the far side of the palace complex from the tower that housed the king's apartments and the council hall. They had been there much of the night, dozing on the stone benches, although they were supposed to be pondering the mystery of the Trinity. This was three gods in one, apparently. God the Father, God the Son and God the Holy Ghost were all one deity, but also three deities at the same time, which was obviously nonsense. Inside the huge round palace chapel, Paulinus and Livinus and half a dozen other priests were preparing the time-honoured ritual, something to do with a spiritual cleansing, that would admit them to the Christ religion: baptism.

'It is just a ruse,' said Tor. 'It is quite acceptable in war to lie to your enemy, to make false oaths, trick him, do anything to gain an advantage. Besides, what do we actually have to do? We acknowledge this Jesus God. Say we believe in this silly Trinity thing. Undergo a ritual. Say some words. And we're free. I doubt the real gods will care much if we pay lip service to this new one. And Valtyr would tell us to do what we have to do to survive.'

'It feels dishonest,' said Bjarki.

'We do this or we die – sooner or later – for the amusement of these so-called civilised people. Trial by combat, my arse. They just wanted to watch our blood being shed. And don't think our trick will work next time, oaf. They will pit us against a hundred Avars. Two hundred. And that will be it.'

'So, what now? We just serve the Frankish king as his loyal soldiers?'

'Three words,' said Tor. 'Guard. Of. Honour.'

'What?'

'When we are members of this *scara* thing, this Auxilla regiment, whatever that turns out to be, we will have the honour of forming a personal guard for their king. We'll be Karolus's bodyguards. I plan to bide my time, wait for the moment and, when they least expect it, slice open his throat.'

'Shhh,' said Bjarki, looking around him at the small, empty anteroom. 'Even if you're joking, Tor, don't say that kind of thing out loud.'

Tor shook her head. 'I'm not joking.'

The door opened and Father Livinus poked his tonsured head round the jamb. 'The king is here now and Lord Paulinus is ready for you,' he said.

The ceremony was a simple one. They stood together as the bishop and his priests chanted a long babble of sacred words in the old Latin tongue – something about being reborn in the light of the Lord, accepting Jesus Christ as their Saviour, or so Father Livinus whispered to them in his translation.

Bjarki did not pay much attention to the priest's words – he was staring open mouthed at the chapel, a huge circular space made of coloured marble, its dome decorated wonderfully with gold and jewels and coloured tiles in vivid blues and reds, and images of the Christ, and his mother Mary, a virgin who had nonetheless given birth to him, apparently, and all the various saints – who were like minor gods. The chapel had a huge stone throne, raised up in the very centre, on which sat the king, beaming down at them. Tor made a point of yawning conspicuously during the ceremony, and while Bjarki, too, was exhausted, a sense of courtesy kept him reasonably solemn.

They both swore to renounce evil, in all its forms, and the worship of false gods and demons, in particular. Then they were liberally splashed with water three times, a big cupful on their heads, taken from the font, which was a big marble basin. Then they were smeared with holy oils, and Father Livinus stepped forward and declared himself Bjarki and Tor's father under Almighty God, responsible for keeping them on the path of righteousness.

There was more unintelligible chanting from the priests, more prayers, and a speech about the Christ's last days in the Middle-Realm, and they knelt and were fed a scrap of bread and a sip of wine by the bishop. And the baptism was done. Father Livinus embraced both of them one after the other, and said it was time to swear the oath of allegiance to King Karolus himself.

This was no prolonged matter either, it was simply a question of kneeling before the king on the steps as he sat above them on his stone throne and placing their clasped hands between his warm palms as he leaned over them, then swearing to be loyal and faithful to Karolus and his heirs, for the rest of their lives, and never to break the oath on pain of death.

'I know you're a man who strives to keep an oath, Bjarki Bloodhand,' said the king, when he had released Bjarki's hands and the ceremony was concluded. 'It is one of the reasons I took you into my service. And I look forward to many more interesting and illuminating conversations with you.'

–

The Auxilla barracks were something of a shock. In the palace complex, and in the city of Aachen itself, they had seen vast quantities of marble and gilt. They had been awed by the soaring columns and beautiful bronze statues, by the arrow-straight paved streets and the towering brick-built apartment blocks, by the extraordinary majesty of the council hall and the splendour of the king's chapel. But when they came into the large walled compound that housed the Frankish standing army, in the rolling fields just outside the city limits, the first building they saw was a longhouse, of a kind they might see in any humble village in Saxony, or the Dane-Mark, for that matter.

It was a low, thatched building, built of wood with wattle-and-daub walls, with a slightly curved roof, the shape of an enormous upturned ship. For the first time in many weeks, Bjarki was pierced through by a shard of homesickness. An image of Freya leapt into his mind. He wondered what his sweet girl was doing at that moment, and whether she was thinking of him.

He thought even more painfully of the oath he had made to her in the dunes, and then of the oath to the Mikelgothi in the Groves, and then of the oath he had just sworn to Karolus in the jewelled chapel. So many oaths. A burden of promises made – and, in the case of Freya – immediately broken.

One day, he told himself, one day soon, he would return to Bago in triumph. And he would kneel before Freya and beg her forgiveness. And she would forgive him. Then he'd take her into his arms and kiss her and…

The other buildings in the rectangular army compound outside the city were constructions of brick and red tile, neat squares, laid out with precision along the sides of the straight, slab-paved streets, but the Auxilla barracks was a slice of his old life on Bago, magically transplanted to this Frankish soil.

Smoke trickled from the 'wind-eyes', triangular holes at the tops of the gable ends of the roof. Bjarki smelled roast pork, and sour days-old ale and the musty stench of seldom-washed bodies living together in a small space.

'These will be your quarters, along with the rest of the king's pack of tame savages,' said the captain of the *Scholares* escort who accompanied them. 'Rations will be brought to you each day, and Lord Grimoald will issue the weekly orders, but on a day-to-day basis you will be under the authority of the leader of this gang of mountebanks. You'd probably call him a *hersir*.'

The man grimaced at the ugly, unfamiliar word. He had made it clear on the way from the palace that he didn't approve of this unit at all.

If the Auxilla barracks was a small shock to Bjarki, the first person he saw when he went into the longhouse was a huge one. It was Freki, the boy from Bago, son of Olaf, who had taunted him and Freya in the sand dunes, along with his elder brother, Jeki, and their broad, dull-witted servant, Ymir.

Freki was standing by the end of the fire-trough in the centre of the hall, leaning against a carved wooden pillar, gesturing with his hands and chatting with a group of others. He was no longer a youth, Bjarki could see that – he had filled out in the chest, the shoulders and arms. He was a man, a warrior, with a fine sword hanging from his tooled belt. Bjarki stopped dead in the doorway at the sight of him, and Tor barged right into his broad back. There was no mistaking the pale, nearly snow-white hair of Bjarki's erstwhile tormentor in Bago, and his large, slightly bulging dark blue eyes.

'What? What is it?' Tor was looking wildly between Bjarki and the interior of the longhouse. Her body was tensed for immediate action.

'See the blond man by the fire-trough? I killed his brother. In Bago.'

By this time Freki had noticed and obviously recognised Bjarki.

'I see him,' said Tor. 'Right. We had better get astride this matter right from the start.' They were both armed, the Black Cloaks had issued each of them with a northern-style sword, a straight yard of sharp steel with a downward curved cross bar, which hung from their waists in leather sheaths. They both had seaxes slung across their loins. But there were about thirty Auxilla in that hall, indistinct figures in the smoky interior, all surely armed.

'You!' said Freki, pointing a finger at Bjarki. 'It's you – Blood-hand!'

Tor marched directly over to the group of young men by the pillar.

'I am called Torfina Hildarsdottir. This is my friend Bjarki Bloodhand – I think at least one of you knows this.' She looked at Freki. A challenge.

Freki said nothing. He was staring balefully over her shoulder at Bjarki.

'I understand that my friend here slew your brother in a fight on Bago,' continued Tor. 'He admits the deed. And he has already been judged and sentenced by his community – by the Thing of Bago – and punished with outlawry. I know this because I was there myself with my master, Valtyr. Your father, Olaf Karlsson, renounced vengeance for himself and the village.'

Freki seemed to have lost the power of speech.

Tor said: 'He also made Bjarki a thrall – although he has since been freed of that yoke by Valtyr Far-Traveller. However, you still may wish to claim kin-vengeance. We understand that. It is only natural. If so, my friend Bjarki will willingly fight you, seax or sword. But tell him now. We have been invited by the king to join the Auxilla and shall be living among you. This must be settled fairly and speedily. Tell me what your choice will be.'

'What is going on?' said a new voice. A short, stocky man of perhaps thirty winters, bald as an egg, strode over to the gathering at the fire-trough.

'Who are you, strangers? And why do you disturb us in our house?'

Tor repeated her name and explained the situation.

'You are the Rekkr?' said the bald man, gazing up admiringly at Bjarki. 'I should have known. I should have been told. I am Otto, captain of the Auxilla, *hersir* of this company. I'm sorry I did not recognise you sooner, Rekkr. I saw you yesterday in the amphitheatre. It was magnificent. We are honoured to have you here, Bjarki Bloodhand, and your comrade.'

'He's a murderer. A blood-lusting maniac. He destroyed my brother and a thrall with his bare hands. Tore them apart.' Freki had found his voice.

'Greetings, Freki,' said Bjarki. 'I am sorry, truly sorry for killing your brother. He did not deserve it. And I will fight you, formally, if you wish it.'

'No, no, no… the king has outlawed feuding between his vassals,' said Otto. 'Don't be a fool, Freki. I saw these two Rekkar kill forty Avars!'

'That's not actually quite what hap—' began Bjarki.

'I know what kind of mayhem he is capable of…' Freki did not seem to know how to continue. 'I know what a brute he is…'

'I forbid you to fight,' said Otto. 'As your *hersir*, I absolutely forbid it! No one here doubts your courage. But I order you *now* to forgo vengeance.'

Freki looked at him, then at Bjarki, his expression unreadable.

'Say it to him,' said Otto. 'Now. Say you forgive the killing. I do not want to lose you, Freki. But this matter must be put to rest without delay.'

Freki looked at Bjaki, towering above him. There was a long, horrible silence, and finally the boy muttered: 'Well, since you order it… I forgo my vengeance. Let it be forgotten. My father has forgiven it, I must as well.'

'Well spoken, Freki Olafsson,' said Otto. 'Well spoken, indeed. Now let us have some ale, a proper drink, to welcome our friends to the Auxilla.'

Tor watched Freki's face as jugs were brought, and horns were filled with foaming ale, and drunk, and toasts to the mighty Bloodhand were made, and to the king, as well, may he rule over Francia for a thousand years.

Forgiveness is for weaklings, Tor thought privately. *What kind of a warrior could overlook the murder of his own brother?* And while Freki made a good show of comradeship, talking easily with Bjarki, introducing him to the other members of the Auxilla, she knew deep in her heart that an old blood-debt was not so easily forgiven – still less would it be forgotten.

–

Bjarki and Tor settled into life in the Auxilla with little difficulty. The small company of warriors was given only light duties guarding the council hall and the outside of the palace complex and apart from an hour or two's exercise and drills each morning on the parade ground of the compound, they had little to do in their waking hours. The days grew shorter as the year turned, and they spent much of their time in the longhouse, drinking and sleeping, telling tales around the fire-trough that ran down the hall's centre.

Bjarki kept away from Freki as much as he could, but Captain Otto seemed to enjoy his company, seeking Bjarki out with the ale jug in the evenings, and urging him to tell tales of blood and glory; something Bjarki found a little trying. He told the story of the fight at Thursby, several times over. Because he could not remember what had happened on the only occasion his *gandr* had come to him, he was forced to invent details of the fight; which made him uncomfortable. Indeed, he felt a little like a fraud.

Captain Otto hung on his every word. And he responded to Bjarki's irksome lies by recounting several feeble stories about the times he had lost his temper and initiated violence in some ale-house fracas. It soon became clear that Otto had almost no experience of real combat whatsoever.

'What brought you to Aachen, sir?' he asked the captain one evening.

Otto blustered and lied about being specially chosen for this elite auxiliary unit in the king's standing army but Bjarki realised that he had been sent here by his aged father, who was a lord of a minor Frankish fiefdom on the west bank of the River Rhenus up near the border with Frisia.

Despite Otto's admiration for the Rekkr, he was an enthusiastic follower of the Christian god. And while all the various Frankish peoples had been converted to this Roman religion many generations back, in the remoter parts of Francia there were still villages who paid homage to their old gods: to the All-Father, his son Thor, Tiw, the god of war, Hel of the realm of the dead, and Loki, the trickster, some of them even still told the old stories about the Irminsul, the tree that linked the Nine Worlds. Bjarki got the impression that Otto's father was half-hearted in his duty to Christ, and that Otto was, in fact, a hostage to ensure his father's good behaviour.

'The king has been admirably firm, and Lord Paulinus, as well, when it comes to stamping out heresy whenever they find it,' said Otto. 'But some of my father's people stubbornly cling to the old ways. And my father finds it hard to execute folk who've been loyal to him for several generations.'

'Execute them for what?' said Bjarki.

'For apostasy, of course; for denying the Christian god. But I have faith that the light of Our Saviour will come to all the unbelievers in due course. After all, even you, Bjarki, a Rekkr, have forsaken your false gods.'

'Hmm,' said Bjarki.

'Perhaps you would like to pray with me in the morning,' said Otto. 'To affirm your faith and cleanse your immortal soul of all its past sins.'

'That is a *very* kind offer, Captain. Very kind. Let me think about it for a while, yes?' said Bjarki. 'Now tell me a little about the rest of our company. How did our brave comrades come to be serving Karolus here?'

In truth, Bjarki wanted to know why Freki Olafsson had travelled down from Bago but could not bring himself to ask Captain Otto directly.

'Some are here because they love the king, as do I, and recognise that one day the whole world will be ruled by Karolus and his line. He will be an emperor one day, like the Roman emperors of old. They are his models, you know, Karolus venerates them like his ancestors. But what was I saying?'

'You were telling me how these northern folk came to serve Karolus.'

'Yes, as I was saying, some love the king and desire to serve him. Others, have found the truth of Our Lord Jesus Christ, and seek to bring His light to all Mankind. And others have... well, there are a whole variety of different reasons… You see Brandt, that big, dark-haired fellow over there? He killed a man in Jutland and fled from the fury of the dead man's family. Yoni, the little blonde one by the fire, she's an adventurer from Hibernia. She was a sea-rover in the northern islands. She nearly drowned one time and made a vow to the pagan god Lir that if he spared her a watery grave she'd never set foot in a ship again. Nonsense, of course, but here she is.'

–

It was Tor who discovered the truth about Freki. 'His father sent him down here from Bago,' she told Bjarki one cold morning when they were sparring gently with axe and shield on the almost empty parade ground.

'He's set to be the Bago *hersir* one day and Olaf thought to make a proper fighting man of him by sending him to Karolus to learn skill at arms.'

They paused for a while to watch Freki thrashing away with his sword against an equally unskilled opponent. His blows were wild, uncontrolled.

'That plan doesn't seem to be working out very well,' said Bjarki.

'Maybe I'll take him under my wing, train him up, just like I did you,' said Tor, grinning at him.

Bjarki lowered his shield and axe and gaped at her.

'I'm joking, Bjarki. Although it's not the worst idea I've ever had. I could "accidentally" maim him in a training bout. Cut off his hand or a foot!'

'You say you're joking – but you're not being very funny.'

'How's this for a jest,' said Tor, and she launched a flurry of axe blows at Bjarki, who only with difficulty fended them off with his shield.

When they broke apart, both panting, Tor said: 'It seems that someone, at least, seems to appreciate my sense of humour.'

She jerked her chin at the side of the parade ground where a heavy four-wheeled travelling carriage was parked, the vehicle drawn by four black carthorses. The lumbering box on wheels was painted black and the symbol of the eagle – the insignia that adorned Karolus's war banner – was inscribed in gold on the door. Bjarki could see that the square wooden shutter above the door that acted as a window was very slightly open. Someone inside was watching them. He caught a flash of jewels, and a glimpse of a white face.

'Is that Queen Hildegard, do you think?' said Bjarki.

'Why would she hide from us?' Tor replied.

'I've no idea. But it's a royal carriage and that's not a man in there.'

Tor shrugged. 'Perhaps, oaf, you have a secret admirer.'

–

Bjarki soon realised that the Auxilla was a rather poorly regarded military outfit. They were, despite their pretensions to being an elite unit, distinctly third rate. Very few of their members would have been good enough to make the ranks of the Barda, he reckoned. In terms of skill, Bjarki and Tor were head and shoulders above any of the others – save perhaps the dark murderer Brandt, who had obviously received some instruction in his youth – and although Bjarki still felt a fraud whenever Captain Otto called him Rekkr, and treated him with exaggerated respect, he and Tor were swiftly accepted as natural leaders in this company of thirty mismatched folk.

One thing, however, that the Auxilla did excel at was dressing for war.

Every third day, two Auxilla members were selected for duties as an honour guard for the royal family. The preparations for this service began well before dawn, earlier than the rest of the company usually rose. The two chosen fighters washed thoroughly; long hair was braided and the twisted locks threaded with ribbons, pierced shells and silver bells; cropped hair was shaved back to the scalp, which was rubbed with oil to make it gleam.

The armour worn by the two sentinels was ostentatious, to say the least: breastplates inlaid with relief images of animals and monsters, greaves polished and leather kilts oiled. Mail was scrubbed and cleaned, rolled in barrels of sand till the dull iron shone. Steel helmets, set with bulls' horns or pure white swans' wings or vicious spikes and sharp ridges, were buffed to a brilliant shine. Weapons were all very showy – double-edged axes, the twin blades buffed to a mirror-like brightness, or long swords with ornate, richly bejewelled polished bronze scabbards and gold-and-silver encrusted hilts.

When the two honour guards were ready, they were inspected by Captain Otto and the rest of the Auxilla. Folk in the longhouse gathered around them to murmur admiringly, and darted in to give a little final polish to a gleaming breastplate, or to remove a smudge from a snow-white shield or arrange the fall of a fat plait more decorously on the warrior's shoulder.

When Bjarki first saw the two men in their finery, he assumed they were destined for a grand party or some sort of high Frankish ceremony. He was taken aback when he heard that these two gleaming, glittering, glowing visions of martial splendour – two figures from a childish fantasy of soldiers – were dressed as such only to stand rigidly on either side of the throne for eight hours; stand without moving a hair, ready to spring into action should a passing assassin try his luck with King Karolus or a member of his family.

All the weapons and armour came from a common pool and were used only for the infrequent ceremonial occasion of the honour guard. It was, in fact, the only kit that was well maintained in the whole company. For training purposes, they used old, notched, tarnished swords and battered shields that barely held together after a single decent blow. The ordinary ring-mail was ripped and rusty; scale-mail hauberks had half the shield-shape scales missing and left large patches of bare dry leather exposed;

the helmets were all dented, some with loose and mouldering leather linings.

Tor and Bjarki had their own swords and seaxes, which they took care of themselves, cleaning, oiling and sharpening them nightly. But Tor always found herself wincing when she had to don something rusty or musty from the communal stock for the daily training sessions on the parade ground.

'Do you think we ought to teach them to look after their weapons and kit properly?' asked Bjarki one day when he was wedging tight an ancient and blunt bearded axe that had been rattling alarmingly on its shrunken handle.

'They know how to do it, most of them; they just can't be arsed.'

'Still, shouldn't we show them, and make them understand—'

'These are not *our* people, Bjarki,' snapped Tor. 'These are lackeys of the king; traitors and turncoats all. Don't waste your breath on them.'

Tor was in a foul mood. Her courses had started during the night, and she felt dirty and weakened by this inconvenience. Her belly ached and her back, too. Yet it was not something she ever wished to discuss with Bjarki.

-

Towards the end of their second week in the Auxilla, Lord Grimoald arrived at the longhouse in the late afternoon, with an escort of a dozen Black Cloaks, and asked for the whereabouts of the two newest recruits to the *scara*.

For a mad joyous moment, Tor believed that they were to be invited to form the honour guard at some point in the near future. Her mind began to whirl with murderous possibilities. How close would they be to the king's person? Would there be any *Scholares* there? If so, how many?

In the event, it was nothing to do with the honour guard, and after Lord Grimoald had spoken with Captain Otto privately in the officers' quarters at the end of the longhouse, Bjarki was summoned by the King's Shield.

The young warrior had been invited, it seemed, to an audience with Queen Hildegard in her private chambers. Tor was not required to attend.

'Watch yourself, oaf,' Tor whispered to Bjarki as he followed Lord Grimoald out of the door. 'She probably wants to ride you down to a nub.'

Bjarki paused in the doorway, frowned down at her and shook his head. 'I shouldn't think that's it,' he said. 'She barely considers me human. For someone like her that would be like bedding one of her pack-horses.'

After he was gone, Tor found herself all alone by the dying hearth fire with an empty ale horn at her feet that she could not remember drinking, and for no good reason at all, great fat tears were running down her cheeks.

Chapter Eighteen

In the queen's chamber

As they marched down the arrow-straight stone-paved road, Bjarki was struck once again by the size and sheer oddness of the city of Aachen.

Everything was arranged in lines and squares. The 'islands', as he had heard them called, were the strangest of structures of them all. These were great brick blocks rising three- or four-storeys high in terrifying square towers, each level containing a small dwelling big enough for one family. Rickety wooden staircases curled around the blocks allowing the residents to enter their unnaturally high homes. As Bjarki looked up he could see women and men, children, too, leaning out of their windows, gossiping with each other, or with families in other islands across the street. He could not even imagine living like this: he would be continually afraid of plunging to his death. Yet these people seemed unconcerned about being suspended all day at the height of a tall pine tree above the constantly thronging thoroughfares.

One small boy of about ten or eleven summers, hanging out of a low window, caught sight of Bjarki marching down the main road with Lord Grimoald by his side and a dozen Black Cloaks all around him and called out, 'Hey-o, Beast-man!' to him in an excited but not at all unfriendly way.

Bjarki raised one hand in acknowledgement and the cry was taken up by dozens of people looking from their windows in almost as many islands.

'Beast-man! Beast-man! When will you fight again, Beast-man?'

Bjarki found he was smiling at all the attention and, indeed, enjoying it. He had never been popular; never been recognised by total strangers before.

'You think these people love you?' snarled Grimoald. 'They do not.'

Bjarki looked across at him and said nothing. He was slightly taken aback by the poisonous rancour in the big man's deep, hard-edged voice.

'I don't think they exactly hate me,' Bjarki said.

'You are this week's novelty; the foreign oddity on every tongue today. Forgotten tomorrow. They would as happily see you bleed in the gutter.'

'Show us your beast-self, barbarian,' shouted an old man on the street corner. 'Come on, show us! Change into a wolf and I'll give you a coin!'

One of the Black Cloaks barked something and menaced the old man with his spear and the fellow retreated to his doorway, muttering to himself.

'You have some personal experience of this, I think,' said Bjarki.

Lord Grimoald stared hard at him. For ten strides he said nothing at all. Bjarki assumed he would not bother to reply. Then…

'I too fought a trial by combat, Dane, long ago. Like you, I bled before the public and I triumphed. Like you, the king took me into his service.'

'I see,' said Bjarki. They were approaching the palace complex. A gleaming white marble portico, supported by six elegant fluted columns, filled his vision. A dozen more *Scholares* were guarding the entrance to the jumble of palaces and gardens. They snapped to attention when they saw Grimoald approaching. The big man stopped; seized Bjarki by the shoulder.

'I know you faked it, barbarian. In the amphitheatre. I could see what you and the Svear woman were playing at, even if others could not.'

Lord Grimoald's hairy face was a hand's width from Bjarki's – Bjarki could smell sour wine on his breath and the faecal stench of his rotting teeth.

'You are no true beast-man,' he said. 'It was paint and tricks and misdirection. And that woman is very competent. But you are no Rekkr.'

Bjarki was shocked to hear that last word from Grimoald's mouth.

He stared at the big man, now quite speechless.

The huge man's heavy paw was squeezing his shoulder painfully.

'Yes, my tricksy Dane,' said the King's Shield, his words coming out in a hot, stinking gust, 'I know all about the Rekkar – and the *gandir*, too. Growing up in my village, far to the east, beyond the River Elbe, we heard all the old stories of the bear-warriors who feel no pain, or the wolf-people, and the boars. I am a Wend, what you Danes would call a Vindr, and before I found Christ and came to Aachen, before I made my oath to the king, we used to tell the tales of these fabled warriors around the hearth-fire. And I know you are *not* one of them. You used bluster and mummery; roared and danced like a madman; you had a bucket of luck and, for some reason, the king decided to tip the odds in your favour in the amphitheatre. He had your enemies slaughter each other, then face you wounded and weakened. You fought well, yes; you triumphed and won glory. But you are no Rekkr.'

–

Bjarki was still feeling a little ambushed by that conversation when he was shown into Hildegard's quarters, which was not helped by the fact that the young queen was wearing few clothes and was sitting on a large bed and powdering her long neck and upper torso with something that looked like fine milled flour and smelled like flowers.

'Stand over there,' she said, pointing at a spot on the black-and-white tiled floor, 'and remain silent. I will attend to you in a little while.'

The ground-floor room was painted plain white, pale yellow and pink and was inordinately large, about half the size of the longhouse where thirty Auxilla spent so much of their days. There was even a small fountain tinkling in one corner, several stands filled with lit candles and various tables and chairs, as well as the huge bed covered in a fine woollen blanket.

Perhaps Tor's right, thought Bjarki, *perhaps she just wants to copulate with me.* He caught a whiff of the flour/flowers powder and sneezed loudly.

'By the Virgin, you're not sick, are you?' Hildegard said, looking at him in disgust. 'Stand further away, go over there – go, go, shoo.'

Bjarki moved a few steps away. They were alone in the massive room, Lord Grimoald having being firmly told by the queen to leave them in peace, and wait with his Black Cloaks on the other side of the heavy door.

Bjarki watched the young lady as she powdered her half-dressed upper body. She was beautiful, yes. Slim, well made, with pleasing curves where you might expect them; and her face, while a touch long, thin and pointed, was no hardship at all to look upon, either. If she wanted to make love with him, he would oblige her. Indeed, it might well be very pleasurable…

He felt a sudden deep pang of homesickness: and Freya's face sprang into his mind. The two girls were about the same age – although from vastly different worlds. He pictured making love with Freya in the dunes; her laughing freckled face, the warmth of her breath on his face, kissing her soft neck… Would he ever see her again?

Yet it seemed that, for once, Tor was wrong. Hildegard did not desire him carnally. She was now putting on some sort of gauzy dress, covering up her freshly powdered skin. A long robe followed, embroidered with gold thread and belted snugly at the waist, then a pair of delicate slippers with pearl buttons. Then, at last, it appeared she was ready to speak to Bjarki.

'You are probably wondering why I summoned you here,' she said as she walked over to a table and poured herself a large beaker of red wine.

He remained exactly where he was, following her only with his eyes.

'So, yes, well, I needed to ask you something; to seek your help…'

Bjarki said nothing. He inclined his head and smiled encouragingly.

'You *can* understand my language well enough, can't you?'

'Yes,' he said, 'I understand you perfectly, my lady.'

She nodded, threw back her head and drank off her wine in one long swallow. Bjarki got the impression she was nervous but trying to hide it.

'It is a delicate matter,' she said, at last. 'A matter of the heart. A matter of… well, a stupid infatuation, I can think of no better word…'

Bjarki remained silent.

'The thing is, sometimes a young heart wants something desperately; yet it is not really appropriate, and then, well… No. Let me start again.'

Bjarki was deeply puzzled by this performance. A queen, obviously used to having whatever she wanted, whenever she wanted it, why could she not speak plainly. She had all the power; he was little better than her thrall.

'It's about my brother, Gerold. The Duke of Swabia, you know.'

'Yes, I know him. I saw him in the council hall.'

'Well, yes, that's right. It appears that Gerold has conceived… no that's not the right word… not the right word at all. It appears Gerold has somehow decided that he is… in love. He claims he is in love. It's a silly infatuation, of course. But lusty young men never recognise that, do they?'

Bjarki's jaw fell open. 'The duke is *in love* with me?'

'Not you, imbecile, with your pretty little companion. Duke Gerold is infatuated with your girl. He has been watching her. On the parade ground, practising with her weapons. He made me come too, to admire her fighting style. He wants her. He claims he's in love. He says he must have her. The barbarian girl. Whatever she is, your servant, slave. Wife. Is she your wife?'

'You mean Tor? She is none of those things. She's my friend.'

'That's good.'

'Why is that good?'

'Because you can have no legal objection, then. He would take her as his concubine for a season, an *affaire*, set her up in the palace somewhere. Jewels, clothes, whatever she likes – within reason. I would like to help my brother in this matter. He is clumsy with women. And he does not care to risk… shall we say, an embarrassment. So I had thought we might come to an arrangement between us. As it has always been done. I would make you a payment in silver, a fee, or perhaps a favour, if you'd help arrange things.'

Bjarki was bewildered; then suddenly blindingly angry.

He clenched his teeth and breathed out through his nose. He knew that if he chose to he could rip this stupid, pampered girl into bloody rags with only his bare hands. He also knew that, if he did so, he would not live more than a few heartbeats longer than her first scream. Lord Grimoald and his Black Cloaks would be through that door in a flash. He breathed in, and out.

'So, will you help me, then? You would be handsomely rewarded.'

'Stop… talking. Just stop talking about this, please.' Bjarki could feel the thick veins in his neck pulsing, writhing. He knew he was red in the face. His hands were clenched so tight that his nails were digging into his palms.

'I'd part with a purse of gold, if you could get her for a night…'

'*Shut up!*'

Queen Hildegard looked as shocked if she had just been slapped hard.

Bjarki briefly wondered if *anyone* had ever told her to be silent before.

'I don't see why you are getting so upset, barbarian. You admit she's not your lover, nor wife. She's unmarried. He's a lord. What's the matter?'

'Where I come from, friends don't serve up their friends to other men like a plate of tasty honey cakes. Why doesn't he ask to meet her? Give her some flowers. Invite her to take a walk with him. Do whatever you people normally do in these situations. Not that she'd accept him as her husband.'

'You are insolent. He doesn't seek to wed her. And you are making this far harder than it ought to be. I wish you to tell your friend that she's caught the eye of the Duke of Swabia himself. Tell her how lucky she is. I told him he should just force her. Take her into some hay barn. But he's too proud.'

Suddenly, like a passing rainstorm, all Bjarki's anger was swept away. He began to chuckle. The lurid image of a petulant Duke Gerold trying to have his way with a stubbornly unco-operative Tor popped into his mind.

He laughed out loud.

Tor would beat the horny fellow into a bloody pulp. She would knock him round the bedroom. She could *literally* kick him to death. And if he did manage, somehow, to couple with her, he'd end up with a thumb in his eye-socket before the patch was dry. And the balls ripped clean off his body.

Bjarki laughed. He laughed again and suddenly found he couldn't stop.

'Stop that stupid noise. Stop it right now,' shouted the queen.

Bjarki was folded over himself. He couldn't control the storm of mirth.

'I command you to stop that ridiculous braying – now!'

Yet the tears continued to run in torrents down Bjarki's face.

'What is all this merriment? What is going on here?' said a new voice.

And Bjarki saw through blurry eyes that His Majesty was with them.

–

A half hour later, Bjarki found himself sitting on a long padded bench and sipping a cup of extremely good wine in one of the king's private halls.

'The duke could have his pick of any of the slave girls, of course. There are dozens of them, pretty little things, all different colours, shapes and sizes, in the kitchens or the bathhouse. But Hildegard says he's always liked girl-fighters, shield maidens, and they're few and far between. When I was younger, before I married, I remember, there was this one lady…'

Karolus stopped. He had been pacing up and down the marble floor while Bjarki sat and sipped his wine. He turned to face the younger man.

'I'm sorry if you have been embarrassed by this grubby business, my friend. Hildegard should know better. But she dearly loves her brother. And Gerold… well, young men don't use their heads to think with, do they? But he is a powerful man, an important vassal. I'd like to keep him happy, if I can. Don't suppose there is a chance your friend might consider…'

'Not a chance,' said Bjarki. 'If the Duke tried to force her, he would swiftly end up dead. She is careless of her own life. It doesn't matter to her that killing him would mean her own end. She'd think it a glorious exit.'

'So Death holds no terror for her – nor for you, either?'

Karolus poured himself wine from the jug stand and came over to sit on the end of the bench, a yard or so from Bjarki. The young man noticed the Black Cloak standing by the wall a dozen paces away, had shifted his stance a fraction. Not that Bjarki had any intention of trying to harm the king.

'No one wants to die,' said Bjarki slowly. 'But if the manner of your death is pleasing to the gods, then there is a suitable reward in the afterlife.'

'Eternal feasting in the Hall of the Slain, isn't that what you believe?'

'That's what all the skalds and *gothi* claim.'

'*Gothi?*'

'Our priests – but also law-givers and sometimes healers, too.'

Karolus scratched his beak of a nose. 'An eternity of feasting with a gang of boozy warriors; boasting, burping, bellowing at each other down the benches. I'd quickly find that very tedious. Sounds more like a punishment.'

'There would be singing and story-telling, as well. And the presence of the All-Father, Odin – it's his feasting hall, of course. And the other gods.'

'You know you are speaking heresy, don't you?'

Bjarki stared in shock at the king, who smiled mischievously back at him. 'If our good Bishop Paulinus were with us right now he'd be yelling "Abomination!" and calling for you to be executed without delay.'

'I humbly beg pardon, Your Majesty,' Bjarki stammered.

'Pardon granted. Your heresy is hereby forgiven. I can't expect you to be a pure Christian soul after only a week or two. Lord Paulinus is a tedious buffoon anyway. He is blinded by his devotion to God – and it is preventing him from fulfilling his duties properly. He thinks that strict adherence to the Faith is the answer to every problem in the kingdom; that all men must be either good or evil. And the men he deems evil must all be exterminated.'

Bjarki had nothing to say to this.

'But I'm boring you with my own problems. Let us forget Bishop Paulinus and God and heresy and all that business, and take our ease. Tell me a story, friend Bjarki,' said the king, sipping his wine. 'One you might hear in the Hall of the Slain. Tell me something shockingly heretical.'

'Me?'

'Yes, you, Bjarki Bloodhand. I command it of my faithful vassal, my newest convert to the light of Christ. I've a feast to attend tonight and some of the greatest men of Francia will be there – dukes, lords, bishops and priests – and it's sure to be as dull as a feast filled with the drunken heroes of the Northlands. So tell me a tale, Bjarki, tell me one I haven't heard before.'

The warrior finished his wine and dutifully got to his feet, striking a heroic posture in the manner of a skald at a feast. But his mind was blank.

Then, almost as if another man was speaking through him, he began:

'Once, when the world was fresh, before the first men were made, even before the gods came into being, there existed but a single tree, a mighty oak called the Irminsul, which was so huge and vast that it connected this Middle-Realm with all the other eight worlds of the universe below and above, its great thick trunk running through the centre of them all…'

Chapter Nineteen

A blade in the darkness

Tor did not find the revelations of Duke Gerold's infatuation with her in the slightest bit amusing. When Bjarki returned to the longhouse that night, cheerful, content and more than a little drunk, he found her waiting for him.

'It's not funny at all,' she said, scowling. 'It is a dangerous, even potentially lethal situation for me – for both of us.'

'The king will sort things out. I made it plain that you would not be Gerold's – what? – concubine or bedwarmer, under any circumstances.'

'The king? Why should he help us – against his own brother-in-law?'

'He's a good man. And, well, he seems to like me. He's friendly.'

Tor lost her temper. Her yells echoed through the sleeping longhouse.

'A good man? Are you fucking *insane*. This "good man" would crush all our countrymen like worms beneath his boot heel; he would kill all the Saxons, the Danes, the Svears, all who fought him, enslave all the rest, and force his Christ-worshipping nonsense across the whole of the North. He is our enemy, oaf. He's our mortal fucking enemy; our foe until death and even beyond. He is not, and never will be, your *fucking* friend.'

'Hey, keep it down over there, girl. Some of us are trying to get some sleep,' said a man's voice from the darkness at the back of the longhouse.

'You pipe down, dick-breath, or I'll put you to sleep permanently,' Tor retorted. But she seemed to have regained a little of her usual composure.

'You are becoming one of *them*,' she said, in a more moderate tone.

'But you're the one who made us swear an oath of loyalty to Karolus,' Bjarki replied. 'You insisted we should submit to their Christian god.'

'We had no other choice,' said Tor, her voice a whisper. 'But don't think we must become like them. Become like poor old Henk, the happy slave, content with his servitude, having no memory or notion of freedom.'

'What shall we do, then?' asked Bjarki.

'That's obvious. We must get out of here. The question is how. And how do we stop them coming after us and dragging us back here in chains.'

They left it there and went to their sleeping blankets. Bjarki was snoring within a few moments, but Tor lay awake, staring into the darkness.

-

Bjarki did not know exactly what it was that woke him: a clink, perhaps, of steel on iron; a shuffled misstep; a creak of leather. Some insignificant noise that his deep-sleeping brain told him was out of place, simply wrong.

He opened his eyes in the darkness. Sensed something. A presence. A disturbance in the space directly above him. And rolled. He heard something heavy thud down into the straw pallet where his sleeping body had lain only a moment or two before. He saw a shape, darker than all the surrounding blackness. And a gleam from the last of the hearth-fire embers on steel.

A sword.

He yelled out – not a word, a war cry – and hurled his body directly at the dark shape. He caught the attacker with his shoulder, forcing a bellow of air and pain from him and then they were both on the floor of the longhouse, rolling, grappling, the sword trapped uselessly between the writhing bodies.

The assassin's head butted hard into Bjarki's face, a disorientating blow to the cheekbone. The attacker reared back and repeated the manoeuvre.

Bjarki got one good punch in, a looping overhand right, and felt the crunch of cartilage, and a spurt of wet over his hand. He punched again and felt the slice of broken teeth across his knuckles. *Good*, he thought, punching a third time, much harder. *I'll have marked the murdering bastard at least.*

'What in the name of Christ is going on?' Otto's cry rattled round the longhouse. Bjarki's opponent had slipped loose from his grip. Someone was sparking tinder and flint; another Auxilla was blowing on the hearth-fire, bringing it back to life. Bjarki fumbled at his feet, trying to find his seax in the darkness. But he knew the fight – if you could call it that – was over.

'Are you hurt?' Tor was beside him, gripping his arm. In the newly kindled light of candles and lamps, he could see that she had a short-handled axe in one hand and her seax unsheathed and stuck through her leather belt.

He felt his battered face; his left cheek was already beginning to swell.

'I'm fine,' he said. 'But whoever it was that attacked me will have a freshly broken nose and he'll be lacking more than a few of his front teeth.'

–

When all the lights had been lit, the hearth-fire stoked, and the longhouse roused to full excited wakefulness, Captain Otto gathered all the members of the Auxilla in a circle. Bjarki looked at each face carefully but no one bore the marks of his fists, which he believed could not possibly be hidden. The Irish girl Yoni had a fine black eye, but her small button nose was perfectly intact, and she claimed the bruised eye had been earned on the training square two days ago in a pole-arm bout with her best friend, Brigitte.

The other girl confirmed her story. And the eye was evidently not fresh.

'Where is Freki?' said Tor.

Bjarki looked round the circle of faces. The Bago youth was nowhere to be seen. They searched his sleeping place and found his possessions still there. His blankets and furs rumpled and recently slept in by their look.

Tor, rummaging in the rushes on the floor of the house by Bjarki's bed, found a sword, a fine one, with a grip made of silver wire and a large piece of polished amber set in the top of the iron pommel.

'Is it his sword?' asked Otto. It was. A crony of Freki confirmed it.

They took Freki's possessions apart, then. Tearing the seams of his clothing, emptying his chest out on the floor of the longhouse. In the toe of an old pair of dirty woollen stockings, they found a small leather bag containing twelve gold coins – a fortune. On one side of the coin was a profile of Karolus, his famous beak of a nose making identification obvious. On the other side the coin was marked with letters and a Christian cross.

They searched every corner of the longhouse, the latrines and the area outside the building. Then ranged over the whole compound.

There was no sign of Freki.

'I'll have to report it in the morning, if he hasn't come back,' said Otto gloomily as they sat at the table an hour later and passed round the ale jug.

'Not just because he attacked you, Bjarki – I have full authority to stand in judgement over small disputes in the Auxilla – but because it looks like the fool has broken his solemn oath and deserted. It's punishable with death. But Lord Grimoald must be informed. I'm sorry, but he must be told. They will hunt him down, they have special *cabellarii* companies designated just for that purpose, and if they catch him, which they will—'

'Somebody paid him to kill Bjarki,' said Tor, pouring out a cup of ale.

'We don't know that,' said Otto.

'I do. Why else would Freki Olafsson have twelve gold *livres*?'

Otto declined to reply.

'Freki may be gone,' she said. 'But the person who paid him is still in Aachen.' Tor's logic was unassailable. 'So Bjarki is still at risk.'

-

They celebrated the twelve days of the midwinter feast of Jul in the longhouse, bringing in boughs of green stuff, eating roast goose and pork, drinking a strong, specially brewed ale. There were games and songs and old jests, and they did no military training or work of any kind. Even the ceremonial honour guard for the king was suspended during this time of drunken jollity.

The snow fell and covered the world in a thick white blanket and, on more than one occasion, Bjarki wondered where Freki was – was he out there in the snow somewhere, friendless, hunted by squads of Frankish horsemen without food or clothing, or even his sword, trying to make it back to Bago?

He pitied Freki; there, he admitted it. But he did not dare mention these thoughts to Tor, who would, he knew, have been scathing. The fellow had tried to kill him. He was an enemy – a *mortal* enemy, as Tor would no doubt phrase it. You weren't supposed to pity your mortal enemies. Let 'em freeze.

The threat of another assassin, Bjarki took seriously. He and Tor never slept at the same time, always one of them would be keeping watch, no matter how much Jul ale had been taken. But they were not attacked again.

Bjarki soon became bored with the endless singing and drinking. And when Karolus summoned him for a private audience in the last days of the festival period, he was actually eager to see the great man once again.

He did not tell Tor where he was going and passed a pleasant and relatively sober afternoon with the King of Francia, during which they discussed many things to do with Bjarki's homeland, and the customs and beliefs of his people. He seemed particularly interested in the Groves of Eresburg, and the great Irminsul, and the story of Odin's nine-day ordeal on the One Tree – and the shrine that held the wealth of the Groves. Bjarki was flattered that the king should concern himself with such matters outside his realm, and always answered Karolus's questions as honestly as he could.

And the passage of information was not all one way.

While Karolus and Bjarki conversed over the next few days and weeks, sometimes for hours, they were regularly interrupted by messengers and courtiers, and by visits from counts and bishops and other high functionaries.

Father Livinus had been away much of the winter on a long trip to the North, overseeing his county of Westphalia, no doubt, and the priest returned one cold February day in triumph. He and the king were closeted together for a time, before Karolus returned to his conversation with Bjarki and it was clear there had been some sort of victory in southwest Saxony.

The picture emerged slowly, Bjarki putting the news together from fragments of conversations that he caught over the next few days and weeks.

Theodoric had been forced to summon his jarls in the depths of winter – an unheard of practice – and with five hundred men he had hurried south to counter a large Frankish incursion into Westphalia led by Father Livinus.

The wild charge of the Saxons had disintegrated on the tightly packed disciplined infantry formations of the Red Cloaks, and the massed assaults of the *cabellarii* that followed rolled over the shield wall of *hersirs* and their followers. The Saxons had been broken, routed, and slaughter had ensued.

Duke Theodoric had fled the battle, retreating with his remaining jarls through the cruel snows rather than fighting on and risking death or capture – and this was, perhaps, a wise course. Theodoric was the symbol of the united tribes of Saxony. If he were killed, his realm could be eaten up piece by piece. Most of Westphalia had already been gobbled up by the Franks. Even Karolus admitted that his enemy had made the right choice. But the once-all-mighty Saxon leader was now penned in the northern part of his territory – in the lands of the Nordalbians – while the victorious Franks built churches on what had once been Saxon lands and divided the spoils of war.

When Bjarki passed on the news to the other members of the Auxilla, the response in the longhouse was mixed. Captain Otto insisted they must all drink a loyal toast to the noble king and his glorious victory, but some members of the company, Bjarki noticed, did not taste their ale. And Tor went so far as to spit noisily on to the floor rushes when Otto hoisted his horn.

Bjarki felt undecided about the battle. On the one hand, a people similar to his own folk in the Dane-Mark had been defeated. The bloodshed must have been terrible and he wondered whether any of the Fyr Skola people, any of his friends, had been involved in the fight, and had perhaps even lost their lives.

On the other hand, what did the deaths of a few hundred Saxon *hersirs* really mean to him? He did not know any of them personally; they were not his kin, nor even his neighbours. Was he not now an oath-sworn soldier of Francia? His side had won a great victory. His lord Karolus had triumphed.

There was other information he gathered that was less troublesome to his conscience. And Bjarki recounted his latest snippet at the supper table in the longhouse one night as an amusing diversion, more than anything else.

'There is a region called Thuringia, I am told, in the southeast of the king's domain, east of Swabia,' he began. 'And in this remote region there is a village called Eggeldorf, which has been plagued by a dread monster!'

'Eggeldorf, what a stupid name!' giggled Brandt, who was drunk. 'It means Egg Town. Are they famous for their huge eggs?

Ha-ha! They should be famous for their poor chickens who have to squeeze out those eggs.'

'I was in Thuringia once, long ago,' said Otto. 'The old King Pepin was doing a tour of his territories. I'd just been recruited to the Auxilla—'

'Tell us of this dreadful monster,' said Yoni in her sweet lilting accent.

'Quiet, everyone! Let the oaf tell us his story,' yelled Tor, banging her hand down hard on the table and, as had become usual, she was obeyed.

'The monster is a massive creature from the depths of Hel's realm,' intoned Bjarki, 'three times the size of a grown man, wilder than ten angry bulls, with eyes that glow with an other-worldly fire, and huge fangs that drip with venom. It is a foul beast straight out of your very worst nightmare.'

'More, more,' shrieked Yoni happily. 'Tell us more about it!'

Bjarki grinned. 'It has sword-blades for hands, which can cut through even the toughest scale-mail, and its skin is armoured with iron or protected by some magic. An ordinary blade can never penetrate its flesh; warriors' spears and arrows bounce right off its thick hide. And it eats men – and women – whenever it can catch them. Its favourite meat is newborn baby.'

Bjarki was enjoying himself. He could see by the expressions around the long table that his comrades' flesh was creeping most satisfactorily.

'Six folk have already been claimed by this fell demon – all from Eggeldorf and the surrounding forestlands.' Bjarki paused and looked around the table. 'All were eaten alive, crunched down and swallowed whole, with nothing left but scraps and bones and a huge pool of blood.

'Before long the good people of Eggeldorf grew desperate. They knew this monster would destroy them all, one by one, if they did not do something. They hired a champion – a warrior from Aquitaine, a noble *cabellarius*, the victor of a dozen such dangerous quests – to come and kill the fiend. He travelled to

Eggeldorf, and they paid him in silver, in advance, to rid them of this curse. And one dark night the bold hero strapped on his full armour, and went alone into the deep forest in search of this cruel and terrible monster, his long, steel-tipped lance grasped tightly in his hand…'

Bjarki paused then and took a long, slow pull from his ale cup.

'What happened then?' Yoni was hanging on Bjarki's every word. *She really is quite pretty*, Tor thought. *But does she really need to make her eyes so big, so round, and to snuggle up quite so close to the storyteller?*

'The villagers of Eggeldorf heard the noise of a colossal battle taking place in the woods nearby, the clash of steel on claw, the angry roars of the creature, the screams of the brave *cabellarius*, such terrible screams…'

Bjarki took another unnecessary sip of his ale.

'And? Don't stop there!' Yoni seized Bjarki's large right bicep and squeezed it. *The bitch is utterly shameless*, thought Tor, *but then my oaf is quite oblivious to her interest in him, so maybe she needs to be that obvious*.

'The Aquitainian was never seen again. All that the villagers found next day were his boots, torn to shreds, drenched in his heart's blood.'

Bjarki revelled in the total silence that followed his tale. He smiled: 'And to this day, none in Eggeldorf dare to venture into the forest that surrounds them. And no one who wishes to live goes out of doors at night.'

The silence in the longhouse was absolute.

'They sound like a cowardly bunch of *nithings*,' said Tor. 'Pathetic.'

She found she was glaring at Yoni. The Hibernian girl saw her fierce look, released Bjarki's arm and moved away, further down the bench.

'They're just ordinary villagers,' said Bjarki, now feeling deflated. 'Not everyone is as fearless as you, Tor. And since when have *you* been a monster-slayer? Sensibly, they sent word to the king begging for his help.'

'I'd kill that monster soon as look at it,' she said. 'Is that where you heard this pack of nonsense? Sitting like a good dog at Karolus's knee?'

'It's all true. I heard a royal messenger read the Eggeldorf petition yesterday.' Bjarki was becoming irritated with his friend. Why was she being so unpleasant about a piece of after-supper fun – a nice scary tale.

'Well, if it is true, then let's do it.'

'Eh?'

'I said, if your monster is real, and these Egg-folk need help, let's do it. You and me, Bjarki; two warriors of Eresburg. We'll do this together.'

'What are you talking about, Tor?'

'Let's go to Thuringia, just the two of us, and kill us a monster.'

–

Bjarki, Tor and Captain Otto stood in a straight line at strict attention in front of the dais at the western end of the massive council hall of Aachen.

It was the first time that Bjarki had used his right as a member of the Auxilla to request an audience with the king since most of their other meetings had been informal, in the palace complex a few hundred paces away, and at Karolus's invitation. As he looked up at the stern figure on his massive throne, crowned in gold, clad in purple robes, surrounded by the soaring magnificence of the council hall, he wondered if he knew this great man at all. Karolus seemed so different to the homely fellow who had been amused by his rambling stories of Bago, the Dane-Mark and the Fyr Skola.

He had approached Lord Grimoald the morning after his recounting of the tale of the monster of Eggeldorf, visiting the bearded giant in his large brick house at the entrance of the compound. At first, the King's Shield had flatly refused his request. But Bjarki had insisted, and when Grimoald asked why he wished to see his royal master, Bjarki refused to tell him. It was his right, he repeated, granted to him by the king himself, after the fight in the amphitheatre, when he had first been sworn into the Auxilla.

Reluctantly Lord Grimoald had agreed and here Bjarki was, a day later, with Tor and Otto, standing stiffly before the world's most powerful man.

Father Livinus announced him formally – as if the king had never set eyes on him before – and there was yet another strangeness that Bjarki found deeply uncomfortable. The priest was no longer wearing the plain, undyed robes that for so long had seemed a part of his personality. He was clad in a series of robes even more gaudy than his war mantle – the bright raiment he had last seen on the Bishop of Aachen. He was even carrying the shepherd's crook of office, too, a long golden pole with an elaborately curled top piece.

'Bjarki Bloodhand, Trooper First-Class in His Majesty's Auxilla, craves a personal audience with you, sire,' boomed Father Livinus.

'He has it,' replied Karolus, in a frosty tone. 'Speak up, Bjarki, tell me what is in your mind. You've not come to tell another fairytale, have you?'

Bjarki was unsure how to begin. Tor and he had discussed the idea of travelling to Thuringia and killing the monster of Eggeldorf long into the night – and, while Bjarki had at first thought the idea fantastical, absurd, Tor had persuaded him that it would be an excellent way of winning renown. If they succeeded, every citizen in Francia and beyond would know their names.

'You want to be famous,' Bjarki had asked. 'Is *that* all it is?'

'No, oaf, it's not just that. Use your thick head, will you?'

Bjarki shook his head: he was still baffled.

The other occupants of the longhouse had all gone to bed, and Tor brought her head in very close to his. 'We wish to save our homelands, yes?' she whispered. 'We hope to overthrow this foul nation of Franks, with its silly religion, and to destroy the person of Karolus and all he stands for?'

Bjarki wasn't sure what he wanted. But he nodded along anyway.

'To do that, we must rise. We must rise until we are close to the seat of power. Close to the king himself. And the fame we will earn by killing this monster will ensure that we are folk of great renown and high regard throughout his realm. We will seek a promotion, perhaps even out of this ramshackle gang of incompetent boobies. Perhaps we might make officers in the *Scholares*. Senior officers. We could even one day perhaps replace old Grimoald as the King's Shield. As Karolus's personal bodyguards. Trusted absolutely. Just think what we could achieve if that were the case?'

'What could we achieve then?'

'Think!'

'Why should I? You seem to insist on doing my thinking for me.'

Tor glared at him.

'All right,' said Bjarki. 'We kill the monster of Eggeldorf, we rise through the ranks of the Black Cloaks; we get close to Karolus, and – what? – we cruelly murder him and all his family. Is that your bloodthirsty plan?'

'With one death we could cripple the whole of Francia. Almost all power resides in Karolus – you know that. He is the glue that binds it all together. With him dead – and his family – chaos results. We could preserve Saxony, the Dane-Mark, Svearland – *our world* – for a generation or more!'

Bjarki felt slightly sick at this stark outlining of Tor's brutal plan. But when Tor described it as saving their world, he felt he could hardly refuse.

'Your Majesty,' Bjarki said finally, speaking particularly loudly and clearly for the whole council hall to hear, 'we have heard tell of a terrible monster that is ravaging your eastern domains, in the vicinity of Eggeldorf, in the province of Thuringia. We come here today, my companions and I, with an offer of service. We would travel to Eggeldorf and destroy the fiend in Your Majesty's name, for your glory and the relief of your subjects.'

'You want to go to Thuringia?' said Karolus.

'We do, sire – to defeat the dread monster of Eggeldorf.'

'Have you ever been to Thuringia? Do you even know the way there?'

'Our brave commander, Captain Otto, here, has been there, sire, with your late father, many years ago. We also hoped you might furnish us with directions or even a map…'

Bjarki glanced at Captain Otto. Their brave commander looked utterly terrified. And Bjarki began to feel uneasy in himself. This was a silly plan.

Lord Grimoald, who had been standing behind the throne glowering at the three petitioners before the dais, stepped forward then. He leaned in and whispered in Karolus's right ear for what seemed an inordinately long time.

Grimoald will surely block it, thought Bjarki. *He must suspect us.*

When Lord Grimoald had finished speaking, Karolus beckoned Livinus to his side and another hushed conversation took place.

Finally, the king dismissed the priest.

He looked coldly at Bjarki and said: 'There is one thing I must insist on. I require an undertaking that you will return here, to Aachen, after you have encountered this creature. Do you now give such an undertaking?'

The three of them chorused their assent.

'In which case, your request is hereby granted,' said the king. 'Bishop Livinus's people will furnish you with a map, coin for your expenses, and whatever equipment and stores you may need. I also desire you to depart on your mission as soon as possible. Now… is there anything else?'

'No, sire,' said Bjarki. He was feeling dizzy with sudden relief.

'Yes, Your Majesty,' said Tor. 'Whatever happened to old Paulinus?'

It was Livinus who answered her: 'Father Paulinus has decided that his talents lie in another direction. He has taken up the simple life of a travelling apostle, a missionary, bringing the light of the

True Faith to the benighted heathen in Moravia. He will be gone for some years, alas, ministering to the savage pagan hordes. But our loss is surely a gain for the souls of Moravia.'

Chapter Twenty

A night to remember

They travelled by river. Firstly heading upstream, broadly southwards along the River Rhenus, being poled along in a flat-bottomed barge. The weather was inclement and a constant drizzle made sitting in the open barge a trial.

Bjarki shivered and snuggled further into his furs. His buttocks ached from sitting on the pine boards for so many hours, but he did not want to rise from what little warmth he had managed to gather in his wet furs and find some padding for his behind. Captain Otto had succumbed to a cold and was sweating and moaning in a swaddle of blankets in the cabin near the stern.

Tor was standing erect at the prow of the boat, clad in leather breeches, boots and jerkin and with a fine green woollen travelling cloak around her narrow shoulders, which along with new weapons – a good sword apiece and several hand axes, some money and a good deal of dry stores – had been provided by Livinus. She discovered that she never tired of watching the steeply wooded hills of Francia drift by on the eastern side of the barge.

To the south, beyond a range of hills, were the uplands of Swabia, one of the first provinces to have been conquered by the Franks and joined to their heartlands of Austrasia and Neustria more than two hundred years ago.

It was the third day of travel and her mood had steadily improved since they had left the confines of the longhouse and the city of Aachen. She was now almost joyful and relished the feeling of motion, even at the snail's pace produced by the two powerful pole-men, heaving away at either ends of the narrow barge. She couldn't contain a swelling sense of escape from danger combined with the pleasurable promise of novelty and fresh adventures ahead.

Bjarki was not nearly so content. He was bored and uncomfortable. He was also perturbed by the sudden change in attitude in Karolus. The king, once so open and friendly, had seemed cold and distant at the audience in the council hall and had not summoned Bjarki for a farewell conversation, nor sent him any kind of message of encouragement, before their departure. The great man was doubtless very busy ruling the world, of course, but Bjarki could not help but feel that he had been slighted. Summarily dismissed.

On the morning of the fourth day, Captain Otto threw off his head cold and his warm sleeping blankets, rose before dawn and tried to persuade Bjarki and Tor to join him in his morning devotions. Tor refused abruptly.

'We shall all need the help of Almighty God in the task before us,' said Otto. 'And the danger of death is not inconsiderable. It would be better for us to be at peace with our Heavenly Father, I would think, just in case...'

Bjarki demurred. He still did not entirely understand this strange new Christian religion. But it seemed to him that he would rather have hammer-wielding Thor on his side in a fight with a monster, or battle-wise Odin, than the new god he had been introduced to so recently. The stories he had heard about Jesus seemed to be about avoiding violence, turning the other cheek.

But he was curious, and he did not wish to offend the little man, so he sat quietly next to Otto as the captain knelt on the gunwale lifted his voice in prayer. '*Pater noster*,' chanted Otto as the red lip of the sun peeked over the distant mountains, '*qui es in caelis, sanctificetur nomen tuum*...'

When he had finished his prayers, Bjarki watched Captain Otto closely. The man seemed serene as he washed his hands and face and went into the small cabin aft to have his breakfast. Otto even seemed to have a soft inner glow about him that reminded Bjarki of the Mikelgothi praying in the Groves.

–

It took them five long, boring days to reach the top of the River Rhenus, whereupon the three of them hired a mule at the Frankish town of Strasburg, packed up their gear, and set off across high country on rough muddy tracks, heading southeast for the village of Esginga, high in the hills that loomed above them. Esginga was on one of the headwaters of the mighty Donau – the very long river that would take them all the way east to Regensburg.

Three days of brisk walking in the fresh mountain air, beside the over-laden mule, appeared to be a tonic for Otto, who seemed filled with cheerful energy and regaled them with many tales of the royal progress he'd taken part in under Pepin the Short as a youthful new recruit to the Auxilla.

'It was a very different *scara*, back in those days,' he said as they laboured up a steep zig-zagging stretch of rough road; the blue sky crowned by snowy peaks far to the south. 'Truly elite. Captain Marcellus was in charge then, and he was a right tartar. He's a count in eastern Neustria now, of course, and an old man. But he was a fearsome fellow when I first joined the Auxilla. And we had over a hundred troopers on the strength then. Parade every morning at dawn, and God help you if you weren't as neat as a pin, with your arms and armour polished and shining like a mirror.'

Apparently unaware of the damning comparison he was drawing with the condition of his own Auxilla, Captain Otto continued: 'And the progress itself was a sight to see. The king took five whole *scarae* with him on the march – fifteen hundred men, not counting the Auxilla – four *scarae* of Red Cloaks, and one of his black-cloaked *Scholares*. It was a show of strength, you see, he was showing the provinces that he was a man to be respected, even feared – that's always the problem for Frankish kings, the far-flung territories get ideas above their station, start thinking they could do much better on their own. And in those days, Thuringia was only half-pacified, a new acquisition, the western part wrested only a few months earlier from the Moravian clans after several hard-fought battles on the marches. That's why Pepin brought so many men with him. To overawe the rebellious locals.'

'How many men does he have in total,' asked Bjarki. 'Does anyone know?'

'Of course someone knows. The king's chancellor is responsible for every soldier in the army, the clerks of the royal household under him arrange pay and rations for the whole lot, and keep records for every single trooper. There are twenty-eight *scarae* in all – but only a few of them are in Aachen, most are scattered in garrisons all across Francia from Aquitaine to Thuringia, from the warm vineyards of Gascony to chilly shores of Frisia. And, apart from the king's *scarae*, every vassal, every duke, bishop and count must bring his liegemen when the *bannum* is called. Every year there is a great muster – the Marchfeld. Karolus can call on thousands of fighting men from all his many territories, if he chooses. And he's going to need an awful lot of them in the spring – or whenever he chooses to take on the armies of the powerful Lombard princes on the other side of those Alps.

Otto waved vaguely at the impossibly white peaks to their south.

'In total, His Majesty has nearly a hundred thousand men he can call on – and that doesn't count all the clerks and servants and dog's bodies who toil daily in the palaces, in the cities and in smaller local towns. You might bear that in mind, Bjarki, if you wonder why the king has so little time for *you*!'

Bjarki was beginning to wish he had kept his mouth shut about his feelings of neglect. The numbers were staggering – a hundred thousand Red Cloaks! The full strength of the North, if every man and woman capable of bearing arms could somehow be mustered, was no more than one tenth of that. What were he and Tor thinking to challenge such impossible might?

–

At Esginga, they engaged the services of a striking river-captain called Master Bohemus, a strapping fellow whose antecedents came to Francia from Libya, with gleaming dark eyes, skin like old leather and a voice that could be heard across the grey waters of the Donau in a thunderstorm. A day later, they found themselves scooting down the wide river in his twenty-foot, clinker-built dragon-ship, the one big square sail drum-taut above them.

Bjarki and Tor conferred under Master Bohemus's striped awning in the evening after a fine supper of pork stew with bread and fresh butter.

'In your opinion, Master Bohemus, how long will it take us to get to Regensburg?' asked Tor. She seemed to have taken a liking to the dark boat captain and was treating him with, for her, an unprecedented level of respect.

'In this wind? And barring fuck-ups? Three days, maybe less.'

Tor exchanged a glance with Bjarki. This was good news. Captain Otto was already fast asleep on a pile of old sailcloth beside the steering oar.

'Whisper is you're hunting the monster of Eggeldorf,' said Bohemus.

'How do you know that?' Bjarki was astonished.

'Word travels fast on water. Two bold heroes from the North, they said. Folk of unusual powers, they said. *Wizards*, not to put too fine a point on it. You don't look much like wizards, to my eye, meaning no offence.'

'We're not wizards,' said Tor. 'Just ordinary folk with a bit of steel in our spines. That's all. We aim to make a name for ourselves.'

'I tug my lock to you, nevertheless,' said Bohemus. 'That Eggeldorf creature, whatever it is, has the whole o' the Donau talking, and the stories get wilder and wilder. Some folk say it can fly. Though that's news to me.'

'You've seen it?' Tor sat up straight on her stool. 'You saw the fiend?'

'Not I. My cousin Jubal down in Regensburg, he claims he saw it once on the bank, eyes glowing like flame, fangs of steel. Not flying, though.'

Tor subsided a little. 'What did your kinsman say it looked like?'

'It was dusk, my cousin said, and all he could make out was a huge black shape, vast, bigger than a small house, and the eyes, glowing like coals in the gloom, and it was feeding on something by the river, a dead body of some kind. It gave a mighty roar when he saw Jubal in his little skiff; my cousin said it shook the Heavens themselves. He just put his craft about and skedaddled for the middle of the stream. The creature didn't care to swim after him, or so it seems. It didn't attempt to fly after him neither.'

Bjarki gave Tor a slightly nervous look. 'So it can't fly,' she said, nodding. 'That's good. Then it won't be able to escape from us too easily.'

Regensburg, when they arrived there on the afternoon of the third day, was something of an anticlimax. Otto had informed them that it was the easternmost city of Francia, perched on the northern lip of the independent Duchy of Bavaria, which was ruled by Duke Tassilo, an old ally of Karolus.

Tor remembered Father Livinus telling her that it boasted a royal palace. When they disembarked at the dock on the south side of the river Donau, and bid goodbye to cheery Master Bohemus, Tor craned her neck to look for something as magnificent as Aachen's council hall and palace complex.

She was disappointed. The walled heart of Regensburg was only about twice the size of the *castrum* they had fought at in Thursby six months before. A square fortress of sharpened pine logs with high guard towers at the corners and a massive stone building in the centre of its courtyard with a great circular window made of coloured glass high up on the eastern walls.

Admittedly, the *castrum* or palace or fortress or whatever it was looked like a tough bastion to conquer if the Moravian hordes ever came spilling out of the surrounding forests to attack them.

But it was nothing compared to the beauty of Aachen. This was the edge of Karolus's realm, Tor realised; the frontier, with all the roughness, dirt and danger that the word entailed.

Around the square fortress walls of the so-called palace, the town of Regensburg sprawled outwards along the southern bank of the Donau, on either side of a stone bridge that crossed its wide grey waters and carried a road north, deep into the forests of Thuringia. Eggeldorf and its monster lay about a dozen miles up that unpaved road.

The town was low, squalid, cold and unwelcoming. As they humped their belongings off Bohemus's craft and on to the slimy wooden quay, predatory eyes watched them intently. A gang of four tough-looking young men in plain tunics, with cropped hair, and all with daggers at their belts, watched them pile their belongings on the platform, occasionally murmuring among themselves but never taking their eyes off the labouring newcomers.

Tor bristled at their unabashed staring.

She dumped the bundle of heavy hunting spears she had been carrying on the wooden deck, loosened the seax in its sheath on her belt, squared her shoulders and… suddenly found Bjarki standing foursquare in her path.

'They're doing us no harm,' he said. 'Just looking. But, if you like, I'll go over to them, have a little chat and see if I can find out what they want.'

Bjarki turned and ambled over to the men, a friendly smile on his face.

'Hail, good citizens,' he said. 'We are strangers in this country, new-come to your beautiful town. We mean no disrespect but how would you like to earn a coin? We seek accommodation, if you can recommend a good place – clean, inexpensive – and help in carrying our baggage there.'

The four men looked at Bjarki, looked at the sheer size of him, and at Tor who was standing slightly behind him, leaning on a hunting spear. One of them muttered something unintelligible and all four of them peeled away, slouching off down the road, only one man casting a backward glance at the two figures, one slender, one huge, silhouetted against the river on the quay.

'They seemed *very* nice,' said Tor. 'I wonder if all the folk hereabouts are as welcoming.'

Although they had letters of introduction that would allow them to demand accommodation inside the walls of the Regensburg fortress, Tor had argued that they should not alert the authorities to their presence in this grim frontier town until they had accomplished their mission. Tor feared that if they engaged with the local commander, he might forbid them to go after the monster of Eggeldorf or, worse, send large numbers of troops to accompany them when they went off to kill the creature and so dilute their glory.

If they were to make a name for themselves, she said, they had to do this alone. There would be plenty of time to feast and drink and accept the admiration of the Regensburg garrison after the matter had been settled satisfactorily. Bjarki agreed with her logic – fewer fighters, more glory – although he privately thought that having a company of heavily armed Red Cloaks to back them up against this foul fiend would not be all that terrible.

Captain Otto, however, was utterly bewildered by their refusal to enter the high walls of Frankish officialdom.

'We are on a mission for the king himself,' he said. 'We would be treated with honour. Why choose, instead, to spend the night in this hole?'

The Red Hart was indeed a hole. To be precise, a shit-hole.

Bjarki had parted with three silver pennies and secured the top room of this ramshackle two-storey inn a hundred yards south of the river, a stone's throw to the west of the fortress. For that steep price, the landlord also promised to include supper and plenty of freshly brewed ale.

The room they were given smelled strongly of urine, which seemed to be mostly coming from the one huge straw-filled mattress that occupied almost all of the tiny space. One of the previous occupants, Captain Otto observed with a chuckle, seemed to have suffered badly from incontinence.

'I wouldn't say *suffered* from,' replied Tor, wrinkling her pretty nose. 'More like *revelled* in.'

They leaned the soggy mattress up against the wall to dry and decided to bed down after supper on the wooden floor. They had enough blankets and furs with them to take the worst of the sting out of the bare boards.

'We all need to get used to sleeping on the hard ground anyway,' said Otto piously. 'There won't be any comfy beds in the deep forest!'

They trooped down the stairs a little while later to the large, smoky, low-ceilinged common room, where a fire was burning in the long central hearth trough. The room held several small tables with stools, one long communal table with long benches, and a wooden counter across one side of the room behind which a beefy maiden bustled with foaming jugs and horns of sweet freshly brewed ale. Tor led them to a table at the back of the room.

The food the landlord brought them was predictably foul – cold, greasy sausages that seemed to be mainly composed of gristle, long-boiled cabbage that smelled like a midden, a loaf of stone-hard bread. But the ale was good.

They ate joylessly, finishing the ale jug quickly and calling for another.

It was a little after sunset and the inn began to fill with folk who had completed their days' labour and were seeking food and drink before bed.

Tor watched the door idly as it banged open again and again, admitting a gust of rain and wind and the latest weary Regensburger looking for his supper. The customers took their places at tables in the large room and called for the pot boy to bring them sustenance, or stood by the long, wooden counter that ran across the right-hand side of the common room.

One of the men who came in caught her eye. He was middle-sized, with cropped dark hair, and a plain tunic and cloak. His boots, she noted, were heavy and well worn. He was one of the men who had watched them unload their belongings on the quay.

He came into the common room, went up to the counter but instead of ordering ale or meat, he turned his back on the server behind the wooden shelf and casually surveyed the whole room.

The man's eye ran over the trio sitting at the table at the back; stopped, came back to look at them again, and hurriedly moved on again. It was reasonably well done, but not well enough. Tor immediately knew this fellow had been looking for them, had found them and then tried to disguise his interest. The man did not order anything from the counter; he waited a few moments, then shoved off the bar and headed back out of the door.

Tor's hand went to the handle of the seax she always wore across her lower belly. Bjarki had a decent blade, too. Otto had only an eating knife.

She slipped off her stool.

'I'm just going to fetch something from the room,' she murmured.

When she came back a few moments later she was carrying a heavy bundle wrapped in a blanket. She sat down at the table, putting the clanking cloth package on a stool beside her left knee. She saw that the man she had spotted before was back, sipping a small horn of ale at the counter and, so it seemed to her, deliberately not looking in their direction.

She looked about the room – there at the long communal table were two more of the men who had watched them on the quay. There were several dozen inns in Regensburg, Tor reasoned; this could not be a coincidence.

'Captain Otto, I'd like your opinion, as an experienced military man, of this fine old sword,' she said, passing a sheathed blade over the table to him.

'And perhaps you, Bjarki, might like to give me your opinion of this bearded axe. I chose it from the Aachen armoury but I am not so sure it will serve. Would it be a suitable tool for tackling our monster, do you think?'

'What are you doing?' Bjarki said.

'It's a fine old blade,' said Otto, who had unsheathed the long sword.

Tor watched the room, looking between the bodies of her companions, who had their backs to the common area. She saw the first man, the one with the dark hair, talking to the landlord. A purse was passed. She saw the innkeeper speak to the beefy girl who served the ale, who argued briefly and then began to angrily take off her ale-wet apron. He signalled the pot boy too, and the lad grinned and slipped into the back of the inn. The landlord then began moving along the counter to speak to his other customers. He spoke to an old man who quickly drained his horn and hurried for the door.

'Looks like we're going to have to sing for our supper, oaf,' said Tor.

Bjarki turned around slowly and cast his eye over the tavern. Men and women were all leaving the common room. The space was rapidly emptying. He turned back and reached for the handle of the bearded axe.

'I don't understand why they can't just leave us alone,' he said.

'Where would be the fun in that?' said Tor.

'I wanted to have a nice quiet evening and a good night's sleep.'

'Ah, well,' said Tor, 'you know what they say about Regensburg.'

'What do they say?'

'They say there's never a dull moment in this town.'

'Who says that? You've never met anyone from Regensburg before.'

'Nobody says it,' said Tor, 'it's just a… oh, never mind.'

'I think this sword dates right back to the time of the mayors,' said Captain Otto. 'It's a fascinating piece, you see this faint patterning here—'

Bjarki stood up, turned round and faced the room, the bearded axe held loosely, low in his right hand. There were only twelve customers in the room now – all fairly similar in appearance; fit young men, hair snipped short, good, solid boots. They looked like soldiers to Bjarki, but out of uniform. Experienced, confident men. A squad of Black Cloaks, maybe, incognito.

‘It would be a lot healthier for all of us if you just left now,’ Bjarki said loudly. ‘Whatever you boys are being paid, it’s not enough to die for. Why not go home, leave us be. Simply say you couldn’t find us. How about it?’

‘That’s not going to happen, Beast-man,’ said one of the older-looking men at the communal table. An officer, perhaps. He stood up, swept aside his short cloak and pulled a thick stabbing sword from the sheath on his belt.

Tor, still seated at the table, peered round Bjarki’s bulk at the standing man. She lifted a light throwing axe from the stool next to her and threw it hard, laterally. The axe spun across the room and thunked into the officer’s ribs.

Mayhem.

The gang rushed them, all at the same time. Bjarki swung and sank his bearded axe into the cropped head of the quickest man, as he leapt towards him, snarling, with a pair of daggers in his hands. The man gurgled, coughed, dropped his blades and folded at the knees. The axe, stuck vice-like in his skull, was tugged from Bjarki’s grip.

He saw another attacker coming at him, chopping with a long, curved sword. Bjarki ducked the blow at the very last moment, and the sword smashed into the table, dashing splinters everywhere. Captain Otto gave a wail of surprise and dived under the nearest bench, chased by a thin ginger fellow with a sword, who stabbed downward at the Auxilla commander through the wooden slats. Jabbing, jabbing, as Otto dodged and squealed.

Tor hurled another hand-axe, which whirred through the air and embedded itself into the shoulder of a charging man, knocking him to the side. She leapt over the table to join the melee; her seax in her right hand, another axe in her left. She buried the seax fist-deep in one man’s stomach, and knocked teeth out of another’s jaw with a backswing of the axe’s butt.

Someone barged heavily into Bjarki’s side just as he was trying to draw his seax, and the blade flew out of his hand and clattered across the floor.

He turned, saw a fellow behind him about to strike; blocked the knife stroke, his left forearm sweeping out and thumping against the man's grip on the hilt. Then Bjarki punched him full in the face – with everything he had.

The man flew up, back and crashed down on to another table, smashing it to kindling. Bjarki looked around wildly for a weapon; someone swung a sword at his face, he ducked, seized the empty sword-sheath from their table, swung and crunched it into his attacker's screaming mouth, mashing his lips, knocking him to the floor and snapping the wooden sheath in the process.

Tor was fighting like a whirlwind, laying out men left and right, her blades flying, blood droplets looping in the air and splattering on the ground. Captain Otto was dodging round a small table now, feinting left and running right, still being pursued by the same furious, flame-haired attacker, who was now *ordering* him to stand and fight.

Bjarki took two steps forward and seized the nine-foot-long bench that lay alongside the big communal table. He picked it up by one end, using both huge hands and all his considerable strength and, using it like a massive club, he whacked the angry redhead who was pursuing Otto across his chest, crushing his ribs. The ginger fellow was bowled two strides clear across the room before he crashed into a wall, and slumped in a heap.

Bjarki went on the attack then. He swung that bench like an enormous club, swatting his attackers this way and that, battering down men before they could get close enough to him to strike with their swords or daggers, swinging the heavy wooden seat in wide, lethal arcs, sweeping the room, left and right, and occasionally surging forward and lunging like a swordsman, and smashing the blunt end of the bench into this man's face or that one's body. In one fortuitous swing, he knocked three men over at the same time. One fellow, one of the few remaining attackers now on his feet, came howling at Bjarki, swinging a pair of long swords. The man ducked Bjarki's first swipe, bobbed up and threw himself at the northerner. But Bjarki reversed the swing of the cumbersome bench; flicking it the other way, he smashed the fellow in the shoulder, breaking bone with a loud crack.

The attackers knew they had lost then. And some of them, battered, bruised, bleeding, but able to limp, were already heading for the inn door.

'Kill them all!' shrieked Captain Otto. He had found his antique sword again and, apparently, his courage. 'Kill every mother-fucking one of them.'

A broken man, sitting on the filthy floor, his half-crushed torso propped against a shattered table – one of the men crippled by Bjarki's swinging bench – got the first taste of the good captain's righteous wrath. Otto carved his sword down on his half-conscious head, burying the blade deep in his skull.

Tor hurled her last hand axe at a fellow, right in the doorway, the man in the very act of leaving, and buried the spinning blade in his side. With a yell of outrage, and a glare that would have curdled spring water, the man plucked the axe out from between his own ribs, tossed the gory item to the floor and, quick as an eel, slipped out the door, which banged behind him.

Bjarki dropped the bench with a long, reverberating clatter. He felt suddenly sick and weak. He had fought, yes, and he had won, but once again his *gandr* had not come into him. What Lord Grimoald had said to him in the street was undoubtedly true. He was no Rekkr. And he never would be.

'Is everybody all right?' he said at last. He could see that Captain Otto had blood streaking down his right leg. And then looked down at his own left arm, which had a bloody gash in the meat beneath the elbow. He had no recollection of receiving the wound at all. Now he saw it, it began to burn.

'I killed him, Rekkr, did you see me? I killed this bastard here!'

Bjarki looked into the excited face of Otto, and then down at the split-open head of the man on the floor, his brains a bloody porridge in his lap.

'Don't call me that, Captain. Don't *ever* call me that again,' he said.

Chapter Twenty-one

The never-ending forest

They departed before dawn, leaving the landlord of the Hart in considerable pain and a state of abject terror. Tor had started crushing his knuckles with the steel pommel of her sword, one by one, till the man told them all he knew; Bjarki held the man still, and Tor asked her question. When he didn't answer, she whacked down her heavy sword hilt on the offending digit. Sometimes she smashed his finger, then asked the question, just for variety.

When he had told all he knew, she crushed a few more of his fingers as a punishment for betraying his guests – an unforgiveable crime in her view. He was lucky. She had wanted to cut his throat, but Bjarki had restrained her.

The landlord had, in fact, known very little of use. The dozen men who had attacked them were off-duty Black Cloaks, as Bjarki suspected. They had been tasked with killing Bjarki and Tor under the fig-leaf excuse of a drunken tavern fight. The men were all part of the same elite *Scholares* unit – Third *Scara* (Austrasia), Fifth *Cunei*. One of the few surviving soldiers confirmed this intelligence before Captain Otto eagerly slashed his throat wide open. The fifty Black Cloaks of the Fifth *Cunei*, and another fifty men of the Sixth *Cunei*, were housed in the Regensburg fortress as part of the five-hundred-strong garrison there. The orders had come from on high, higher even than the Governor of Regensburg, but neither the wounded soldier nor the landlord knew where exactly. The Fifth *Cunei* had searched most of the town that evening before finally locating them in the Red Hart.

'We made it harder for them by staying away from the fortress,' said Bjarki. 'If we'd stayed there we would have been murdered in our beds.'

He and Tor looked at Otto. 'Do you think the king has taken against you now?' the captain said. 'You think Karolus ordered your deaths?'

'Doesn't make any sense,' said Bjarki. 'Why send us off to the edge of Francia only to dispatch us by assassins here. He could have ordered our deaths in Aachen. Or thrown us back into the cells under the amphitheatre.'

They did not tarry long in the Red Hart.

They dressed swiftly in their best war gear – Bjarki donning boots and greaves, and iron-reinforced leather vambraces on his brawny forearms. He wore a padded linen shirt and over that a long mail hauberk that covered his body to his elbows and knees. He chose a solid steel helmet with a nasal guard and cheek pieces, heavy leather gauntlets, a good round shield, and a long sword. Tor and Captain Otto also dressed for a full-pitched battle, then Tor slung a small bag of provisions over her shoulder, and a skin of ale, and they each took one heavy hunting spear. They reluctantly abandoned the rest of their gear. They locked the landlord, weeping over his ruined hands, in his own cellar and left the inn.

It was still pitch dark when they pulled the door shut behind them and cautiously emerged into the quiet, foul-smelling back streets of Regensburg. It was cold, too. An hour or so before the town's curfew would end, Tor reckoned, and the city gate opened. As they trudged through the slush of the narrow street, heading north towards the river, feathery flakes began to fall.

They knew they would soon become hunted. They had killed half a dozen Black Cloaks and they would not be forgiven for that. Bjarki's biggest fear, which he did not express aloud, was that the few men who had escaped the Red Hart, battered and bruised, would return to the fortress and rouse an army of their comrades to come and finish the job.

Their best plan, so it seemed to both Tor and Bjarki, was to complete their mission: go to Eggeldorf and slay this terrible monster. They would be heroes if they could accomplish that, acclaimed by all frightened civilians in Regensburg and the surrounding areas – in all Francia, in fact – and it would then be more difficult for whoever it was that wished them ill to arrest them or have them executed. Or murdered in their beds, for that matter.

They would kill the dread creature, then immediately seek out Master Bohemus for a speedy return back up the Donau and on to the route back to Aachen. Once back in the capital, the deaths of a handful of out-of-uniform soldiers in a faraway place could be denied; it would seem less important, anyway, compared with the victory of these heroes over a terrible monster.

There was no record of them being in Regensburg, after all. They had not registered at the fortress and, with a bit of luck, the landlord would be too scared to talk. It was the only thing to do. Kill the monster and go home. The alternative – to march up to the fortress and voice their indignation at the attack, seemed suicidal. And going back to Aachen without even *seeing* the beast they had come all this way to slay would make them ridiculous.

So, as the sky in the east turned grey, the three would-be monster-killers found themselves shivering in the shuttered front of a blacksmith's forge – the wide door was bolted but there was some heat seeping out from the banked fires inside – stamping their feet, their breath pluming like smoke in the air, and watching the scales of snow fall in ever thickening veils.

Thirty yards from the blacksmith's door, across the empty street, was the fortified gate in the Regensburg town walls, which led directly to the great stone bridge over the River Donau. Tor could make out a couple of steel-capped sentries on the wall beside the gatehouse, huddled in their heavy cloaks, around the cosy glow of a brazier. As far as she could tell, no hue and cry had been raised. There was no activity on the walls. No noise in the streets of the town. She craned her neck around and looked east for the hundredth time. Was it getting lighter?

After a dozen years, or so it felt to Tor, one of the sentries got slowly to his feet and disappeared from the wall. A year or two later, there was a terrible grinding and creaking noise and the huge wooden gate began to creep open. 'About bloody time,' muttered Tor, and, shouldering her spear and slinging her pack, she stepped out into the snow-crusted street.

-

They walked in a silent grey mist of fat whirling flakes and a cloud of their own dragon's breath. On either side of the road the forest edge was a dull impenetrable wall. Somewhere in there, in the endless wilderness of black tree trunks and snow, was the monster of Eggeldorf. Was it prowling around, even now, seeking fresh man-flesh to gorge on?

Unlikely, thought Tor. If the creature had an ounce of common sense it would have found a snug hollow tree to bed down in, or a dry cave, where it could sleep through the storm, only waking when it was hungry. She wished now she hadn't thought about sleep… or hunger for that matter.

Neither Bjarki nor Otto had yet made any complaint – and she had been initially pleased to get out of Regensburg and across the bridge without being challenged, they were simply waved through the gate by the sleepy guards – but after walking for several hours in the freezing, blinding cold, their boots slipping and stumbling on the frozen ruts and ridges of the track through the thick woods, Tor was thinking more and more in terms of snug hollows and large hot meals. They had not slept the night before, of course, nor eaten very much. But she wouldn't allow herself to be first to call a halt.

'We should stop soon,' said Bjarki, 'and rest, and eat something. Do we know how far it is to Eggeldorf?'

He had to bellow his words through the whistle and howl of the wind, putting his hooded face right up close to his two companions.

'According to the map, there is a fork in the road just a mile or so up ahead,' yelled Captain Otto. 'We take the left-hand fork and then it's about three or four miles from there to Eggeldorf.'

'Then let's rest now and eat. And we will do the last part later.'

'We should push on,' said Tor. 'The days are short and we need to be in Eggeldorf before it gets dark. It will be night in a few hours. I say we push on.' Even as she said it, she regretted her words. *Bjarki will insist we take a rest*, she thought. *Captain Otto will refuse to go on.*

But they did not.

'Makes sense,' yelled Bjarki. 'But chew on this as you walk. If we push it, we could be there in an hour or two.' He handed his companions thin sticks of dried venison, tough as leather, but nourishing nonetheless.

'Can you hear something?' said Captain Otto, a little while later. 'Sounds a bit like someone rattling a drum.'

Bjarki and Tor both pushed back the hoods of their cloaks and listened.

'Horses?' said Tor.

'Get into the trees, now!' bellowed Bjarki.

They raced towards the wood to the right of the track, sliding and slithering on the icy road, and dived into the cover of the trees, taking refuge behind a heavy fallen log about ten paces beyond the tree line.

The scuff marks made by their running feet were clear to see in the virgin snow, and Tor wondered about trying to disguise them somehow, perhaps brushing them away with a tree branch. But there was no time.

The drumming noise was growing louder and louder, even over the whistle of the storm. In a matter of moments, they saw horsemen, perhaps thirty of them, wrapped tight in black cloaks, scale-mail just visible, and pinched faces raw under their ridged helmets, cantering past in a clatter, jingle and great cloud of breath-steam.

Then they were gone.

They waited a while until the rattle of the iron-shod hooves on the rock-hard track had faded into nothing, then very cautiously they emerged again on to the road. The horsemen had been completely swallowed by the grey of the storm. As if they had never been there. But for the hundreds of hoof-marks pitting the snow on the track, each one now filling with fresh flakes, Tor might have imagined the episode.

'*Scholares*,' she said. 'On our scent from the Red Hart.'

They proceeded with a great deal more caution from then on, walking up the edge of the road, close to the trees, ready at any moment to flee for safety into the vast trackless forest beside them.

Before very long they came to the fork in the road.

The left-hand fork was the larger of the two; the road that according to the crude leather map supplied by Bishop Livinus led to the village of Eggeldorf. Tor peered down the track, straining to see through the swirl of snowflakes, her eyes streaming with the icy wind. She thought she could see a glow of fire, red-yellow, just a prick of light at the very limit of her vision, and a dark line across the road.

'I think they are just ahead, waiting for us. I can see a light,' she said.

'Could that be Eggeldorf?' asked Bjarki.

'No, it's a fair few miles yet to the village,' said Otto.

'So… they are waiting for us,' said Bjarki. 'Blocking the road.'

'And there are probably some more of the bastards, Red Cloak infantry coming up more slowly on foot behind us,' Tor said.

Tor and Bjarki exchanged a glance. Captain Otto said: 'What then shall we do? Could we surrender? At least they'd give us something hot to eat.'

'We'll have to go round them,' said Tor. 'Once we get to Eggeldorf we can pay someone to hide us. We've plenty of coin. Or we could find a remote shed, or a barn to shelter in. If we stay out in this tonight, we won't enjoy it.'

'Come on then,' said Bjarki cheerily. 'The sooner we start, the sooner we'll be in Eggeldorf, and somewhere warm. Just three or four miles, you said, Otto, yes? We can make it before nightfall if we step out just a little.'

Bjarki began striding away into the grey blustering weather, up the smaller right-hand fork. His two companions reluctantly started after him.

-

Bjarki was cold, wet and completely exhausted. His hunger seemed to have passed but he could no longer feel his toes even inside the boots and woollen hose he wore. Worse, it was getting dark and they were, he knew, lost.

Perhaps the map was faulty – this was the back of beyond, after all, the very edge of Francia, where cartographers were thin on the ground – or they had taken a wrong turn somewhere in the storm. It was pitch dark now, and he spent most of his energy trying to avoid walking into trees looming in the darkness, and not always successfully. He had a lump on his forehead and his face had been scratched by branches. When exactly the sun had gone down was a mystery in the gloom of the forest; it must have been hours ago.

They had walked a mile, fifteen hundred of his counted paces, up the track on the right-hand fork, which had grown progressively narrower and more overgrown as they followed it. Then they had turned left, exactly a half turn, and plunged into the snowy forest aiming to hit the road behind the Black Cloaks' roadblock and continue into Eggeldorf via that easier route. But whatever happened, whether the map was off, or they had miscalculated, they were now stumbling in freezing darkness through untamed wilderness.

'That's it,' he said, turning to the two huddled forms behind him. 'We have to stop for the night. We could walk past Eggeldorf and never know it.'

Neither of them disagreed.

Bjarki was no stranger to sleeping out in the snow; he had done so on hunting trips with Ubbi, and he was reasonably certain he could keep them all alive for the night. He began by clearing a small area of snow under a tree, scraping the snow into low walls in a rough circle, then building up the walls with the fall from around the growing shelter. Once he had cleared most of the forest floor he was relieved to find dry-ish sticks, branches and leaf litter, and in a few moments he had a flame kindled and a fire going, with a cooking pot packed with snow suspended over the crackling flames.

'Aren't you worried about the enemy seeing the flames?' Otto said.

'If we don't have a fire we're probably going to freeze to death,' said Tor. 'If we have a blaze and the Black Cloaks see it, at least we die warm.'

They managed to get the pot to boil and made a sort of weak venison stew from scrapings of the dried meat and some stores from Tor's pack. It was watery fare but at least it was hot, and when everyone had got down a good cupful, the three of them lay down next to the fire, pressed close together and covered with all their blankets, cloaks, furs and spare clothes. For the first time that day, Tor felt her bones begin to thaw.

They lay in silence for a few minutes, but Tor was oddly wakeful.

'You know where we are, oaf,' she said. She was snuggled right into the comforting bulk of Bjarki's back, with Captain Otto pressed into hers.

'We're lost, Tor. Of course I don't know where we are.'

'I do. I know. We're in the First Forest,' she said.

Bjarki thought about this. Or perhaps he had already fallen asleep.

Tor continued, murmuring the words quietly: 'This is the same ancient forest that we travelled through with Valtyr, one year ago next month. This vast woodland stretches right across the world, east to west, and it contains the Irminsul, and the Fyr Skola, and the Lodges… and all that we love. Hundreds of miles to the west of here, perhaps a thousand miles – I don't know how far – there are boys and girls from the Groves who are out Voyaging, alone in the First Forest, and frightened, with nothing but a scrap of fur to keep them warm. They want nothing more than to discover their own *gandr* in these woods, to become Rekkr. And here *we* are, as well…'

At which point, still awaiting a reply from Bjarki, she, too, fell asleep.

Chapter Twenty-two

The Beast awakens

The storm passed in the night and the sky cleared to a magnificent blue with the dawn. Even so, when the three travellers awoke and climbed out of their snow-encrusted blankets, somewhat dazzled by the sunlight filtering through the trees, they could feel that the temperature had dropped significantly.

They broke their fasts with dried venison sticks, oatcakes and half frozen ale from Tor's water-skin. Then, shivering, teeth chattering, they packed up their little camp with as much speed as they could generate.

The trees marched off around them in all directions, their trunks closely packed. There was no sign of any path or track. The snow lay like a smooth, crisp, blanket over the whole earth, untouched by any living thing. Bjarki looked at the shadows the sun cast from the trees, he walked around the trunks looking at patterns of moss, and at which side it grew. Then he said, 'I think we go this way,' sticking out his arm to the west.

'Since we are hopelessly lost, does it matter which way we go?'

Captain Otto had not had a good night. Apparently Tor had thrashed and turned wildly in some sort of sweaty nightmare, and kicked him several times painfully in the shins, each time as he was just getting to sleep. He was not in a pleasant mood.

Bjarki said patiently, 'The Eggeldorf road is west of the smaller track we took last night. So we should head west. Unless you have a better idea?'

Captain Otto merely grumbled inaudibly to himself and hefted his pack.

'Well, then, let's get on…' And Bjarki turned and began to forge his way through the heavy snow drifts, in the direction he believed to be west.

It was very hard going. The snow was as deep as Tor's waist in some places and, although she tried to tread in Bjarki and Otto's footsteps, she could feel her strength and energy draining away with every laboured stride.

The ground began to rise and became rockier, the trees appearing to grow sparser, with wider gaps between the trunks and less tangling undergrowth. They found they had to negotiate huge round boulders, as well as smaller ones covered in snow that turned dangerously under their boots.

On a brief rest, to gulp down a mouthful of ale and an oatcake, Bjarki said: 'I aim to get us to the top of this hill, then maybe we will be able to see something from there. Even a tiny village should be visible from a decent height. There'll be hearth smoke, of course, which we must be able to see.'

Neither Tor not Captain Otto offered any comment; they leaned on their spears, tried to steady their breathing and swallowed down their oats and ale.

An hour later, with the white summit of the hill still a fair distance away, they came into a natural hollow in the hillside, a clearing with a wide apron of snow-shrouded turf between walls of silver birch, and saw at the far end, half covered by a curtain of ice-crusted greenery, the dark mouth of a large cave that appeared to burrow horizontally straight into the rocky hillside.

Tor stopped and pressed a fist into the small of her aching back. 'It might be useful to remember the location of this place,' she said, 'particularly if we have to spend another freezing night out in the wild.'

'I say we stop here now – and make this place our camp,' said Captain Otto, his face drawn with tiredness. 'We can make a fire, cook some food, scout out a path to Eggeldorf from here. One of us could climb to the top.'

Bjarki looked up at the sun, it was only a little after noon. But he was very tempted. At least they would be warm tonight if they did camp here…

'What is that smell?' said Tor.

Bjarki breathed in through his nose. There was a definite odour on the wind: meaty, musty, a tang of faeces. A smell of old corruption and rot.

Captain Otto had shrugged off his heavy pack and leaned his hunting spear up against it and was clambering up a spill of icy rocks towards the black mouth of the cave. He was smiling happily for the first time that day.

Tor had wandered to the edge of the clearing and was stirring the butt of her spear in the crust of snow at the base of a small huddled shrub.

'Oh gods,' she said. 'Look at this, oaf!' And she lifted an object on the butt of her spear, something soft and floppy.

It was a boot, the remains of an old military boot, the leather shredded into strips and slimy with mould.

–

The monster of Eggeldorf waddled slowly out of the cave interior on all fours, blinking in the light, like an elder awaking from a deep snooze.

It was an enormous creature, almost as big as the stories had claimed, and black as midnight, with a huge square head, small round ears and very pale brown eyes that were almost orange or yellow: the colour of flames.

It saw the humans and gave a long, low warning growl, sounding more exasperated than angry, to Bjarki's ear. It was a bear, of course, an old she-bear who had lived long past thirty summers and grown to a prodigious size.

Bjarki could not take his eyes off her. He was lost in admiration.

The massive animal reared up on its hind legs and roared: another warning. A blast of sound that seemed to shake the air in the placid clearing; a shelf of snow on the branch of a nearby silver birch slid off with a whump.

The she-bear roared deafeningly once more: 'Who dares disturb me?' she seemed to be saying. Indeed, she seemed to be speaking directly to Bjarki, a deep ancient voice inside his head. He saw that her belly and chest were a lighter colour, a paler brown hue, and stood up on her hind legs like this she was twice Bjarki's height. He noticed something else: jutting from her left flank, below the ribs, was an object that looked like a tree branch, snapped off.

'Mother Bear,' he said, his voice shaking with emotion, 'we greet you as a comrade; Mother Bear, we respect your strength and your wisdom.'

The bear had now fixed Bjarki with her fire-coloured eyes.

'I see you there, man-child,' she said, silently inside his skull.

'Have mercy on us, Mother Bear, we weak creatures, we foolish—'

A long, high-pitched warbling scream – Bjarki jerked his gaze to the right. And there was Otto, with his sword drawn, yelling out a Frankish war cry and charging straight at the she-bear. It was a very courageous move.

And utterly senseless.

The massive animal dropped on all fours again and lollopped to meet the charging captain. The Auxilla captain never stood a chance; his sword swept downward and the blow hit her left shoulder but its power was easily absorbed by the layers of thick, dense black fur and humped muscle, like a man being struck with a goose feather. The sword bounced off, untouched by blood. And the bear's massive right paw licked out at the same time, four claws extended like a handful of spear blades, and swept across Otto's body, ripping away his stomach and much of his chest from his spine.

Otto's eviscerated body wobbled on its legs for a moment. The Auxilla captain looked down at the bloody space where his belly had been, his eyes rolled up and he slumped to the ground.

The bear licked the man-blood from her claws, gave a shiver of pleasure, and turned her burning eyes on Bjarki.

'Wait, no!' said Bjarki. Now Tor was running in from the left of the clearing towards the bear's vast black flank. She had the heavy hunting spear levelled and ready to plunge deep into the animal's side.

'No! Tor! No! Stay right back!' yelled Bjarki.

The girl ignored him. She was four strides away from the gigantic animal. The bear turned, faster than seemed possible. The spear blade was only a foot from her black fur when she swept it aside with a casual flick of one huge paw. Tor was committed to her run, and momentum carried her straight towards the she-bear. The animal opened her jaws wide, exposing several long sharp yellow teeth and an ugly purple-tinged mouth.

'Mother, no – she's my friend!'

The enormous jaws snapped shut but, at the last moment, Tor managed to twist her slim body out of the way of the creature's teeth. Instead she crashed hard into the bear's shoulder, rebounded, just managed to keep her feet, when the bear whacked her with one massive sweeping paw and sent her flying across the clearing to crash into a stand of ash.

Tor's head smashed directly into the bole of one of the thick trees with a clonk, and she fell boneless in a heap, twitched once, and moved no more.

The bear began to plod towards Tor. Saliva dangled from her jaws.

'No, Mother Bear, I beg you. Leave her be.'

The bear stopped, turned and looked once again at Bjarki.

'I will not harm you, Mother,' said Bjarki, showing his empty hands and spreading his arms wide. 'But you must not hurt my friend any more.'

The animal was forty feet away from Bjarki. If she chose to, she could leap on him in a couple of bounds and tear him to bloody scraps.

She slowly rose up on her hind legs once more. Bjarki could smell the creature strongly now, the rottenness of her. The tree branch that was jutting from her flank was, he now saw, a spear shaft. The blade was still buried deep inside her body. It had been there for a long time. The wound had festered, the flesh around it was greenish-black and crawling with maggots.

Bjarki could feel her pain. He could smell her death on her.

Yet she lived.

'You and I are one,' said the she-bear inside his head.

'Yes,' said Bjarki. 'You are my *gandr*.'

'You see my pain, man-child,' she said. 'Show mercy. Release me.'

'If that is what you desire, I will do it gladly,' said Bjarki.

The bear roared, a vast meaty blast of sound that sent Bjarki reeling backwards several paces with its force. He stumbled over his own pack and baggage, which he had set down by a boulder in the centre of the clearing, and stood up again holding his long, heavy, hunting spear in both his hands.

'I will release you from this life, Mother, if you wish it,' he said.

The enormous bear was waddling towards him now on her two hind feet, coming at him fast, her paws held high, in an almost human-like gesture of surrender. She was growling too – not growling, humming, deep in her throat. Bjarki recognised the four-note tune like the greeting of a friend.

He set the butt-end of the heavy spear against the boulder, and took a firm grip on the shaft, keeping the blade low, a foot above the snowy turf.

The bear lumbered forward, gaining speed, the humming rose steadily in volume and became a hard snarl and then a full-on howl of rage and pain.

At the last moment, Bjarki hoisted the blade of the hunting spear, and the charging she-bear barged straight into the steel, impaling herself on the razor-sharp blade. The spearhead entered the centre of the bear's chest, just below the sternum, and slid deep into her maggot-corrupted lungs, driven deep inside by the onward momentum of the enormous lolloping beast.

The bear screamed then, massive purple mouth open wider than ever, the months of agony she had endured pouring out of her in an avalanche of deafening sound. The thick spear shaft snapped in Bjarki's hands and he only just managed to dive out of the way as the dying bear stumbled, tripped and fell like a mountain on top of the boulder – and lay there wheezing and slobbering and gurgling, leaking blood and green and yellow pus from its months-old rotting wound. Bjarki got to his feet, ears still ringing from the huge animal's death howl, and looked into the hot yellow eyes of his *gandr*.

And she returned his gaze.

She was still breathing, and he could feel her ancient pain as an ache in his own heart. 'Release me,' she growled. 'Keep your promise, man-child.'

Bjarki drew his seax from the sheath at his waist. Its foot-long, single-edged blade was always kept as sharp as it could possibly be.

The bear was slumped on its front, its massive head resting on the round boulder, the spear-shaft driven deep into the earth. The vast body was still twitching and the muscled forelimbs occasionally shuddering.

Bjarki swung his leg over and sat astride the animal's wide furry neck, feeling the soft warmth of the bear beneath his thighs. He reached forward with his right hand, the seax blade gripped tightly, stretched his arm around to the front of the bear's throat, plunged the knife deep into the bear's fur, then ripped the blade sideways. He felt a great hot gush of blood drench his right hand, and the beast's body shudder beneath him like an earthquake.

Then it was still.

He suddenly felt freezing, colder than he had ever felt before; he heard the urgent sound of rushing water in his ears like the noise of a giant cataract. He found he was humming, deep in his throat, the same simple, four-tone tune, his mind was spinning, whirling. Time seemed to crawl, his vision blurred, then became tinged with red, then suddenly sharpened.

He felt the spirit of the dead she-bear, his *gandr*, humming deep inside his own chest, he felt his own heart begin to swell and engorge, he could feel the blood pounding, slow, ominous drumbeats, in his hot, wide veins; he felt light, buoyant, stronger than ever, as if he could leap whole mountains in a single bound, reach out and touch the sky itself…

Still sitting astride the dead creature's neck he looked up and saw that there were men in the clearing, dozens of them coming in through the trees. Dark-clad men with scale-mail and steel helmets, all sporting black cloaks.

His enemies.

The Rekkr smiled.

-

He hopped off the body of the dead bear. He didn't count the enemies, two score, three dozen? Who cared? There was no point in tallying them: they were just bodies, dead bodies who were for some reason still standing, walking around ignorant of their doom. And still more were emerging from the snowy trees in ones and twos, advancing cautiously. He pulled his sword from its sheath, tossed the sheath away, and walked briskly towards the nearest Black Cloak. His right hand was covered in hot, sticky bear blood and still held the dripping sax. His left hand held the shining naked sword.

He was dimly aware that one of his foes, a big fucker, a leader, black beard, piggy eyes, was saying something about surrender. He didn't listen.

He was eager to begin the slaughter.

The Black Cloaks were still drawing their swords when he slipped in among them, fast as the wind, and cut down the first man, and the second.

They all seemed to move slowly, when he was so nimble. He sliced the seax through windpipes, slammed it into eyes, and plunged the slick blade into armpits, chests, thighs. His deep four-note hum became a chuckle, then a laugh; before long he was cackling with glee and he danced and cut and hacked and dropped man after man. The blood sprayed in wide slow *glorious* arcs, spattering on the white snow, so beautiful, so utterly perfect.

He took blows, too, feeling weapons clang against his well-armoured body, but he heeded them not at all; he was in and among them leaping, striking, faster than a hummingbird, a heart-beat quicker than any of these dull men, and that made it easier for him and harder for the *Scholares* not to strike their friends. He was tireless, killing with a springy energy, which seemed almost to be replenished, redoubled even with each victim he felled.

The big fucker, the black-bearded giant, struck at the Rekkr's mailed left leg with his pole arm, and he felt *that* blow. But he recovered and dived like a cat on the man's chest, his own weight knocking the big fellow down to the snow, and his right hand jabbed and probed with the long seax blade under the rim of the giant's iron cuirass. The big one roared in agony, leaking hot, delicious gore, and hurled the Rekkr away from his prone body with the strength of his arms. The Fire Born landed lightly on his feet and the dance continued.

Then another check to his gory flow, he jammed the long sword in a skinny fellow's ribs, and the blade became wedged tight in the heart cage, he couldn't haul the blade free. He cursed, tugged, twisted to no avail: then he booted the dying man away, relinquishing his long blade.

He killed, then, with seax alone.

He sank it deep into backs and necks, dodged and ducked down to jam the blade up into men's exposed groins. He sliced, stabbed; he punched, scratched and even bit his enemies, when flesh came within range of his snapping teeth. He scooped up a discarded ridged iron helmet with his left hand and battered blurred faces with this makeshift weapon. He snarled at wounded men, already down. Stamping on them. Pounding and stabbing just to feel the sweet sink of the blade in a warm body. And then, suddenly, there was no one left. He stood upright, blade dripping, on the bloody field alone.

A few dark shapes were fleeing through the trees; he saw black horses there too, and heard the muddled thudding of their departing hooves. And the snow, the snow, churned pink and brown and pure scarlet, was strewn with bodies, dead and dying all around him. Dozens of men destroyed. He could hear screaming, on and on, and could taste the fresh blood on his lips, salty, metallic, sweet. He wanted one more. Just one more enemy to kill; just one more soft white belly to thrust his slick blade inside…

There were none left. He was aware of a great weariness, pressing down on his neck and shoulders. And a great, dark heaviness of mind. He looked down at his own body, slathered, dipped in gore, sorely wounded too.

His *gandr* was leaving him. Slipping away. He felt dizzy, cold, empty.

On the far side of the clearing, away from the blood, the ripped snowy turf and the bodies, he saw Tor, standing alone by the stand of ash. She was pale and shaky, holding a drawn sword, and gazing at him in amazement.

'It came to you,' she said. 'At last. Oh my gods, you lucky, lucky oaf. Your *gandr* came. And I… and mine… mine never did…'

'The monster of Egg… that great she-bear, yonder, she was my g…' somehow Bjarki could not form the words. They just stared at each other mute across the churned and bloody snow.

The sound of pain-filled laughter interrupted their silent communion. Bjarki turned and saw a huge, bearded man lying on the ground about two paces away. His lower body was sheeted in blood, his legs awash from deep wounds in his belly, up under his iron cuirass. His face and neck seemed to have been savaged, ripped by the teeth of a beast. Yet he was recognisable.

'You followed us all the way here,' said Bjarki.

'I didn't believe it,' said Lord Grimoald. 'I thought you were a sham, a fraud. I thought it was all tricks and mummery. And now I have seen it with my own eyes. Felt it. Been slain by it. You are, after all, one of the Rekkar.'

'Why?' said Bjarki. 'Why are you here?'

Tor was coming over, picking her way delicately through the wrecked bodies of the dead and dying Black Cloaks. 'I think I know,' she said.

Bjarki looked at her. He wanted to ask but found he had lost his words.

'Captain Otto was always your man inside the Auxilla, wasn't he?'

Lord Grimoald tried to smile; his expression a pain-racked grimace.

'Otto told you who was loyal to the king in his company, and who was not to be trusted. I was not to be trusted. We were both not to be trusted.'

'He was a fool. But a useful one for some years,' grated Grimoald.

'I could not understand,' said Tor, 'why such a poor soldier, such a sad ninny as Otto, should command an elite *scara* – I do now.'

'He served the king well, in his pathetic little way.'

'Why did you not simply have us executed in Aachen? Why follow us all the way here and attack us in secret? You have more power than anyone.'

Lord Grimoald did not answer, his eyes were tightly closed in pain.

Tor kicked his boot. 'Don't die on me yet, old man,' she said.

The King's Shield opened his eyes a fraction.

'*He* likes you,' he hissed. 'The king. Karolus likes your man, says he sees something in him.' Grimoald made a jerk of his head towards Bjarki. 'He's right – but also badly mistaken. The Dane has the Beast inside him.'

'We admitted we were Rekkar,' Tor said. 'We were open about that.'

'But dishonest, too. You never meant to keep your oaths – to His Majesty or to God. I told him you would prove treacherous. I saw that plain as day. I knew you'd never serve the king, or Francia, or Christ willingly. You only wanted to get close to Karolus and stick a blade in him.'

'So why not just execute us?'

'I urged him. He decided to spare you. He said we must put you to the test. If you returned from this absurd mission, if you willingly came back to his side in Aachen, then you could be trusted. I said no. But he's the king.'

Lord Grimoald began to laugh again, more weakly, and as his chest convulsed in mirth, something tore and a squirt of fresh blood shot out from under his cuirass and spattered his already gory legs.

'What's funny?' said Bjarki. 'Why do you laugh at your own death?'

'I have… achieved… my aim,' said Grimoald, fighting for each breath, forcing the individual words out through his mirth and his red agony.

'I have… protected… the king… after all.'

'How so?' said Bjarki.

Tor answered for him: 'Because we can never go back to Karolus now. Not now we've slaughtered half a *cunei* of his Black Cloaks – and this big old bastard, too. If we went back to Aachen, we'd be dead inside the hour.'

Grimoald's laughter had subsided to a few soft heaves and wet coughs.

'There is more… that makes me… content,' he said. 'Karolus will hear of this bloody day… and come after you… with all his strength and power. To avenge me… and because you broke… your oath to return.'

The King's Shield was suddenly racked with a coughing fit. He spat a gobbet of something red on to the snow and said, 'I am being called to the Lord's side now… this is my end. I am dead. And so are… both of you!'

Part Three

Chapter Twenty-three

A walk in the woods

'So you like cheese then, do you, little one?' said Tor in her softest voice.

Bjarki opened his eyes. He had no idea where he was for several moments – then his mind adjusted and he peered through the gloomy half-light and recognised his friend, sitting with her back against a rocky wall on the far side of the space, holding what looked like a large black dog upside down in her lap. She was feeding it small pieces of a crumbly substance and playing with its thick, stubby paws at the same time.

'What is that thing?' said Bjarki.

'Oh, you're back in the world, are you, oaf?' Tor gently set the animal down on the floor of the cave and came over to the mound of blankets and furs upon which Bjarki was lying. 'Nice of you to join us at last!'

Bjarki looked down at his own naked body, which was covered by a blanket. His right shoulder was bandaged with linen, as was his middle, and his left thigh, too, he discovered as he moved the limb sideways out from under the bedclothes. His body was covered in cuts, scrapes and bruises and throbbed, his head was splitting and he'd never felt so thirsty in his life.

'You knew that monstrous beast was female, yes?' said Tor. 'Well, I found this little one in the back of the cave when I hauled your arse inside.'

She gestured at the animal and Bjarki saw that it was a jet-black bear cub, only a few months old. The chubby little animal stared solemnly back at him. He noticed it had bright yellow eyes, the exact same shade as its mother's.

'I decided to call him Garm because his fur is so dark… after the fierce guardian of Hel's realm, you know?'

'I know. Good name.' For a moment, the image of Freya flashed into his mind. In the dunes, with the three youths standing on the slope above.

Tor handed him a large bowl full of water, which Bjarki drank down in three large gulps. 'Where did the bowl come from?' he said, wiping his lips.

'Oh, I salvaged quite a lot from the baggage of the Black Cloaks.'

'How long have I been lying here?'

'Five days – or is it six?'

'What? Why? We should have left. They will be coming for us.'

'I could barely shift your great fat carcass inside the cave; I couldn't go on the run with you, dragging you through the snow like a dead bullock.'

'You should have left me and gone on alone. Tor, they *will* come looking, and they *will* find us here.' Bjarki began to struggle out of his bed.

'They won't be going anywhere. The mother of all snowstorms hit, just after I got your unconscious bulk in here. And the blizzard has not stopped since. No force of Red Cloaks is going to venture out of Regensburg in this. And if they did, they would never get up here. We are safe while the storm rages. When it's done, we'll go before they find us. What are you doing?'

Bjarki had got to his feet, and was painfully hobbling over to the entrance to the cave, which was almost entirely blocked with snow. A small window at the top of the space had been cleared, and kept open, an air hole, and Bjarki peered out of it into the grey maelstrom outside. The bitter icy draught stung his cheeks. Tor was right: nothing could be out in this and live.

He ate a little soup, and slept some more, keeping one ear on the pitch of the moaning wind outside the cave. At one point, the little cub Garm came and licked his face with his fat pink tongue, and cuddled down in his arms to sleep. Tor huddled in under the blankets with them, too, for an hour or so, sharing the warmth, before getting up and pottering with bits of fir tree branch and rawhide thongs, constructing something, at the back of the cave.

The next morning the storm died down and Tor, with help from a very stiff Bjarki, broke down the wall of snow and ice in the cave mouth. It was painfully bright outside, wide blue skies and a big pale sun, but the snow was several feet thick on the ground, deeper in the drifts; when Tor waded out into the clearing, the snow came right up to her skinny chest.

'I know some of the Black Cloaks escaped the fight,' said Bjarki. 'But could they have made it back to Regensburg before the storm came down?'

'We must assume they did. We must assume they know where we are.'

Bjarki felt his heart sinking. He was weak and very sore, his head still ached, and the prospect of a long journey did not appeal. He wanted to rest.

'We have to leave this place,' he said.

'And go where?'

'Isn't it obvious? We're folk of the North. Clearly, we head north.'

-

Tor had fashioned snowshoes, of a kind, for them to wear on their feet. They were crude and clumsy – the smaller branches of fir trees lashed inside a circle of ash wood and strapped to their boots – but they made the going much easier. They packed their belongings, weapons and food – and a bulky mysterious package that Tor insisted they must take – and Bjarki scooped up Garm into his arms. By midday they were off, tramping over the unmarked snow in their new shoes, through the eerily silent woods.

They followed no road, heading north as best they could through the trees, following the tracks of snow hares and deer, when they came across them, forging through virgin white crust when they did not. Bjarki found the going very hard; he soon had to give Garm over to Tor to carry inside her leather jerkin. His breath was short and his head light.

The wounds he had suffered had been salved and bandaged by Tor, and he was a preternaturally fast healer but, nevertheless, by mid-afternoon, when it began to gently snow again, he could feel hot blood trickling down his ribs inside his shirt. He said nothing to Tor and they forged on. He knew that the further they could get away from the cave, the safer they would be.

Just before nightfall, when it began to snow properly again, and they were forced to stop, Bjarki reckoned they had covered only three or four miles.

They made a fireless camp under the low boughs of an old yew tree, ate dried meat and drank water, with the little bear sitting on Tor's lap and whining. 'At least the snowfall will disguise our tracks,' said Bjarki.

'If they *are* coming after us at all,' said Tor, stroking the bear's soft fur. 'We could be snug in the cave with a fire and some hot soup right now...'

She stopped and looked at Bjarki. He had heard it too. The neighing of a horse somewhere close at hand. As quietly as she could, Tor got to her feet, passing the bear cub over to Bjarki. She loosened the seax at her belly, and peered round the trunk of the yew. Twenty paces away there was a rider, a Red Cloak, sitting on his dun-coloured horse and drinking from a flask.

Tor kept her body flat to the trunk of the tree. The rider seemed to be alone. But that was very unlikely. They knew what Tor and Bjarki could do. There would certainly be many others near by even if she couldn't see them.

The rider put away his flask, and clicked his tongue at his horse to get it moving. It was coming closer to Tor, heading almost straight at their tree.

The snow had been falling for a good hour by now, and when Tor looked round to see if there were any footprints that would lead to their little camp, she was relieved to see that there were none. The rider was a dozen yards away, his horse breathing grey smoke, and looking a little wild eyed and agitated. Tor wondered if it could smell the cub. She could see the face of the Red Cloak clearly: he was unshaven but handsome; his cheeks mottled with cold. She made her plans. It had to be silent, otherwise the other Red Cloaks would come and there'd be no end of blood. Her hunting bow would be good, yet he might cry out when shot and raise the alarm.

No. It had to be the seax. She had to swing up behind him on that big dun horse, and slice his throat wide open before he could scream. It was a tall order, the silent part. But it could be done. He was six paces away...

'Marco, where are you?' The call was a shocking breach of the silence.

The rider looked back over his shoulder. 'I'm up here, Sextus.'

'Any sign of them?'

'Nothing. They're long gone by now for sure. We should be too.'

'Yes, well, that's for the captain to say. Get on back down here.'

The rider turned his horse, and walked it back the way he had come. Tor realised that she had been holding in her breath for a very long while.

-

They saw nobody on the second day, trudging on endlessly through the trackless wilderness, Bjarki occasionally using the lichen on the trees to keep them heading northwards. Neither of them knew how long they would have to travel before they came to a settlement of any description, nor what they would find when they got there.

Bjarki spent much of the day in a pain-filled trance, mindlessly putting one foot in front of the other, his head down, his wounds leaking. When they made camp that night he fell down in the snow and immediately went to sleep. Tor had to cover his body with a blanket or he'd have frozen to death. She had to slap him briskly awake next morning.

On the third day they came to a narrow track, not really a road, a path no wider than two men abreast, and saw the fresh hoof-marks of horsemen in the muddy snow, a large group, heading south. It was unnerving to think the enemy had been in the north, ahead of them.

They bickered briefly about whether to take the track: easier going but more risk of encountering Red Cloaks. Tor won. They eschewed the track and continued on through the forest. Bjarki was too weak to argue, anyway.

They now had about three days' food, by Tor's calculation, most of it hard bread and cheese, and dried sticks of venison, which she had looted from the Black Cloaks' saddlebags before putting the horses to flight after the battle at the cave. Tor figured they could hunt game, if they ever saw any, and kept her ash-wood bow and arrow she had constructed to hand.

On the fourth evening they came across a small hunters' hut with a big hole in the ancient shingle roof, and they risked a fire inside and a hot meal.

Tor had managed to shoot a snow hare and they roasted the animal inside the hut, and slept relatively warm for once. The bear cub was quiet, and subdued, though; he seemed to be pining for the cave, the only home he had ever known, or for his dead mother. He curled in a ball and whined softly for much of the evening, refusing to eat the scraps of roasted hare or even nibble the dwindling stock of cheese that Tor offered to him.

She tried cuddling the creature in her arms and singing to him as if he were a baby, while Bjarki snored like a drunk. But the little bear buried his head further in, curled himself tighter and cried softly until he fell asleep.

On the fifth day, the forest began to thaw. The sun came out strongly and the trees were filled with the sounds of dripping, and the merry gurgling of streams and brooks. The animals began to reappear, and birds called from the newly bare branches, and Tor shot a fallow deer in the belly in the early afternoon and, while Bjarki and the cub rested beside a fallen oak tree, she tracked its trail of scarlet droplets till she came upon the corpse of the animal. She cut a haunch from the young buck and hefting it onto her shoulder, she ported it back to their camp in triumph. That night they all feasted. Even the cub perked up and discovered an interest in the fresh meat.

Tor changed Bjarki's bandages and was astounded to discover that despite the rigours of five days of hard marching through the wilderness, his wounds were almost closed now and there was no infection that she could see or scent. He was a very long way from healed and whole but he was on the mend. She felt cheerier in herself, as well. Even the cub seemed happy. They'd seen no sign of the pursuing Red Cloaks for two whole days.

With their stomachs full of hot roasted venison, snuggled down in their furs and blankets, and a small blaze warming their toes, they felt cosy, comfortable, content and even relaxed for the first time in a very long while.

'So, oaf, tell me what it's like,' said Tor.

'What is what like?'

'You know.'

Bjarki leant forward and shoved a log further into the fire, causing sparks to fly upwards in a cascade of orange and gold. The bear cub, Garm, dreaming beside Tor, gave a soft snore, rolled over on his back and farted.

'Tell me, oaf – I don't believe I'm ever going to find out for myself.'

Bjarki still seemed unwilling to speak. Eventually, he looked at her and said: 'It's wonderful – and horrible – both at the same time.'

'Keep talking.'

'You feel so powerful, so fast and clever, like a god, somehow, or a hero, as if you could do anything, anything at all. Soar like an eagle or jump over a lake, knock down a mountain with your bare fists… And when you kill a man, when you rip away his life, it feels as good as… actually, it feels as good as fucking. It's like sex, when you plunge into a girl for the first time.'

Tor, who had no experience in this field of combat, said: 'Ah, I see.' Then, when it seemed that Bjarki would say no more: 'So why horrible?'

'It is horrible because a part of you – the human part of you, the real part of you – is standing outside the body of the Rekkr, watching as it slays and stabs, laughs and destroys his enemies. It is horrible because you can feel the jolt up your arm as your blade strikes home; and you smell the fresh hot blood and spilled bowels… but it isn't you who is doing the fighting. The Rekkr is killing them, not you. You feel you are being dragged along behind the *gandr* as it tears a delightful bloody path through the enemy's flesh. And when you come back, when your *gandr* leaves you at last, you feel ashamed, you feel dirty and sore all over, and not just from the wounds you've taken while it was in control. You feel – how can I say it? – used.'

They sat in silence for a little while.

'Did I ever tell you my father was a famous Rekkr?' said Tor at last.

'I think you may have mentioned it.'

'I don't remember his face much; he died when I was young. But when I was growing up I remember his presence: a powerful presence in the house, looming, filling the whole space, and more than a little frightening. I think my mother truly feared him. Hated him. And there is something else. I told you, I think, that he died gloriously in battle. Sometimes my mother told me that story. He had been a big hero in the wars against the Kingdom of the Vestfold. She said that was how they met: the King of Svearland, whom he loyally served, rewarded his valour with lands and a village and a bride – one of the king's wards – my mother, Gytha. He was appointed *hersir* and the people in the village he owned all respected him – and feared his wrath.'

Tor pulled the blankets tighter around her. 'You still awake, oaf?'

'Yes – your father was a very great man, it seems.'

'No, that's not the point. I think my mother lied about his death. She used to have bruises, on her face and her arms, all the time; she had cuts and abrasions. She looked like you do now. Sometimes she could not get out of bed for the pain and claimed she was sick. Or she would say that she tripped and fell but… I know she cringed away from him. She encouraged me to learn how to fight, to protect myself. And she told me that my father went off to war and died fighting the king's enemies, falling bravely in battle…

'But I don't think that is true. I heard other stories growing up; stories whispered in the village. I heard that my father had killed himself. There was a local high place, a great big rock overlooking the sea near our village, it was called Thor's Rock. I heard that my father went there in despair one dark night, and threw himself off that rock and into the wild sea below.'

'Why would he do that?' asked Bjarki, sitting up and looking at Tor.

'I think… I suspect that he went mad, that all his valour in battle and his status later did nothing to stop him going Galálar. His *gandr* took over his mind. Like Brokk, of the Bear Lodge, you told me about him, remember? I think my father used to beat my mother, frequent brutal beatings, till she was near to death, and he was ashamed that he could not control himself, that he could not control his *gandr*. So, in the end, I believe he took his own life.'

Chapter Twenty-four

The Spring Market

Ten days later, an hour after dawn, dirty, hungry and footsore, Bjarki, Tor and Garm found themselves walking out of the forest and beside a wide, placid blue lake. They approached a weed-covered field, where a ploughman and his ox team were carving out the first furrows of the year.

The snows had shrunk and finally disappeared as they walked, and the trees had become thinner before dissolving completely as their feet found a definite track leading them back into the lands of men. There had been no more evidence of the Red Cloaks since that brief encounter, and both Tor and Bjarki were convinced that they were beyond the reach of their foes.

Three weeks after the battle at the cave, and after hundreds of miles of hard travel on foot, Bjarki – astonishingly – seemed almost fully recovered from the wounds he had taken. But he was very thin, and tired beyond belief.

'It's not natural,' muttered Tor, who had twisted an ankle on a root in the woods three days before and was still limping. 'It's downright freakish.'

In the distance, a mile or two away, they could see the long mossy wooden walls of a decent-sized town built on the banks of a slow brown river. 'Any idea where we are?' Bjarki asked.

'I'm not sure but I think we are somewhere east of the River Elbe,' said Tor. 'In the land of the Vindr, or the Wends, as they call themselves. Valtyr used to speak about them from time to time. Stubborn fighters.'

The map they had been given in Aachen, long abandoned, had been vague about anything beyond the walls of Regensburg, merely marking the territory they had walked through as indistinguishable forest with little tree symbols. Tor thought they must have travelled a good three hundred miles on foot, roughly north, and were now completely out of Francia in the Slavic pagan lands to the east. That meant, presumably, that they were safe from the king's wrath. However, the Wends, despite sharing a deep hatred of the Franks, were not the natural allies of the many peoples of the North.

According to Valtyr, there had been much thrall-taking and pillaging by pirate bands from the lands of the Svears and the Gottar, and from the Dane-Mark, too, over the years. These rovers descended suddenly on the northern shores of Wendland, coming across the Eastern Lake in their swift, narrow dragon-ships to murder and rape and steal and burn the farms of the locals.

Indeed, several full-pitched battles had been fought between boatloads of warriors from Svearland and the stolid shield-men of the Wendish tribes.

So Bjarki and Tor kept their weapons handy, guarded their tongues, and had Garm well hidden inside Bjarki's cloak as they joined the mass of people waiting patiently to cross the wooden bridge over the river and enter the gates of the town. The language spoken around them was different to their own tongue, yet so close to the Saxon border there were a few people here who spoke their northern language, although with a thick Slav accent.

It was a special day, apparently, for on this sunny morning hundreds of people from all the surrounding villages had come to this town – which was called Brenna, they quickly learned – for their famous Spring Market.

Bjarki exchanged a few pleasantries with an older man and discovered that this was a celebrated annual event and folk came from hundreds of miles to buy and sell goods – Brenna was renowned for its fine pottery – and greet their friends and neighbours after the snow-bound seclusion of winter.

The man, who was named Hufnar, came from the northwest of Wendland, not very far from the Dane-Work, in fact. He was a salt trader, making his own product in the pools of the shallow bay where he lived with his family and moving it by mule for sale all over the eastern lands.

'So where do you come from, young fellow?' he asked Bjarki.

Bjarki hesitated for a moment then, his imagination completely deserting him, he told the man the truth: 'From Bago, in the Dane-Mark.'

'You're a long way from home, son. What brings you to Brenna?'

'We are sell-swords looking for a generous lord,' Tor interrupted. 'Do you know if the big chief hereabouts might have need of two bold warriors?'

'Lord Ostoja has half a hundred fighters already but I guess he might take on a couple more. But they are a rough bunch. You sure that's what you want, missy?' He looked doubtfully at Tor's wiry frame.

'Where would we find this Ostoja person?' she said.

'*Lord* Ostoja will be in the Old Tower, if he's here today. Can't miss it. East side of town. Tall square building. Lots of soldiers lounging outside.'

Hufnar had decided that Tor and Bjarki were not his kind of people after all and began edging away from them. The skinny young woman was clearly mad – or was mocking him in some way. As the gates of the town opened, he guided his loaded mule forward and positioned the beast between his plump body and these two filthy, emaciated, yet heavily armed lunatics.

–

The town of Brenna was home to nearly a thousand souls, a significant settlement by any yardstick, yet to Tor and Bjarki, after the glories of Aachen and even Regensburg, it seemed slow and comically provincial.

It was laid out in an oval shape, fenced by sharp logs, with the main gate at the western end by the river. There was one long, wide street, which ran west to east towards the wooden stronghold, or the Old Tower, as Hufnar called it, at the town's east end. It was, Bjarki thought, not much more than the large courtyard of a big fortress, which was probably the town's origin.

Dozens of little side alleys branched off this wide main street, forming little blocks between them that were occupied by the various allied trades and professions: the potters and the brick-makers had pride of place in the centre of town; the butchers and tanners were near the main gates; the grain merchants, millers and bakers occupied another block to the south of the main street. The jewellery-makers and the gold and silversmiths occupied one such block on the north side about halfway down.

Pausing briefly to admire a street stall that was set out with a scatter of glittering trinkets – brooches, pins, gold rings and clasps – lying on a faded purple cloth, Tor found herself looking into the face of Valtyr Far-Traveller.

The two just stared at each other for about three heartbeats.

'Tor – you live!' said Valtyr. 'I assumed… I never imagined—'

'What in the name of Thor's hairy hole are *you* doing here?'

'My usual trade, of course,' he said. He looked beyond her shoulder. 'And Bjarki! Well met! You look different, son. Older. Wait! Wait…'

The one-eyed man peered at the hulking warrior. 'By the One Tree, it came to you. I can see it in you. Your *gandr* came to you. I'm so pleased.'

Tor grimaced.

'But you both look half-starved. I'm sure there used to be a good deal more of you, Bjarki. Wait, just wait till I pack this up and we'll go and eat.'

Half an hour later, they were sitting at a rough wooden bench at an inn beside the Old Tower, where Valtyr had taken lodgings for the three-day market, all munching hot mutton pies and drinking strong new-brewed ale.

'I saw you last in the autumn, Tor, in the depths of the First Forest, ten miles north of the Groves, and you were utterly determined to Voyage till you found your own Wolf spirit,' said Valtyr. 'Don't tell me you've been in the woods all this time. You can't have been! And instead of a *gandr*, you found a bear cub!' He gave the wide-eyed animal a chuck under its chin.

Tor gave Valtyr a brief account of their adventures since they had parted company. The old man listened patiently, only stopping her once.

'You say that Lord Paulinus has been sent packing and Father Livinus has been made the king's chaplain and chancellor? Is that right?'

Bjarki and Tor confirmed it.

'This is grave news for our people,' he said. 'Livinus is even more of a fanatic than Paulinus. And he's much more cunning than the other fellow too. He will not rest till the whole North is subjugated to the Christians.'

Bjarki took up the story of the journey to Regensburg, and the cave and the great bear. How he found his *gandr*, at last, and slew Lord Grimoald.

'That was bravely done, Bjarki,' the one-eyed man said. 'Grimoald was a powerful force, and no friend to us. I rejoice in his death at your hands.'

They ordered more ale and, since Bjarki was still hungry, cheese and fruit and fresh bread, too. It was wonderful to be able to eat too much.

'What news of the Groves?' asked Bjarki. 'Have you been back?'

'The news is bad, I am afraid,' said Valtyr. 'All across Saxony the Franks are encroaching. Duke Theodoric has lost another two regions, and a dozen more churches have been built. The duke himself has retreated almost to the borders of the Dane-Mark. He has called for all free warriors of the North to come to his banner to resist the steady advance of the Franks.'

'We should answer his call,' said Tor, looking at Bjarki. 'I am sure we would soon earn ourselves positions of honour among Theodoric's jarls.'

Bjarki helped himself to another slice of bread and broke off a piece of cheese. He was avoiding their eyes. He fed some cheese to Garm.

'You heard Valtyr,' said Tor. 'Duke Theodoric calls for warriors.'

'Do you not wish to fight for him?' asked Valtyr.

Bjarki looked down at the table. 'I'm tired,' he said. 'I'm not fighting anyone until I have rested. Until I'm ready. Even then, I don't know...'

'You have a gift, Rekkr,' said Valtyr. 'The gods have given you strength. Will you not use it in defence of our land, to fight for all we love?'

'A gift, is it?'

'Yes! Of all the warriors in the world, only a handful find their *gandr*. You have the divine spark inside you – you have been touched by the gods.'

'In Francia, they call it possession by an evil demon. They say that something wicked takes control of a Rekkr's body and corrupts his soul.'

'Francia? What do they know? Nothing. Their hectoring priests see everything as either good or evil, nothing in between, either sanctioned by their ridiculous Christ god or benighted and vile. They even try to deny the existence of the other gods. How insane is that? How would it be if I said that only Tiw was real – and that all the rest of the gods were imaginary? You would laugh at me. But this is how they see the world. Their god and only their god can be allowed. No other deity may be worshipped – on pain of death. And you, Bjarki, you know for sure, for certain, that there are other unseen forces in the world. Your *gandr* has come to you – does it speak to you? Yes? And is that not real? Is it not holy – a sacred thing. A gift, I say.'

'So that is my fate, is it?' said Bjarki, his temper was beginning to fray, his usual restraint loosened by strong ale and bone-deep exhaustion. 'Because the gods say so, because I have been *chosen*—' he spat out that last word '—because of that I am destined to fight and kill and kill until...'

'All life is struggle,' said Valtyr. 'We're born, we fight, we die. Folk will always struggle for power and land, for silver, for fame, women and slaves. The gods know that; they show their favour by bestowing courage and strength on those they chose to uphold the old ways. You *have* been chosen, Bjarki. You're special. You *must* fight for what you know is right.'

'And because I'm so *fucking* special—' Bjarki was red in the face now, and loud, and he was beginning to draw looks from the other tables in the inn '—I must wade in a lake of blood, on and on, till it closes over my head.'

There was a long and painful silence.

'I think Bjarki is right,' said Tor, breaking it. 'We need to rest properly before we make any decision about what we should do next.'

Valtyr nodded. 'Let us get all your gear up to my room. A few days of good food and rest, Bjarki, and you will see the world in a whole new light.'

-

Valtyr was right. When Bjarki had slept for fifteen hours, and eaten some more, and slept again, he did feel a good deal better.

The next day, a little before noon, he rose from the big mattress that they were sharing in the small room in the attic of the inn and went out to look at the Spring Market of the town of Brenna. He wandered the busy main street alone, stopping only briefly to greet Valtyr at his stall on the jewellery quarter, and to enquire where Tor was.

'She went to see a master tanner of my acquaintance, took the bear cub with her too,' said Valtyr.

'What does she want with a tanner?'

The old man shrugged. 'We are meeting tonight at sundown, in the inn for a feast,' he said. 'I leave tomorrow and I've asked the landlord to cook us all something special as a last decent meal before I go back on the road.'

Bjarki nodded vaguely, and wandered off down the street. It was a warm day and he was feeling good in himself. He had slept well and was well fed, his wounds hardly troubled him at all, nobody was trying to kill him, so far as he could tell, and after such a long period tramping alone in the woods with only Tor and the little bear for company, Bjarki relished the sensation of being in a noisy, jostling crowd of his fellow human beings.

He looked at the numerous stalls set out in the sunshine outside the shops. He admired the bright bolts of cloths on display outside the drapers – vivid blues and greens and bold reds, even a rare roll of jet black cloth that the stallholder indicated was more expensive than all the rest put together.

He contemplated buying a new sword with a gold-inlaid ivory handle that he greatly admired – they still had a number of Frankish coins from the purse they had been given before departure from Aachen – but when the stall keeper made him understand the full price in his rough Frankish dialect, Bjarki recoiled in genuine shock and quickly walked away empty handed.

He waved at Hufnar, who was standing beside a pile of salt sacks and weighing out a small cupful of his product on a set of scales for a customer. But the man frowned at him and did not bother to wave back. Bjarki then bought himself a big bag of sweetmeats – hazelnuts baked in honey – for a copper coin and crunched them as he walked along. He realised he was enjoying himself, for the first time, in… well, he could not remember since when.

His eye was arrested by a painting on a wooden board, as wide as both his outstretched arms, and by a man with extremely long brown hair – it hung in a thick shining curtain well below his belted waist – who sat below the board on a stool, a stack of parchments on a table at his elbow.

The image on the painting was of a longhouse with a humped roof, thatched with straw, and there was a figure sitting outside, with a jug of ale at his side and a cup in his hand. Smoke was rising from the wind-eyes at either end of the dwelling. The seated figure had stretched out his long legs and was looking over a small garden, apparently filled with cabbages, onions and leeks, with a happy-looking pig tethered in a small hut at the end of the patch. Beyond that were several large fields, neatly ploughed and planted, and beyond them a forest of oak and beech, a swathe of greens and browns. On the other side of the longhouse, just glimpsed, was the silvery blue flash of a stretch of sea, and a one-masted fishing boat drawn up on the sand.

Bjarki stopped dead and stared at the painting. It was a bewitching scene and he found he could not take his eyes off it. He could well imagine himself sitting there after a long day's work, legs stretched out, sipping good ale, surveying his own well-ordered lands. He would fatten the pig in those woods in the autumn on beech mast and acorns, slaughter it in the early winter and have bacon and salted pork all through the cold season. And he would take that little boat out to sea to fish, for a change of diet, mackerel and herring, he reckoned those rich seas would be full of them, and, in the season, he would harvest his own cabbages and leeks, and maybe plant—

'Beautiful, isn't it?' said the long-haired man sitting below the picture.

Bjarki agreed; he could have looked at the picture for hours.

'And it could all be yours, you know,' said the fellow. 'All of it.'

That got Bjarki's attention. 'What do you mean by that, sir?'

'I mean there is free land on offer. East, up on the coast, for any man bold enough to take up Duke Leszko's generous offer.'

'I don't understand,' said Bjarki. 'This fellow is *giving away* land?'

'My name is Goran, why don't you sit down with me and we'll talk.'

He used his leg to hook out another wooden stool from under the table, and Bjarki thumped down next to him. Goran handed the warrior a piece of parchment, which was covered with black writing and had a large red wax seal dangling from the bottom of the page. Bjarki looked at it blankly. He glanced at the table; there were dozens of other similar pieces of parchment.

'Not a reader, eh?' said the man, sweeping the hair away from his face and tucking it behind his ear. His accent was Svearlander. 'It's a charter; it says who owns a particular stretch of land, once it's witnessed and sealed.'

Bjarki gave him back his piece of parchment. He had never learnt his letters as a boy, his master, Thialfi, seeing no need for reading in a fisherman.

'Allow me to explain what that parchment represents,' said Goran. He had produced a jug and two cups from somewhere and was pouring out ale.

'Leszko's lands are rich and vast,' he began. 'But his territory has few people, at present. And this troubles the Duke of the Polans. That is his first problem. His second is that the northern parts of his lands are plagued by wild tribes of Pomeranians, Prussians and Lithuanians, savage brutes, little better than wild animals, who plunder our people's farms without mercy.'

Bjarki shifted uncomfortably on his stool. He'd heard this song before – in Francia. Every lord, it seemed, claimed his enemies were less than human.

'So the wise duke has come up with a plan,' said Goran. 'He is willing to offer land and title to any warrior who has the strength to hold it.'

'Anyone?'

'He must be brave and strong, and willing to fight for his lands but, yes, anyone. Leszko will grant any man a hundred acres, and make them a *druzyna* – that is a sort of *hersir* – if they will swear to hold the land for the duke, and come and do homage before his throne in Poznan every spring. By the look of you, you are no stranger to a good hard fight. Am I right?'

'So I'd have to swear an oath?' said Bjarki. He got up from his stool.

'It's a simple homage ceremony,' said Goran. 'Just a few moments.'

'I've sworn too many already. I don't think I can make any more.'

'This new oath of fealty would supersede all others. Your slate would be wiped clean by this one act. Whatever oaths you've made in the past, they would count for nothing. Duke Leszko would be your sovereign and your only lord, and you would hold lands of him, and owe loyalty only to him.'

Bjarki took one long final look at the picture, sadly shook his head, and began to walk away.

'Hey, where are you going?'

Bjarki did not turn his head but he lifted a hand in farewell.

'Think about it, young man,' called Goran. 'Just think about it. I'll be here for the next two days. Just imagine: the chance of a wonderful new life in the vast expanse of the east. Free land! You could bring your father, bring your brothers, your friends, too, the Duke of Polans has land for everyone.'

But Bjarki had already disappeared into the market crowds.

Chapter Twenty-five

The long road back

The landlord gave them a suckling pig for supper that evening. A neat little animal with crisp brown skin, and its belly stuffed with boiled grains and dried fruit and seasoned with saffron. It was a dish fit for a royal table, and best of all, in Tor's opinion, Valtyr was paying, which made it all the tastier.

Bjarki was still in the strange humour of the day before, silent, almost sullen. But, she noted, he ate with a wolfish appetite, which was a good sign.

'You asked yesterday about the Groves of Eresburg, Bjarki,' said Valtyr, when they had demolished most of the piglet, and were sitting back picking scraps of pork meat from their teeth, 'and I have received some news, specifically about the Fyr Skola, since we spoke. The Spring Market is an excellent place for gossip and news of all kinds, as you can imagine.'

Tor watched Bjarki's expression. He said nothing but he cocked his head respectfully, as if to invite Valtyr to continue speaking.

'Yes, a marvellous place for gossip, is Brenna, in the springtime.'

'Are you going to tell me your news or not?' said Bjarki.

'I'm trying to gauge your mood, Bjarki; the news may not please you.'

'Just tell me, old man.'

'You remember Ivar Knuttson, the Boar Lodge Rekkr.'

'He's not a Rekkr,' said Bjarki. 'He's a fraud and a coward.'

'Be that as it may,' said Valtyr, 'he is now Father of the Boar Lodge.'

Bjarki sucked a scrap of pork from one of his molars and swallowed it.

'I don't care,' he said. 'If they were so stupid as to choose… I don't care. What do you think, Tor? Does it make your piss boil – a sham Rekkr as Father of a Lodge? That's what Valtyr's trying to do. Make us both angry.'

'What do I think? I think fuck the Groves. They kicked me out for trying too hard to become a Rekkr.' Tor suddenly realised that she was, in fact, very angry. 'Whatever happens in the Groves, whether they pick that idiot Ivar Knuttson or another idiot, doesn't change a thing. Fuck them all.'

'Why do you believe I want you to be angry, Bjarki?' asked Valtyr.

For a long time, Bjarki did not answer. Then he said: 'Who are you, Valtyr Far-Traveller? A man who sells trinkets across the world. A gatherer of gossip. A recruiter of likely young folk for the Fyr Skola. Who are you?'

'Who do you think I am?'

'For a while I thought you were the Old One. You have one eye, as the god Odin has, and you are a great wanderer. I don't think that any more.'

'What do you think now?'

'I think you should stop answering questions with questions and give me some truth: what do you want? What do you seek in this life? Why do you try to make us angry with silly tales about a *nithing* like Ivar Knuttson?'

Bjarki glared defiantly across the table at Valtyr.

The old man held his gaze. 'Obviously, I am not a god, nor am I some sorcerer or shape-shifter or anything like that. I am just a man. A trader in trinkets, as you said. But I am also what is called a Guardian of the North, a life-long servant of Odin and all the ancient gods of our people.' He said this very quietly but there was a definite ring of immense pride in his voice.

'I live to serve our people – all the folk of the Dane-Mark, Saxony, Svearland and Vestfold, and elsewhere – I fight to preserve our way of life, our ancient customs and beliefs. I have spent my life defending the freedom that you and Tor and many thousands more people just like you enjoy.'

'A Guardian of the North? What is that?' Tor was frowning at the old man. 'Are there more of you?'

'It is like a guild, a small fellowship of dedicated men and women of knowledge, ability or power, who are committed to the cause of the North. I do not think you know any other Guardians, except Skymir the Mikelgothi, of course, who was once my wife. And Duke Theodoric will not object if I tell you that he is also one. But we seldom reveal who we are to outsiders.'

Neither Bjarki nor Tor knew what to say to this odd revelation.

'You asked why I tried, so clumsily, to make you feel anger, Bjarki,' said Valtyr. 'It was a crude attempt at manipulation. I am sorry for it. But the North, and its way of life, *our* way of life, is in terrible peril. The danger is immense and comes from the Franks, from the Christians, who are a threat to all our people and to our whole world. They would crush us, enslave our people, or make us bow to *their* god – unless… unless we can resist them.'

Valtyr had fixed Bjarki with his one eye, which seemed to blaze like an icy blue jewel in the candlelight of the inn.

'Our civilisation is balanced on the edge of a crumbing cliff, one good hard stamp and we fall to our ruin,' said Valtyr. 'I mean to strike back with all my strength, all my powers, at those who would shove us into the void.

'I hope to gather the North in battle array against the king of the Franks, to defeat him, and force him to leave us in peace. But I need every fighting man and woman to stand in the shield wall beside me. I had hoped you would be such a man, Bjarki. I had hoped that you would spend your strength and courage in our cause; that as a Rekkr, you would *choose* to use your holy gift to protect your own people. I can see now that I hoped in vain.'

Tor said: 'I'm with you, old man; I will fight for the North with all the strength in my bones. How could I not after such a heart-squeezing speech?'

'Thank you, Tor. I accept your offer and rejoice that your courage and battle skill will be ours,' said Valtyr. 'We are the stronger with you beside us.' He looked across the table. '*We* stand for the North, Bjarki Bloodhand. Tor and I believe in our folk and our way of life. What do you stand for?'

They both looked at Bjarki, who could feel their combined will almost physically pushing up against him. He, too, had been moved by Valtyr's speech, but he instinctively sought to resist the old man's invisible pressure.

'I met a long-haired man today,' he said.

Tor frowned.

'I met a man today who offered me the perfect life; or rather the dream of a perfect life, if I would only swear an oath to his master, a great Polans lord of some kind, a duke, he said, and go east and take up new lands in this lord's domain. I refused him. I refused immediately. I refused him because he wanted me to make a solemn promise. And I know that I have broken the last three solemn oaths I made – which shames me deeply. So I said no to him. I turned my back and walked away. No more oaths, I thought. I decided I'd had enough of people trying to bind me to their will. I'd had my fill of people trying to use me to achieve their own ends – I thought of you then, Valtyr, and the Mikelgothi, and Karolus. I told myself I wanted to be free to choose my own path and not be fettered by more oaths and obligations.'

'What oaths you have broken?' said Valtyr.

'I will tell you, although it is painful for me to admit my shame. I broke my oath to Freya. I swore to love and protect her all the days of my life. And only one day of my life later, I was expelled from the village of Bago. I have not seen her since. The second oath I made under the One Tree in the Groves of Eresburg. I swore I would not speak of the secrets of the Fyr Skola to others and, as you may remember, I did not make that choice in any great haste. Yet, in Aachen, I was so grateful to have a friend, to have anyone speak to me in a kindly way, that I spilled out much of what I knew about the Fyr Skola and the Groves… to the king of the Franks. I knew I should not be speaking of these things to him, yet I could not stop myself. Karolus is a good friend, I told myself, and at the same time I knew that he was not.'

There was a painful pause at the table. Valtyr cleared his throat loudly and said: 'Please carry on, Bjarki.'

'The third oath I swore,' said the young warrior, 'was to that same man – to Karolus. I promised to be his faithful vassal. And I broke my oath to him, too. I plotted with Tor against his person – we spoke together in secret about murdering him – then I fled Francia, after killing his servants.'

'Men *do* break oaths, Bjarki,' said Valtyr. 'It is regrettable but true.'

'I know that. But that does not make it acceptable. You speak about the customs of the North, Valtyr, and how you wish to defend them with all your strength. Are oaths not a central part of our way of living; are they not, in fact, the core of what it means to be us? We swear oaths to our kings and jarls, we promise to serve them faithfully. We swear to our wives, to our friends. To the people we trade with. A man's word is sacred. If a man is a known oath-breaker, all shun him. He is no true man; he is a mere *nithing*.'

'We *had* to swear that oath to the king,' said Tor, 'or we would have been slain. I swore the oath at the point of a sword and therefore I feel no shame in breaking it now. He was an enemy. We owed him no fidelity.'

'The oath I made to the king was, as you say, extracted at the point of a sword. But does that really make it less binding? All oaths are made with the knowledge that *not* making them has consequences. Swear and I shall reward you, says the jarl; do *not* swear and you shall be shown no favour.'

Once again there was an awkward silence.

'I do not mean this as an attack on *your* personal honour, Tor,' said Bjarki, 'only on mine. There is some merit to your point-of-a-sword argument. But my own oath-breaking troubles me. I have thought about this long and hard and I have come to realise that I feel the most shame because I broke the vow I made on joining the Fyr Skola by sharing its secrets with its mortal enemies – as you'd put it. So, this is what I have decided to do. In order to expiate my shame, I will journey to the Groves of Eresburg, and beg the Mikelgothi for forgiveness in the shade of the One Tree where the oath was made. I shall undertake whatever punishment she sees fit to give me.'

'So you *will* come west with us then?' said Tor.

'I will go with you to the Groves, if that is where your road takes you,' he said. 'But when I have received forgiveness, I'll come back here and seek out this long-haired dream-seller and his duke and make one final oath, which I shall never break as long as I breathe. This is what I have decided.'

'If you went to the Groves, you could call out Ivar Knuttson – expose him as a cheat and a coward – you saw him flee at Thursby, yes?' said Tor.

'This is so,' said Bjarki gravely. 'And I will gladly fight him again in the Fyr Pit.' He fingered the dent in his face where the man had bitten him.

'To see that,' Tor said, 'I would happily risk a visit the Groves.'

'You know that the Mikelgothi may well order you, for your penance, to go north immediately and fight for Duke Theodoric?' said Valtyr.

'She might. But when the last battle is over. I shall return to Brenna – if I survive the slaughter – and seek to make a new life out east.'

'So be it,' said Valtyr. 'It is agreed. And may the Bear guard you.'

–

They bought horses the next morning, using the last of the Frankish coin, and fresh provisions and new boots for both Tor and Bjarki as theirs were worn to shreds after their long march. They debated whether to sell Garm to an animal dealer they saw at the Spring Market, and both agreed that it was the sensible thing to do – but when it came to it, they could not.

'The cub would be raised as a freak, a tame wildling,' said Bjarki.

'Someone would offer people the chance to kill a live bear,' said Tor. 'Or they would set the dogs against him in the pit when he was bigger.'

So Tor fashioned a padded leather sling in which they could carry the animal as they rode along. Valtyr told them they were mad.

It was gone noon the next day before they rode from the gate of Brenna, crossed the bridge and took the road heading southwest. Bjarki turned back in the saddle when they had gone not more than a few hundred paces down the road – it was a rough, muddy track that would have been despised in Francia – and took a last look at the place he hoped to return to.

The Spring Market was already winding down, and there were wagons and carts streaming out of the main gate, which was flung wide open as those who had sold all their goods or bought everything they were looking for began to make their way home. Most of the traffic was heading north towards the distant coast, and Bjarki wondered whether he would ever be able to catch up with the long-haired man – Goran – when he came back to Brenna to take up his master's offer. What had he said? A man who wished free land must do homage to Duke Leszko in Poznan, wherever that was.

Poznan – he would remember the name.

-

They rode hard, pushing themselves and their horses, and were lucky in that the weather was dry and warm. Bjarki was a poor rider but he was determined not to slow the others down. Tor, who had learnt to ride well as a young girl in Svearland as part of her military training, told Bjarki he looked like a sack of wet barley in the saddle, and made a series of jokes about the suffering horse, named Spot, which had to carry his enormous bulk.

'Be quiet, Tor,' said Valtyr eventually. 'You are wearing my old ears out. And besides, these frontier lands are far from safe. There are said to be swarms of bandits – both Slav and Saxon – in these parts. Keep your mouth shut, your eyes on the skyline and your mind on any potential dangers.'

'The greatest danger is to poor old Spot,' said Tor, 'who must be at the point of expiring, having to bear that unwieldy sack of lard all day long.'

'Go and scout the road ahead, Tor,' said Valtyr testily. 'Go on.'

After that they took up their former practice of travelling mostly in silence, and making all their conversations in the evening around the fire.

There were other familiar aspects of travelling with Valtyr. Tor used her bow to hunt for game, and they ate well most nights. They crossed the River Elbe, swimming beside their horses, and entered Saxony, into the homelands of the Eastphalian tribe. The farms and small villages they passed began to have a homely comforting air; the houses and barns were all the right shape and size, the hedges and fences fashioned in the normal way. The alien-ness of the Wendlands, and before that of Francia – which they had only been aware of in the deepest parts of their minds – fell away. Familiarity re-asserted itself. And always on their left flank as they rode, sometimes close enough to touch and sometimes several leagues away, was a green ocean of a wilder, older countryside: the First Forest.

Bjarki was interested to note, on a day when the road took them hard up against the mossy barrier of ancient, tangled trees, that the local people here followed the old practice of their western compatriots and nailed up living sacrifices to the spirits of the forest: here a skinny spring lamb, pathetically pinioned to the bark of an ancient oak and slowly rotting to pieces; there the severed head of a surprised-looking bull balanced atop a thick beech bough.

Every day, when the sun began to sink in the west, they sought out a place to make their camp. Bjarki would fetch water and wood, Valtyr would usually cook the stew and keep an eye on Garm as the little beast rambled about sniffing and exploring, and Tor took herself a little way away and worked on something involving the mysterious bulky bundle they had carried all the way from the cave. It was a secret, she said. It was meant to be a surprise – and she refused to say any more about her activities. All Bjarki learnt was that it was strenuous work, whatever she did out there, for she came back flushed and sweaty to the fire when it was too dark to see.

It was usually full night by the time they ate, gathered round a decent blaze, and afterwards when Valtyr was in the mood, he would tell a story.

On the fifth night of their journey, Tor said: 'Tell us about a battle, Valtyr! Since we are heading off to the war, tell us something heroic.'

The one-eyed man, who was teasing Garm with a piece of rabbit gristle, looked across the fire and said: 'In that case, Tor, I shall tell you of the battle of Blundfjell, in which your own father, Hildar Torfinnsson, took part.'

He passed the cub over to Tor, who set the animal on her lap, wrapped in her cloak. Valtyr took a large swig of water from the leather skin, and began.

'The events I am to relate took place more than twenty years ago, before either of you were born, in the hard lands known as the Little Kingdoms, north across the sea from the Dane-Mark. In those days, the kings of Varmland and Vestfold were the greatest of rivals; they were cousins, you see, and their fathers had been brothers who hated each other from birth. Vestfold was rich, though, from fishing and good husbandry but Varmland was poor, mostly covered as it was with thick forests and lakes. No man can say why the war began, both sides often raided over the border into their neighbours' lands, coming through the high passes to lift the cattle and sheep and take them home. There were always casualties, always some blood feud between the farmsteaders who lost family to the violence.

'But one year, Ole, King of Varmland, married one of his daughters to Harald Fox-Beard, the powerful king of Svearland and, to seal their new alliance, he invited the great lord of the Svears to come one spring with his warriors and join him in a raid on his neighbours in the Vestfold. Harald agreed and summoned his jarls and his *hersirs* and their warriors and he personally led them through the thick forests of Varmland to Ole's hall.

'Harald's army was five-hundred shields – a formidable force in those days – Ole supplied only a hundred men, and he stayed snug in his hall that spring, not from cowardice, but because he had suffered a broken leg. But after a long, dull winter by the hearth, his young men were eager to fight alongside the Svears, even without their king, all of them in a lather to take plunder and thralls. And the untested warriors of Svearland were equally keen to make names for themselves and prove their valour to the women folk back at home. It always astonished me,' said Valtyr, 'how often I hear stories of a bold young man doing something impossibly reckless to impress a pretty girl he fancies...'

'Was my father trying to impress a girl?' asked Tor.

'Not him. Not then,' said Valtyr. 'He was a lost man then; a ragged, homeless vagabond. He had come to Harald's court the winter before, in the middle of a terrible snowstorm, and begged to be allowed to serve the king, in any capacity at all. And Harald Fox-Beard took pity on him—'

'Wait,' said Tor. She looked perplexed. 'Surely he was then a great hero, a famous Rekkr, why would Harald take pity on him? And where had he come from to be lost in a storm? You're not making any sense, Valtyr.'

'He had come from the Fyr Skola. He had been expelled from the Groves. He killed four servants and two Barda. I am sorry, Tor, but your father went Galálar shortly after his Voyaging. He came back from a month in the forest, where he met his Wolf, but the meeting was too much for his heart. He just exploded one day and began slaying every person in his path. The Ropers quickly netted him, of course, and the fit passed. But…'

Tor's expression had not changed. 'They kicked him out; just like they did me. Sent him packing. Made him a vagabond.'

'They did. Perhaps it would have been kinder to kill him. But you would not be here today, if they had done that, Tor.'

Tor said nothing. She stroked the bear cub and stared into the fire.

'This story isn't very heroic, so far,' said Bjarki. 'Does it get better?'

'Would you rather I did not speak of this, Tor?'

'No, it's all right. I suspected that my father was not… perfect. Continue with your tale, Valtyr. Let's get to the heroic part, if there is one.'

'There is.'

Valtyr took another long swig of water. 'So Hildar Torfinnsson, exiled and hungry, presented himself at the court of Harald Fox-Beard in the deep midwinter, and was taken into service. And all the cold season he was meek and mild, never hurt a fly. Some of the other young men in the retinue thought he was a weakling, thought he was no warrior, a *nithing*. Hildar kept his head down, he accepted the insults of his comrades, and bided his time.'

Bjarki got up and added another log to the fire. The faces in the firelight and the sparks rising upwards, the soothing hum of Valtyr's voice, all made the old man's word-world come to life. Bjarki could imagine the taunts of Harald's jarls, and Hildar, knowing what he did of his true self, knowing what things he was capable of, keeping his eyes down. Saying nothing. Taking no offence. Serving his new Svear lord in humble silence.

'At first, King Harald's grand raid into the Vestfold lands was a great success. The combined Svearlander and Varmlander army surprised a rich lowland town and sacked it, carrying away great booty, and leaving it in flames. They descended on dozens of remote farmsteads and took many cattle. A small force of Vestfold *hersirs* and some of the braver local farm boys, a few scores only, confronted the invading army, but they were easily swept aside. All the while, the king of Vestfold – Anders Black-Tooth was his name – was quietly raising an army, calling his jarls to his banner. Summoning his *hersirs* from across his land, all the men who owed fealty.'

The bear cub was restless, and whining softly, scrabbling at Tor's chest. She handed him silently over to Bjarki, who fumbled in his pouch for a few morsels of hard cheese he always carried there: the cub's favourite snack.

'Harald called a halt to the pillaging after a few weeks. The harassment from the small, swift-moving army of local farmers and *hersirs* was becoming a nuisance; a few of his men died every day. They had gathered a vast herd of cattle and many wagonloads of plunder. It was time to go home.

'"Black-Tooth is too cowardly to confront us," Harald told his men. So they would come again next year, and the year after that. But now it was time to go home and enjoy all that they had gained by war. So they formed a long column, hauling their booty by slow-lumbering ox-carts, and set off north back to the mountain pass that would take them east into Varmland.

'But King Anders was no coward, nor was he stupid, nor yet had he been idle. He had slowly and surely raised a formidable force from all across his own lands, a muster almost twice the size of Harald's invading army, and he set them to watch the pass through which he knew Harald and his warriors must eventually cross, beneath a mountain called the Blundfjell.

'The slow-moving column of ox-drawn wagons was being attacked constantly by the rag-tag army of Vestfolders, angry men who had lost everything to the invaders, and who crept in by night and took their revenge, slaughtering the warriors of Svearland in their blankets, before fleeing into the darkness, disappearing into the countryside they knew well. The spring rains began then, and the wet did not cease for many days, which turned the roads into quagmires and made the ox-carts move more slowly. The wagons became stuck in the mire daily and needed to be lifted out by brute force.

'The Vestfolder attacks came by day now, as well as by night. The Svearlander casualties mounted, hour by hour. Harald Fox-Beard rode up and down the column, urging his men and women to move along faster. When the carts full of loot became stuck in the glutinous mud, he told his warriors to abandon their treasures and ride on. But few obeyed him. They had bled for that plunder. They would carry it home, or die in the attempt. The mountain of Blundfjell loomed over them as they struggled onwards. "We'll soon be safe in Varmland," Harald told his exhausted, mud-slathered troops. "One last effort, and we'll be in the lands of our friend and ally!" Then the beleaguered column came to the saddle of land beneath the high mountain where, to their surprise and horror, they saw the mighty army of Anders Black-Tooth waiting for them, blocking the only road home.'

Valtyr yawned. 'Are you sure you want me to continue, my children?' he said. 'It is late. You look sleepy, Tor, shall I stop now and tuck you in?'

He was grinning slyly at them both.

'You stop now, old man, and I'll cut your other eye out the moment you fall sleep,' said Tor.

'As you wish, my little firebrand,' he said. 'Now, where was I? Oh yes, the Svearlander column was surrounded beneath Blundfjell: behind them was the rag-tag militia of dispossessed and angry Vestfolders; on either side loomed impassable mountains; and before them a fresh army of mail-clad jarls and doughty *hersirs* – a thousand shields blocking their path.

'The invaders abandoned their plunder-wagons now; they were forced to. They released all the thralls they had taken and drove them away. And the Svearlander army drew together in one compact mass. But there were fewer than four hundred left alive after the bloodletting of the past weeks.

'King Harald addressed his demoralised troops. "We cannot go back down into Vestfold," he said. "We would be hunted down, chased around the enemy's lands until we were all dead. And we cannot fly over these accursed mountains. There is only one thing to be done," he said. "We must go forward together and smash the impudent enemy who dares stand before us."

'His jarls pointed out that the enemy had more than a thousand fresh men in their shield wall, while they had only a few hundred wounded and exhausted ones. "Look at them, Fox-Beard, look! Three men deep in a wall that stretches across the whole pass. We cannot hope to beat them."

'That was when Hildar Torfinnsson stepped forward out of the throng of noble jarls and proud *hersirs*. "Great Lord," he said, "if we cut off the head of the snake, the body will surely die. I will kill their king for you personally. I can break their shield wall alone and cut down Black-Tooth. If you will follow after me, when I make my charge, we can split the enemy line asunder. When they are leaderless, then we can make our escape down the other side of the mountain and into the safety of our ally's lands."

'The king's hearth-men laughed and taunted Hildar, calling him mad and boastful, and a liar if he made these foolish claims. But the king listened to his voice. "Who else has a plan to save us?" he said. Not one warrior answered. "Very well, Hildar Torfinnsson, if you can break their wall and kill King Anders, I shall follow you into the fray, and we shall have victory."

'In the chill of the mountain air, Hildar stripped himself of his clothing, he took only his long axe, a seax and a shield, and wearing no armour but fur vambraces on his forearms and greaves over his boots, he began to hum.

'He hummed, and he hummed some more, and his *gandr* came to him. Nearly naked, and all alone, he charged into the shield wall of the king of Vestfold's jarls. It was just one man against a thousand foes, so the stories tell us. Yet this was not quite true. The Fire Born charged the very centre of the enemy line, where Anders Black-Tooth had set his personal banner.

'Hildar Torfinnsson hurled himself into the shield wall, three men thick, and wrought bloody destruction with his long axe and with his shield. He slew the jarls, and he scattered the *hersirs*, he smashed open the wall, and fought all the way to the king himself.

And there, after a bloodbath the likes of which had never been seen before, the lone Rekkr slew King Anders and every man in his personal bodyguard, with his axe and seax he ripped their ranks apart… and Harald Fox-Beard, King of Svearland, kept his word to his liegeman. He followed Hildar Torfinnsson with all his men, charging in the footsteps of the Fire Born's one-man assault upon the far superior foe.

'And when Hildar broke open their wall and killed the king, Harald's whole army – or what was left of it – poured through the gap the Rekkr had made and streamed down the mountainside into the forests of Varmland. And the army of the Vestfold, shattered, leaderless, and demoralised by this disaster, could not follow after them, and so they allowed their enemies to escape.

'And that, my friends, was how Hildar Torfinnsson saved Harald, King of Svearland, from defeat in the mountains and almost certain death.'

Valtyr stopped talking. And a silence fell over the little camp.

'That is a good story, old man,' said Tor sleepily. 'I shall allow you to keep your one remaining eye.'

'You are generosity made flesh, girl,' said Valtyr.

'Do you think it's true?' said Bjarki. 'That just one man could break a well-formed shield wall like that? Sounds like a fanciful story for children.'

'It's true,' said Valtyr. 'I know for sure that it is true.'

'How can you be so certain?' said Bjarki.

'I know because I was there. I was a young spearman in the army of Harald Fox-Beard on the ill-fated Vestfold raid.' He put a finger to his empty socket. 'I left my right eye on the field at Blundfjell. But I made it home to Svearland nonetheless. And I have Hildar Torfinnsson to thank for my deliverance.'

Chapter Twenty-six

Return to the Groves

They left the road the next day and plunged into the First Forest, heading roughly south and west. They released the horses, slapping their rumps to send them cantering away, and packed all their belongings into their back-sacks. There was not much food left, and beside their weapons and spare clothing, they did not have all that much to carry except for Tor's mysterious package. Valtyr claimed that he was leading them on a well-known path through the tangled trees, but to both Bjarki and Tor it seemed as if they were struggling through virgin woodland, almost as thick as the snowy wastelands they had negotiated with such difficulty north of Regensburg.

Bjarki took the lead, hacking at the undergrowth with his axe, trying to locate this path that Valtyr insisted existed. But when he complained that he could see no trace of it, the old man answered just as vaguely as he had last time he had been questioned about the exact routes, and times and distances of travel through these primeval woodlands.

'The First Forest is a magical place, Bjarki,' Valtyr said. 'No journey through this place is ever the same twice. The old trees are alive, for they contain the ancient spirits. So go easy with that great big axe, will you?'

'I can't walk through wood,' snapped Bjarki. 'I must cut a path.'

'Think of the trees as the hairs growing on the Middle-Realm's beard,' Valtyr said. 'Your axe is a razor. So take the proper care when you cut.'

When they camped for the night, Valtyr refused to let them have a fire yet Bjarki made no complaint. He was regretting his former ill humour. In fact, if was rather pleasurable to be reliving their previous journey in the First Forest together. 'I wonder if we will meet another bear,' said Bjarki.

'I haven't got over the one near Eggeldorf,' said Tor. 'And speaking of that monster, I have something for you, Bjarki. I have been trying to find the right moment to give it to you. I guess this is as good a time as any other.'

Tor rummaged in her back-sack, and pulled out her package. She untied the leather thongs that held it all together, and shook out the contents. It was a vast bearskin cloak, very thick and black as midnight.

Garm gave a little snuffle and waddled towards it; its scent striking a powerful chord in his memory.

'It's a gift,' said Tor. 'For you. To celebrate you becoming a Rekkr.'

'Oh,' said Bjarki. 'Oh… it is… magnificent. But how did you…?'

'I worked on it while we travelled through the snow, while you were asleep, scraping the fat off the skin and rubbing in salt and oil. I had some help from a tanner in Brenna and, well, that's not important. You like it?'

Bjarki, who had never been given such a splendid gift, was rendered speechless. He opened up his massive arms and enfolded Tor in a giant hug.

They held each other for a long, long time, feeling the warmth and comfort of each other's bodies. Bjarki found he was weeping with joy.

'That's enough of that,' said Valtyr. He seemed oddly disturbed by this physical show of their affection for each other. 'Put her down, Bjarki.'

'Try it on,' said Tor, sniffing too, and Bjarki draped the heavy fur around his broad shoulders and clasped it. The cloak fell exactly to the right length, the hem just brushing the forest floor. Garm sniffed the edge of the fur and began making happy squeaking noises. 'I will sleep warm and dry tonight,' said Bjarki, 'and I believe Garm will be curling up with me, too.'

–

The first thing they sensed that told them something was wrong was the smell of smoke. It was faint but persistent. They all looked at each other in alarm. No one made campfires in the First Forest, no one – and the smell was too pervasive for a small cooking blaze anyway.

'Hurry,' snapped Valtyr, his vague, old-man pose entirely gone.

They rushed through the trees, the low branches seeming to grab angrily at them as they pushed through. Valtyr led, moving surprisingly fast, dodging under branches, sliding round trunks, and Bjarki and Tor, who was carrying Garm, had a good deal of difficulty in keeping up with him.

They came out on the bald ridge to the north of the valley of the Groves and stopped dead, utterly appalled.

The Groves of Eresburg had been destroyed. Where there had been a high, island-like oasis of bright green sticking up in the centre of the river valley there was now a blackened mash of mud and broken timber. The One Tree, the mightiest of oaks, the fabled Irminsul, was a massive twisted charcoal skeleton. A haze of smoke hung over the whole valley. Not one of the Lodges was still standing, nor any of the other buildings atop the stronghold. The Thing House, the largest building on Eresburg, was a rectangle of ash.

And the destruction was recent. The One Tree was still smouldering, wisps of smoke rising into the clear air from its tortured limbs. And there were flocks of ravens circling the incinerated settlement, where Bjarki could just make out the tiny, scattered bodies of his folk, his friends.

'Yesterday,' said Tor. 'The fires were raging yesterday, or possibly the night before that. They took their time with it; set them all cunningly, against every wooden wall, to be thorough.

If we had only been a little faster on the journey, if we had not dawdled, we could have—'

'We would have been slaughtered with the rest of them,' said Valtyr.

'Who could have done this?' Bjarki's brain was having difficulty encompassing the scale of this disaster. 'The Irminsul, the Groves…'

'We know who did this,' said Valtyr, and he looked hard at Bjarki.

They went slowly, blades at the ready, Valtyr leading the way down the steep path to the valley bottom. Bjarki found he was weeping again, and trembling a little, but he was also filled with a pure, cold rage. And one ice-hard word was bouncing around inside his head: vengeance.

They found the place where the main battle had been fought down in the valley. It was a little to the west of the heights of the Groves on the northern side of the river. Some sort of shield wall had been formed, they could tell by the fall of the bodies, and then swiftly broken, with heavy cavalry triumphant by the look of the hoof-torn ground – many hundreds of *cabellarii*. The defenders had battled on individually until they all fell.

He could imagine the thick knots of Frankish horsemen surrounding each Rekkr or Barda, swamping them with their superior numbers. There were bodies everywhere, even in the shallows of the river, and Bjarki found his eyes misting with tears again as he saw face after torn face that he knew so well. He sensed a sudden movement and turned quickly but it was only Valtyr falling suddenly to his knees, and picking up a slight, limp corpse and crushing it to his breast. It was Skymir the Mikelgothi.

Here was Angantyr, lying in a lake of blood. He had very nearly been cut into pieces and it was clear that the Father of the Bear Lodge had fought to the last like a true Rekkr. He had been pierced deeply in both thighs, and had lost one hand and was wounded deeply many times through his bare torso. The lower half of his face was entirely missing, yet Bjarki was still able to recognise him. The Bear triangle between his brows was untouched.

It suddenly occurred to him that there was no sign of his enemies. The scores of Frankish troops Angantyr had fought against, the Red Cloaks, or the heavily armoured *Scholares* or whoever it had been who ended his life; they were nowhere to be seen. Neither were there any wounded. All the Grove people were stone dead, throats opened, finished off by their enemies.

Bjarki lifted his eyes from the churned-up ground and the puddles of gore and saw a huge mound of freshly dug earth over by the tree line.

The Christians had buried their own, it seemed, but ignored the corpses of their foes. Almost two-thirds of the membership of the Groves was lying here, scattered, dismembered, bloody, cold and still. Bjarki saw Helga, or rather just her sightless severed head: she had been Tor's Elder Sister before becoming Rekkr, and had treated Tor indifferently, he remembered. She was nobody's sister now. A few paces later he came across Hymir, the Bear Lodge master-at-arms, and endured a fresh shaft of agony. He remembered the kindly man's backhanded compliment that had pleased him so much: 'Just do the simple routine that *I* teach, little bear, don't go showing off.'

He had to cuff his hot eyes clear at that moment. And there were more corpses that he knew: Sif, another of the Bear Lodge's Rekkar, a woman with a lusty appetite for young warriors; Edmund the Angelcynn, another brave comrade; Floki the White, one of the senior Barda; Little Sven Half-Finger, a Bear Lodge servant, a clumsy little fellow; and many more whose names he could not recall.

He found himself standing next to Valtyr.

'We should bury them,' he said.

'No,' said Valtyr, 'we have not the time. There are more than seventy dead here and Tor says more are lying up on the summit of the Groves; Lodge servants and *gothi*, those who chose not to fight. Just as dead. We must bear the news to Theodoric, tell them what has befallen the Fyr Skola.'

‘We can’t just leave them here, lying out like this—’

‘No!’ There was steel in Valtyr’s voice. ‘The only woman I ever loved is lying over there, cold as contempt. Do you think I would leave her if this were not far more important? We must go to Theodoric *now*.’

‘Hey, hey, help me…’ a distant voice was shouting, and Bjarki turned to look at the tree line. A gaunt figure was emerging from the wall of green.

‘Is that… no, is it? Can that really be old Bjarki Bloodhand?’

The figure came closer, running a little in his eagerness, and Bjarki saw that it was Gunnar, the boy who had been his Elder Brother and then his good friend, and that one side of his face was crusted black with dried blood.

-

They got the tale from Gunnar as they hurried north through the First Forest. Two days ago a massive Frankish force had appeared, coming from the west along the river, filling the little valley with their vast numbers – a thousand Red Cloaks, five hundred Green Cloaks and about two hundred mounted *Scholares*, that’s what Angantyr had estimated when they mustered for battle. The Fyr Skola had fewer than a hundred shields. And nine Rekkar.

‘We couldn’t work out how they had discovered us,’ Gunnar said. ‘For generations the location of the Groves has been a closely held secret – you remember that solemn oath we all had to swear, Bjarki, under the Irminsul?’

There was an awkward silence. Nobody answered him.

‘Well, however they did it, they found us, and came in overwhelming force. We made our battle line down in the valley, two-men thick, Rekkar in the centre and on the wings. The Mikelgothi said we should remain on the summit of the Groves, and fight behind the palisade, but Angantyr said they would be able to scale the cliffs and come at us from all sides. And anyway, we were seeking to keep the fighting far away from the One Tree, so we came down to the valley and made our thin line across it, barring their path.

'We made our shield wall there and we all sang the "Death Song of Tiw", that miserable old dirge – I am a Barda now, Bjarki, did I tell you? They finally allowed me to join the ranks. Not that I really wanted to. I'd rather have been up in the compound with the servants and the *gothi* than standing in that feeble line in the valley, quaking with fear, warm piss dribbling down my legs, waiting for those massed Frankish horsemen to charge into us.'

'You wouldn't have been any safer in the compound,' said Tor.

'No, I suppose not. Some folk retreated up there after the first Frankish assault, those who survived it. And the Green Cloaks – those are their mountain troops – came scrambling up the cliffs, on all sides, just as Angantyr predicted. He was dead by then, of course… And I saw them torch the Groves afterwards – hundreds of Red Cloaks with oil and bundles of faggots. They carried away the contents of the treasury first in carts, all that gold and silver in Odin's shrine beside the Thing House, all gone. Well, nothing could have survived that fire, anyway. And if I'd been up there—'

'How *did* you escape with your life, Gunnar?' said Bjarki. 'No wait, shush, absolute quiet now.'

They were in the deep, gloomy forest, but something was moving up ahead. Bjarki could hear the crackle of a heavy body moving through the undergrowth. He drew his sword; Tor, beside him, had an axe in her hand.

Whatever it was, it was approaching them. And very close now. Bjarki found that he was humming, softly, deep in his throat. A long hairy snout appeared through a tangle of brush at knee height, below a pair of red piggy eyes. It stared at them for a moment then crashed away noisily heading west.

'It's just a boar,' said Valtyr. 'It's just a wild pig looking for food.'

They walked on a little in silence. 'Carry on, Gunnar,' said Bjarki. 'How did you manage to escape them?'

'They had archers,' the Barda said, 'and they filled the sky with their arrows. We lost about a third of our strength before they got within a sword's length of our shield wall. Then the heavy horsemen charged home. They cut through us like a knife through wet curds. The Rekkar were all humming, and chanting, and they fought like heroes, as you would expect. Slaying left and right. But the Franks cut them to pieces in the end; then their infantry came in, all marching together, fifty men in each company. Hundreds of them, row upon row, not like men at all. It was… horrible.'

'You haven't answered the question,' said Tor sternly. 'How did you get away when all the rest of our people died?'

For a moment, Gunnar said nothing.

'Gunnar?' said Bjarki.

'All right, all right. I ran – there, are you happy now? I played the coward. I got knocked down by a horseman; took a nasty whack on the head. My helmet split and I had blood in my eyes. By then, the line was broken, and our people were fighting in ones and twos, some running back up to the Groves, Franks riding everywhere slaughtering the Barda, Red Cloaks coming up in vast numbers… and I ran. I sprinted for the trees at the edge of the valley and hid there whimpering like a craven till you came today.'

There was a shocked silence.

'Not all men are made to be warriors,' said Valtyr finally. But even he seemed a little disappointed. The other two could find nothing at all to say.

–

Two days later, Bjarki was peering out from behind an oak, looking at a *cunei* of Red Cloaks marching across his line of sight. He had seen dozens more companies – each fifty men strong – passing that morning, heading northeast. The flat Saxon countryside beyond the forest, traditionally the territory of the horse-breeding Angrian tribe, was crawling with them.

'It's a full-strength invasion,' said Valtyr at Bjarki's elbow. 'They have come north to end Theodoric's rule for good. To destroy the North.'

'How can we get past them?' said Tor. 'Can't you summon up a magic mist to hide us in? Or make us invisible?'

'I could turn us all into birds? We could fly over their heads and shit all over them, if you like,' said Valtyr.

'Could you really do that?' said Tor.

'Of course not,' said Valtyr. 'Don't be idiotic. How many times must I tell you, I'm neither wizard, nor sorcerer, I'm not even much of a conjuror.'

'But, surely, as a Guardian of the North—'

'Listen to me, Tor, as a Guardian I gather information and pass it on to those who can best use it in defence of our folk and our lands. That is what I do – all I do. I gather news, pass messages, sometimes do a little persuading and whispering in the right ears. And right now we must find a way to get to Theodoric quickly and tell him the Groves have been destroyed.'

'What's the hurry?' said Tor. 'The Fyr Skola will still be a pile of dead folk and damp ashes in a week's time – or even next month.'

'Theodoric may be expecting aid from the Fyr Skola. I'd be surprised if he did not expect a powerful contingent to help him in the coming battle. Also, it will light a fire under his troops to know what the enemy has done to the sacred Groves. We must tell him the news as soon as possible.'

'There *is* a powerful contingent coming to his aid,' said Tor, making a little circling movement with her finger. 'We are coming to rescue him.'

Valtyr laughed, a little hollowly. 'Yes, indeed.'

'I think I know how we can pass through them without being arrested,' said Bjarki. 'It will take more than a little luck but it might suffice.'

–

They marched in a compact group on the road north, four of them all clearly armed and armoured, no disguises, no attempt at all at subterfuge.

They were challenged once that day, towards nightfall, when they came to a *castrum* – a newly built one where there had once been a little Saxon village – which had several pickets posted outside the new pinewood gate.

'Name yourselves and state your business!' came the order from a Red Cloak officer standing in the half darkness; his spear levelled at them.

Behind him were three other spear-armed Red Cloaks. For a tiny moment, Bjarki was tempted to pull out his sword and annihilate them all. His raw anger at the destruction of the Groves was like a coal burning in his chest, which could only be quenched by buckets of Frankish blood. He knew he could do it alone, and without even troubling his *gandr*; and with Tor's efficient help it could all be over in a matter of a few heartbeats.

Instead, he controlled himself, snapped to attention rigidly and yelled out: 'Bjarki Bloodhand, sir, Trooper First-Class in His Majesty's Auxilla, sir. Detached on special duties, sir.'

'Auxilla, eh? I know of them. Scruffy bunch. Remind me, soldier, what is the name of your commanding officer? Captain Rollo, isn't it?'

'Captain Otto, sir,' said Bjarki.

'Oh yes, of course,' said the officer. 'Good old Captain Otto. Big hairy fellow, very tall, blond, massive beard, if I recall. Is that right?'

'Small and bald, sir, begging your pardon. No beard to speak of.'

The officer chuckled. 'Forgive my caution. Lots of spies about.'

'Can't be too careful, sir,' Bjarki said.

'So what are you doing here, trooper?'

'I'm trying to find the front lines, sir. Scouting duties for the Auxilla.'

'You're a long way from the front, man. You'd better come inside the *castrum* and spend the night here. We'll give you a decent bite of supper.'

'No, sir, thank you, sir. We have orders to get forward as quickly as possible, sir. Our captain is waiting. We don't mind a bit of night marching.'

'Suit yourself. What is that trooper carrying in the sling. Is it a dog?'

'*Scara* mascot, sir,' said Bjarki.

'Right. Well, carry on then. Straight up this sorry excuse for a road for about twenty miles and you will find the front lines eventually. Off you go.'

'Thank you, sir.'

–

They camped an hour later in a spinney of alders and made a small fire, over which Gunnar cooked a slop of oat pottage. All of them were feeling nervous and subdued. They had been reminded during the long day's march of just how powerful Francia was. On the journey to Regensburg, Captain Otto had told Bjarki that the king had a hundred thousand men under arms, and Bjarki had duly marvelled at the figure. But saying a big number was a great deal different to seeing the actual men who made up that huge force.

All day they had passed units of Red Cloaks, hundreds, perhaps thousands, and a few score Green Cloaks, too, the sight of which made Bjarki's ears fill with the sound of rushing water. But he controlled himself. A company of *Scholares* horsemen had cantered past around noon, going south for some reason, and Bjarki had taken a moment to study their arms and armour as they thundered by. They looked truly formidable: clad in good scale-mail, ridged steel helms and greaves, bearing nine-foot lances, two swords, some with axes and maces, and big black round shields painted with the Christian cross in white. Even their horses looked fearsome; some were even covered like their grim riders in scale-mail.

They had seen hundreds of civilians, bald men, frowning at scrolls before directing gangs of slaves to start repairing the poor Saxon roads. They had passed at least three new churches, too, and heard the communal singing from inside as the Frankish soldiers raised their voices to honour their god.

No one felt much like talking that night and, when the tasteless pottage was all eaten, they wrapped themselves in their cloaks – Bjarki and Garm sharing the big bearskin – and slept uneasily until a little before dawn.

They saw the first signs of fighting the next day, corpses and scorched crops and, once, a village where it looked as if some sort of extremely bloody rearguard action had been fought. There was a pile of about twenty dead warriors of the North, stripped of their arms and armour, white flesh, gaping red wounds and dead eyes staring into the next world. The village had been torched either during the battle or after it, and the remains of its four thatched longhouses still smouldered.

They hurried past, with Gunnar trying hard not to stare at the gashed bodies or the destruction of life. Valtyr muttered: 'Ottersfeld, that was the name of this place. Knew a woman here who brewed fine ale, the best—'

There came the sound of brass trumpets and drums, very loud and getting louder, and the harsh clattering of a mass of cavalry approaching.

'Off the road,' said Tor. 'Keep well clear of the horses.'

The four of them jogged off the track and into a small wood of silver birch. They passed round oatcakes and water skins, and watched as a grand cavalcade of *Scholares* cavalry trotted up the road, two hundred troopers at least. Bjarki wondered whether they knew that Lord Grimoald was dead, and guessed they did. It had been several weeks since the battle at the cave. Who, he wondered, had taken over as high commander of the Black Cloaks?

It was Valtyr who recognised the danger first. 'Get behind the trees, you two. Now!' He shoved Bjarki hard towards the nearest trunk.

Right there in front of them, not thirty paces away, on a magnificent black horse, was Karolus himself. Above him fluttered his eagle banner, black and gold. Tor and Bjarki kept their faces hidden behind their trees but Valtyr and Gunnar gaped like yokels as the great man, surrounded by a sea of Black Cloaks, clattered past. Beside him, on his shield side, rode the Duke of Swabia, in dark cloak and scale-mail. Gerold's youthful face was contorted, as ever, in a petulant scowl. Beyond these two there was a flash of colourful robes, scarlet and blue and gold, a flamboyant presence amid all the black wool and iron armour and Tor caught a glimpse of the man riding at the king's right hand, almost like an equal. It was the king's chancellor and chaplain, Livinus, the new Bishop of Aachen.

'Are you sure you can't just lob a magic fireball at them and blow them all to bloody rags in a flash of blinding white light?' whispered Tor.

'If I could do that, girl, it would already be done,' Valtyr replied.

The king, the duke and the bishop were past them now, and the Black Cloak escort too were disappearing in a whirling cloud of their own dust.

'What does it signify,' said Bjarki, 'that the king himself is here?'

'It means they seek to crush us all completely this time,' said Valtyr.

An hour after that, when the shadows were lengthening, Bjarki could just make out the looming black bar of the Dane-Work on the northern horizon, two or three miles away.

Suddenly, he and the others found themselves surrounded by a ring of hard eyes and drawn bows, and a voice saying in Saxon: 'Take one more step, big lad, and I'll skewer you.'

Chapter Twenty-seven

A council of war

The ten-man Saxon patrol that escorted the travellers into Hellingar Fortress was one of the last to have ventured out beyond the Dane-Work before Theodoric gave the order that the only drawbridge over the channel – a great lumbering wooden structure on wheels – should be removed and every man who served the Duke of Saxony must remain behind its ramparts.

They told the captain on duty in Hellingar who they were, and Valtyr asked for an audience with Theodoric immediately. As the old man was led away, one of the patrol leaders, a fellow named Kundar, said: 'If you'd like to follow me, my friends, I will take you to the rest of your comrades. They are lodged in the third quadrant, in Ash House. This way, if you please…'

Bjarki was mystified, glanced at Gunnar and Tor, who just shrugged back at him, and followed the broad shoulders of Kundar as the warrior set off at a brisk pace walking down one of the two log-paved roads that, set at right angles to each other and running north–south and east–west, neatly divided the circular fortress of Hellingar into its four numbered quadrants.

They were taken to a longhouse in the third quadrant and once they reached the door, or rather the thick piece of cowhide that hung over the entrance, Kundar, with a bow and cheery wave, left them.

'Comrades?' said Bjarki. Gunnar swallowed nervously. Tor loosened the seax in its sheath on her belt. Garm gave an interested little snuffle.

They lifted the leather flap and went into the longhouse.

It was very hot inside Ash House: the long fire-trough that ran down its centre had been piled high with logs as if it were the deep midwinter rather than early spring. After so many nights spent out in the cold, Bjarki immediately began to sweat. Few people took any notice of the three newcomers, not even of the bear cub poking its shiny black nose out from the swathe of cloth at Tor's hip. Almost every eye was fixed on the far end of the hall, where a bowed figure appeared to be affixed somehow to the rough log wall, arms and legs spread wide.

The fellow on the wall, a clean-shaven man with his dark hair cut short in a military style, looked terrified, and Bjarki could see that the crotch of his once-white linen breeches were stained dark where he had pissed himself in fear. He was securely attached by leather thongs at wrists and ankles tied to heavy nails hammered into the logs. There were several heavy knives and axes embedded in the wood, some just inches from his body. As Bjarki looked on, a squat, muscular figure with his back to the doorway, a man almost as broad as he was tall, drew back his right hand and hurled a bearded axe. The long weapon spun through the air and – *thunk!* – smacked blade-first into the logs a finger's width from the wretch's face.

The prisoner gave a little cry, not far from a whimper, which was drowned out by the huge roar of approval from the watching crowd.

The squat man who had hurled the axe so successfully turned with both his bare muscular arms lifted in triumph and he was cheered to the rafters by the dozen or so folk who were crowded around him at that end of the hall.

It was Ivar Knuttson, the new Father of the Boar Lodge.

They stared at each other for a long moment. But Gunnar broke the tension by crossing between them and calling out greetings to people he knew in the hall, and being welcomed with pleasure in return. The Barda began telling the eager throng about the disaster in the Groves, and Bjarki was dimly aware of the general cries of horror and sadness – and anger too – erupting all around him. Even Tor was being welcomed by some of the inhabitants of the longhouse she knew, but perhaps with less enthusiasm.

Bjarki continued looking steadily, unblinkingly at Ivar, and then began to move towards him, pushing through the crush of folk and their questions.

Ivar dropped his eyes; then raised them again immediately, knowing he had somehow already lost the silent battle of wills between him and Bjarki.

Bjarki was closing on him, only three steps away. Ivar called out: 'By the gods: it's Bjarki Bloodhand, of Bear Lodge, back from the land of the dead! Welcome, Bjarki! Welcome to Ash House! Bring ale for our guest!'

Bjarki stopped one stride from Ivar. He stared at him in stony silence.

'Where have you been, Bjarki?' Ivar's tone was jolly, and comradely, but with a wobbling edge of falsity. 'We thought you killed at Thursby? I only got away by the skin of my teeth myself; had to chop my way clear. But, here you are; obviously, you didn't get cut up with the rest. Captured, were you? Held by the Franks? Enslaved? I imagine that was very hard. But you're back – that's the most important thing! And you're welcome!'

Bjarki still did not utter a word. Someone offered him a foaming horn of ale. He ignored the out-thrust hand. His blue eyes bored into Ivar's.

Ivar's face began to change. The false bonhomie faded away. His expression showed a flash of fear, then grew uglier, flushed with hatred.

'Many things have changed since you left us, Bloodhand,' he said quietly. 'Lot of changes in our little world – I'm Father of the Boar Lodge now and, if the rumours I've just heard are true, I'm the most senior Rekkr left alive. I am, therefore, the leader of the remnants of the Fyr Skola – and all these people look to me for leadership. So you… you'd better watch your step. You'd better be very careful what you say to me – or about me.'

'I know what you *truly* are, Ivar Knuttson,' said Bjarki in an equally quiet voice, almost a whisper. He could feel his *gandr* hovering just outside of his body. It was eager to enter him, eager for the inevitable bloodshed to begin. He heard rushing water in his ears, and had to fight the urge to hum.

'And you know what I am, don't you? I am what you only pretend to be.'

Ivar looked into Bjarki's eyes and recognised the Beast inside him.

'Take the h-horn of a-ale, Bjarki. Quench your thirst, my old friend. Be welcome here! We are all on the same side. There is no need for ill feeling, or petty quarrelling between comrades. You must have had a hard time as a prisoner of the Franks. Here, take revenge for your hurts on this cringing Frankish worm – we caught him on our last patrol, but he didn't have anything useful to tell us. So I decided we should have a little fun with him. Have a turn, go on; I promise it will put you in a much better humour.'

Ivar had a throwing knife in his left hand, held out hilt-first; he was offering it to Bjarki. 'The rules of the game are simple, my friend: you try to get the blade into the wall but as close to the target as you can without cutting him. Make him squirm, go on. It's a fine game; here, take the knife.'

Bjarki took the hilt of the heavy knife. He thought about his options; plunging it deep into the man in front of him and ripping out his entrails seemed the most interesting idea. He could feel his *gandr* urging him to take the first step down this bloody path. But then he'd have to kill almost every person in this hall, all his friends and comrades, all the blameless Fyr Skola folk. No, he could not take that step. He shut his mind to the pleading of his *gandr*. There was a battle coming, an epic struggle for the North; they would need every hand that could lift a sword, even *nithings* like Ivar Knuttson.

He weighed the throwing knife in his hand and looked at the terrified prisoner hanging from the wall. *Vengeance for the Groves*, he thought. *Yes*, and he heard his *gandr* somewhere close chuckle darkly with anticipation.

He accepted the horn of ale, tipped back his head and drained it. Then he tossed the empty vessel to a bystander, drew back his hand and hurled the knife with all his strength at the wretch at the far end of the house. The blade flew true, spinning over and over, the dull steel catching the firelight, and it smacked hard between the eyes of the man tied to the logs, and split his skull like a walnut. The man's brains and blood splashed messily across the wall.

There were several groans, even derisory hoots. 'Now you've gone and done it, oaf,' said a voice at his elbow. 'You've ruined everybody's fun.'

'Sorry, Tor,' he mumbled, looking down. 'That was clumsy of me.'

–

'We're summoned to a council of war,' said Valtyr. It was early the next morning, and the old man had joined Bjarki, Tor and Gunnar in Ash House for a breakfast of ham and eggs, toasted bread, butter and fruit preserves.

One thing the Dane-Work and Hellingar Fortress was not short of was supplies. Siegfried, King of the Dane-Mark, and Duke Theodoric had known this day would come for many months, perhaps even years, and between them they had been stocking the granaries and storehouses of the defensive line with fresh, dried and salted provisions until they were full to bursting. There was no danger of the army of the North being forced from its position by hunger. And even if they were to be pinned here for months by the hordes of Frankish troops on their doorstep, they could always bring down food from the rest of Jutland or even from further afield by ship.

'Who else will be there?' asked Bjarki, stealing a piece of buttered toast from Valtyr's over-flowing plate. He and his friends had already eaten mightily that morning, after a late and fairly drunken night in the Ash House, but he found when there was food available it was hard for him to resist it.

'The Duke of Saxony, of course, and his eldest son, Widukind, and King Siegfried and Jarl Snorri Hare-Lip, Master of Hellingar, also Ivar Knuttson, Father of the Boar Lodge – I trust, Bjarki, that you will comport yourself with the proper decorum around our good friend Ivar.'

'I believe we came to an understanding last night,' said Bjarki. 'We'll co-operate with each other while the enemy is at our gates. Afterwards…'

'Good. And there are two other respected Fyr Skola folk who sought refuge here,' said Valtyr, 'both from your own Bear Lodge, Bjarki. Eldar the *gothi*, who is one of the finest healers I've ever met; and Nikka the Dreamer – a true Rekkr but one who has not fought a battle for many years.'

'I know them both – and value them highly,' said Bjarki.

'None of the Wolf Lodge people survived?' said Tor.

'Alas, no,' said Valtyr. There was a moment of awkward silence.

Last night, Bjarki had learnt, over many horns of ale and a raucous feast in which a whole roasted ox had been consumed, how the Fyr Skola folk – sixteen people, including the arrivals – had come to be in Ash House.

As Duke Theodoric had been pushed further and further back north by the ever-advancing Frankish tide, he'd sent a stream of desperate messages to the Groves imploring the Fyr Skola for help. After the drubbing they had received at Thursby in the autumn – a battle with unusually high casualties for the Groves, in which two famous Rekkar and nine Barda had lost their lives – the Mikelgothi had been reluctant to sacrifice yet more of her people. But the Mother of the Wolf Lodge, a cousin of Theodoric's, had volunteered three of her Wolf Rekkar and a dozen of her Barda to support her Saxon kinsman. They had all died in a bloody rearguard action a dozen miles south of the Dane-Work, at Otterfeld, in Nordalbian territory, heroically holding up the enemy advance and allowing Duke Theodoric to get the bulk of his retreating Saxon forces back behind King Siegfried's massive earthworks.

On the eve of the fight at Otterfeld, Skymir the Mikelgothi had dreamt of a terrible disaster engulfing the Fyr Skola and, on waking, she sent immediately reinforcements north, a mixed force from all three Lodges, under the command of Ivar Knuttson, Father of the Boar Lodge. They had narrowly missed the bloody massacre at Otterfeld, arriving a day too late to help, but had managed to get themselves safely into the stronghold at Hellingar despite being constantly harassed by the Frankish foot patrols.

'So who's the top dog here?' said Gunnar. 'Siegfried or Theodoric?'

'That remains unclear,' said Valtyr. 'Duke Theodoric has many more men – two thousand battle-hardened Saxon fighters under his command, while Siegfried has no more than five hundred shields. But the Dane-Work is Siegfried's pride and joy, the achievement of his lifetime, and it is on his lands. In theory, Theodoric is Siegfried's hearth guest. In reality you might say that – like Bjarki and Ivar – they co-operate with each other.'

–

The council of war was held, not as one might expect, in one of the longhouses in Hellingar Fortress, but in a draughty command post – not much more than a long cowshed – which had been constructed on the brow of the east rampart, and overlooked the countryside for miles around. As Bjarki toiled in full war-gear and heavy bear cloak up the man-made hill, one of the two enormous earthworks that he had seen the year before when travelling south with Valtyr, he was awed once again by the size of Siegfried's achievement.

He paused at the summit of the east rampart to catch his breath and admire the view. Leaning on the chest-high wooden fence at the top and looking south into Nordalbia, he could see a wasteland of trampled fields and broken hedges, territory crossed again and again by bodies of marching men. The small woods and copses that had once been a pleasant feature of the lands hereabouts had all been cut down to bare stumps for firewood by bivouacking soldiers. The landscape bore no resemblance at all to the rich, placid farmland he had walked through with Tor and Valtyr only a year ago.

On the horizon, a mile or so away, he could see a great low bank of pale grey smoke and the dark line of the Frankish encampment under it. The wise word in the fortress had been that the Franks had fielded four thousand against them, which was already an impossible number – how would they feed such a multitude? What about water and firewood? Fodder for their animals? How would they prevent siege-fever running rampant through the lines? Yet, knowing Francia's resources as he did, Bjarki had believed it.

Now that he looked out at the great sweep of enemy tents, horse lines and carts moving back and forth, all toy-sized in the distance, the dull, brown earth diggings, the blocks of red-cloaked marching men and black-clad *Scholares* cavalry, he wondered if there might not be more than four thousand men assembled here. Five, perhaps? Or even six thousand men?

There was no point being downhearted: the Dane-Work was strong; it had been designed for this purpose. The Fortress of Hellingar in the centre of the defensive line was a circular structure of high wooden walls, the logs reinforced with iron bands and double the usual thickness. It was devised to be held by just a few hundred warriors on the high perimeter walls.

The fortress lay between the east and west ramparts like a gigantic walnut held between two massive index fingers. On the south side of the fortress was the channel, as daunting a defensive barrier as Bjarki had ever seen, which would halt the attackers before they even came close to either of the two massive ramparts or the thick round walls of Hellingar Fortress.

The channel was twenty paces wide and filled almost to the lip of the bank with silty brown water. Now that the enormous task of digging it was done, this massive artificial river ran a full ten miles, in a long gentle curve from the fort of Hollinsted above the impassable Eider marshes in the west, all the way to the fortified port of Hedeby on the coast in the east.

There were no bridges or fords anywhere along the channel's length. The only way across was via the drawbridge, a massive vehicle, a dozen feet wide, made of wooden planks on eight iron-rimmed wheels. The machine had a twenty-five-yard-long bridge part that could be lifted into the vertical position by a system of ropes and pulleys. Accordingly, the enormous drawbridge could be wheeled to the northern edge of the channel and the bridge section dropped to the horizontal, so that it spanned the brown water, allowing men and horses to cross. Or, as was the case now, the bridge section could be lifted into the vertical position, making the whole contraption the shape of a right angle, and the drawbridge wheeled away from the water's edge, back across twenty yards of flat turf and stationed out of reach of the enemy beside the huge double-gates of Hellingar.

The channel was wide enough for two dragon-ships to pass each other in comfort and, without the drawbridge providing a convenient crossing point, it was a truly formidable obstacle for any attacking army. The enemy would have to swim their men across the deep water, perhaps in their heavy armour – a risky endeavour likely to lead to many drownings – or construct a suitable bridge of their own on the south bank under the onslaught of showers of crossbow bolts, arrows and javelins from the fortress defenders.

Once the enemy had crossed the channel, if they could even manage this feat, they had a choice. Directly attack Hellingar – the Dane-Mark's strongest fortress – under a barrage of deadly missiles from the west and east ramparts on either side, or attempt to overrun the ramparts, sending their men scrambling up the steep grassy slope that rose thirty feet above the surface of the earth, and then fighting on the summit at the stout wooden fence that ran all the way along the top of the ridge, from east to west, which would be packed with hundreds of ferocious Saxon and Danish warriors.

The enemy could not go around the ramparts to the east, for at the port of Hedeby a few miles away Siegfried had massed a squadron of warships from his fleet, the most powerful in the

North. In the west, the ramparts stretched as far as the marshy Eider River, which flowed into the sea.

It was cleverly designed, Bjarki thought. Siegfried had done well.

He glanced behind him to see where Tor had got to. Gunnar had been charged with looking after little Garm this morning and had remained in Ash House. But Tor was supposed to be up here. Bjarki saw she had stopped three-quarters of the way up the slope and was staring out, as he had, over the wheel-shape of the fortress, which was now swarming with fighting folk.

Bjarki looked north of Hellingar, behind its long protective bulk, and saw that the sprawling village of grubby make-shift tents – the channel diggers' sad lodgings, through which they had passed on their previous journey – had been swept away and replaced with rows of long wooden barracks for the influx of Saxon soldiers and log storehouses for their food and provisions. Latrines had been dug, and horse lines laid out. He could even see a small herd of penned sheep. It had all been meticulously planned. He could see the smoke of at least three forges and hear the tinking of iron on anvil as smiths worked to fashion weapons for the huge garrison.

However, beyond that neat military encampment, the fields and heathland stretching north as far as the eye could see were filled with small bedraggled groups of people, mostly women and children, camping any old how on the ground, although some had made scrapes in earth banks or stick-walled huts, or crude, low turf-roofed shelters to keep the rain and sun off. These were the poor of Saxony, who had been driven from their homes by the advancing Red Cloaks; some burned out of their villages to make room for new settlements built around churches. There were many hundreds of them, homeless, hungry and owning no more than the rags they stood up in.

He felt bad about his lavish breakfast, then, and the feast of the night before. But the orders were clear – food was for fighters, and that was that.

Tor finally emerged, pink-faced and puffing, at the top of the hill, and immediately came over to Bjarki's side.

'I don't believe we can hold them here, oaf,' she said. 'Not if they come in sufficiently large numbers. They can swamp us. There is too much frontage for us to cover – ten miles of it – and we simply don't have enough shield-men. We're spread too thin. I don't see how we can beat them here.'

'I don't know,' he replied. 'They will have trouble getting their men over the channel. And maybe with a bit of good luck—'

'Unless the gods intervene, we're heading for the Hall of the Slain.'

'The word is that Theodoric sent messages to Svearland and Varmland and Vestfold and the rest of the Little Kingdoms some weeks ago begging for fighting men. They will answer the call, I'm sure of it. They'll send us a slew of brave warriors in our hour of need, just you wait and see.'

'If the message was sent weeks ago, why aren't they here? They're not coming, oaf. We're on our own – and we're going to be butchered like pigs.'

Bjarki frowned. Surely Tor was wrong. Siegfried had spent a lifetime, and the gods knew how much of his silver, in creating this extraordinary defence. It would hold. It must hold now it was to be put to the ultimate test.

–

'I insist, my lords,' said Jarl Snorri Hare-Lip, his words coming with a light rain of spittle through his cloven upper lip, 'that the bulk of the Saxon men are assigned to me in the fortress. I need at least fifteen hundred men. It is clear where the Frankish hammer blow will fall, on Hellingar itself—'

'Nonsense,' said Duke Theodoric. 'I have been fighting these people for years now, and if I have learnt anything in that time it is that Francia teaches its soldiers always to take the simplest option in warfare. In this case, they will come at us straight up the ramparts. East or west, don't know which, but we *must* keep the bulk of our strength on both summits.'

'My lords, please,' said King Siegfried, a tall and very slender man. 'We cannot know exactly what is in the enemy's mind. We must try to be prepared for all eventualities. I have heard several rumours to the effect that Karolus himself is here, which may well affect their—'

'He *is* here,' said Valtyr. 'My friends and I saw him with our own eyes on the journey here. And Gerold, Duke of Swabia, his second-in-command, and the general of his armies, and Bishop Livinus, too. This Christian bishop is the Frankish king's chaplain, chancellor and the so-called Count of Westphalia. He seems to be in charge of the administration of all Francia, so I've been told.'

'What do you say, young fellow?' Siegfried was looking at Bjarki, who was next to Valtyr at the long table in the centre of the command post.

'I understand you have met Karolus in person, several times, while you were his captive in Aachen. What do you think the Frankish king has in mind?'

Bjarki was struck stupid. This great man before him was king of the Dane-Mark. And he had just sought out Bjarki's opinion.

'Ah, um, my lord…' he said. 'Ah, well, now, you see…'

'Spit it out, boy, you're the only one of us who knows him well,' said Valtyr. 'What'll he do? How will he come at us? What kind of man is he?'

'He's a subtle man,' Bjarki managed at last. He wanted to blurt out: 'He tricked me into telling all I knew about the Groves, into betraying my friends to their deaths…' but decided against it at the very last moment.

'He is a thinker, a planner. Not reckless. Not impulsive. He's actually quite a humble man, plain in his dress, relatively simple in his tastes—'

'Not so humble, I think,' said Duke Theodoric, slapping a pudgy hand down on the tabletop. 'He didn't show a great deal of humility when he barged into my lands and claimed them as his own, or when he drove out or slaughtered my people when they stood in his way. A humble man, pah! He's a tyrant, a blood-drunk monster, an overweening bully…'

Bjarki waited politely until the duke had finished his angry tirade. He was grateful for it, in truth. It gave him time to marshal his own thoughts.

'The Frankish king will have a plan,' Bjarki said. 'Something clever. He cannot have been ignorant of the Dane-Work all these months. He has more than enough spies and traitors in his pay. So he must know what has been built here. And he will not just throw his Red Cloaks at our defences in huge numbers for us to slaughter. Not because he is tender-hearted about the lives of his men. He is not. He will do it because he enjoys deception. He likes to play games; he loves pretending to do one thing and then doing something different. He wants to be seen as a cunning man. He is vain in that way.'

'A feint, perhaps?' said Siegfried. 'He'll make us think he is coming with all his strength from one direction and, in fact, come in from another.'

'That sounds about right,' said Bjarki.

'But you don't *know* what he plans to do,' sprayed Jarl Snorri, 'I'll wager nobody does except, perhaps, this Livinus character. Until our scouts report in, the spies and what-have-you, we are quite blind. We don't really know anything. And, if nobody can give us an accurate idea of Karolus's intentions…' The jarl wiped his spit-wet lips and glared at Bjarki. 'I see no value at all in speculating on where he might – or might not – assail us.'

'You make a good point, Jarl Snorri,' said Theodoric. 'We must wait for all our spies to report back. We have sent enough of them out there.'

'Indeed,' said Siegfried. 'It is true that we may not very usefully speculate; but we can make our dispositions intelligently. Fortunately, I designed this fortification to be supremely flexible in defence. I propose…'

Bjarki listened hard as Siegfried outlined his troop placements, naming this jarl and that one, this captain or another, all men he did not know until they acknowledged their orders with a nod from their position at the table. Siegfried informed each leader where they and their men should take up their positions on the east or west rampart or in the fortress itself. The Master of Hellingar then complained again that he had far too few troops to successfully defend his fortress and Siegfried allocated him another five hundred, after some wrangling with Duke Theodoric, whose men they were.

Bjarki gazed over the heads of two dozen or so people seated at the table and out of the open shutters that granted a panorama of the battlefield. He wondered what Karolus was doing now – was he over there, a mile or two away, planning out his attack with Duke Gerold and Bishop Livinus? Discussing who should command which bodies of troops? It seemed likely.

'And am I right in thinking that you, Bjarki Bloodhand, claim to be a Rekkr?' King Siegfried's question took him completely by surprise.

'I, um, I have not been formally acclaimed a Rekkr by the authorities of the Fyr Skola,' said Bjarki. 'Since it is now destroyed, it seems unlik—'

'He is a Rekkr – I can attest to it,' said Valtyr.

'Has he done his Voyaging? Has he survived the Fyr Pit?' This question came from a frowning Duke Theodoric. 'There have been worrying tales circulating recently about some Fyr Skola fighters masquerading as Rekkar.'

And far, far too late, Bjarki noticed that the duke, a fat, grizzled, red-faced old fellow, who had seen more than sixty summers, had a faint mark between his bushy grey brows. It was a long thin triangle – Boar Lodge.

Valtyr answered. 'He has been through the Fyr Pit, and emerged with great honour – saving the life of one of his comrades from the flames. In fact, he rescued that red-headed shield-maiden there, who sits beside him.'

The old man indicated Tor, who smiled sweetly and made a half-bow to the assembled company. 'He has also Voyaged in the

First Forest, and has found his *gandr*, who entered his heart, and who can be summoned at need. He is Rekkr, I swear to you. By my oath, and on my honour, he is a Rekkr.'

'Good enough for me,' said Theodoric, who nodded and smiled warmly at Bjarki for the first time since they had sat down at the long table.

'In which case, would you be willing to accept another, less prestigious honour?' said King Siegfried. 'Will you accept the position of commander and captain, under my authority, of the Fyr Skola contingent in the battle to come?'

Chapter Twenty-eight

The paths of peace and war

'Keep still or I will never get it straight,' said Tor. She grabbed a hank of Bjarki's blond hair, which had grown back since the Fyr Pit six months ago and was now long enough to fall into his eyes. She sliced through the greasy strands with one motion of her razor-keen seax.

He was seated comfortably on a stool at the summit of the west rampart, with his back against the thick wooden fence, looking out over the ruin of north Saxony. It was the first time he had been able to relax in twenty-four hours. The sun was shining and the sky was entirely clear of clouds. It looked as if it might well turn out to be a beautiful spring day.

If he had stood up and walked a few paces to his left, he could have looked down over the ring of Hellingar Fortress. If he had really wanted to, he could have hawked and spat a thick gob of phlegm that would have spattered down on to the log walls of the stronghold between the ramparts.

This was Bjarki's allocated position. This was the section of the defences give to the refugees from the Fyr Skola. As their captain, Bjarki had fifteen men and women under his command. He had been expecting resistance from Ivar Knuttson – perhaps a confrontation or a refusal to fight under his authority. But Ivar had shrugged and said: 'If that is what the duke and the king of the Dane-Mark have decided, who am I to disagree?'

This reasonable response completely wrong-footed Bjarki. He had expected to have to dominate Ivar, force him to accept his authority, maybe fight him. But he had no time to ponder the Boar Lodge man's acquiescence. Since the council meeting the day before, Bjarki had been too busy organising weapons, armour, rations, provisions and shelter for the people in his charge.

Nikka the Dreamer, once more a fighting Rekkr, was clad in rusty knee-length ring-mail, moth-eaten fur vambraces and an ancient steel helm, and armed with sword and a long spear. She was given the left flank of the Fyr Skola position with five young Barda to support her; Ivar Knuttson, with another five Barda, was given the right flank to guard, and Bjarki, Tor, Gunnar, Eldar the *gothi*, and a none-too-bright Boar Lodge man called Erik held the centre of the twenty yards of fence that they'd been given to defend.

They were at the end of a long line of defenders, the extreme east of the west rampart. Beyond Ivar was Duke Theodoric's son, a handsome young Saxon warrior called Widukind, and his forty oath-sworn men, and beyond him a crusty old Jutland *hersir* with his retinue, and so on into the distance. Below them and behind them, down on the reverse slope of the rampart were ten fifty-man-strong companies of *hersirs* and seasoned warriors. They were stationed on a rough dirt road that had been hacked out of the turf of both the east and west ramparts ten paces below their summits, and which ran miles in both directions. When the Frankish troops attacked, these Storm Companies, as they were called, could easily be moved along the ramparts behind the front line to where they were needed. It was a flexible defence structure, as King Siegfried had rightly boasted.

Yet Bjarki suspected, deep in his heart, that Tor might be right. They were simply too few defenders. If the king were to send in two simultaneous attacks of a couple of thousand Red Cloaks each, and they got over the channel somehow and up the ramparts in great numbers, the defenders would be overwhelmed. They'd fight to the bitter end, of course, and die bravely but… There was no point thinking like this, Bjarki told himself. No point at all. And if this battle *were* to be the end for Bjarki Bloodhand, he would do his very best to make it a death for the skalds to sing about.

Tor sliced away a final clump of hair, cursed, tilted her head to the side, squinted and said: 'That will have to do, oaf. At least it's out of your eyes.'

Bjarki stood up, thanked her, ran a hand through his crudely shorn locks and said: 'I'm going down to check on the spare javelin stocks—'

Tor stopped him. She gripped his arm. 'Look,' she said, pointing south.

Karolus, mighty king of the Franks, had come to the Dane-Work.

–

The massed troops of the King of Francia completely filled the horizon – rank after rank, *scara* after *scara* of Christian warriors, all slowly coming forward together. Thousands of men – in the front two ranks of red-cloaked men alone there must be two thousand, at least, advancing as if they shared but a single mind. Bjarki felt a cold ripple of awe right down to his boots.

They came tramping forward in their *scarae*, about three hundred men in each regiment, warriors from Austrasia, from Neustria, from Burgundy, Province and Aquitaine, swords at their sides, spears in hand, many with the red cloaks and red shields of the standing army, still more in their own dress and arms under their regional counts and bishops; green-clad men from the mountains of Swabia – Gerold's men – as well as warriors in brown leather jerkins or dun-coloured cloaks from as far away as Septimania and Gascony.

The *scara* were grouped into blocks of six companies, known as *cunei*; each *cunei* – or company – being made up of about fifty fighting men. Bjarki did a tally of the *scarae* he could see; even the ones in the distance, which were no more than smudges of red or brown. He must be imagining it – could there be thirty-two *scarae* here? Surely that was not possible.

He counted again. No. He was right. Bjarki watched the approaching horde with his mouth open. He could scarcely believe the evidence of his eyes. He had supposed that the king might bring five thousand men to this conflict, or six thousand, outnumbering the defenders by a very comfortable margin. But this was an unheard-of force, more than nine thousand warriors. It was an extraordinary display of Karolus's might and power.

'Looks like the whole of fucking Francia's come out to play,' said Tor.

It was a sea of enemies, an ocean of Franks… In the centre of the field, at the heart of this huge army in a dense, defined, thousand-man block, were the *Scholares*, the king's bodyguard – three *scarae* – some companies of them on horseback, but most of the men on foot.

'How many do you think, Tor?' said Bjarki, trying to keep the tremble out of his voice.

'Looks like…' Tor sucked her teeth. 'All of them.'

'Seriously, how many?'

'Ten thousand? How should I know? Enough to swamp us easily.'

At a distance of about three hundred paces, far beyond the range of the defenders' mightiest bows, the front line of the Frankish army came to a halt. The *scarae* shook themselves into perfect squares; the *cunei* formed, leaving neat lanes between the individual blocks of fifty men. The officers of the *scarae*, helmets decorated with plumes, brought their black, green and scarlet standards, and the symbols of their honour, to the front and stabbed them into the turf. These were mostly Christian crosses sewn on the material, along with a symbol of their lord or region – lightning bolts, bulls, lions, sunbursts – flapping at the end of poles adorned with bells and streamers.

He seeks to intimidate us with the enormous numbers he has brought, thought Bjarki. *It is a tactic. Do not let it succeed. Don't let fear rule you.*

'Look at all those lovely meat-bags,' whispered his *gandr*. 'More than we could ever need. So many soft white bodies, ripe and ready for a blade.'

There was movement in the centre of the mass of the *scarae* – in its dark heart – and Bjarki saw that a group of horsemen, perhaps fifty of them, all Black Cloaks, was coming forward. There was a flash of bright colour in the centre and he saw that there were several priests in the midst of them, and – there – Karolus himself under his eagle banner in glittering mail and a golden crown, in the centre of the group of his guards. *Now for a parlay*, Bjarki thought. *A little chat before the bloody business of the day begins.*

Then Bjarki noticed something a little unusual. Clean open spaces divided the front *cunei*, and the *scarae* they belonged to; wider lanes between each regional unit. And the *scarae* behind the foremost ranks were also clearly delineated. But at the rear of the vast army before his eyes, where it stretched into the far distance, there were no lines or lanes, or so it seemed, the troops there were formed in one solid block. It was as if the men at the back were one super-*scara* containing scores of *cunei* all mingled and mixed together. They looked like a rabble, although it was hard to be certain.

Was it just the sunlight shining in his eyes? It seemed that the further back he looked into this dazzling array of Frankish martial splendour the worse their order became. *So what?* he thought. *Karolus's most disciplined troops have all been stationed near the front. A very sensible arrangement.*

He dismissed the thought from his mind.

The *cunei* of fifty Black Cloaks was approaching the channel. One of the lead riders was now holding a large white flag, and riding out in front of the pack. Bjarki turned left, glancing over at the command post on the east rampart, where both Siegfried and Theodoric had placed themselves.

He saw a corresponding white flag appear through the front shutters of the post, and then the Duke of Saxony and the King of the Dane-Mark strode out of the wooden shelter and climbed up to the top of the wooden wall, staring down, contemptuously, or so it seemed, at Karolus, Duke Gerold and Bishop Livinus, who trotted out from the mass of Black Cloaks and came up to the very lip of the channel, about sixty paces from the position of the two leaders of the North.

A skilled bowman, Bjarki thought, *a keen-sighted one might just be able to hit*… and then he cursed himself for entertaining such a dishonourable notion. A warrior who broke a truce under an acknowledged flag of peace would never be accepted into the Hall of the Slain. Odin would never reward him. He would be reviled as a *nithing* for as long as he was remembered.

'People of Saxony,' said Karolus. He spoke loudly, in a clear, ringing tone that was perfectly audible up on the summit of the rampart.

'Men and women of the Dane-Mark – I come with one last offer of peace. An offer of peace and prosperity for all our people.'

Bjarki saw that Valtyr had emerged from the command post too, and was standing beside Duke Theodoric, listening to Karolus's words. Looking down at the gatehouse of Helligar Fortress, he saw that Jarl Snorri had come out on to the open platform above the heavy wooden double-gate to hear the proclamation from the great Frankish monarch on the far side of the water.

There were no more than forty paces separating Jarl Snorri from Karolus and Bishop Livinus and the company of Black Cloaks. And most of that space was wet. Since the drawbridge had been wheeled back there was no dry way of crossing the deep channel without a boat – or a pair of wings.

He was aware that his own Fyr Skola folk were all around him now.

'I want nothing more than peace between our peoples,' repeated the King of Francia. 'That is all I desire!' Bjarki remembered how reasonable the man could sound. He had to fight to recall how treacherous he truly was.

'All I ask is that you come down from your ramparts this very hour and submit to me. You will do homage before me, and swear to turn away from your false gods and heathen practices. If you will swear to follow the teaching of the priests, and accept Jesus Christ as your Lord and Saviour and to follow the One True Faith evermore, we shall all become good friends.'

An eerie silence fell over the field. The King of Francia conferred with Bishop Livinus, who gestured at the huge gate of Hellingar. Karolus nodded.

'If you will agree to this very modest request,' said the king. 'I shall be more than generous with you – you may return to your homes and take up your lands and your lives again. I shall not seek to enslave or persecute any man nor woman, nor to punish your leaders – I have no quarrel with you, my noble duke, nor you, Siegfried Siegfriedsson. Let us talk and be friends.'

'Friends?' called down Theodoric. 'Why would I choose to be friends with a man who butchered my people and stole my lands from under me?'

'I would be a friend to you, nonetheless. I can find a use for a man of your talents, Duke Theodoric, but within the realm of Francia. I could make you a count and royal counsellor and give you dominion over Thuringia or Frisia or Septimania, if you so choose. You would be a great lord of the Frankish nation! And for you, Siegfried, King of the Dane-Mark, a high governorship, perhaps, of Jutland and the islands and the Little Kingdoms.'

'I believe I *already* rule Jutland and all the islands,' said Siegfried.

'Yes, but for how much longer?' came back the calm reply.

Siegfried turned his back rudely on Karolus. 'I've heard enough,' he said, and the king of the Danes hopped down from the wall, landing lightly as a tomcat on the turf, and began walking back towards the command post.

'Do not choose the path of war, O King!' shouted Karolus. 'Nor you either, Duke Theodoric. You can see the vast might of my holy realm spread before you. I could crush you like a toad beneath the ploughman's blade. Choose, instead, the blessed path of lasting peace!'

'I am a warrior of the North,' yelled back Theodoric. Bjarki could see he'd gone bright red in the face. 'We are bred in the bone here to fight for our land and our honour. More than that, I am Rekkr; the gods have chosen me as their red instrument. War lives in my heart. I shit all over your peace.'

-

The Green Cloaks came at them first. Bjarki watched as five full *scarae* of these light infantry troops, some fifteen hundred men, came trotting forward towards the wide channel from the centre-left of the vast Frankish army.

He remembered from conversations with the Auxilla in the longhouse in Aachen that the Green Cloaks were specialists, trained for mountain warfare and to fight in thick forests. They were Duke Gerold's men, bred in the uplands of Swabia, and they were used to traversing the frozen passes. Lightly armed, fast, able to march great distances at speed over very rugged terrain.

The Green Cloaks crossed the three hundred paces of no man's land in a terrifyingly short time. They were heading straight for the west rampart.

'Get ready!' yelled Bjarki. And all the way along the line the *hersirs* and jarls were exhorting their own men to prepare to receive a full assault.

The first wave of Green Cloaks reached the southern edge of the channel. Bjarki could see that they were armed only with slender ash spears, short, thick stabbing swords, round shields and their steel-cap helmets. They wore no armour over their moss-green tunics, and their footwear was light, kidskin shoes, rather than the iron-studded boots the Red Cloaks favoured.

Then he remembered the other skill for which the Green Cloaks were so renown. He watched in amazement as the first of the enemy soldiers reached the channel and demonstrated it. He saw the lead man hurl his round shield, like a discus, right across the twenty-yard stretch of water to bounce on to the grassy ground on the other side. The other Green Cloaks were all doing the same, skimming their shields across the water. Their spears were next; they tossed them high, sending them arcing over the water barrier twenty yards to the far bank where they stuck, quivering, in the turf.

Then, without the slightest hesitation, the Green Cloaks dived one by one into the murky channel. In a few short strokes they were climbing out on to the far bank, dripping, retrieving arms and forming up in squads.

Now it came back to him. Swimming – the Green Cloaks were famous all across Francia as champion swimmers. Not that the narrow channel would be much of a challenge for such accomplished water-folk as they.

The Green Cloaks took only a little time to organise themselves in their companies. And then they charged.

'Javelins!' Bjarki bellowed, without looking round at his Fyr Skola comrades to see if they were ready. 'On my signal! Wait for it, wait…'

The foremost Green Cloaks, a couple of dozen lean men, were sprinting straight up the steep grassy slope of the west rampart as if it were as flat as a table. Bjarki could see the lines of determination on their pale, sweaty faces as they pounded up towards him.

He hefted his javelin.

'Kill them!' he shouted and launched the light spear in his hand at the nearest Green Cloak, a long-faced man, who was leading the charge.

The javelin took him right through the throat, the ash shaft sliding in to its midway point. The Green Cloak was jerked back down the slope by the force of the throw. All around Bjarki, the Fyr Skola fighters were hurling their spears over the wooden barrier, skewering the charging Green Cloaks, punching the sharp points through their unarmoured green chests, transfixing limbs, knocking the lightly armed men down in their dozens and scores.

Bjarki snatched up another missile and threw it into the green swarm, adding it to the lethal rain of missiles that was decimating their bold, uphill charge. They were throwing all along the line now, pelting the enemy with wood and steel. He could hear Ivar

Knuttson calling out, 'Ha!' with every javelin he launched. Tor beside him was a blur of motion, too fast to see, as she grabbed spear after spear and flipped them into the attacking Green Cloaks with an awful precision.

Bjarki reached for another javelin from the stack leaning beside him on the chest-high fence and threw it hard into the face of a wild-eyed man just a few strides away from the summit. It took the fellow in his rolling right eye; his head snapped back and he gave out a horrible scream of rage and pain, clawing at his own face, and slithered back down the blood-greasy side of the rampart, tangling the feet of the Green Cloaks pounding up behind him.

Bjarki put out his hand for another missile but, by the time he had lifted it, there was a Green Cloak right at the fence line, only a foot or two away, who lunged at him with his own spear, and he had to twitch his head to one side to avoid the strike. The spearhead hissed past his face and Bjarki's left hand shot out and he grabbed the fellow by the front of his green woollen tunic. He dragged the man forward to the fence, slammed his face into the top of the wood, and jammed the point of his own uncast javelin down into the hollow by the struggling man's collarbone; forcing the shaft deep into his torso, right down, shoving it inside him till the man stopped wriggling.

There were Green Cloaks all along the fence now, pressing up hard, jabbing with their spears at the defenders, lunging over the barrier, swearing, screaming, spitting at the enemy – and the men of the North fought back with their own long weapons, cursing and shouting, jabbing at their faces, smashing mouths, slicing into scalps. The sunlight was spotted with gore.

Some of the Greens were tearing at the wooden fence with their bare hands, trying to pull it down. One of the Storm Companies came up the slope behind Bjarki's men – reinforcements. Their bowmen hauled back their strings and loosed into the enemy line from a dozen strides away, showering the Green Cloaks with their arrows, picking them off in ones and twos, forcing them back, sweeping them away from the line.

Bjarki's hand clutched below the fence for another javelin but he was snatching at air. All gone. He seized the long handle of his bearded axe, which was leaning against the wattle by his knee, and swinging it high over his head he chopped down and split the helmet of a Green Cloak who had just drawn back his spear. The man crumpled, dropping his lance.

He lashed out laterally and carved the jaw from a man. A screaming face slashed at him with a short sword; he ducked the blow, and punched the heavy butt of the axe into the enemy's mouth; he disappeared in an instant.

And suddenly there were no more foes before Bjarki's section of fence.

He could see the thick scattering of dead and wounded on the ground beyond it, an undulating mass of blood-spattered flesh piled up before the wattle barrier. He looked to his right and saw that one of the young Barda, a man under Ivar Knuttson's command, was lying on the ground on his back, mewling, his face a mass of wet blood. Another of his men was sitting with his back to the wooden fence, his face pale grey, clutching with both hands his own gory stomach from which a long, slender spear shaft still protruded.

Yet the rest of his people seemed mostly unharmed. A bloody cut or two here and there. He caught a flicker of movement to his front, ducked instinctively, and was aware of a spear hissing past his face. But the man who threw it was five paces away from the summit, on the slope. It was a half-hearted assault, a gesture; he did not seem inclined to close and fight.

Bjarki did not choose to come out and engage him, either. There were hundreds of Green Cloaks still milling around on the slope below the fence now, a few still climbing, but more slowly, reluctantly. Their green-plumed officers were shouting, urging the Swabians onwards, upwards, but the energy of their attack was failing, subsiding, its cutting edge blunted.

He looked left and saw that a knot of five Green Cloaks, under an officer, was trying to creep round the flank where the fence ended on the eastern shoulder of the rampart. He heard Nikka, the nearest section leader, give a blood-curdling scream and hurl away her shield; she now had an axe lifted in one hand and short sword in the other. She charged into the flanking Green Cloaks alone, a plump matronly woman, long past her youth, who had not tasted the blood and filth of war for many a year, but who was now launching herself at the foe, yelling nonsense and frothing like a madwoman.

He felt a shiver of kinship. He heard his own *gandr* gibbering, begging to be let in... But he knew he must set his face against it for the time being.

Nikka ripped into the five Green Cloaks with axe and sword like a whirlwind and literally tore them all into pieces. Her axe cracked down on bone and hacked through skin, ripping into fat and muscle; her sword carved into flesh and sliced clean through limbs. The enemy were transformed into reeking mounds of meat in less than a dozen blood-splashed heartbeats, with Nikka still cutting and capering, leaping, screaming nonsense war cries and slashing at their hacked, fallen bodies long after they'd stopped moving.

The rest of the Green Cloaks began pulling back in an orderly manner. All along the summit of the west rampart they were peeling away and retreating down the slope. Now that Bjarki was able to draw a breath, he saw that the east rampart, over to his left, had also been attacked with a similar force of these Frankish light troops, which had also been similarly repulsed.

This had been merely a probing action, he now realised, Karolus was testing their fighting spirit, feeling for weaknesses, and spending the lives of his Green Cloaks to discover that crucial intelligence a little more quickly.

Bjarki could clearly see Karolus; just there, on a little hillock only about three hundred paces away, a bump in the mostly flat battlefield that lifted him a few feet above the rest of the plain. He was gazing up at the slope, strewn with the broken bodies of his brave light troops.

Beyond the Black Cloaks of the bodyguard, and the brightly coloured gaggle of priests around the king, Bjarki could make out several new blocks of troops advancing. He thought he counted a full ten *scarae* of Red Cloaks this time, heavy infantry, coming up the centre of the field from the south – three thousand men – heading for Hellingar Fortress, between the ramparts.

The attack by the Green Cloaks had just been a skirmish, a feint to test their mettle. Now the Frankish king was taking the fight seriously.

Chapter Twenty-nine

The price of treachery

The surviving Green Cloaks were milling around at the bottom of the slope, where the land flattened out before the channel bank, and Bjarki saw that there were still a large number of them alive and unharmed – several hundreds, at least. A sudden thunder of hooves and peal of trumpets heralded the Saxon cavalry. Pounding around the shoulder of the west rampart, between the earth mound and the walls of Hellingar, it slammed straight into the green-clad infantry. It was only a small force of Angrians from the middle of Saxony, perhaps sixty horse, mainly made up of the second sons of jarls and *hersirs*, who were trained to ride from an early age.

Yet they were all brave northern boys and girls – and all eager for battle.

The Angrian cavalry came hallooing around the shoulder and hacked down at the heads and bodies of the lightly protected infantry with their swords, axes and maces. The Green Cloaks responded in the most sensible way imaginable; they ducked away from the galloping horses and their excited riders, dodged the wild sword blows, and dived into the channel, swimming quickly and efficiently to the other side – and to safety.

The scene reminded Bjarki of a time in Aachen when he had walked beside an ornamental frog pond in the palace complex at night after a late meeting with the king. The frogs had been croaking happily on the edge of the pond, summoning their lovers, perhaps, or boasting of their prowess, but, as he walked along the paved edge of the pool, one by one, the creatures had abruptly plopped into the black water.

So it was, as the cavalry of the North galloped along the edge of the channel, the Green Cloaks tossed away their equipment, shields and spears, sometimes even their helms, too, and hopped like frogs into the brown water. The bank was littered with abandoned gear but now it was swept clean of enemies, and the exuberant young Angrians began cheering as they rode away westwards, as if they'd won a great victory single-handed.

Bjarki knew that they had not. If the Swabians had chosen to stand and fight, or if they had received the orders to do so from their officers, they could have made it very hard for these inexperienced young horse troops.

Nevertheless, the Green Cloaks were now all gone.

The Red Cloaks, however, were not.

The Frankish army was advancing on the Dane-Mark with a slow, measured tread, heading directly towards Hellingar. *Scara* after *scara* marching forward as one man. Trumpets blared, drums rattled. The Franks were now only three hundred yards from the channel, the first units coming up level to the mass of Black Cloaks clumped around Karolus on his hillock. They saluted him as they passed; thumping their right fists against their metallic chests. Three thousand Red Cloaks: big, hard men in iron mail, with steel swords and daggers, iron greaves, and heavy iron-shod marching boots.

They'll not be able to swim, thought Bjarki. *They'll sink like anvils.*

'What in the name of Odin's arsehole are they playing at?' said Tor from Bjarki's side, apparently hearing his thoughts. 'They'll never get over the water.' She cupped hands round her mouth and bellowed: 'Go home, you great fat idiots; don't waste any more of our time.'

He glanced down at her and saw that she had a spray of red dots right across her pale little face, a blood splatter. She seemed otherwise unharmed.

'Oh,' she said. 'I see it now. That *fucker*. The weaselly turd. Snorri.'

She pointed down, to her left, and Bjarki followed her finger. The two heavy wooden gates of the Fortress of Hellingar were swinging open.

Jarl Snorri Hare-Lip himself was standing on the top of the gatehouse, with one of his hearth-men, a standard-bearer. And the standard that the man bore was marked with a huge black cross on a long pole, adorned with bells and streamers: the Christian flag of their enemies spreading out in the breeze.

The gates of Hellingar were now fully open and Bjarki could see a knot of Snorri's *hersirs* gathered round the mobile drawbridge, kicking away the blocks under the massive wheels and putting their shoulders to the wood. The Red Cloaks were now a hundred paces from the channel. And closing.

The truth came to Bjarki all at once, the pieces all falling together: a memory of Livinus and his bodyguards in the hall in Hellingar a year ago, after a private meeting with Jarl Snorri; the *scarae* of Red Cloaks marching nonsensically towards the deep channel they could not cross in their heavy gear; Snorri's *hersirs* beginning to roll the drawbridge towards the bank…

'With me, all of you,' Bjarki was yelling at the Fyr Skola folk. 'Now!'

He looked at the captain of the Storm Company that had supported them during the Green Cloak attack. 'I need your warriors, sir,' he said.

The Storm captain, a dull middle-aged Saxon, frowned back at him.

'I'm going to attack them,' Bjarki could feel a panic rising in his chest.

'Down there, I mean to stop them before they let the enemy across…'

The captain did not understand.

'Support me!' Bjarki said, then turned away, and called the Fyr Skola to him. He saw Tor and Gunnar looking at him, expectantly. 'On me, all of you, now. Ready? Charge!'

Bjarki hefted his axe, swept up his shield and started to race down the shoulder of west rampart, skidding on the blood-slippery grass, sliding on his arse most of the way down. He regained his feet at the very bottom, unharmed, and pelted straight towards the drawbridge, which was by now trundling noisily towards the edge of the channel, slowly gathering speed.

'Let me in,' his *gandr* was hammering at his heart in time with his own thudding pulse, his own panting breath. 'Let me help you, I beg you!'

Bjarki was just yards from the nearest *hersir*, a big, black-bearded fellow. He let out a scream of battle-rage and, as the fellow turned towards him, Bjarki swung his axe, the blade sinking in and splitting his face in two.

He was aware that Tor was by his shoulder, and Gunnar was yelling something behind him. There were dozens of enemies all around him now, and they turned on him and his little band as one. He got his shield up just in time to receive a tremendous axe blow from a giant of a man with blond swinging pigtails and a roaring red mouth. The massive blow rattled his teeth in his head, the elm planks of the shield split and splintered into shards, the whole only held together by its circular iron rim. He shook the broken wreckage of the shield off his arm, ducked another colossal swinging cut from the axeman, bobbed up and buried his own axe in the fellow's belly.

More of Snorri's men were pouring out of the gates, scores of warriors, coming to join the fight around the drawbridge. For a fleeting instant, Bjarki wondered how many of them knew about the Jarl's treachery. He could not have convinced them *all* to abandon their faith in the old gods. Surely not.

But two score of Hellingar's finest fighting men were running at him, nonetheless. He saw Tor effortlessly maim a grizzled Saxon who was shoving at the front wheel. She dealt him a quick sword thrust to his knee, then dodged an axe blow to her own head from a fat man standing atop the vehicle. Nikka the Dreamer was there too, still gibbering and frothing and waving her bloody sword in a loose and terrifyingly unco-ordinated fashion.

Then someone chopped an axe into the back of her plump neck and she flopped and fell. Gunnar had a spear in his hands and a grim expression; he was thrusting it wildly at a Saxon, who easily fended him off. Bjarki saw Ivar and one of the young Barda clashing swords with two veteran *hersirs*. Ivar killed his man, but the less-experienced Barda took a thrust through the belly and screamed like a vixen. Ivar took revenge on his killer an instant later.

The drawbridge was only a dozen yards from the edge of the channel. A couple more shoves and it would be there and the bridge part could be lowered to open the way for thousands of enemies to pour across from the far bank. The Red Cloaks were thirty paces from the edge of the water now.

Bjarki ducked a sword swing and punched the head of the axe into the face of a skinny bald man, who was looming over him and yelling from the bed of the drawbridge, bloodying the fellow's nose. Then he reached up and hauled the man off the drawbridge by his mail hauberk, tossing him right over his shoulder to thump down on the turf. He saw Erik, one of his Barda, close in and chop the bald man down with his axe as he shakily tried to rise.

He could see the Red Cloaks – so many of them – massing on the other side of the channel, waiting right on the lip. He vaulted up on to the vehicle.

In front of him were the thick ropes that held the bridge part upright. 'Tor,' he yelled. 'I need you, Tor. Ward my back! Keep them off me!'

'You don't need *her*,' hissed his *gandr*, 'I am all that you need.'

Tor jumped up on to the bed of the vehicle: she had a sword in one hand and her seax in the other. Their eyes met in perfect understanding.

Bjarki turned his back on his swarming foes and swung the axe at the thick, taut rope on the right that held the bridge section upright. His blade sliced into the woven strands, cutting the hawser about halfway through. The strands began to unravel. The drawbridge was still wobbling forward. He heard a bellow of rage behind him, and Tor's hiss of breath, the clang of steel on steel, and again. But he did not turn. He swung his axe at the last strands and they flew apart. The bridge section lurched to one side, hanging at an angle, and he now had a clear view of the far bank of the channel. He was looking straight into the eyes of an officer who was holding a standard with a black cross like the one Snorri's man was brandishing on the gate.

The Frank was gaping at him. Mouth open and as red as his plume.

Bjarki hurried to the other side of the vehicle, swinging the axe at the second rope, and it bounced right off the taut hemp. Bad angle. He had hurried his stroke. The drawbridge was only eight yards from the edge, now. He could hear the officer on the far bank calling for archers to come up, fast.

Tor alone was fighting two big, hairy *hersirs* at the same time, blocking sword cuts with her seax, sliding her slight body under massive blows that would have cut her in half. Bjarki longed to help. He gritted his teeth, focused his strength, and swung the axe at the second and final rope. The blade struck, the angle was true, the cable parted with a mighty crack, and the bridge toppled over the edge of the vehicle, slithered down the muddy bank and splashed into the water, slowly sinking, sliding like a knife blade into the brown silt and finally disappearing from view.

He distinctly heard the officer say: 'Fuck me, it's the Beast-man!'

Then he turned and saw that Tor had killed one of her opponents and gashed the other deep in the right thigh: he'd be a cripple for life, if he lived.

Scores of soldiers were streaming down both shoulders of the ramparts now, Theodoric's men from the East and the captain of the Storm Company, belatedly understanding what Bjarki had been trying to tell him. And there was Widukind, the duke's eldest son, and his men, joining in the fight. They plunged into the Hellingar men, screaming and slicing, howling and killing. More joined the fight from the slopes, overwhelming the traitors completely.

Snorri was no longer on the top of the gatehouse – that traitor at least had the sense to realise when his cause was lost. And suddenly it was over.

All the fighting around the drawbridge somehow magically stopped as if by mutual consensus with the loss of the bridge section. The surviving Hellingar men were throwing down their weapons and raising their hands, some were even kneeling. Bjarki stooped to pick up an abandoned shield.

And saved his own life.

A Frankish arrow whizzed over his bent back, and a moment later he was enveloped in a blizzard of shafts, pattering into the turf all around him. He ran then, covering his mailed back with the big round shield, dodging, zigzagging, sprinting up the slope to the protection of the wooden fence.

And all his surviving Fyr Skola folk ran with him.

–

'It seems that it was Snorri and only about a dozen of his closest *hersirs*,' said Valtyr. Bjarki, Tor and he were sharing a skin of red wine at the Fyr Skola post on the west rampart. 'A few of the *hersirs* had converted to the Christ god, as Snorri had; others just took the view that their loyalty lay with their lord, whatever he might do and whichever side he might support. They've all been executed, anyway, so it doesn't matter what they believed.'

'What about Snorri?' said Tor. 'I'd like to gut that weasel myself.'

'He's disappeared,' said Valtyr. 'Gone completely. Once he saw you destroy the drawbridge, he fled. We think he went north, through the Saxon refugees' encampment, but he'll be taken up eventually and then – *phitt*...' Valtyr made a fast cutting motion with a hand across his own neck.

Bjarki scratched at the bandage on his hand. One of the Frankish arrows had sliced the skin on the back of his fist as he fled the battlefield, the very lightest of wounds, but it hurt more than it should. It throbbed. He wondered if the arrows could have been poisoned. He didn't know if the Red Cloaks did that… Thinking about his irritating scratch meant that he missed the first part of Valtyr's speech.

'…so you would have a completely new garrison of Theodoric's men under you, plus your own Fyr Skola contingent, what is left of it. It was Widukind's idea. He saw you fight and, apparently, he was impressed. He spoke up for you in the council and suggested that you be given the fortress. They are clearing out all the warriors who were in there under Snorri, just a precaution, they're probably all loyal but it doesn't make sense to tempt the gods to mischief, does it? So… I can tell them you'll accept the position?'

Tor was beaming at him.

'I'm sorry,' said Bjarki stupidly. 'I wasn't listening. What position?'

'Men, eh, Tor?' said Valtyr. 'Can't concentrate for three heartbeats!'

'Imbeciles,' she replied. 'Particularly this ugly specimen.'

'All right, that's enough. What is it you want me to do?' said Bjarki.

Valtyr gave a great sigh. 'Jarl Snorri's treachery has caused a rift between Duke Theodoric and King Siegfried. Theodoric blames Siegfried for not recognising that Snorri was the rotten apple in the barrel. They both insisted on nominating the next Master of Hellingar, but neither would accept their other's candidate. So Theodoric's son Widukind suggested you for the post. And this was generally agreed by all to be a good choice.'

'Me?' said Bjarki.

'Did you get a knock on the head in the drawbridge fight, Bjarki? You seem to be unusually stupid today.'

'That's unfair,' said Tor. 'He is *not* unusually stupid today.'

'Thank you, Tor,' said Bjarki, 'I'm glad at least you—'

'He is exactly as stupid as this almost every day,' she said.

'If I do accept the position of Master of Hellingar,' said Bjarki, 'the first thing I shall do is demand the proper respect from my subordinates.'

–

Bjarki stood on the top of the gatehouse of the Fortress of Hellingar and looked out at the retreating enemy. The Frankish archers had been matched by the bowmen of the North who shot from behind their fences on the ramparts and dropped lethal arrows down on the Red Cloaks standing impotently, without cover, on the edge of the channel. After an indecently long time, during which many a Red Cloak dropped screaming with a shaft in an exposed limb, an order was given for the Franks to pull back.

Bjarki wondered what was to come next. The channel had defeated them; but surely that was only a temporary respite. They might attack again with swimming Green Cloaks, but he doubted it. They'd received a mauling at the fight on the summit, and he doubted the king had brought enough Swabians to overwhelm the Dane-Work without aid from the other *scarae*.

Behind him, Tor, appointed his deputy master, and assisted by Gunnar, was organising the food and lodgings in the long-houses for the new occupants of Hellingar Fortress. Bjarki had also reluctantly taken the time to congratulate Ivar Knuttson on his bravery in the fight at the drawbridge. He had been surprised, again, by the Boar Lodge man, who had followed his orders willingly, and charged down to attack Snorri's men right beside him.

'I decided it was better not to invoke my Rekkr powers that time,' said Ivar, not meeting his eye. 'It seemed unnecessary in such a petty skirmish.'

Bjarki avoided his gaze, too, and said: 'Wise, Ivar, very wise.'

'I noticed that you refrained from using them as well,' said Ivar.

Bjarki was on the verge of saying something unkind in retort, but bit his tongue. 'You did well, Ivar,' he said. 'You did honour to the Boar Lodge.'

Then he gave him a section of the fortress walls to command.

Now, standing on the roof of the gatehouse, Bjarki wondered if that had been a wise choice. This was his first experience of command and already he was not sure if he liked it very much. Could he trust, Ivar? He had no idea. If he had made a mistake, it could be disastrous. The fortunes of the garrison, nearly a thousand men and women, now rested solely in his hands. More than that: the future of the North. If he failed to keep Karolus out of Hellingar, then the Dane-Work would fall, and if the Dane-Work fell, it would be the end of them all, and the destruction of their whole way of life.

How *could* he keep the Red Cloaks out? They would find a way across the channel soon enough, and with their vastly superior numbers it would then be all over. They simply did not have enough warriors in the Dane-Work to win this fight – ten thousand men against two thousand. It was impossible. For an indulgent moment he thought about Goran, the long-haired man he had met in Brenna, and the dream of happiness he had dangled before him: the image of that longhouse on the edge of the forest, with the little fishing boat and the contented pig and the well-tended barley fields.

He sighed. There was something missing from that picture, though. A woman – and perhaps some little blond children running joyfully about the courtyard. But first a good woman. He tried to imagine Tor sitting quietly beside him after a day's work – and could not. Tor was too restless a spirit, too spiky a companion, and besides, while he knew he loved her, and although she was undeniably pretty, he did not think of her in the warm, urgent way he sometimes thought about other girls when he noticed them.

Freya, then? She had been less in his thoughts of late. Had it really been a year since he had seen her? Did he still love her? He could not say. But he *had* made an oath to her. And he could easily imagine her beside him after the long day's work in that perfect eastern homestead. They could be happy together. Yes. Freya. If she agreed. And if he survived the battle, of course.

Bjarki lifted up his face to the sunny heavens and closed his eyes.

'All-Father,' he prayed, 'Odin, hear me now. If I must fall in this battle, make my death a good and noble one. Grant me one fine blazing moment of glory and, afterwards, accept me into your eternal feasting hall.'

He took a deep breath. 'But, All-Father, if you do not wish my life to meet an ending here, then allow me, O Great One, to survive and make a life in the east. If you have some purpose for the great honour, this gift you have bestowed on me, show me, I beg you now, show me a sign of your intent.

'Old One, I *am* truly grateful that you have allowed the *gandr* to come inside me; all that is holy comes from you, I know this, and I am humbled by the favour you have shown. But am I to be so highly honoured only for such a brief period of time? If not, if you wish me to continue to serve you for a little while longer, grant me this boon. Show me a sign, and let me survive this field of blood. Help me, All-Father, help *us* all in our time of need. Our enemies are mighty – their host is as uncountable as the stars. But you are the Lord of War who can shatter their spear-shafts, crack their swords, and split their shields in two. Help me now, mighty Odin, this I beg of you; if it is your divine will that I survive the coming test.'

Bjarki opened his eyes. The sun was setting in the west, in a blood-red sky. An omen, perhaps, of the battle to come. Or, more likely, just a sunset.

He felt foolish for praying; for begging for his life like a coward.

Then he looked east, and all the hairs on his neck stood up at once. For the old god had answered his prayer. The All-Father had given him a sign.

A mile away to the east along the muddy channel, Bjarki could see a large square sail, red-and-white-striped, and the low black form of a dragon-ship beneath it. A large flag depicting the fighting stags of Svearland flapped at the top of the mast, round shields adorned the sides of the ship, and Bjarki could see the glints of steel helms inside the vessel in the last rays of the sun. There were more sea-steeds behind the first, many more, too many to count.

The All-Father had sent aid to his people.

Chapter Thirty

Nose to nose with the future

Tor's head was splitting. It wasn't because the cub Garm had befouled the store cupboard he had been locked in all the day before, and the thrall responsible for cleaning it up was complaining loudly in her ear. It wasn't because she now had to find food and lodgings for another five hundred Svearlander fighters in the cramped longhouses of Hellingar Fortress – she was delighted that her compatriots had answered Theodoric's call and sent ten ships full of warriors to his aid. It wasn't because Bjarki, the Master of Hellingar, seemed to be living in his own world, watching the enemy from the top of the gatehouse hour after hour while there was work to be done.

It was the hammering. For two days, the sound of hammers on wood, of nails being driven home, had rung out over the battlefield. It was not too loud, for the work was taking place behind the Frankish lines three-quarters of a mile away, but it *was* constant, insistent and menacing.

King Karolus was building his own bridges. Three of these contraptions – wheeled machines with an upright bridge section that could be lowered to give a platform across the water; in fact, very similar in design to the one that Bjarki had destroyed two days ago – had already been pushed forward of the enemy lines and left with only a small guard of Blue Cloaks, the corps of Frankish engineers, about five hundred yards from the channel. It was almost as if the king was taunting them with his imminent attack, as if he were saying, 'I can cross your little beck and crush you whenever I choose!'

In the meantime, the hammering and sawing never ceased, day or night. It felt sometimes as if the work was taking place inside Tor's aching head.

She had just got the last of the Svears settled in their allocated longhouses and had arranged their daily rations from the stores, with the help of one of Theodoric's clerks, and was sitting down for the noonday meal at the long table in Ash House with a sulky Garm and a bowl of barley soup, when she became aware that Valtyr was standing in the doorway, with Bjarki behind him. They were both looking at her with grave expressions.

'There is someone from Svearland who wishes to speak to you, Tor,' said Valtyr. He and Bjarki ducked under the lintel and came into the hall.

'If it's another boozy spearman whining about the amount of ale he will receive each day, he can shove his complaint right up his hairy—'

Tor stopped. Behind Valtyr and Bjarki was another figure, tall, even looming. He came forward and stood in a shaft of sunlight from one of the open shutters. He was a warrior; that was plain from the scars on his face and on his muscled bare arms, a tall, broad, brute of a man of middle years in cross-gartered trews and embroidered tunic. A wolf-skin cloak fell from his shoulders to his knees, a sword and a seax hung from his belt.

Tor looked into his face and the shock was as sharp as a slap. The resemblance was uncanny. The man looked almost exactly like Bjarki, an older, more battered version of Bjarki, and with brown rather than blue eyes. But this man bore the face that Bjarki would have in twenty-odd years.

'I am Hildar Torfinnsson,' said the man, in a rumbling growl of a voice. It was the voice that did it. The memories came crashing back: his ale-breathed face bending to kiss her goodnight when she was a child in her cot, the bristles of his beard against her cheek; his smell of man-sweat, horse and leather; the scent of her father; the scent of her childhood in Svearland.

'No,' she said. 'No… I'm not going to… no!'

'This is your father,' said Bjarki. 'He is also, it seems, my fa—'

'You're dead. You died. You jumped from Thor's Rock and—'

'I lived,' rumbled Hildar. 'I jumped from that high rock and fell so far and was swallowed by the storm-tossed waves below. Yet I lived.'

'No, my mother said you… and where have you been… Because I thought you were…' Then Tor, to her everlasting shame, burst into tears.

–

Bjarki summoned a thrall to bring them ale, bread and cheese, and Hildar sat on the bench with his two grown children gazing at him from the other side of the table, and Valtyr, leaning against the wall, watched with a sly smile.

'Did you know he was alive?' Tor asked the one-eyed old man.

'I did – but I was sworn to secrecy.'

'So you have kept this from me all the time I have known you. Some friend you are,' she said bitterly. She was still embarrassed by her weeping.

'He has also watched over you, Torfinna, all these long years, in my absence,' said Hildar. 'And over you as well, Bjarki, my first-born son.'

He turned very fast and snarled at Valtyr. 'Although not as well as I might have wished. I gave you instructions about the boy, Valtyr. No Fyr Skola! None of that. He was *not* to become Rekkr. I was clear, I believe.'

Valtyr shrugged, and smiled more broadly, but Tor could see that he was tense and trying to hide his fear. 'They were going to hang him, Hildar. I had to get him away. Also… well, fate, blood, call it what you will.'

'We will discuss this on another occasion,' said Hildar. It sounded a little like a threat. 'There'll be reckoning with the Bago folk, too. Olaf Karlsson took my silver but he, too, broke faith when he thought me dead.'

'Where have you been?' said Tor. 'Why did you leave me… us?'

Hildar looked at Tor, then at Bjarki.

'Aye,' he said, 'I owe you the telling of it.'

He took a long pull from his ale horn, and wiped his mouth. 'You know, of course, *what* I am?' he said, touching a thick finger to the centre of his brows where there was a long Wolf Lodge triangle in faded black ink.

They both nodded. 'I reckon you must understand a fair amount about the Fire Born by now,' Hildar said, looking directly at Bjarki.

'But, let me tell you this, son. Whatever gnaws at you now, you can expect more of it. Then more still. It lives in you; it grows. It takes your body, your mind, then your soul. There's not a thing you can do to stop it.'

'I know,' said Bjarki.

'I did not want this for you, son, truly I didn't. But it runs in the blood. I thought if I put you as far away from me as possible that you'd be safe…'

'If it runs in the blood, why can I not find my *gandr*?' said Tor. 'Why am I not Rekkr as well?'

'Only Odin knows that. But thank the gods that you are not, sweet daughter of mine. And pray that you do not attract a *gandr* to you in future.'

'Ha!' said Tor. 'Come on, then. Tell us, why did you abandon us?'

'This…' Hildar touched his tattoo again, 'this thing cannot easily be controlled, sometimes not at all. If you do not know it yet, son, you will one day. It is different for each of us. I lost control soon after the Wolf came to me in the forest. We used to have a special word for it in the Fyr Skola—'

'Galálar!' Bjarki laid the word down like a stone slab.

'Yes. That is what they call it. I am losing my words. The Wolf is very great in me now; it gets stronger every year. I went… uh, Galálar in the Fyr Skola. There was a boy I hated. A bully, a swaggerer, and I ripped him apart with my hands. And some others. The Wolf overcame me. The Wolf *was* me. All of me. I don't have the skald-skill now to describe it properly.'

'I understand,' said Bjarki.

'I had to leave the Fyr Skola and I became a vagabond, travelling the North. I stole. I killed men for money. I was… a bad man, an outlaw.'

Neither Bjarki nor Tor said anything. But Tor felt Bjarki take her hand under the table and squeeze it. His hand was very warm; she gripped it tight.

'I came to Svearland with nothing but blood on my fists, but the king there was good to me. He took me into his hall and fed me, gave me a place on his benches. And I fought for him. I killed for him at a great battle under the mountain peaks. Blundfjell was the place. And I earned his favour there by slaying the king of his enemies. After the victory, the Wolf was strong in me. I wanted to go on, to kill and kill and wallow in the blood of my foes for ever.'

Hildar was twitching slightly, his hands jerking, his limbs shuddering just at the act of remembering the bloodshed he had committed so long ago.

Valtyr said: 'You don't need to talk about this.'

'I *do* need to talk about this… I *must*…' Hildar was bellowing. Tor instinctively jerked back at the volume of his familiar voice. This huge man, she saw, was holding on to his humanity by the very slenderest of threads.

Hildar slowly regained his composure.

He whispered: 'I went north. When I do not know what to do, I always head north. I went to the frozen lands of the Sami, and there I met a woman, a fine woman, a beautiful woman and… and she saw me, and she loved me.

'She was a *gothi* of their people, one of their wise women, though she was young and beautiful then. She beat her holy drum and chanted her ancient words and breathed in the sacred smoke – and she travelled into the Spirit World and she found my Wolf, and she spoke to it, she soothed it; she fed it reindeer meat, stroked its fur. She calmed its ravening, she tamed it like a dog, and, for a while, my troubles eased. I, too, was tamed by her.'

Hildar poured himself more ale and Tor saw his hand was still shaking.

'She died, of course,' he said more calmly. 'She died giving birth to you, Bjarki. She went off to dwell in the Spirit World. She left me behind.'

'What was her name?' asked Bjarki.

'She was called Mist-in-the-Morning. She was a fine, strong woman, your mother. But when she left me, I was lost again.'

Hildar stared at the table in silence for a little while, remembering.

'I went south then, with the baby, with you, Bjarki, walking for a month – you were strong, too, even then, my son, for you did not cry once. Not once in a whole month on that snowy march. I took you over the seas to Jutland, and to Bago. And at Bago, I gave you over to Olaf Karlsson, whom I had known in my earlier travels, and I gave him a bag of silver, a fortune – ill-gotten – and told him to care for you, and give you a good home. He was to treat you well, teach you a trade, and on no account was he to send you to the Fyr Skola. Ever. Not that for you. Did he treat you well, at least?'

Bjarki shrugged. 'Not well. They were cruel. But it's not important.'

'Cruel,' said Hildar slowly. 'Cruel. Is that so? And Valtyr here says there was a girl in Bago that you cared for.'

'I did – Freya was her name. I loved her. I made an oath to her. But I had to leave her when they banished me. They took her away from me.'

'Hmm,' said Hildar. 'It is dreadful to be left behind. I know it, son.'

'How did you meet *my* mother?' asked Tor.

'I went back to Svearland, after that,' said Hildar, looking at Tor. 'I went to claim my reward from Harald Fox-Beard, for

Blundfjell. He kept his word, he gave me a village by the sea and a woman: your mother, Gytha.'

'You hurt her; I remember the bruises and the tears,' said Tor.

'I did. The Wolf was in me, and growing stronger. I… wanted her to be Mist-in-the-Morning and… she was not. So, I was… angry with her.'

'You think that's an excuse?'

'I make no excuse for the things I have done. The Norns spun my fate, not I. The Wolf was in me. I tried to kill the Wolf. I failed. I jumped into the wild water from Thor's Rock but the sea god spat me out. Aegir rejected me. I crawled to land; I went north, to the Sami, to the soothing snows and ice.'

'Did you ever love my mother?' asked Tor. She found her eyes were leaking again. 'Or was she just a person who was *not* Mist-in-the-Morning?'

'We loved each other, a little, for a while. Does she still breathe?'

'She died two years ago. A summer fever took her.'

'I grieve for her. You have her look; her hair held fire as yours does.'

Tor found she was suddenly raging at the huge man on the other side of the table. 'You grieve? You say you grieve now? The nights I have dreamt of you; imagined you coming to me, to save me, to save my poor mother, to make everything right again; and all you can say is the Wolf was in me. The Wolf made me do it. Oh, the Wolf made me batter your mother to bloody pulp. I grieve. I'm *so* full of grief. You are pathetic, a cowardly *nithing*—'

'Tor,' Valtyr said, 'you cannot understand what is inside him.'

'I don't *want* to understand.' Tor was shrieking now.

Hildar got to his feet; he seemed to have grown even more massive. His face was flushed red and twisted ugly with rage. He looked ready to explode.

Bjarki stood up as well. He was of a height with Hildar. He leaned one large fist on the table, pushed his face forward and said, quietly and calmly: 'I think you'd better take your leave of us now, Father. Thank you for sharing your tale with my sister and me – but it is time for you to go now.'

Hildar grinned at him. It was a horrible smile: all yellow wolfish teeth and bloody-red gums. They locked eyes, faces close together, and for a tiny moment a cataclysm of raw violence shimmered in the space between them.

'Do you know what you are looking at, boy?' Hildar growled.

'What am I looking at?'

'You are looking at your fate, my son.'

Abruptly, Hildar turned on his heel and stalked out of the hall.

–

On the third day, the hammering stopped. Tor, who was stacking bundles of javelins at regular intervals on the perimeter walkway of the Fortress of Hellingar, immediately stood upright, listened and rubbed her sore back.

No more hammers. The Franks had completed their work. That was bad. She went in search of Bjarki and found him in the command post at the summit of the east rampart. He was standing with Valtyr, Theodoric and Siegfried and looking out of the open shutters at the battlefield. There was an odd air of levity over them. Duke Theodoric appeared to be chuckling.

Right across the spread of the field there was movement: large blocks of men in red cloaks, red shields and steel helmets, advancing, and out in front of them six dark objects like huge land-boats were spearheading their attack. They were still half a mile away but Tor could clearly see what they were. Around each of the objects was a little fringe of blue – the blue-cloaked men of the *scara* of engineers, urging these freshly built wooden drawbridges along on their massive wooden wheels towards the channel.

She caught Bjarki's eye and he beckoned her close to him and said: 'Want to hear some good news, sister?'

She raised one eyebrow.

'Look beyond the Red Cloaks, Tor; look beyond those ten or so *scarae* in the vanguard, the ones that are formed and coming towards us.'

She did so, squinting at the horizon, at the larger, indistinct mass of soldiers behind the moving blocks of troops in front of the Dane-Work, a thin wall of red, which stretched many miles across the landscape.

'Looks like they brought about half of Francia's entire military strength to crush us here, doesn't it?' Bjarki said.

Tor shrugged.

'It's a trick. It's a ruse. Karolus is trying to fool us.'

'What do you mean?' she said.

'The Saxon scouts have come back at long last to report the truth. That force in the extreme distance is not an army, it is just thousands of sticks and planks, with some red cloaks tied to them, and a few battered old helmets and shields. I wondered why they didn't move at all, day after day; or change their battle formations. And how even mighty Karolus could feed such a multitude of men. It's a straw army. Scarecrows. But the king of the Franks thought they'd be too far away for us to see he was hoodwinking us.'

'You are sure about this?'

'Four of our spies – all experienced scouts, good solid men, apparently, and unknown to each other – have confirmed it. The king only brought two dozen *scarae* with him, and some odds and ends. Some Swabians and his bodyguard of *Scholares*. He sent the rest of his force south only a few days ago, there is something important happening in Lombardy, their Pope – some sort of grand Mikelgothi – begged him to come with his army over the high Alps and rescue some of Karolus's kin, who have been imprisoned by the king of the Lombards. I don't understand it but he's gone there, immediately, with much of his army and all his *cabellarii*.'

'Karolus is gone? But we saw him just three days ago.'

'He is tricking us – or trying to. That's why he came forward and made that ridiculous proposal in person. Offering Theodoric and Siegfried what they already had. He *wanted* to be seen – now he's gone south to Lombardy. He's left the young Duke of Swabia in command to complete the task here.'

'That doesn't change the fact that there are thousands of Red Cloaks down there about to cross the channel.'

'No, that's true. But they have fewer than five thousand shields in all.'

'And we have fewer than three thousand,' said Tor. 'Even including the new contingent of Svearlanders. It's still poor odds – two against one.'

King Siegfried looked over at her and smiled. 'But we have the Dane-Work, young lady. This is the rock on which Frankish pride will shatter.'

Tor looked unconvinced. The six wooden drawbridges were slowly lumbering closer to the channel, only a few hundred yards away now, and when they were in place, and their bridges clunked down, thousands of Red Cloaks would flood across the water and surge up against the Dane-Work.

And they would easily outnumber the defenders. Two against one.

Chapter Thirty-one

The battle to end all battles

Bjarki took up his position on the perimeter wall a little to the left of the main gate. He turned and surveyed the faces of the men and women under his command. The front half of the Hellingar walkway, a semi-circle from the east rampart to the west, was crammed with hundreds of warriors: grey-bearded axemen from the woods of Eastphalia, in the far east of Saxony; blond, whey-faced Westphalians clutching javelins and maces; proud Danish *hersirs* from villages not unlike Bago; spearmen from the smaller islands in leather armour and steel caps; dour Svearlanders in full-length mail, gilded helms, with long swords at their waists; even a sprinkling of outlanders from Frisia and two grim, cold-eyed Angelcynn, battle-hardened adventurers who had sworn an oath to serve Duke Theodoric many, many years ago…

The warriors were arranged in two lines, front rank and second, the plan being to take turns in the assault to repel the enemy and clear the walls.

The rear of the fortress, the part facing north into Jutland, was only lightly manned by the very old and the very young, plus the walking wounded. Bjarki did not expect to be attacked from this direction. But he also had four Storm Companies, one in each quadrant, who could be called upon to defend the vulnerable rear, if necessary. Their main role, however, was to reinforce any sections that came under too much pressure.

I should speak, Bjarki thought. *I should say something stirring. I should at least try to act like a leader – like Theodoric or Siegfried, or even Valtyr.*

'Warriors of the North,' he bellowed, looking around to see that everyone on the walls could hear him. 'The time has come. Can you feel it? Can you smell it? Can you taste it? This is the hour of our greatest glory!'

His words were answered with a cheer from hundreds of throats.

'Those Franks are coming. See them! They are coming to kill you, to kill all your children, to seize your goods and lands. These proud Christians believe they have already won. They believe they will triumph this red day. They think they can roll over us, grind us down and trample our bones.'

He paused for a beat.

'They are wrong!' Another gigantic cheer split the air.

'Stand fast. Obey your orders. Summon your strength – and we will show these foreigners the meaning of courage. May the Bear guard you all!'

–

The attack, when it came, happened very fast indeed. One moment the mass of Red Cloaks was safely on the other side of the channel, and the bowmen of the North were lobbing a light but lethal rain of shafts on to them from the east and west ramparts; the next, the enemy were surging up against the walls of Hellingar, a sea of red-faced shouting men with swords and spears. The enemy hurled javelins up at the walls; their arrows flew thickly as the defenders'. They had many ladders – Bjarki had somehow not expected that – and swarmed up the defences of the fortress like monkeys.

They were assaulted all along the curving front wall simultaneously. Bjarki quickly exhausted the stock of javelins to hand, skewering five, six, seven enemies with the hurled missiles, whose places were all immediately taken by other men. He found he was frantically clearing the wall in front of him with his axe, hewing at screaming Red Cloaks, slicing down at mailed shoulders, steel helms, battering faces away with hard jabs from the butt end.

He hacked into the side of a man's head, bursting the skull open, and no sooner had the fellow flopped away than another Red Cloak lunged forward, stabbing with his short sword. Bjarki felt sure he had killed this same fellow not twenty heartbeats ago; but here he was again.

He deflected the sword strike with his shield, then punched the shield's iron boss into the man's roaring face, knocking him off his ladder. For an instant, nobody replaced him and Bjarki gripped the top rungs of the ladder and with a great heave he hurled it away from the pine wall, tumbling Red Cloaks to the ground like apples dropping from a shaken branch.

The noise was incredible, the screams and yells, the clash and screech of metal on metal; the air stank of blood and foulness. Bjarki could hear trumpets calling, and officers shouting orders, but his whole world was contained in the yard of sharpened pine logs in front of his body; and the folk who popped up and needed to be battered away. Another ladder top appeared, a little to his left, and a steel helmet with a red plume. Bjarki stepped to it, swung and slipped in a patch of blood, mistimed his blow, and the Red Cloak ducked, then hacked at him and sliced right through the shaft of his axe, the severed weapon falling from Bjarki's fingers.

His shield was way down and the man's sword blade was now lancing towards his face; Bjarki could see it coming but was powerless to evade it.

Tor's spear suddenly ripped into the man's neck below his helmet strap, tearing out his windpipe and knocking him sideways; the Red Cloak's sword swiped harmlessly over his head. But hot blood sprayed over Bjarki's face.

'Front rank, switch. Second rank, forward,' yelled Bjarki through a greasy mouthful of the dead fellow's gore. The cry was taken up all round the perimeter. He stepped one pace back and allowed Tor to slide forward into his place. She immediately began punching her spear blade down, one-handed, again, again, into the crush of Red Cloaks below the lip of the wall.

Bjarki was panting like a dog; covered in blood – other men's so far, thank the gods. He felt as battered and bruised as if he had been rolled down a mountain in a barrel full of sharp stones. As he caught his breath, he saw that the strip of muddy once-green land between the channel and the walls of Hellingar was now completely filled with Red Cloaks. There was no way on earth they could kill this many foes. They'd need a week to finish the job.

He looked left and saw that the slopes of the east rampart, too, were carpeted with red bodies and glinting helms; the battle was raging savagely all along the fence at the top. Frankish archers below were shooting volleys at the command post and javelins were showering back down the slope in response. To his right, on the west rampart, the situation was little different; but a section of the heavy fence had been torn down, and the summit was one vast melee of struggling Red Cloaks and grim warriors of the North – all madly stabbing, hacking, killing, dying.

His own wall was only just holding, there were scores of broken bodies below on the inside of the fortress, men and women who had been wounded and fallen backwards inside the walls, probably hastening their deaths. The battle lines on the walkway were thinner, too. Where the warriors had once been crammed together, now there was ample room to swing a long axe.

'It's time,' whispered his *gandr*. 'You *know* it is time.'

He set his face against the voice and looked out beyond the channel. The Duke of Swabia, the Franks' overall commander, was over there on the little hillock, just three hundred paces away, the same spot that Karolus had occupied. Duke Gerold, surrounded by an escort of mounted *Scholares*, was calmly watching the battle. Bjarki wished the unpleasant young nobleman were within the reach of his sword. He remembered the foul conversation in Queen Hildegard's chamber with fresh distaste. If only he were closer…

Wait. Just three hundred paces away? The channel was no obstacle now, there were six new wooden drawbridges spanning it.

He could see his people were tiring. There seemed to be no end to the surging Red Cloaks.

'Second rank, switch. Front rank, forward,' he yelled, drawing his sword and stepping in front of Tor.

She had taken a wound, he saw as he slipped past her, a gash to her left arm. The leather sleeve was wet with blood and her face was pale with pain. He had no more time. A Red Cloak was in the act of throwing his leg over the sharpened pine, when Bjarki punched him in the jaw with the hilt of his sword and, as he toppled, he slashed his tunic at the shoulder. But the man was not the only one: a dozen yards to his left three of the enemy had made it on to the walkway, and were coolly fighting off his warriors, back to back.

He yelled: 'Storm Company, here, now! Need you here, right now!'

A helmet appeared in front of his eyes, and he swung the sword at the rising Red Cloak, the fellow blocked with his own sword. Their steel clanged like a bell, and the trooper dropped his blade. Bjarki sliced at him again. The man yelled: 'No!' and held up his hand and Bjarki's sword sliced down between his spread fingers, opening his hand like a blossoming flower.

He yelled again and Bjarki punched him with his shield, knocking him back into empty space. There were half a dozen Red Cloaks now on the walkway. But the Storm Company had heard him and they were racing up ladders and barging along the walkway to crash into the interlopers.

The man leading the charge was Hildar Torfinnsson, in his full Wolf Lodge attire, fur cloak, heavy fur vambraces, leather greaves and boots, his tanned torso as bare as a baby's, his brutal, scarred face contorted in a wolfish snarl, his drawn-back lips already speckled with a soapy foam.

Hildar ploughed into the enemy on the walkway, his axe swinging. Red Cloaks were hurled into the air every which way, body parts cartwheeled over the wall, blood gouted, gore flew, the screaming reached new heights.

Bjarki leaned on the wall, gasping for air, his section of the wall momentarily clear. The Rekkr was truly magnificent, his raw power and violence dazzling. The Storm Company following on his heels were left with little to do but finish off the wounded as Hildar cleared the walkway of enemies in one snarling charge, his axe swinging with a horrible rhythm.

'See – see – the lovely blood, all the lovely man-blood!' his *gandr* was chittering with glee. 'Come on now, let *us* do this!'

Bjarki peered over the wall – could it be his imagination or were the Red Cloaks actually falling back? He looked right at the west rampart, and saw that the Angrian cavalry of the North were in and among the thinning enemy on the summit, hacking and slicing, riding them down, screaming with delight. The wooden fence was down and trampled under foot as the Saxons surged forward to battle one-on-one on the summit with the Franks.

And it seemed they were actually pushing them back down the slope.

On the left, the east rampart was still holding too. The momentum of the Frankish attack had been stalled all across the front. Now, there was fresh movement on the east rampart, and the sounding of brash trumpet blasts over the din of battle. No, it could not be! There was Theodoric, in an ancient Boar Lodge headdress, long sword in his hand and he was charging out from behind the wooden fence with a dozen of his jarls and *hersirs* at his back – no, more, many more – a score, several scores, hundreds of men.

The lord of Saxony no longer seemed old and fat – he was huge and vital; he was Fire Born. Bjarki imagined he could hear the old man's cries as he and his warriors fell on the mass of his enemies like a collapsing sea cliff.

Three yards away, Hildar had a double grip on a huge round shield, holding it by the upper rim, he was standing at the wall, staring out over the enemy below, his gigantic arm muscles writhing like snakes, and he seemed to be gnawing at the top of the thick wood with his teeth, worrying the fitted planks of elm like a dog with a bone. He suddenly spat out a mouthful of wood pulp and roared a deafening challenge at a particular foe below him.

Bjarki could resist the urge no more. He let himself go; and he began to hum, deep in his throat. A rhythmic four-note tune, repetitive, hypnotic…

He felt his *gandr* swell; its mad laughter echoing around in his head.

He shouted: 'Hildar! Father! Hear me. Recall the battle of Blundfjell? Where you slew the King of Vestfold and won the day single-handed?'

Hildar heard him and turned, eyes very large, expression as keen as a hunting dog: but his face also oddly twisted, the cheek muscles writhing.

He grinned at Bjarki, showing bloody yellow teeth.

'My son,' he growled. 'My Fire Born son…'

Bjarki was holding on to the real world now only by his fingertips.

'There is our enemy, Father. Karolus's man. The duke. There. Over there. Come with me, Father! Come – let's cut the head off the snake!'

Hildar grinned horribly. He threw away his chewed shield and climbed on the top of the log wall. Bjarki joined him, scrambling up on to the perilous pine summit of the defences. The young Rekkr threw back his head and bellowed at the sky. Then he drew his seax; holding his long bloody sword in the other hand. Humming, grinning, laughing… Bjarki felt suddenly freezing cold; he heard the sound of rushing water in his ears like the noise of a waterfall. He felt his *gandr* huge, black and triumphant, swelling inside his chest, he felt his heart engorge with power, he could feel blood pounding hot in his veins; he felt light, buoyant, stronger than ever before…

Tor yelled. 'What are you doing, oaf! Don't be an idiot.'

Bjarki jumped.

Chapter Thirty-two

The life of just one man

Tor watched in disbelief as Bjarki, grinning, blood-covered, a blade in each hand, leapt off the wall and crashed into the mass of Red Cloaks below.

So she did the only thing she could. She jammed the butt of her spear against the floor of the walkway and vaulted over the pine barrier after him.

A mound of dead and wounded Red Cloaks below broke her fall as softly as a pile of brushwood, and she staggered upright, stepping hard in the middle of a crying young man's gory open belly, but still gripping her spear.

Bjarki was in a space all his own, blades slicing, blood spattering, and he was surging forward as he killed, ever forward, heading for the channel.

She heard a savage yell behind her and Hildar crashed down, landing partially on an empty ladder, snapping it to kindling but not seeming to notice. Hildar rocketed to his feet, kicking bits of broken wood away from his greaves, and hacked the head from a terrified Red Cloak with his axe.

He plunged into the fray after Bjarki. Tor ran after her father, yet oddly she faced no resistance – the Franks were utterly bewildered by this sudden apparition: two gore-wet madmen and a slip of a girl suddenly thumping down among them. Not a man lifted his hand against her – at first.

Then an officer bellowed, 'Kill that bitch! Kill her right now!' and Tor made two savage cuts with the spear, ripping one man's face wide open and causing another Red Cloak to leap back and stumble over his own feet.

The way in front of her was now open.

She ran after her brother and her father, following their bloody trail. There was a drawbridge before her now, too. She saw Bjarki, howling with joyful rage, hacking his way through the scatter of frightened blue-cloaked men guarding the big wooden structure – the enemy wisely fleeing before him and his two swinging blades. A moment later, in the body-filled wake of the charging Rekkar, Tor found herself clumping alone across the deserted wooden planks and simply walking over to the enemy's side.

For Tor, everything had a dream-like quality, the armed men around her, her Frankish foes, stared at her in blank amazement, stunned by this unexpected turn of events. Hildar and Bjarki were two dozen paces ahead, surging onwards, almost shoulder to shoulder, cutting and killing, carving a gory channel through the knots of men. Slicing and stamping; battering and barging a way through the shifting disorganised crowd of enemies.

The Red Cloaks were distracted; not looking at her, nor even at the two blood-splashed madmen ploughing through their loose ranks. They were all now looking behind her, north, over the channel, at the carnage taking place on the slopes of the ramparts and before the gates of Hellingar.

There was Duke Theodoric, in a Boar Lodge war costume, boar-skull helmet, pig-skin cloak and armour, screaming and slaying, butchering Red Cloaks left and right, and hundreds of screaming warriors of the North at his back. It was an astounding scene, like something out of a nightmare, and little wonder the enemy stared in fear. Theodoric was driving all before him, his mad charge down the slopes had cleared the enemy from the rampart.

He was fighting in front of the central drawbridge now; she saw the gates of Hellingar suddenly thrown open and its thousand-strong garrison pour out to join Theodoric in the jostling blood-bath on the channel's bank.

The scattered sheaves of Franks around her, instead of surging forward to join the melee, were edging backwards, away from the horror.

Those Red Cloaks on the north bank were pouring back across the drawbridges. Some were already running from the field, streaming south.

But not all.

Tor craned to look for her family, and saw them twenty yards away, demolishing a knot of foes. Now a squad of twenty Green Cloaks, the duke's men, was forming up in a neat line, with spears and shields raised. The line charged straight towards Bjarki and Hildar and their pile of fresh victims, the Franks coming in at an angle to block their bloody path towards the knoll and the Duke of Swabia's sea of *Scholares*.

Bjarki saw them coming, turned abruptly and ran at them frothing and howling. At the last moment, he rolled under the reaching spears, and came up killing under their shield rims, slicing up into groins and bellies.

Hildar saw his son's actions – and immediately followed him. He smashed into the wavering Green Cloaks, shattering their line, tossing the Frankish soldiers here and there like leaves in a gale with wide sweeps of his axe. Hildar was giggling, or perhaps weeping, Tor saw, as he crunched his blade through the unarmoured side of a Green Cloak, plucked the blade free of his ribs and crushed another's skull with an elegant backwards sweep.

Tor ran in fast to join them. She lunged with the spear at the desperate officer who was trying to re-establish order in the line. She caught him in the inside thigh, ripping through muscles, tendons and veins, feeling the jar as her blade hit the femur, but dropping the man screaming and pissing blood.

The Green Cloak line was completely disintegrated, and Bjarki and Hildar were well past them all now, with Tor running a few paces behind.

Ahead of the running trio was a mass of black-clad *Scholares* on horseback, just in front of a little rise: the Duke of Swabia's hillock. Tor caught a glimpse of the familiar petulant face, open-mouthed. The young duke himself. And that bastard Livinus, too. Scowling and pointing at them.

Bjarki, a couple of strides ahead of Hildar, was leaping at a Black Cloak on a shiny black horse. He swarmed up, stabbing, grabbing and pulling the man out of the saddle. And she saw an enemy's sword blow take him across the back, smashing into his iron mail. She saw him react, too. He spun round and lashed out with his own sword, slicing the top clean off the attacker's helmeted head. Hildar was right in among the *Scholares* by then; she saw puffs of blood, and a wave-like ripple as her father chopped his way forward through the mass of black mounts and dark-garbed guards.

A Black Cloak horseman was suddenly above her, lashing down with a shining sword at her helmeted head. She dodged the blow, twirled her spear and jammed the blade up and into his belly. He yelled out a curse and tried to turn the horse away. She stabbed him again, pushing him off the other side of the saddle with the shove of the spear. In an instant, she was in the saddle herself, the leather slippery with the man's blood. The horse was terrified and tried to buck her loose. But she soothed and calmed it, pausing only to hurl her spear into a yelling Frank who rode at her swinging a mace.

She turned the horse round and round, trying to get her bearings in all the chaos. Red Cloaks were streaming past her now, in full retreat.

She saw that the slopes of the Dane-Work were empty of foes. They were all pulling back. They were beaten. She saw Theodoric in the middle of a bridge lifting both his arms in the eternal pose of triumph; his men around him, crossing the channel, chasing the beaten foe. A gory sword was in each of the Fire Born Saxon's fists. He was chanting his victory to the heavens.

She saw the Frankish arrow that struck him in the centre of his chest, just a moment later, and buried itself right up to the fletching. And a second shaft punching in right beside the first. And the catch of surprise on his face.

She looked away. Looked south. There was Bjarki, with Hildar just behind him. They were only yards from the Duke now, who had drawn his own sword, a long, silver, glittering item. Bishop Livinus, she saw, was already urging his mount to the rear, out of the mad crush of Black Cloaks.

But the Duke of Swabia wanted to fight.

He slashed at Bjarki, shouting something ugly. Her Fire Born brother blocked the blow but, at the very same time, she saw a Black Cloak officer knee-to-knee with Gerold lean down from the saddle and plunge his sword deep into Bjarki's side. The Rekkr ignored the wound, spun, and pulled the man down from the saddle, ripping out his throat with one sweep of his seax.

The duke yelled again, his horse cavorting, and he smashed his blade down hard on to Bjarki's steel-helmeted head. She saw her brother stumble under the blow and fall. But Hildar was swarming forward, he leapt in the air, his long axe licked out and crashed into the mailed chest of the duke, the keen blade driving right through the overlapping iron scale links.

Gerold reeled back in the saddle, then lurched forward; then he slowly began to slip to one side, finally sliding off his mount to vanish in the crush.

A huge moan of sorrow rose from the enemy ranks.

The Black Cloaks surged forward. Hildar came staggering out of the pack, spinning away, swinging his long axe, scattering drops of ducal gore.

A shrill Frankish cry rang out: 'The duke is down. Gerold is hurt!'

A Black Cloak on foot leapt on to Hildar's back, arm round his throat, a dagger plunging down. Hildar plucked him off his back one-handed like a man removing a wet cloak and hurled the fellow to the ground with a crash.

Tor spurred forward, sword in hand, batting swarming *Scholares* out of her path with her blade, still battle-mad yet gripped with sudden, piercing grief. There was no sign of Bjarki at all. He was trampled somewhere under the melee. Yet the tide of black-cloaked men was moving back, away from her, shifting swiftly like a shoal of dark fish, away, southwards. The still body of the duke, chest sheeted in glistening red, now held high above the rest – and men were shouting: 'Back, back!' and, 'Carry our lord to safety!'

They were all moving away, gathering momentum, bearing the body of their commander. Tor reined in; the frightened horse skittering under her.

There on the ground, in a tangle of dead beasts, and the dozens of dead and wounded Black Cloaks, she could see Bjarki, half-sitting, half-lying on the muddy, bloody earth, his eyes half open. He was oozing from a dozen open wounds, but smiling faintly. And Hildar was there too, hunched and kneeling a yard or two away with his back to Tor, equally wet and filthy, his head hanging down, his face hidden by his thick curtain of greasy hair.

A block of Red Cloaks, formed and under perfect discipline – a whole *scara*, she assumed – now trotted smartly past, and paid them no mind at all.

Tor got down from the horse and walked unsteadily over to the only two living members of her family. She looked back at the Dane-Work and saw that her compatriots were visible everywhere; some were even across this side of the channel, too. Warriors of the North were strutting and bellowing, others were collapsed with exhaustion, or bent over their wounds. Some were just standing, leaning on their spears. Everywhere the Red Cloaks were retreating, some still intact as viable units, but most just fleeing across the field, their formations dissolved, a beaten rabble.

She took a step nearer to her father, who turned his head to look at her. His skin was pale as milk under the spatter, but he was grinning like a Wolf.

'I think,' said Tor. 'I think, Father, that we may have won this bout.'

–

When Bjarki awoke he was lying on his back on a straw pallet in a dim room. He recognised it immediately as the rear of Ash

House. Somebody had rigged a curtain to separate him from the main part of the longhouse. Gunnar, with a neatly stitched cut below his cheekbone, was sitting on a stool near by, fiddling with the metal attachment at the head of a long spear.

The hall was eerily silent. No voices, no murmur or clink of pottery.

'Where is everyone?' said Bjarki.

Gunnar looked at him: 'They've all gone to attend Duke Theodoric's funeral pyre. The whole Dane-Work. But I thought I'd stay here with you.'

Bjarki slowly lifted a trembling finger and indicated the spear in Gunnar's hands. 'You here to finish the job the Black Cloaks started?'

'No, no. Tor has been giving me lessons with the spear these past three days, since… since the battle. She's rather disappointed with my progress. But even if I were a spear-prodigy, I don't believe that it is possible to kill you. You seem to be entirely indestructible. Eldar the *gothi*, who's been looking at your wounds, is convinced there is some sort of sorcery at work.'

'I don't feel indestructible. I can barely move my limbs at all.'

'How do you feel?'

'Everything hurts. My legs, arms… everything. I'm very thirsty, too.'

'I'll go and get you some ale. There's an open cask in the brew yard.'

Gunnar got up; he leaned the spear against the wall by the curtain and went out into the hall.

Bjarki lay there, hurting. He tried to lift up his head a few inches from the pillow, and found he could not.

A shadow crossed his face. 'Back already?' he said, looking up at the figure standing over his body.

It was Ivar Knuttson. He was smiling down at him.

'I heard you got cut up pretty bad, Bjarki-boy,' he said. 'At Hel's black gate, that's what I heard. But you wouldn't go through, would you?'

Bjarki struggled to rise. He got his arm under him and pushed his torso up. Ivar's foot lashed out and swept the arm away from under him, Bjarki thumped back down on the pallet. He had to bite his lip till the blood ran to prevent himself from screaming out in agony. Ivar gave a little snigger.

'What… do… you… want?' Bjarki managed.

'Wanted to see you. Maybe give you a little push through that old black gate I mentioned before.'

'I thought… we had… resolved our differences,' panted Bjarki.

'Is that what you thought? You humiliated me. You took from me the respect of the Fyr Skola. You think I didn't hear all the little whispers, the sly jokes? Ivar's not a real Rekkr. He's just a sham. That was *you*, that was!'

'You *are* a sham,' Bjarki said. 'But, truly, I don't care what you claim to be. And I have never spoke ill of you since we came here to Hellingar.'

Ivar shrugged. 'I'm Father of the Boar Lodge – nobody can take that from me. But enough. Time for you to succumb tragically to your wounds.'

Ivar Knuttson pulled his seax from its sheath at his belly.

'I'd look behind you, if I were you.'

'Really, Bjarki? *Really?* Has anyone *ever* fallen for that old chestnut?'

'Honestly, have a look. There's a warrior about to skewer you.'

Ivar half-turned in time to see Gunnar jump forward and thrust the spear hard into his belly. The point sank in smoothly and burst bloodily out of the other side. Ivar screamed and collapsed beside Bjarki's cot. He flapped and writhed, legs kicking, blood seeping from his open mouth.

Eventually he stopped jerking; but his continued breath was a horrible wet laboured sound in the silent hall.

'Told you,' said Bjarki.

'I am Fire Born,' Ivar whispered. 'I *am*. I can't be slain by a *nithing*.'

'You have not,' said Bjarki, their faces were close now. He could see the flesh on Ivar's cheeks fall; the eyes roll upwards, the last rattling breath come from his lungs. 'You've just been killed by a Rekkr-slayer,' he said.

But, by then, Ivar Knuttson was no longer able to hear him.

Bjarki looked up at Gunnar, who was standing, pale-faced, with his left fist crammed into his open mouth. He looked horrified by his actions.

'Good technique, Gunnar,' said Bjarki. 'You're improving.'

There was the sound of pounding boots, a clatter as a table or a bench was overturned, and the heavy curtain was wrenched wide open.

Tor stood there, panting slightly, with a naked sword in her right hand. 'I heard somebody scream,' she said.

Then she took in the scene: Gunnar deep in shock; Bjarki lying on the pallet; and Ivar Knuttson curled around the bloody spear that transfixed him.

'You all right?' she said to Bjarki.

'I've had better days.'

'Who did this – you, Gunnar?' Tor kicked Ivar's corpse.

The pale young man managed a jerky nod.

'Nice spear work,' said Tor. 'We'll make a warrior of you yet.'

'That's what I said!' Bjarki was grinning up at his sister.

–

'…nobody has seen him since the battle. He's gone. And to be honest, I am a little worried.' Tor was sitting on the stool by Bjarki's bed. Gunnar was dragging Ivar's corpse out of the sick room, grumbling, sighing and retching, displaying his disgust at having been made to do this messy task.

'You kill 'em; you have to clean 'em up,' said Tor. 'That's the rule.'

'He will have gone north,' said Bjarki. 'That's what he always does.'

'Back to the Sami – to some witch-woman he has up there? I'd have thought he would stick around after the battle to enjoy some of the praise. He *did* just put his axe into the Duke of Swabia. With our help, of course.'

'I don't know. Did Hildar say anything before he went?'

'Valtyr says he was muttering something to himself before he left,' said Tor. 'Two words. Over again. Something about money.'

'Two words?'

'He said "silver" and "cruel" again and again, like a chant. The Wolf *gandr* was still strong in him, I think. Or he'd gone completely Galálar.'

'No, oh no.' Bjarki was struggling again to rise. 'I know where he's gone. To Bago. We have to stop him. Or… oh, gods. Tor, help me up.'

'You're not going anywhere; let alone walking up to Bago!'

'We'll take a ship. The Svear dragon-ships, they're still here, yes? It will be faster, anyway, and he has a long head start on us. It will give me a chance to heal a little, as well. Come on, Tor! Every moment is precious!'

Chapter Thirty-three

The reckoning

Hildar Torfinnsson ignored the main entrance of the barricaded longhouse in Bago and went in straight through the east wall, hacking through rough wattle-and-daub exterior and thin inner planks with his axe.

It took him no more than a few moments, and his huge fur-clad shoulders were erupting into the gloomy interior, like a monstrous chick emerging from the egg. His humming had reached the pitch of fury.

A doddering greybeard tried to stand in his way and Hildar skewered him through the loins with the ancient sword and, turning and swinging the bloody axe with his other hand, he hewed the head clean off the howling matron who tried to stab him in the belly with her roasting spit.

The rest of the inhabitants cowered by the long rectangular fire-trough in the centre of the hall, resigned to their fate, all except for a white-faced boy, who charged at the Rekkr from the shadows, yelling shrilly, the sharp eating knife in his hand. Hildar killed him with a sideways flick of the axe, a casual, almost friendly blow, which smashed the little boy's right cheekbone into several pieces, driving the shards deep into his small skull.

Hildar loomed over the last few folk huddled by the long hearth, breathing from his exertions. His gaze crawled all over them like a fly on a freshly made corpse. Then he fixed on one of the older girls, a pretty blonde.

'Freya, my sweet,' he said. The words were clogged in his throat, as if they were too large or too jagged to come out. 'I have come… for *you*.'

'You leave her be, Father,' said Bjarki, stepping heavily through the wreckage of wattle-and-daub kindling beside the hole in the wall. He had a drawn sword in his right hand, an unsheathed seax in his left.

'My son,' gurgled Hildar, 'my Rekkr son!' turning from the fire-trough. He saw a smaller, slimmer shape emerge behind Bjarki's huge form.

'There's my sweet daughter, too. Come, give your old father a kiss.'

Tor stared at him; she looked slowly around the longhouse, noting the headless corpse, the skull-smashed child and the cowering survivors.

'You have no idea how much I missed you, Father,' she said. 'I grieved for you, every day of my childhood. I wept for you, I prayed for your spirit to come back to me, even though I knew in my heart what you had done to my mother. I built my life around a memory, a false memory, of your greatness. I would be like Hildar Torfinnsson, I told myself, and anyone who would listen. I would be a hero, a Rekkr, the greatest of all warriors.'

Tor swallowed painfully. 'Then I met you. Alive… in the flesh. Not conveniently dead as I had always pictured you. I saw what you truly are.'

'I am still your father,' said Hildar, staring at her. His eyes were huge.

'I don't think you are,' Tor said. 'My real father is dead. He's been dead a long time, and I venerate his memory. Perhaps he never existed at all. But *you* are a monster – a slab of horror on two legs. You've gone Galálar.'

'Words,' said Hildar. 'Pretty little words. Come, kiss me, daughter.'

'Keep your distance, Tor,' said Bjarki. Then, looking at the pathetic little group crouched by the hearth fire, he said: 'Freya, it's me, Bjarki, remember? Come away from that man. Now. Come round here behind me.'

The blonde girl hesitated only for a moment and then scampered over to him, widely skirting Hildar, and coming to shelter behind Bjarki's bulk.

'I wasn't going to hurt *her*, son,' said Hildar, he sounded deeply insulted by the suggestion. 'I was going to bring her back to your bed. You said you were forced to part from her by these *nithings*, these vermin—'

'Vermin?' Tor was barely able to control her own rage now. She had a naked sword in her hand. 'That's how you see them. So you killed them all.'

'They were cruel to my boy,' said Hildar plaintively. 'I paid Olaf Karlsson handsomely – a big bag of hack silver – to raise my Bjarki, but he cheated me. He was cruel. He wanted to hang my boy by the neck—'

'So you killed him,' said Tor. 'I saw Olaf's body in the street, with the others. You slew the whole village: the mothers, their babies, the children.'

Bjarki had shooed Freya into a dark corner and was moving clumsily around the hearth trough, circling Hildar. Widening the angle between him and Tor. He moved stiffly, dragging his left leg a little, he looked horribly thin and weak, as if even a moderate puff of wind could knock him over. Even the weight of his long sword seemed too much for him.

'We have to take you before the Thing,' Bjarki said, gritting his teeth against the pain of his wounds. 'For justice. You have killed folk with no good cause. You must answer for it, Father. We've a ship on the beach; if you submit to us, we'll bind you and take you to the king of the Danes.'

Hildar threw back his head and laughed, a horrible crackling sound.

'You make a fine jest, son,' he said. 'We both know how this must end. I *am* Galálar. Torfinna knows it well enough too, don't you, my girl?'

'I'm not your girl,' she said. 'But, yes, I know how this must end.'

'He doesn't look as if he could fight off a crippled kitten,' said Hildar, jerking his head towards Bjarki. 'But you, my girl, my beautiful, brave and fiery daughter – your mother, whom you so resemble, sent *you* to practise sword-work with the boys. We shall see now if you ever learnt anything.'

Hildar flew at Tor; impossibly fast. He moved as smoothly as a leopard and before Tor could properly react, he had struck at her with the long axe, a vicious downward chop that would have divided her skull – if it had landed.

Tor got the sword up just in time and deflected the massive axe strike to her left – but the force of the blow knocked her to her knees and the blade thudded into the beaten earth of the rush-strewn hall floor beside her left leg.

Hildar howled in pain. And Tor saw that Bjarki, behind and to the left of the Rekkr, had lunged with his sword and jammed the steel point into his lower back. Hildar shuddered, as if he was throwing off the pain; he whirled, fast as a whip and the axe lashed out horizontally, hurtling towards Bjarki's unguarded belly. The young man leapt back, stumbling, staggering, and the sharp blade merely sliced through a fold in his baggy grey tunic as it passed.

Tor, still on the ground, flailed with her sword. The blade whacked into Hildar's calf, cutting into the bulge of muscle. Once more the Rekkr cried out in pain. He turned fast and smashed the axe down at Tor's prone body.

She rolled, and rolled again, becoming tangled with a pile of pots and pans. The axe clanged against an iron skillet. The other people in the longhouse, the Bago villagers who yet lived, were scrambling for the hole in the wall, scurrying away from the hissing blades. Hildar lashed the axe down at Tor again, and again she just managed to squirm out of its lethal path.

Behind him, Bjarki took a staggering step forward and swung his long sword; the blade thunked into Hildar's right side, opening a dark gash in his lower chest. Bright scarlet blood bubbled out immediately. Hildar was now panting hard, still grinning like a madman, but running with gore from three fresh wounds. Yet he was not finished. He stood swaying, swiped at Bjarki with the axe; a half-hearted blow, yet Bjarki dodged only with difficulty.

Tor was back on her feet by now, she raised the bloody sword high above her head and hacked down at Hildar's shoulder; the blade slicing in deep, almost severing his right arm. The long axe slipped from Hildar's wet fingers. He fell to his knees by the fire-trough, his weight thumping down hard. He was facing both his children now, weaponless, bleeding.

He lifted his dripping chin, looked straight into Bjarki's blue eyes.

'You're a good boy,' he said, his voice raw with pain. 'And you, too, daughter of mine. You both make me proud. Now, enough! Finish it.'

Bjarki dropped his seax. He took a double grip on his sword hilt. The blade swung, hard and level. And Hildar's head jumped from his shoulders.

–

Bjarki had to lean heavily on Tor's shoulder, but he stood more or less upright before Freya in the street outside the longhouse and said his piece.

'We have been apart for a year now, my love,' he said softly. 'And even now I do not mean to remain in Bago for more than a day or two. But I once made a solemn oath to you, and I mean to honour it…'

The girl looked bewildered, as if she had never seen this huge, blood-splashed man before in her life. She was still very pretty, Bjarki noted, but somehow she seemed a little less lovely, less perfect than he remembered. He was struggling with his exhaustion, and the pain of his many wounds, so recently abused, ripped open in the fight with Hildar. He could not grasp on to the slippery words. He mumbled: 'I'm going to go east… there is a place I have been promised… good farmland, by the sea. A good place. Duke Leszko's land. But it needs a wife… to come with… Do you want…?'

He ran out of speech then and just stared at her dumbly.

'This oaf wants you to go with him. To be his woman on some remote farmstead in the east,' said Tor. 'Bear his snotty children; that family stuff.'

Freya said: 'But… but…'

'If you're worried about me, I'm his sister. Half-sister. But I can tell you that he's a good man. Bit stubborn sometimes. But brave and kind.'

'But,' said Freya. She too seemed to be lost for words. She gestured mutely at a white-haired young man who was standing on the fringe of the small circle of Bago survivors. He stepped forward nervously. Tor saw that he had a swaddled baby in his arms, a chubby infant only a few months old. Then she recognised him. It was Freki Olafsson, once of His Majesty's Auxilla; the boy who had been paid gold by Lord Grimoald to murder her Bjarki in his sleep.

'Freki is my man,' said Freya. 'He has been since… since you left.'

Bjarki stared at Freki, and at the baby. He felt a flush of blood through his whole body. Then anger, a pure, black, boiling rage. He heard his *gandr* whisper: 'Kill them all. She betrayed you. He tried to murder you, let me in; let me in now, and we'll take a sweet, sweet revenge.'

He glared at Freki, and the baby again – then let out a long, long breath.

'Congratulations to you both, Freya and Freki,' he said. 'I wish you joy of your family with all my heart. May the Bear guard you all your days.'

With that Bjarki turned, and began to hobble painfully down the street.

Epilogue

One month later

Bjarki wiped the sweat from his brow, and threw down the muddy spade. That was the last of them. All now properly buried at last.

He looked round to see where Tor was and saw that she was sitting on the grass by another of the freshly dug mass graves filled with the Groves of Eresburg folk, playing with Garm, getting the cub to chase a pretty black-and-white magpie feather on a string. The bear was not so little now, he saw. It had grown alarmingly in the past month, and its playful bites and clumsy paw-strikes were becoming surprisingly powerful.

One day, probably quite soon, they would have to think about what to do with him. A full-grown bear was not an ideal travelling companion. The food requirement alone could make things very difficult. And what if Garm grew too hungry and ate somebody? But that was a problem for another day.

The sun was shining, the river was gurgling merrily in the centre of the valley, and the hard work was done, for today at least. Gunnar was approaching him from the direction of the high valley-island that held charred ruins of the groves. He was pushing a barrow full of muddy tools and had a solemn expression on his face.

'Valtyr wants to say the old prayers around the remains of the Irminsul before supper,' he said. 'With all of us. You're finished here, are you?'

Bjarki nodded. 'I'll be there,' he said. 'As long as he doesn't plan to go on too long. I need to get to bed early. I'm off in the morning, first light.'

'You don't have to go, you know,' said Gunnar, putting a hand on his brawny arm. 'You could stay here a few months, help us get things going. Heal yourself fully. Get stronger. Teach us; share what you know about the *gandir*. It would be useful. Tor could be the master-of-arms, make all the novices jump. You'd be Father of the Bear Lodge, when we've rebuilt it.'

'You don't need me, Gunnar. You'll manage just fine without me.'

'We *do* need you, Bjarki. You're the last of them, you know. All the others are dead – Theodoric, Angantyr, Nikka the Dreamer... all of them gone... You are the last of the Fire Born. The last *berserkr*. You can't deny us your knowledge. What would the Fyr Skola be without a single Rekkr?'

'That's just the point. I don't want to be a Rekkr; I don't choose to live that life – they all die too young. I want the chance to see the world a little before I start knocking on the door of the Hall of the Slain. I don't want to end up like my father, Galálar, killing for pleasure, murdering ordinary folk for no good reason...' He paused for breath, fighting off unexpected tears.

'Anyway, Gunnar, you'll soon find some more people just like me.' Bjarki sniffed and roughly cuffed his wet nose. 'Valtyr brought in two boys just yesterday, twins – Fidor and Fodor – he says they are both very talented and both likely to find their *gandr* very soon.'

'Will you come back and visit us?' Gunnar sounded wistful.

'Of course, I'll visit whenever I'm passing... and I'm sure Tor will, too.' Bjarki could not look at his friend. He could foresee no circumstances in which he would be passing the Groves of Eresburg again. He was bound for Brenna, to find the long-haired man and take up his offer of a farmstead by the sea and swear an oath – with the gods' blessing the last oath he would ever make; and he meant to stay there in the east until he was old and grey.

As they strolled together up the long track to the summit of the Groves, towards the One Tree, they chatted of less painful things. 'The rumour is the Duke of Swabia is not dead,' Gunnar said. 'He's very badly wounded, Valtyr says, near to death, but Francia's healers are working on him night and day. Karolus is fighting in Lombardy – winning victories, or so I hear.'

'Do you think Karolus will come back and attack you here again?'

'Maybe. Widukind is harassing the retreating Red Cloaks with all the unwounded Saxon troops he has. I suppose I should call him Duke Widukind now that his father, Theodoric, is gone. He will make a good duke, I think. He seems a good soldier – resourceful, brave, even rather cunning.

'Francia is not defeated,' Gunnar went on, 'the battle of the Dane-Work was a small setback, a humiliation for Karolus. But the war is not over. Francia is vast, and they have the manpower to come at us again – you know this better than I, Bjarki. So, yes, maybe, they'll be back here again.'

They had reached the top of the track and were approaching the charred ruins of the groves. The beginnings of a new, stronger perimeter wall were being constructed by a handful of Angrian volunteers, farmers from north of the forest, and the air was filled with the crack of axes and the rasp of saws.

'You see that tall construction there.' Gunnar pointed to a rickety watchtower that soared up in the blue sky, one of several new buildings in the fire-blasted landscape. 'We'll keep a Barda up there day and night, and when the Red Cloaks come again, if they come, we'll all hide in the First Forest. Some of us are quite expert at that, you know,' he said, and grinned.

–

They all gathered that evening around the charred One Tree in a loose circle. They were too few to join hands and make a ring around the massive blackened trunk: and only a few of them there were former denizens of the Fyr Skola – Eldar the *gothi*, his friend Gunnar, Eric the big, slow-witted Barda who had fought with them on the west rampart, and Valtyr Far-Traveller, too, of course, who would be taking on the role of Mikelgothi.

The rest were new faces: the twins Fidor and Fodor, who were refugees from Frank-occupied Westphalia; and a strange raven-haired girl, half-mad with hunger, who had just turned up unannounced out of the First Forest…

Humble beginnings. And Bjarki was glad that the Fyr Skola would continue to exist – even if he meant to have nothing more to do with it.

He stood beside Tor and looked up at the blackened branches of the Irminsul. As Valtyr began to chant the prayer to the ancient spirits of the First Forest, Bjarki looked up into the twisted limbs of the mighty oak. And there on a high branch, just visible, he saw a little sprig of green, a new leaf.

Historical Note

There has been a spate of stories in the media in recent years that seek to persuade us that our traditional image of the Viking – the ferocious Northman, hairy, merciless and intent only on plunder and rapine – is completely wrong. The Norse people, we are now told, were in fact peaceful traders not rampaging psychopaths, folk who cared deeply about their personal hygiene and appearance, as evidenced by their combs, tweezers and the copious use of make-up by men.

This may well be true. But they were also warriors, from a society that revered strength and courage, and which produced epic poems about war and bloody revenge, about oaths and honour. They were living in a time of almost continual conflict and frequent violence, and often grew up in harsh lands in an unforgiving climate where making any kind of living required a certain grit and ruthlessness.

So, if you were a defenceless Christian monk in a remote monastery, sitting on a trove of gold and silver church accoutrements and praying for the Lord to deliver you from the fury of the approaching fleet of dragon-ships, you were probably about to experience first-hand a less-cuddly side of their culture.

Whether they were well-coiffed peaceful traders or ill-kempt priory-sackers – and I think they were probably both, depending on the circumstances – there is no figure that encapsulates the image of the Viking better than the berserker. And I must admit I've been fascinated all my life by these Norse super-warriors.

The genesis of this novel, and the whole Fire Born series, came from reading tales about berserkers as a child in various

Viking adventure novels. Then I began to do proper historical research and I came across a real tenth-century Icelandic warrior-poet and berserker called Egill Skallagrimsson, who fought for the English King Athelstan at the Battle of Brunanburh in AD 937. His tendency to go berserk, one researcher suggested, may have been caused by a rare bone condition called Paget's disease, which causes severe pain, giving rise to sudden rages. The disease also thickens the bones by up to four times their normal size and gives the sufferer the appearance of being impervious to blows. After Egill's death, his remains were exhumed and an enemy tried to drive an axe into his grossly enlarged skull. The blade bounced right off the bone.

I started investigating what else, apart from rare bone diseases, might cause someone to behave like a berserker. Some academics suggested that it might be the result of taking hallucinogenic drugs – perhaps mushrooms or other plant extracts – but my experience at music festivals and parties of people who have taken magic mushrooms is that the last thing they want to do is fight like a rabid badger. They usually giggle.

Others have suggested that berserkers deliberately entered a trance-like ecstatic religious state that made them impervious to pain. This was familiar territory to me, since I spent a short period in the 1980s as an anthropologist studying the Balinese belief-systems, which often involve entering a trance during religious festivals. The Balinese claim this state is caused by possession by the witch-god, Rangda, or by other deities, and during it they sometimes perform feats such as walking barefoot across burning coals.

Some Viking researchers suggest that chanting and music might facilitate the berserk state – in Bali it is ritual dance and the soft bell-like music of the *gamelan* orchestra that induce a trance – and this gave me the idea for the special four-note humming that my Fire Born practise to summon a *gandr*, an Old Norse word for spirit.

In Bali, and indeed all over Southeast Asia, they also have the tradition of people running amok, suddenly entering a murderous frenzy in which the person kills other people and animals indiscriminately. Malays claim that an evil tiger spirit enters the man – it only affects men – and makes him go crazy. Men who run amok are usually killed by their community – or they commit suicide.

I began to think about *how* someone would become a berserker and what sort of structures and institutions would be needed in a society to produce a steady supply of them – for it seemed clear that, because of their ferocity in combat and utter disregard for their own lives, and the fact that they may have fought armoured men completely naked, a berserker would rarely survive more than a single battle.

So I came up with the idea of an academy for berserkers, and the fictional Fyr Skola was born. But where would such a training school for frenzied fighters be located? Since the role of a berserker seemed quasi-religious – I see them as sort of elite warrior-priests, rather like the Knights Templar of a later age – this academy had to be somewhere holy, somewhere deeply sacred in their pagan culture.

The Irminsul is the World Tree of the Germanic North – the people of Scandinavia called it Yggdrasil, but it's the same thing – and it is said to run through the Nine Worlds of the universe like an enormous axel. I was excited to discover in the course of my reading that archaeologists believed they had found a location for this massive tree – or perhaps a gigantic pillar – which was worshipped by the eighth-century Germanic tribes.

The Irminsul was to be found at (or near) a place then called Eresburg, which is now a quiet town in north Germany called Obermarsberg. It is set on a very curious geographical feature of the landscape – a small, almost sheer-sided, oval hill that rises out of the Diemel Valley. Archaeologists have also discovered the remains of an Iron Age fort at this ancient site. This was apparently the spiritual hub of the Germanic pagans – their holiest of holies – and it was also a place of great strategic value, as its height dominates all the surrounding countryside. I decided that it should be the location of the Fyr Skola, my berserker academy.

In AD 772, the real Eresburg fortress was attacked by Charlemagne – King of the Franks and lord of lands stretching from Brittany to Bavaria, and the North Sea to northern Spain. Charlemagne – or Charles or Karl or, as I have him, Karolus, from the Latin version of his name – was later crowned Holy Roman Emperor by the Pope and is a towering figure in European history. His well-disciplined household troops (*scara*) captured the Eresburg fort (the topiary of the Groves of Eresburg is an invention of mine) and put the holy Irminsul to the torch at the beginning of his thirty-year crusade against the neighbouring Saxons.

The heights of Eresburg changed hands several times during that long struggle but the end of the conflict was inevitable and a Christian church now occupies the site of the One Tree in the town of Obermarsberg.

–

The massive ditch and rampart system running across the bottom of the Jutland Peninsula, which I call the Dane-Work in this novel (Modern Danish: *Dannevirke*), is a real fortification. Work began on this defensive system as far back as AD 500, and it was improved and upgraded by successive Danish kings, between AD 737 and 968, including King Siegfried (or Sigfrid) who was a staunch ally of the beleaguered Saxons.

The Dane-Work clearly defined the border between Denmark and Old Saxony, and is probably the reason Denmark has remained an independent kingdom. It was last used as a military barrier as late as 1864 in the Second War of Schleswig against Germany. It had a deep ditch and a high earth wall topped with a wooden fence, and the remains of its ten-mile length can still be seen to this day. Sadly, I have not been able to visit it due to restrictions caused by Covid-19 and I had to imagine its earthen majesty when writing this section.

However, I must confess that I invented the great battle at the Dane-Work at the end of this novel. I wanted to end the book with a great, bloody slaughter in which Bjarki could fully come into his berserker-hood and my excuse for this is simply that I always see historical fiction as a blend of history and invention.

That final battle was pure fiction, although I am sure there would have been some clashes at the site of the Dane-Work during this period, and I hope I may be forgiven for including it in *The Last Berserker*.

Duke Gerold of Swabia was a real person. He was Charlemagne's brother-in-law and one of his closest allies, and we will see more of him in future in the Fire Born series. Father Livinus is an amalgamation of several eighth-century English missionaries who came to bring the light of Christ to the benighted pagans. Many of them suffered martyrdom and some historians say that the Saxon slaying of so many apostles was one of the main causes behind the wars. And Charlemagne himself did indeed cut short his 772 campaign against the Saxons (after capturing Eresburg and burning the Irminsul) to go south and conquer the Lombards of Italy.

-

I would also like to say something about the languages used in this novel. Old Norse, Old Saxon and Frankish all stem from the same linguistic root but they were probably not quite as mutually comprehensible in the eighth century as I have glibly suggested in this novel. However, there was an episode during the wars when a troop of armed Saxons infiltrated a large Frankish war party and were accepted without question as their comrades. The Saxons were even allowed into the Franks' fortified encampment, where they promptly caused bloody mayhem. This suggests that their languages or dialects – not to mention their dress, weapons and general culture – were not so very different from each other.

I have used Old Norse words for certain Fyr Skola terms, even though it is based in south Saxony – *berserkr* (plural: *berserkir*); *gandr* (plural: *gandir*) and so on – to give more of a Viking flavour. This is a bit of a fudge, of course, because they would have had their own Old Saxon words for these things. Also, Old Norse nouns declined, as in Latin, so the word would change according to its grammatical use. I have also avoided the use of accents in foreign words as they can be confusing. For example, Bago, the tiny island that Bjarki hails from, is properly written as Bågø. But I don't know how to pronounce Bågø correctly, and I doubt many of my English-speaking readers do either, so it seemed needlessly nerdy to insist on the accents.

-

A novel is never the work of just one person. I get to have my name on the cover but many talented people have contributed to the story you have just read – and hopefully enjoyed. I would like to thank my brilliant and hard-working agent Ian Drury of Sheil Land Associates for his unstinting support of my career. I owe a huge debt of gratitude to Craig Lye for his rigorous yet surprisingly gentle editing of this book – and to Jo Gledhill for her excellent copy editing – and to the whole of the publishing team at Canelo who have been so warm and welcoming to their new author.

I would also like to thank Neil Price, Professor of Archaeology at the University of Uppsala, for his fascinating book *The Viking Way: Magic and Mind in Late Iron Age Scandinavia*, which gave me much food for thought when considering the spiritual dimensions of the Fyr Skola and its denizens. I thoroughly enjoyed several of David Nicolle's excellent Osprey books on Charlemagne and the long Saxon wars – an absolute mine of information about weapons, strategy and tactics. And Professor Janet Nelson, of King's College London, shed a pool of brilliant light on the life of Charlemagne in her magisterial new book *King and Emperor*. My gratitude and heartfelt thanks to them all – and many others too numerous to mention.

Angus Donald,
Tonbridge, November 2020